Kahsir had their total attention now. Every eye was trained on his face.

"The men who escaped the enemy at Rodja'âno will be trying to move toward you," he told them. "A conservative estimate of four thousand men would give Errehmon eight companies of five hundred each. Adding our eight companies, we'll have sixteen highly mobile forces spread out up and down the enemy corridors. The key here is to strike and disengage.

"Let me emphasize this again. Be especially wary of the enemy. You know what happened to the sentry they captured—how they broke his mind. I repeat: don't engage the enemy unless you have to. Keep at them all the time: pick at them, raid them, but don't be lured in. Spread wide so they'll have to spread out their own attack. And if any of you or your men *are* captured—" Kahsir looked at the men who stood clustered close by. "If you're captured," he finished, his voice very soft, "forget. Forget everything you know, beginning with your life."

TWILIGHT'S KINGDOMS

NANCY ASIRE

TWILIGHT'S KINGDOMS

A Baen Books Original

Baen Publishing Enterprises
260 Fifth Avenue
New York, N.Y. 10001

First printing, November 1987

ISBN: 0-671-65362-8

Cover art and interior maps by David Cherry

Printed in the United States of America

Distributed by
SIMON & SCHUSTER
1230 Avenue of the Americas
New York, N.Y. 10020

DEDICATION

For Susie, who waited longest

For Teo, Dahri, and Nikki, who were there when
I needed them

For Vicki, Jake, Pat, David, Bob, Nancy, and
all my other friends who believed in me

And most of all:

For the Sorceress from her Apprentice

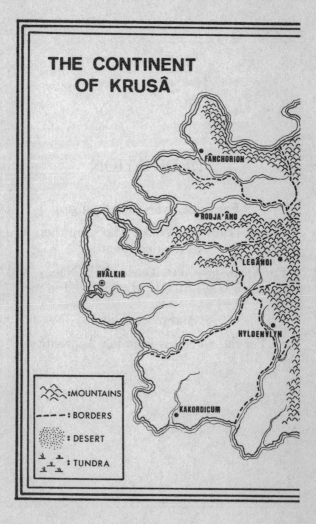

THE CONTINENT
OF KRUSÂ

FÂNCHORION

RODJA'ÂNO

HVÂLKIR

LEGANOI

HYLDENVLYN

KAKORDICUM

≈ : MOUNTAINS

--- : BORDERS

: DESERT

: TUNDRA

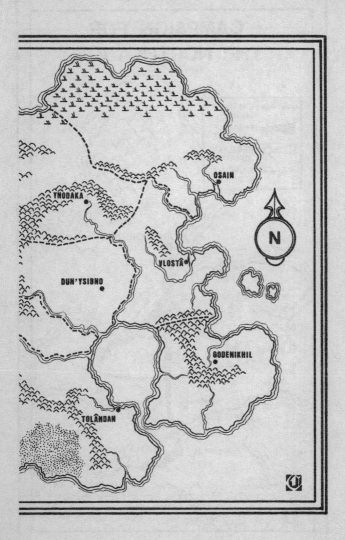

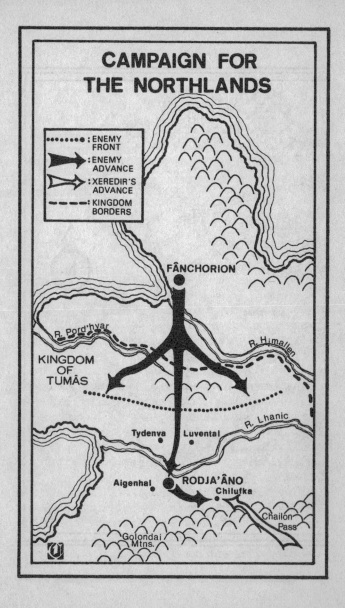

CAMPAIGN FOR
THE NORTHLANDS

•••••• : ENEMY FRONT

: ENEMY ADVANCE

: XEREDIR'S ADVANCE

---- : KINGDOM BORDERS

FÂNCHORION

R. Pord'hvar

R. Himallen

KINGDOM
OF
TUMÂS

R. Lhanic

Tydenva   Luvental

Aigenhal   RODJA'ÂNO

Chilufka

Chailon Pass

Golondai Mtns.

CHAPTER 1

Early spring came late in the northlands; Aeschu shivered and drew her cloak closer as she walked down the echoing stone hall. Torches and hanging lamps lit her way, brighter light escaped from the opened doors at the end of the hallway. She barely noticed the hangings on the walls as she passed. The symbols of the Leishoranya, her people, hung there for all eyes to see: the downward-pointing sword of destruction and death, and the upward-pointing sword of conquest and growth.

The windows she passed to her right offered a twilight view of Fânchorion: a city like all other northern cities she had seen, stone and steep-roofed. The palace of the fallen Krotànya King that was now her home commanded the city's height. Aeschu paused a moment before entering the doors before her, reached out with her mind, and sensed her visitor's presence.

Dhumaric. What is he doing here? The slave who had told her Dhumaric was waiting had said he had come to see the Warlord. Aeschu's hands clenched. She had dealt with Dhumaric countless times and knew he disliked dealing with her. *Damned man! Does he think*

*he can sneak around me to get at my husband? The fool
should know better.*

Squaring her shoulders, Aeschu walked into the room.
Two of her husband's honor guard stood on either side
of the doors of the informal audience hall, mail-clad,
grim of face and bearing, their weapons glittering in the
lamplight. Both warriors snapped to attention and lifted
their spears in imperial salute.

The tall figure standing before the fireplace turned
around and bowed deeply to cover his fleeting expression of surprise. "My Lady."

Dhumaric. One of the Great Lords, scion of an ancient Clan, and—by marriage—distantly related to
Aeschu's husband. She looked at him carefully, keeping
her mind shielded. He stood silent, a living example of
all the traits her people held highest: tall, powerful of
mind and body. Her own hair was a shade darker, her
own eyes blacker, but then her Clan was one of the
oldest, its beauty more refined.

She waited, making him cross the room to face her. If
the failure to get a message directly to her husband
angered him, he did not show it: his every movement
showed arrogance and fierce physical power.

He stopped just short of infringing on the proper
distance of a formal meeting, bowed low again. "Honor
to you, Lady," he said, and straightened. He was taller
than most men, but she was tall herself, and did not
have to look up that far to meet his eyes.

"My Lord Dhumaric." She acknowledged him with a
nod.

Dhumaric served as commander of one of the armies
that had taken Fânchorion from the Krotànya. Lately,
he led his forces farther to the south, seldom returning
from the war. In their past dealings, she had found him
suitable to her needs. And now? Could she still trust
him? Or had he outlived his usefulness? His presence
here this late in the day, and his attempt to go straight
to her husband, could mean he needed something he

could not get on his own—*or* that he had some message too important to send.

"It's late, my Lord," she said, keeping her voice quiet and easy. "What do you want?"

Her blunt approach often took other people by surprise, but he responded with similar directness.

"The invasion of Tumâs, Lady," he said. "We're nearly in control of that kingdom's northern half."

"Nearly? Are there that many resistance fighters out there?"

"No, Lady. They're determined and fight like demons, but we seem to be containing them. We've got our supply bases set up, we've opened a corridor, and we're protecting our flanks. The Krotànya are evacuating the countryside, clearing out the villages and small towns before our line of march, burning everything we could use. There are no great cities left in Tumâs to take save Rodja'âno. The Krotànya have made that city a rallying point in their defense. I'm afraid we're going to face stiff opposition when we try to take it."

"Stiff opposition?" she asked, moving closer to the huge fireplace, the gold embroidery on the edges of her dress catching the ruddy light of the flames. "I take it you're asking for more men. How many do you command?"

"Nine thousand, Lady," Dhumaric said. "What I meant by 'stiff opposition' is that the Krotànya will fight harder for this city than they have for any city in the past."

He's right about that. Rodja'âno's the next to last of their capitals. She quickly called up an inner map of the area he spoke about, showing the various forces deployed in the region. Rugged country lay between Fânchorion and Rodja'âno, hilly and wood-clad; the lack of roads made it damnably hard to cross. The armies could use the mind-road, but that left them too weary to turn back an attack by waiting Krotànya bush-fighters.

Dhumaric and the other generals were pushing southward, their armies lined up in a straight frontal penetration. As commander of the largest of those armies, Dhumaric served as the spearhead of this invasion of southern Tumâs, and his nine thousand men had already camped several hundred leagues north of Rodja'âno, a march of relative ease.

"You command the largest army in the region, my Lord. You said your strength is nine thousand. You have twenty siege engines, plus five full companies of cavalry. And you still think you need more men?"

"Lady," he said, "I do."

"Oh?" She gave him a moment of silence. "What happened to the other thousand warriors who went south with you?"

"Krotànya got most of them, Lady, from out of the night, from out of the woods . . . there aren't enough Krotànya to meet us in battle, but they've picked at us continuously."

"Yet you plan to attack Rodja'âno with the corridor that unstable?"

"Aye, Lady. A lightning strike, unforeseen, with irresistible force. The Krotànya know our relative positions, but they won't expect us to move this soon."

"What about your rear? If you've been having trouble with resistance fighters, they'll come at you unopposed."

"There aren't that many of them, and we could fill the empty corridor behind me with men from the armies close by. So I'm not only requesting more warriors for my army, but additional men for the armies behind me."

She drew a long breath. She had the power to send out supplies and food, but needed her husband's approval to dispatch troops. Holding Dhumaric's eyes, she pointed across the room to a closed double doorway, flanked by two more of the honor guard. "Ssenkahdavic rests in the other room, my lord. Do you want to discuss this with him?"

Dhumaric's face was very still; he shook his head. "No, Lady. Since you're here, you can tell him."

She stood silent, studying his reactions. *Perhaps he*

isn't *trying to go around me to get to my husband. His tale of Krotànya attacks rings true.* She kept her face blank. *It's because I'm a woman, and he thinks women are beneath his notice. We'll see, my Lord . . . we'll see.*

She watched him a moment longer, but he kept respectfully silent. "Is there anything else, my Lord?"

"Tell him I'm here, Lady, and await his order to attack. And ask him if I could have his personal support when I storm Rodja'âno."

She lifted one eyebrow and stared at Dhumaric. *And now the truth comes out. Oh, he wants more men, that's certain. But he made this trip to be sure my husband's power will be behind him when he attacks.* "Very well," she said, and motioned across the room to a set of chairs by one wall. "Wait here, my Lord. I'll speak with my husband."

She turned from him before he had completed his bow. The honor guard saluted her as she crossed the room, and one of the warriors opened the doors. For a moment, Aeschu hesitated just inside the doorway, in the still darkness. A slave had recently lit the fire and several lamps, but the dark hangings and high ceiling swallowed up their light. She drew a deep breath, smoothed the heavy cloth of her dress down across her thighs. For another moment she stood in the silence, listening to the crackling of the fire in the huge fireplace. Lifting her head, she walked slowly into the room.

At first glance, it seemed the chamber lay empty. But she sensed him here—her husband, her lord, the most powerful man her race had ever produced. She *felt* his presence as if she could see him.

The far end of the room, clustered with deeper shadows, seethed with his power. She saw him there, far from the light of the fire and the lamps, a dim shape lost in the flickering darkness.

"My Lord?"

No response came from those shadows—no stirring, no evidence of attention at all.

She drew another deep breath, allowed her shoulders to relax, and walked quietly across the deeply carpeted floor. Not more than five paces from him, she stopped—held motionless in her awe of the man she had married and her fervent desire to avoid his notice.

Somnolent again, he sat in that state of body and mind that much resembled sleep, his broad-shouldered form upright in a high-backed chair, the dim light from the fire catching the rich gold that bordered his black tunic. The pure white streak that ran through his long black hair was easy to see in the shadows. His face, perfect in its handsomeness, was expressionless. Though his eyes were closed, she knew herself watched.

"My Lord?" She waited a moment, then tried again. "My Lord . . . Dhumaric is here."

The smallest of motions caught her eye: his hand twitched slightly on the arm of the chair.

"My Lord." She bowed her head. *I know what he wants*, that hand twitch had said. *Take care of it for me. You're Queen . . . my Queen. Who can gainsay you?*

A brief flush of pride warmed her. She smiled a small smile, one she seldom allowed herself. Queen? Aye, wife to the Warlord Ssenkahdavic—a wife who, like all the Leishoranya, lived to obey him and the Shadow he served.

She bowed to her husband, and walked away to the audience hall. She blinked in the brightness. Dhumaric waited in the center of the room, his eyes seeking hers.

"My Lord is still indisposed," Aeschu said. "He asked that I stand in his place."

A brief tightening of Dhumaric's lips let her read his thoughts as though he had no shields to hide them.

"I realize your impatience, my Lord," she said, going to the sideboard and unstopping a beaker of wine, "and the fact that you must deal with me, who am only a woman. Will you have something to drink? No? Pity. These Krotànya kept well-stocked cellars." She lifted her cup, restopped the beaker, and turned to face Dhumaric. "So. You think you'll be able to storm Rodja'âno if you have more men?"

"Aye," Dhumaric said. "The Krotànya defense of Rodja'âno will be difficult to overcome."

She kept her eyes level with his. *See him dance around the* real *reason he's here. Come, my Lord . . . tell me.*

Dhumaric's eyes flickered with an unreadable emotion; shielded, he was near impossible to Read. "Taking this city might go beyond sheer manpower, my Lady. I realize the Dark Lord has been . . . occupied since we took Fânchorion. But that was nineteen years ago. To overcome the Krotànya, we might well need his help."

Nineteen years? Had it only been nineteen years? She thought back to the fall of Fânchorion. The People had fought hard for the city, her husband spending much of his strength to overcome Fânchorion's mental and physical defenses. For years after taking the city, he had remained to all eyes dead, deep in some healing union with the Dark he served. And during those years she had ruled for him, guiding his lords and generals as best she might, fending off the more ambitious who would use her influence.

And Dhumaric? He was dangerous, and powerful, but fully aware he stood at the pinnacle of his power, and mostly content with that. And what if she had him killed? She had the power to order such an execution, especially if she convinced her husband it was necessary. Dead, Dhumaric might not achieve the status he needed to return, in his next incarnation, as a God of his family.

But not now—he still had his uses. He stood silent, waiting for the answer to the question he had posed.

"If the need arises, my Lord," she murmured, "he will come. In person. Have you so little faith in him?"

"No, Lady. I've never doubted him. But again I remind you: there are no more great cities beyond Rodja'âno until we reach Hvâlkir. The closer we come to the capital of all the Krotànya kingdoms, the fiercer the opposition will be." Dhumaric gestured briefly. "We aren't the Dark Lord, my Lady, only his generals. The Krotànya have strong minds among them—very strong. They have learned, Lady; they've recovered their warlike ways. If we let them organize a defense at Rodja'âno, if we don't take the city quickly, we'll be bogged down in a major campaign. We need your husband's help."

Aeschu took a sip of her wine, her eyes holding Dhumaric's over the rim of her cup. "And he'll be there," she said, and set the wine behind her on the sideboard. For a moment she watched Dhumaric, alert for the slightest hint of treachery. "Are you waiting for his order, then? Is this all you require to attack Rodja'âno?"

Dhumaric shifted slightly. "Aye, Lady. That and your word that we'll have the men we need."

She stood silent, her mind turned toward the darkened room where her husband sat . . . Ssenkahdavic, channel for the very Powers of Darkness. His presence weighed down on her, suffocating in its strength. But she had been born for this, so the priests had said, and she had not shied from responsibility.

"Go, then," she said quietly, motioning toward the south. "I want daily reports from you and the other commanders. Eleven thousand men are yours for the taking: six thousand for your army, and the other five thousand to fill the space behind you. Choose as you will from the divisions that camp east of Fânchorion."

Dhumaric's eyes flashed in the lamplight. He bowed deeply, turned from her, and left the room.

Aeschu stared after him. What he had proposed seemed logical: a surprise attack on Rodja'âno when the Krotànya least expected it, *plus* additional warriors to

add to that attack, could give Dhumaric the city inside
a ten-day.
—*Aeschu*.

She stiffened and looked toward the room where her
husband sat. Gathering her skirts, Aeschu crossed the
audience chamber and passed through the open doors.

There was a stirring in the shadows at the far end of
that room now. She swallowed, hurried past the fireplace.

His eyes were open: void-black, they stared at her,
through her, *within* her. Everything she had ever thought
and done lay open for him to read. A small smile
touched his handsome face.

"And so Dhumaric goes to take Rodja'âno," he said,
his voice rough with disuse. He stretched out a hand to
her; she took it to steady him as he stood.

Taller than Dhumaric, he loomed over her, wrapped
in the shadows that seethed about him, a darkness she
could see with the inner and outer eye, and his Power
flooded out into the room.

"It's time," he said. The firelight struck his profile as
he turned his eyes southward, and despite all their
years of marriage, Aeschu trembled in fear.

Kahsir had taken the mind-road innumerable times
before, but seldom with as much secrecy; thank the
Light the Mind-Born giving them additional shielding
had not asked close questions. Warriors came and warriors went these days, and the harried Mind-Born cloaked
their movements and assisted them on their way in
increasing numbers. No one had asked the Throne Prince
of the Krotànya *why* he was going, or asked for higher
authorizations; the only thing the Mind-Born asked was
where to where, and when. They had their war gear, he
and Lorhaiden and Lorhaiden's brother Vàlkir: were
armed in chain and leather, carried their swords in
sheath, and had their shields bound to the saddles of
the horses they led into the grey, drizzle-bound courtyard.

Kahsir rose into the saddle and reined tight, backing his horse into position with Lorhaiden's and Vàlkir's— contact helped. Around them the towers of Hvâlkir the King-City and capital were obscured in mist, spring weather. He made himself see another courtyard, in Rodja'âno, weather unknown: the details of grey stone walls, a precise *feeling* of being in that place. He felt the touch of Lorhaiden's mind and Vàlkir's, settling into the same recollection, a solidity on either side of him. Then he felt the touch of the Mind-Born as the protectors of Hvâlkir gathered up their thought and shielded it.

And, projecting his will, Kahsir began to build the gateway to the mind-road.

At first indistinct, then solidifying, a shimmering arc formed before them. Kahsir ran a hand down his horse's neck, steadying him, and sending him forward as they took the gate at a walk.

An instant of disorientation then, the bite of intense cold, an impression of dark, and Kahsir rode out into the afternoon sunshine in Rodja'âno, Lorhaiden and Vàlkir on either side of him.

And the impression of the Mind-Born fading from behind them and about them to a single one before them. . . .

A tall, slender man, clad in a long tunic and robe of white, waited for them in the near-empty courtyard. Kahsir recognized Remàdir, chief of the Mind-Born in Rodja'âno and counselor to King Nhavari of Tumâs.

"Welcome, my Lords." Remàdir bowed low as Kahsir and his companions dismounted.

Kahsir pulled the reins over his horse's head and let them drop. Well-trained, his horse would stay in that one spot until the reins were lifted again. "It's good to see you, Remàdir. Have you told Nhavari we're here?"

"Aye, Lord." The Mind-Born gestured toward a tall tower. "He's waiting for you."

"Vahl," Kahsir said to the younger of the two men

who stood by their horses. "Would you mind taking care of our gear? Lorj and I will go on up to Nhavari."

Vàlkir nodded, then smiled at the Mind-Born. "This way I'll have a chance to talk with Remàdir. We haven't seen each other in years."

"Join us when you're done." Kahsir clapped Vàlkir on the shoulder and set off toward the tower, Lorhaiden at his side.

"Damned man," Lorhaiden growled, with a backward nod toward Remàdir. "Shows up with no soldiers, no support at all. What if we'd been the enemy?"

"Rodja'âno's totally shielded by the Mind-Born, Lorj, just like Hvâlkir. No enemy's going to jump past that barrier. And the enemy's not that close. Rodja'âno's not under siege."

Lorhaiden's silver-grey eyes glittered. "Not yet. But if Nhavari sits here on his rear end much longer, it will be."

Kahsir sighed. "Quietly, Lorj."

Lorhaiden threw both hands out to his sides. "Why should I be quiet? It's idiocy! If the enemy's coming, why the Dark not go out and meet them before they get here? If nothing else, it would buy us some time."

"Do you know how many Leishoranya are out there, Lorj? No? I didn't think so. Not even the Mind-Born are sure. The enemy's heavily cloaked and we have only a general idea of their position. Rushing out to meet them could get you all killed."

"It's better than waiting for them to come to us."

Kahsir shot Lorhaiden a warning look as they neared the tower. A group of warriors had gathered by the tower doorway; faces turned and blank looks gave way to instant recognition: Kahsir dor Xeredir dàn Ahzur, grandson of the High-King Vlàdor; and Lorhaiden dor Lorhaiden dàn Hrudharic, the Prince possessed by his deadly Oath.

The two honor guards by the doorway snapped to attention as Kahsir entered the tower. Lorhaiden fol-

lowed, throwing a dark look at the guards as he passed
them.

"Fools," Lorhaiden muttered under his breath, just
loud enough for Kahsir to hear.

"Dammit, Lorj!" Kahsir paused on the stone stairway, turned his back to the wall, and faced Lorhaiden.
"What the Dark's the matter with you? Everything I've
done, you've found fault with! I thought you agreed
with what I'm doing. Eh?" Lorhaiden did not reply.
"—and keep your comments about Nhavari's warriors
to yourself. Do you want to start something again? The
last time you had one of their units under your command, they were convinced you were crazy."

Lorhaiden stood two steps down from Kahsir's position. He looked up, his eyes shadows in the semi-
darkness. "Because I wanted to chase down the enemy?
What's wrong with that?"

"Outnumbered as you were? Lorj . . . it would have
been suicide."

"We could have made it back to our lines in time,"
Lorhaiden said, his jaw set.

"A *fine* point of argument." Kahsir leaned his head
back on the stone wall. "For the Lords' sakes, Lorj!
What *do* you want Nhavari to do?"

"What he should have done a long time ago. Get out
of this city and ride north to face the enemy. They're
moving against us now, and there's no army between
them and Rodja'âno to slow them down."

Kahsir pushed himself away from the wall. "And why
do you think that is? Answer me that one, Lorj."

Lorhaiden stared back in silence.

"You know why. Nhavari's lost too many men to put
an army of any great size to field. He's doing the best
he can with what men he has. And he hasn't got
reinforcements."

"But to sit here like—" Lorhaiden gestured sharply.
"Can't you see what I'm talking about?"

"Aye. But that doesn't mean I agree with you. There

would be nothing wrong with your plan of going out to meet the enemy *if* Nhavari had the men for it. He doesn't, so he's chosen the next best thing: he's evacuated the land north of here, and fallen back to the only position he can possibly defend. Now, leave off, will you? I've got enough on my mind as it is without you badgering me."

Lorhaiden dropped his eyes. "I still think it's a mistake. Better to be mobile than trapped."

"Huhn." Kahsir started up the stairway again, hearing Lorhaiden follow.

The tower which housed Nhavari's working rooms stood flush with the eastern wall. Kahsir blinked in the strong sunlight as he stepped out from the stairway onto the stone pavement that ran atop the walls that encircled Rodja'âno. Around ten of Nhavari's warriors stood clustered together close to the doorway; they came to attention as Kahsir and Lorhaiden left the steps.

"Stay out here, Lorj," Kahsir said quietly, "and cool down. I don't want you and Nhavari going at each other's throats."

Lorhaiden's jaw tightened, but he nodded. Kahsir glanced at the watching soldiers and ignored the dark look that followed him to Nhavari's door.

Lorhaiden glanced away from his sword-brother's retreating back, and stared at the waiting warriors: expressionless, they returned the stare. Anger-heightened, Lorhaiden's sensitivity allowed him to read their shielded thoughts as if they were broadcast: an uncomfortable feeling, for a man's thoughts were his own unless he *invited* someone else to listen. *Damned crazy fool's back. Suicidal, that one. Lords keep him from leading us again. Nearly got us all killed the last time.*

Lorhaiden glowered, but the thoughts still came. *Can't see why Lord Kahsir puts up with him, swordbrother or not. Aye, if Lorhaiden wants to go out and*

*get himself killed, that's fine—but don't drag us into
it.*

Several of the warriors glanced away; one of them
said something in a hushed voice and the others nodded. Lorhaiden pretended not to notice and looked at
the closed door that led to Nhavari's chambers.

*Why can't Kahs see what I'm talking about? Staying
here in Rodja'âno like some vermin in a hole. All the
enemy has to do is come in after us. I know Kahs can
see it . . . he's risking enough coming here.*

For over one thousand years, he had been oathed as
sword-brother to the High-King's grandson; known him
as a friend for close to twice those years. After the
passage of all those centuries, Lorhaiden felt certain he
knew Kahsir better than anyone save the Royal Family.
Though Kahsir understood Lorhaiden's position, he would
do as he thought best.

Lorhaiden looked away from the doors, met the sus-
picious eyes of the watching warriors. *Idiots! What the
Dark do you know about strategy? Huhn. I was fighting before most of you were born.*

He rubbed his chin, remembering the land north of
Rodja'âno. Hills and thick woods; rivers and streams
beginning to swell with spring runoff. The Krotànya
armies were spread painfully thin across the northern
borders, and equally thin to the east and south of
Elyâsai.

For over fifteen hundred years the war had dragged
on. In its early stages, the Krotànya had lost all their
Kingdoms in the eastern half of the continent. Three
more Kingdoms had fallen after the enemy crossed the
dividing mountains, and the Leishoranya had taken
Fânchorion only nineteen years before. The fabled
Twelve Kingdoms of Vyjenor stood reduced to only
two: Tumâs and Elyâsai, and the northern half of Tumâs
was falling.

And, as far as Lorhaiden could see, the end of all
those Kingdoms, of the Krotànya as a race, was not far

off. He snarled silently, denying such an end for his people, but his heart told him his guess was right.

Damn! Nharvi should send the largest force he can to the north, leaving just enough men in the city to hold it until the army returns. If he could draw in a few more men from the general area of the enemy's position, he could attack their flanks and keep them busy. Kahs is right . . . Nhavari doesn't have enough men to meet the enemy in battle and protect Rodja'âno, but he could at least slow the enemy's approach.

Another spate of shielded thoughts scattered across Lorhaiden's mind. He scowled, leaned back against the wall, and dared Nhavari's warriors to start something.

Kahsir stepped into the King's chambers, shut the door, and met the blond-headed man halfway across the sunlit room. "Nhavari! What's your status here? Still the same?"

The King of Tumâs gripped Kahsir's arm in greeting. "Aye. The enemy's mobilized and marching this direction."

"Huhn. We know they're moving south from Fân-chorion; that there are several armies of considerable size deployed in an east-west line across northern Tumâs. Has anything changed? How many men are marching on you? Do you have more accurate positions?"

Nhavari motioned to a group of chairs by an open window. "Between our scouts and the Mind-Born, we're sure as we *can* be of the enemy's number and their position. They've got several thousand men over two hundred leagues north."

Kahsir sat down, rubbed his eyes, and called up a mental map of the area. "Who's leading them?"

"Various of Ssenkahdavic's commanders." Nhavari took a chair alongside. "We're not sure. They're heavily shielded, possibly to keep us from knowing who their officers are."

"Luvental must be in the thick of it then," Kahsir

said, "if the enemy's advanced to within two hundred leagues of here."

"Luvental's gone, Kahs. We got word of its fall not more than an hour ago."

"Damn. I'd hoped to use that city as an outpost."

"As had we all." Nhavari crossed one booted foot on his knee. "Have you seen Alàric yet?"

Kahsir drew a quick breath. "You mean he's still here? He was ordered to leave a day ago."

"He's always one to draw it out to the last instant. He led me to believe he wouldn't be replaced. You didn't see him?"

Kahsir glanced out of the window at the broad, heavily forested hills that surrounded the city. "No. I came straight to you." He drew the shields over his mind and met the King's eyes. "He's not happy being recalled like this, especially with a siege coming."

"Ah? You think it will come to that?"

"Aye . . . in three to four months. Where *is* Ahri?"

"Out with the engineers and the Mind-Born. Do you want me to send for him?"

"No. He'll sense my presence soon enough."

"The High-King said nothing about you coming when he told me he was recalling Alàric."

Kahsir shrugged. "I'm here. What are your plans of defense?"

"I don't have much choice, Kahs. I've lost too damned many men, and those I have left are scattered across the lands north of here. With Luvental gone, Rodja'âno is the last place I can hope to defend."

Kahsir remembered his inner map of the countryside to the north. "What about Tydenva?"

"I had the city evacuated and burned. It's the same story . . . too few men to make a viable defense. And I don't have enough to send as reinforcements."

Kahsir shook his head. "I understand. You've emptied all the villages and towns north of here?"

"Aye. We simply can't defend them, Kahs."

"Spread as thin as you say your men are, I don't doubt it. What about this, then? Could you send a company of men—around three hundred or so—north? If you can spare them from the defense of Rodja'âno, *and* most of them are archers, we may do more damage to the enemy than sending out a larger group."

"Huhn." Nhavari scratched his beard and looked out the window. His eyes were bright with thought as he looked back. "It's a good idea, Kahs. Surely we have three hundred bowmen we can spare."

"Good. I think that will help us."

"And your father? Is he still coming north with four thousand men?"

Kahsir made himelf meet the King's eyes. "Aye. Over the Golondai Mountains and through Chailon Pass."

"That's the best news I've heard in days. Now we have a damned good chance of defeating the Leishoranya, even if it comes down to a siege."

"You've got over six thousand warriors here in Rodja'âno now. If the enemy has—let's say—an equal number, my father's men will nearly double our strength. We'll be able to catch the Leishoranya between us."

Nhavari nodded. "And then we'll have the men to send north to act as a buffer between us and the enemy if they send more troops south."

"That's the plan." Kahsir leaned forward in his chair. "Have you got the time right now to show me what you've done here in Rodja'âno?"

"Aye. You might see something I've missed."

Lorhaiden shifted his weight against the wall by the stairway and glared at the doors to Nhavari's rooms. The waiting warriors stirred: bootsoles grated on the stairs to Lorhaiden's left. He glanced in that direction and stiffened.

An elegant, fine-boned man stepped out from the stairway, his luxuriant blond hair and combed mustache giving him the look of a dandy. Lorhaiden stared down

at the newcomer, keeping his face expressionless. The
officer in turn glanced up at Lorhaiden, who towered
over him—and over all the other warriors present—
nodded briefly, and crossed to the doorway. After a
quick conversation with Nhavari's houseguards, who
stood on either side of the King's doorway, he passed
into the room beyond.

Reordan: Nhavari's commander of the guard.

Lorhaiden snorted a laugh. *Bloody fool! Thinks he
knows everything, and he hasn't seen active service in
the field for decades. Lords! If Kahs and Nhavari in-
clude him in their planning, we'll be stuck inside these
walls until we rot!* His hands clenched. *I'm so damned
tired of running all the time! Give me a pitched battle
with the enemy . . . let me stand up to them, not run!*

Footsteps sounded on the steps again: it was his
brother. Vàlkir paused for a moment at the head of the
stairs, glanced pointedly at Nhavari's warriors, who stood
across the parapets, back to Lorhaiden, and stepped out
into the sunset light.

"Kahsir's with Nhavari," Lorhaiden said, answering
his brother's unvoiced question.

"I see."

Lorhaiden met Vàlkir's eyes, then looked quickly
away. *Dammit, Vahl! What am I supposed to do? Play
dice with Nhavari's warriors? If they didn't have to be
here, they would have left the moment I arrived.*

He felt Vàlkir's mind brush his, seeking the deep
channel that siblings used when they wanted utmost
secrecy.

—*Lorj, you've been tied up in knots lately. What's
going on?*

—*Nothing new. I'm tired of running, that's all.*

Vàlkir sighed quietly. *Can't you forget your Oath for
a little while? You don't always have to be so damned
bloody-minded.*

—*This doesn't have anything to do with my Oath.*

—*Oh?*

Lorhaiden set his jaw. *No, dammit. It's a matter of strategy. Everyone's so intent on defense that they won't think about pushing the enemy* back! *And that includes the Mind-Born. All* they *ever say is:* "defense! defense!" *No one seems to see that we—*

—I doubt that. From what Remàdir told me, Nhavari doesn't have much choice.

—Huhn. I still maintain he could send out a division or two and harry the enemy on their way here.

Vàlkir glanced at Nhavari's warriors, then back again. *I don't think he has the men.*

—He will have, if what Kahsir's doing works.

—Maybe. But we're not sure it will. We can't send men out on the basis of something that might *happen, Lorj.*

The door to the King's chambers opened: Nhavari and Kahsir came out onto the parapets. Reordan followed; spear-stiff, he stalked behind his King, an expression of self-importance on his narrow face. Lorhaiden glared at Reordan, felt Vàlkir's mind brush his own again, and took a deep breath. *That man drives me mad, Vahl. Supercilious little bastard.*

"Lorhaiden, Vàlkir. It's good to see you again," Nhavari said.

"And you, Lord," Vàlkir replied, bowing slightly. Lorhaiden merely nodded his head, his eyes still fixed on Reordan's face.

"Lorj," Kahsir said, "you and Vahl come with us. We're going to take a look at Rodja'âno's defenses."

Followed at a discreet distance by four of his honor guard, Nhavari led Kahsir out from the palace courtyard and into the city of Rodja'âno itself. Kahsir walked by the King's side, Lorhaiden, Vàlkir, and Reordan following.

The city had been evacuated of all but its warriors and the Mind-Born. Now, as Kahsir walked down from the citadel, he saw lifeless houses, empty windows, and emptier streets. Some courtyards of the larger residences were filled with fighting men, now, at late afternoon, gathered around their cooking fires. Horses were stabled wherever possible. A few chickens pecked at the gravel beside an abandoned house, and a yellow dog stood in front of another empty home, wagging its tail as Kahsir and the other men passed.

It had been over a century since Kahsir had been to Rodja'âno and he preferred to remember the city as it had been: streets alive and bustling with people, houses opened to the world but fully occupied, and the calls of children at their play. Only the ghosts of those things remained. Now he was surrounded by the smell of woodfire, dung, and bodies gone too long unwashed. It would become worse if the enemy actually besieged the city.

"How are your supplies, Nhavari?" he asked.

"Good. When we sent the citizens away, they left us most of their perishables. We've got deep wells and plenty of medicines."

"Huhn. How many Mind-Born are here?"

"Counting Remàdir, eighty."

Eighty Mind-Born? That's more than I hoped for. They've alredy got the city under a protective shield, or I wouldn't have been able to mind-road in here without having to send ahead that I was coming. No doubt Nhavari's got them helping the engineers fortify the walls.

"Aye." Nhavari had Read Kahsir's thoughts. "Twenty with the engineers. The rest keep the shield up around the city."

Reordan cleared his throat. "We have the rest divided into fields of specialty, Lord. Let's see—thirty of them are healers, fifteen—"

"We don't need the breakdown now," Nhavari interrupted.

Kahsir glanced at Lorhaiden: his sword-brother walked stiff-shouldered and silent, his expression foul.

—Get that little bastard out of here, Lorhaiden Sent on a private level, *or I swear I'll beat him into mush!*

—Patience, Lorj. He won't be around us much longer.

A small shrine to Tihtàlyir, one of the Dorelya who watched over the Kingdom of Tumâs, stood to one side of the street. Kahsir touched his forehead in respect as he passed by, but kept silent, not inclined to talk. No one spoke much; the sight of the nearly empty city was depressing.

Nhavari turned and led the way down another street, one that ran right up to the northern wall. The King's engineers worked on that wall, walking and kneeling atop it, suspended on scaffolding, and pacing along at street level.

"We're going over all our walls carefully," Nhavari said, gesturing at the engineers. "The eastern wall is structurally the weakest, and we'll need to do the most work there." He paused and looked up, waving to the workmen on top of the wall. With an expression of pride on his face: "This wall's always been the strongest; it was the last erected."

"Lord, both you and Remàdir said the Mind-Born are helping the engineers," Vàlkir said to Nhavari, "but I don't see them here."

"They've already done their job on the western and southern wall. Right now, they should be about finished with the eastern wall. Then—"

"My Lord Nhavari!"

The hoarse cry brought Kahsir and his companions to a halt. A man dressed in soiled woodsman's clothes ran down the street toward them, the expression on his face hard to read in the shadows.

"The enemy, Lord," the man got out, stopping in front of Nhavari. "They be only twenty leagues off!"

"Twenty leagues?" This from Lorhaiden. Kahsir made a shushing motion with one hand.

"How the Dark did they—" Nhavari drew a long

breath. "Did you see the enemy yourself, or is this secondhand information?"

"Myself, Lord. I been a member of one of them northern squads, based up 'round Tydenva. Me and my comrades run head-on into the enemy vanguard. They killed all of us but me. I got away because I been the last to come out of the woods into their path."

"How many?" asked Kahsir.

"In the vanguard? 'Round seven hundred, Lord. I took off into the woods and then come by mind-road a ways farther. Never gone so far in my life. Scared, I guess. 'Fore I jumped, I sensed many more follow."

Nhavari's hands clenched. "How much is 'many more'?"

"Not sure, Lord. I Saw four of them black banners."

Kahsir's heart tightened. Four legions? Fifteen thousand men? None of his father's reports had hinted at that number coming south, only of companies of one thousand or so scouring the land beyond Fânchorion. The enemy must have consolidated those men and then marched toward Rodja'âno . . . unless the situation was far worse than anyone—including the Mind-Born—had foreseen. He thought of Xeredir poised on the opposite side of the Golandai Mountains, coming north with his four thousand men to reinforce the troops in the northlands. Now, with the enemy so close, there would be no chance for his father to make it to Rodja'âno in time, and the four thousand men he led would hardly make a difference.

Nhavari's Sending to Remàdir and the rest of the Mind-Born captains brushed across Kahsir's mind. He met the King's eyes.

"Let's get back to the tower," Nhavari said in a thin voice. "We don't have much time to mount our defense."

Several of Nhavari's commanders already waited outside the tower room when Kahsir, Lorhaiden, Vàlkir, Reordan, and the King of Tumâs stepped out of their quick jump from the northern wall. And there, among those commanders, bearded jaw clenched, stood Kahsir's youngest brother, Alàric.

"Kahs! What the Dark are *you* doing here?"

Kahsir glanced sidelong at Nhavari. "I'll handle Ahri. Go talk with your commanders. We'll join you in a moment." Nhavari nodded, gestured to the warriors, and entered his work room. Kahsir nodded Lorhaiden and Vàlkir after the King. As the door shut behind them, Kahsir faced his brother. The youngest son, Alàric seemed to think he must work longer and harder than his two older brothers to make up for that fact: hence his presence in Rodja'âno the day after he had been ordered to leave.

"Kahs—"

The two houseguards on either side of the door kept their eyes averted, their expressions bordering on embarrassed.

Kahsir pointed to the opposite side of the parapets, and followed his brother out of earshot of the guards.

"Why are you here, Kahs?" Alàric asked in a low voice, his eyes glinting in the fading light.

"I'm here because Father sent me."

Alàric shook his blond head. "He said nothing to me about it. Not a damned thing!"

"So. If you disbelieve me, ask him when you see him."

His brother shot him a confused look. "It's not that I don't believe you, it's that—"

"Ahri, we don't have time to stand here arguing. The enemy's only twenty leagues off to the north. You're going to get out of here—"

"Twenty leagues? The Mind-Born said they were—"

"The Mind-Born made a mistake. Obviously the enemy's taken the mind-road since they last checked."

"An entire army? Damn! They'll be in no condition to fight, then, not for at least a day."

"Or they *didn't* take the mind-road and set up a false impression for the Mind-Born to read."

"Whatever." Alàric's shoulders tightened. "I'm not going now, dammit! If the enemy's that close, we'll need all the officers we can get here in Rodja'âno."

Kahsir bit down on his lower lip. *How the Dark am I going to get him out of the city before he finds out the real reason I'm here?*

"You're going, Ahri, because Father *and* Grandfather recalled you. It's not as if there aren't enough commanders—"

"This is *my* border to fight on, Kahs, not yours! I'm responsible in the north, not you."

Kahsir's shoulders tightened. Here he stood, arguing with his stubborn youngest brother, the enemy marching only twenty leagues away, and Lorhaiden ready to explode into anger. Keeping an eye on Lorhaiden would be difficult enough without having to mollify Alàric.

"Kahs. Ahri. Do you two fight all the time, or only before battle?"

Kahsir briefly closed his eyes in utter frustration, then turned from Alàric to the stairway. There, one eyebrow lifted in mock disdain, stood his middle brother, Haskon, who by all rights should have been off fighting on the eastern border.

"Kona," Kahsir said. "How the Void did you get into the city?"

"Really, Kahs. Do I look like one of the enemy? The Mind-Born are more discerning than that."

"You'd better have a damned good reason for being here."

"So had *you*." Haskon crossed the parapets, glanced at Alàric, and stopped no more than two paces away. "You're supposed to be on the southern border. Last time I noticed, my command on the eastern border is closer."

"O Lords of Light!" Kahsir rubbed his eyes wearily. "If Father and Grandfather ever find out we're—"

"We can fix that easy enough," Alàric said. "We *all* leave . . . like we're supposed to."

Kahsir turned his head and followed his youngest brother's path to the edge of the wall. "You're going, Ahri. I'm staying. And," he swung back to face Haskon, "as for you—"

The door to Nhavari's chambers flew open and the King rushed out onto the parapets, followed closely by his commanders. "Go!" he ordered. "Spread the word! All warriors to their posts!" Remàdir, Lorhaiden, and Vàlkir stood just outside the door behind Nhavari, their eyes shadows in the twilight. The King looked in Kahsir's direction. "The enemy's closer than twenty leagues, Kahs! Remàdir finally breached their shielding. He says we can *see* the Leishoranya outriders now!"

"*Chuht!*"

Without a look at either of his brothers, Kahsir ran off after Nhavari to the tower ramparts that looked north and east.

Bells of alarm rang out through the city. The courtyard below milled in controlled pandemonium, as Nhavari's warriors rushed out of buildings close by. Officers stood rooted in the seething mass and called out orders as warriors went running off to the walls, some of them only half-armed. Kahsir cursed, rounded a corner after Nhavari, and came to a sudden halt.

"There, Lord," Lorhaiden said, joining Kahsir at the edge of the parapets. "Looks to me to be around a hundred of them."

Kahsir's lips tightened as he leaned on the ramparts. Lorhaiden's estimation was likely accurate. Across the river, coming out from the forests, rode the outriders of the enemy's vanguard.

He heard Haskon and Alàric come up from behind. How the Dark could he get his stubborn brothers out of Rodja'âno now? Nothing besides force—

"Kona. Ahri." He turned from the ramparts and faced them. They flinched at the tone of his voice. "I'm commanding you, in Father's name. Get out of here. Now!"

"It's too late, my Lord," Remàdir said. "The enemy's lowered a block around the city. They'll be able to trace anyone who leaves—by the mind-road *or* the world's roads."

Lords! Now what do I do? How will I ever explain this one to Grandfather—or Father? Kahsir glanced over his shoulder at the enemy warriors approaching the city from the north. "Remàdir . . . if you have help, you should be able to cloak these two idiots long enough for—"

Pain exploded inside Kahsir's mind. He staggered, dimly saw the other men waver on their feet. With long-used skill, he threw the shields up around his mind, felt the pain melt away to a dull throbbing.

"Lords!" Vàlkir's voice was rough. "They've got some strong minds to throw that kind of power at us."

"Remàdir?" Nhavari glanced at his advisor.

"Vàlkir's right, Lord," the Mind-Born said. "The enemy's got *brikendàrya* with them."

Mind-Breakers! Kahsir shivered suddenly. *Damn them to Darkness!* He looked at Remàdir, who alone seemed impervious to this mental assault. Slightly built, anything but a warrior, the Mind-Born assuredly had more strength of mind than Kahsir and the other men combined.

"Status?" Kahsir asked.

"We're tightening our shield, Lord," Remàdir replied. Then, pausing as if he listened to unheard voices: "We'll have it under control soon."

Kahsir turned to Nhavari. "Let's get your commanders assembled. I don't think the enemy will attack yet tonight. That may give us the time we need to prepare our defense."

One of the hanging lamps sputtered, flickered, and died, throwing a corner of the large room into shadows.

Kahsir rubbed his eyes, then glanced up as the last of Nhavari's commanders closed the door behind him as he left. In the wake of the volatile discussion that had just ended, the room seemed far too quiet.

Nhavari sat slumped in his chair at the head of the table, his bearded chin propped up on a clenched fist. Shadows lay like old bruises under his eyes. The last three days of the Leishoranya attack had not been easy for anyone, least of all the King whose capital city was assaulted.

"Well, Kahs?" Nhavari said, pulling his blond hair back over his shoulders. "What do you think? Will your father arrive in time?"

"Or will we break first?" Kahsir leaned back in his chair, propped his head on the chair back, and stared up at the ceiling. "Hard to tell. We haven't been able to get any messages in or out of the city since the enemy brought down their block. I can only suppose he's still on schedule."

"Which means, with luck, he'll be here in five more days."

"Huhn." Kahsir closed his eyes and drew his shields tighter. *Lords! I can't go on much longer lying to him like this. Or lying to my brothers. What the Dark possessed Father to order Alàric out of here and not send someone of equal rank to take his place? It's a comfort to the warriors on the walls to know the High-King cares enough about them to have one of his family present.*

"Kahs?"

Kahsir turned his head and looked into Nhavari's shadowed eyes.

"There's no one around now, Kahs," the King said, straightening in his chair. "Out with it. Something's obviously bothering you. What's wrong?"

Lords of Light! He's seen through my lies . . . he must have! I know my shields haven't dropped. Kahsir heaved forward in the chair and lifted his cup. "Seal the door, Vahri," he said, "and I'll tell you. But we can't be interrupted."

Nhavari reached out with his mind and placed a seal on the door so no one could enter without his permission. "Is it *that* bad?"

"I think so." Kahsir took a long swallow of wine, set the cup down, and met Nhavari's eyes. "You were advised to abandon Rodja'âno, weren't you?"

"Aye."

"And your reply?"

Nhavari shook his head. "I said I couldn't . . . that my people were depending on me to stay here and fight."

"No one told me what you'd said, but that sounds like you." Kahsir took a deep breath. "Alàric wasn't lying to you when he said no one was replacing him. The way I read his recall is that it was intended to *convince* you to evacuate. Father thinks this region has become too dangerous for any of his heirs."

Nhavari stared. "So he was leaving me to defend by myself, is that it? Does he think Rodja'âno is expendable? That *I'm* expendable?"

Kahsir shoved back his chair, its legs scraping loudly on the stone floor. "Dammit, Vahri," he said, standing and beginning to pace up and down beside the table, "I don't know. We fought over this for days. I told him we've got to make a stand, that Rodja'âno is too important to give up. He thinks the north is all but lost to us. He wants to deploy his armies into an unbroken line of defense from east to west."

"*Aü'k'vah!*" Nhavari slammed his fist down on the table. "You mean he's *not* sending me reinforcements? Is that it?"

Kahsir nodded.

Nhavari's face went red. "Can't he see that Rodja'âno is the linchpin of the north? Once she falls, the rest of Tumâs falls, and the enemy's got a clean run to the south, with no more great cities to stand against them until they reach Elyâsai."

"That's what I told him. But he didn't listen to me. Delay and run, delay and run. That's his stragety."

"*Aii'ya!*" Nhavari struggled for words. "But strategies change for every new situation."

Kahsir stopped his pacing beside Nhavari's chair and looked down at his friend. "One of these days, Father's going to run out of places to fall back to, and then what?"

Nhavari stood and met Kahsir's eyes. "So you came here against his wishes?"

"Ha! His wishes? Against his specific orders!"

"You did *what?*" Nhavari's face was pale in the lamplight.

"You heard me. He thinks I'm resting back in the capital. I *was*, up until the time he left with his army."

"*Chuht*, Kahs! When Alàric and Haskon leave, they'll tell him."

Kahsir's jaw tightened. "Let them. I couldn't abandon one of my closest friends, *and* lose a point of strategic importance."

Nhavari simply stared. "I know you two don't see eye to eye on a lot of things . . . but to defy him like this. You've never gone against his orders before."

"That's because he's never given me any orders this stupid." Kahsir shook his head. "And I've got to get my brothers out of here before too many more days pass. The three of us are never supposed to fight in the same area, and here we are, in the same city! Fur will fly, mark my words, when Father *and* Grandfather find out."

"O Lords!" Nhavari lowered his eyes, reached out for his own cup, and took a healthy swallow. "What's your plan, Kahs? You wouldn't have done this unless you had one."

"I'm forcing Father's hand," Kahsir said. "When I send Ahri and Kona off, they'll tell him I'm here, *and*

give him the military situation. He'll have no choice but
to come to Rodja'âno with his army."

"You're betting on that?"

Kahsir smiled tightly. "Angry as he'll be, he still
loves me enough to try to rescue me."

"Lords, Kahs! You must be awfully sure of yourself.
He could have you disinherited for insubordination! At
the very least, keep you confined in the capital."

"With our lack of commanders in the field? He'd be
crazy! Look, Vahri." He reached out and drew the map
of the northlands over to face them. "Follow my reasoning, if you can. Fânchorion lies due north of here."
Kahsir's finger moved up the map to the fallen capital's
position. "That's where Ssenkahdavic's been holed up
for nineteen years now." He spreads both hands and
moved them down in the map toward Rodja'âno. "His
armies have been moving slowly southward under the
command of his generals."

Nhavari leaned closer to the map. "And they've taken
their time marching . . . been very thorough in appro-
priating anything we haven't destroyed."

Kahsir's finger moved across the map, to the borders
of the Kingdom of Elyâsai. "The news isn't much better
to the east or south. The enemy's trying to encircle us
in Elyâsai."

"Damn!" Nhavari whispered. "They just might do it,
too."

"Huhn. Rodja'âno is the last great city left, save
Hvâlkir. Once she falls, as you said, the enemy's got
nothing much between them and Elyâsai."

"Save the Golondai Mountains."

"Aye. And here's where Father and I violently disagree. He sees the north—"

"—including Rodja'âno," Nhavari inserted.

"—including Rodja'âno, as a bleeding wound. As far
as he's concerned, the north's as good as lost. Sending
more men to fight a losing battle isn't his style."

"Then what the Dark does he propose to do?"

"For the moment, he's planning to send his men out to the north, reinforcing the troops that have fallen back before the enemy advance. These troops are to draw the enemy farther south, to bog them down in a war of forest ambushes and the like. Meanwhile, Father's going to build redoubts in all the Golondai passes, where he'll have the advantage of height over the enemy."

"Aye," Nhavari mused. "But the enemy will eventually overwhelm those redoubts by sheer numbers, if not from mental attacks."

"I think Father realizes that. Eventually, he plans to fall back *behind* the Golondai, and use those mountains as a shield between us and the enemy."

Nhavari stared at the map for a long moment. "We'd be trapped, then. And if the enemy jumped the Golondai. . . ."

"Aye. That's what I told him. I stressed Rodja'âno's importance—told him that we'd end up with maneuverability if we fought from *this* side of the Golondai, using Rodja'âno as our supply base."

"And he *still* couldn't see your reasoning?"

Kahsir snorted a laugh. "When Father gets wrapped up in his own idea of defense, he's as single sighted as a horse with blinders on." He brought his fingertip back across the map so it lay on the circle labeled Rodja'âno. "If we can make a stand here, we'll hold the enemy far longer than if we give the city up."

"I agree with you, Kahs. But what about your Grandfather? *He* can't be this blind."

Kahsir shrugged. "I'm not sure what got into Grandfather. I think he gets tired sometimes . . . tired of going on. When he gets in one of those moods, he worries about his family. I'll bet that's what Father played on when he got Grandfather to recall Alàric."

"But the enemy. . . ." Nhavari's finger stabbed out at two small cities. One lay to the northwest and the other to the northeast of Rodja'âno. "The enemy's here and here. I know that for a fact. I had reports from those cities today."

"The enemy's there *if* they haven't taken the mind-road," Kahsir agreed.

"Taken the mind-road," Nhavari echoed. "Aye. That must be how the army coming at Rodja'âno got here so quickly."

Kahsir chewed on his lower lip. "If we can depend on that news—if the enemy really *is* around those cities. . . ." He moved his finger from the northwest, down to Rodja'âno, then up again to the northeast. "Do you see it, Vahri?"

"Aye. We've been concentrating on the entire string of enemy armies, lulled by their slow invasion. The Leishoranya have caught us off guard, moving before we thought they could."

"But only with one army."

Nhavari's face lit up. "That means that we might be able to cut this army off from the others, if we split our forces and circle around behind, coming from the east and west."

"Aye. But we can't do it with the troops in Rodja'âno. What about your bush-fighters?"

"You'd draw them into this?"

Kahsir stared at the map and nodded. "If we can get your troops to the north of Rodja'âno and the bush-fighters combined."

"Huhn." Nhavari glanced at Kahsir, then back at the map. "It's worth the try, Kahs. I don't see anything else that could work. I don't have enough men in the field to the north to do the job. But don't count too heavily on the bush-fighters. With winter just ending, those I have aren't in the best condition . . . *and* they'd be hard to find."

"Let's try it. If it doesn't work—" He spread his hands. "—forcing Father to come to Rodja'âno is the last trick I have left. When Kona and Ahri tell him what's going on, he'll see what the enemy's doing."

Nhavari lifted one eyebrow. "After what you've told me, I wonder."

"He will. He and I may be on opposite sides of the tactical fence, but he can be an astute commander when he wants to be."

"Lords . . . that really puts us out on a limb."

"Aye, but we'd be out there anyway, with *no* hope of striking back."

"Huhn." Nhavari shrugged. "To return to my original question: how long do you think we can last?"

Kahsir shoved the map back across the table. "You did a good job of preparing for a possible siege, Vahri. Barring total misfortune, we can hold out until my father gets here."

"With his four thousand men. I see what you mean. And I also see why you want to get Alàric and Haskon out of here. We can't send any messages out, so they'll have to tell your father in person."

"If the Mind-Born can hide their going." Kahsir rubbed his neck, working the stiffness from it. "I might have outsmarted myself. If my brothers can't get out, there's no way Father will know I'm here and he won't come this far north. Or, if they leave too late, he won't be in time even if he *does* come quickly."

"What do *they* think his plans are?"

"That Father's coming north with reinforcements for Rodja'âno. I never said that exactly, but they're not stupid, either of them. Even they can see that we can't give Rodja'âno up to the enemy, so they assumed that's what he's doing."

"And you didn't discourage them in that, I take it," Nhavari said, the hint of a smile touching his weary face. "I've got to admit, Kahs . . . you've got guts to do something like this."

"Huhn." Kahsir walked back to his place, reached for his cup again, and drained it.

"I know why you're here now. But why the Dark did Haskon come here? We've never been close friends."

"I asked him that. The Mind-Born spread the news that the enemy was marching on Rodja'âno. Naturally, having Mind-Born in his own ranks, Kona heard about it. And, close friends or not, he saw a chance to help. He was due for leave, knew Ahri was being ordered out, and decided to come to Rodja'âno." Kahsir set his cup down on the table. "But, good intentions or not, Kona and Arhi have got to go. Keep the Mind-Born busy trying to find a way to get them out, Vahri. I want to know the first opportunity we have to send them off."

"*If* you can make them go."

Kahsir met the King's eyes. "There's only so far they can push me, and they know it. I'll *make* them go, old friend, one way or the other."

CHAPTER 2

The pre-dawn air was chill and Tsingar drew his cloak closer around his shoulders. He looked around the camp again, at the featureless lumps of sleeping warriors, the larger shadows that were the commanders' tents. It was not far to the woods: the countryside was clogged with trees. For a moment he stood on the edge of the forest, but sensed no one close by. He walked into the woods and peered into the darkness, seeking privacy.

His mind slipped easily into the familiar ritual of worship. He knelt between two trees, carefully took longsword, shortsword, and bootknife from their scabbards and laid them at his knees. For a long while, he held himself motionless; then, in a near whisper, he recited the names of his ancestors who had carried these weapons—men he honored and strove to emulate; men who, even after death, strengthened members of his Clan. He closed his eyes, delving into his ancient memories, events of long ago and far away. Well over a thousand years old, he buried detail for the sake of sanity, locked it away in partitions only profoundest effort could reach: and he was old, though not the oldest.

The war with the Krotànya predated him. The Gods had laid the death of that race as a duty on his Leishoranya ancestors, and that task no one could turn from, not even Ssenkahdavic, Void-Son, wielder of the Shadow. For the Krotànya stood as a bulwark for the Powers of Light: their very existence mocked the Dark Gods the Leishoranya served, and prevented their manifestation in the world.

Tsingar repeated his ancestors' names: the sealed places opened and memories flooded his mind—not only his memories, but those of his ancestors before him, tens of thousands of years old. For this hour, he remembered the minutest detail of the course that had brought his people here, through centuries of warfare, to this city, this morning, this assault—

Another land: his people had hunted the Krotànya there. Great battles fought under strange skies and stranger stars. And finally, clan by clan, the Krotànya were forced into their last retreat, out onto the sea. Sensing victory, Ssenkahdavic had set sail after them.

But on a summer's afternoon, virtually within Ssenkahdavic's reach, the Krotànya had sailed through a hidden gateway into another time and place. Aided, some said, by the Gods of Light, they fled beyond even Ssenkahdavic's knowledge.

And then disaster overwhelmed the Leishoranya. The backlash of the power the Gods of Light wielded all but destroyed Tsingar's ancestors. The fleet that had pursued the Krotànya foundered in the open seas and sank, leaving only a few survivors, including Ssenkahdavic, to struggle back to land. And the Leishoranya? In the moment that backlash had poured over them, they became no better than beasts, forgetting their heritage, their purpose, their reason for being. For 30,000 years, they struggled upward from savagery, slowly regaining their strength and skills. And always Ssenkahdavic stood waiting, chosen not long after the disaster by the Darkness itself to be its channel.

Tsingar opened his eyes, forced his breath calm. His hands trembled on his weapons: the memories of Ssenkahdavic's rage—of his ancestors' agony and slow regrowth—burned like a fire in his mind. And the Gods? Their will was still plain.

For centuries after the Leishoranya had regained their strength, and after Ssenkahdavic had finally united them, the Warlord had searched for that gate. The search obsessed him, drove him near madness, drove some of those around him past it. When at last he did find the way, when he had led his armies through, it was to a new land, the eastern shore of a country well-settled. The Krotànya were waiting and it all began again.

And this time, the Krotànya were not ready, though they had grown in numbers and strength of mind. Their kingdoms flourished; descendants of those Ssenkahdavic sought ruled in a land where war was only a dim memory. Those kingdoms were old now, but Ssenkahdavic's hatred was new as ever. And beneath the unknown wheeling stars, war flamed forth once more.

Time wavered—past was present again. Cold and stiff, Tsingar knelt in the darkness, shaken by all he had remembered. He straightened his shoulders, anxious that he still knelt unnoticed. Lieutenant to Dhumaric, who served Ssenkahdavic, who served the Void Itself, he could not allow his inferiors to see any weakness.

"Gods . . . Gods of my people," he whispered. "Let me be your knife-hand today. If I must die, grant me an honorable death that I may be reborn stronger to serve your will." His anger grew, his desire to kill, to fulfill his part in his people's ancient quest. Deep inside he felt the nearness of his ancestors, the ghostly touch of his Gods and his ambition.

He bowed his head to the ground, then rocked back on his heels. One by one, he lifted his weapons, kissed them, and slid them into their sheaths. He stood and walked as far as the forest edge, within view of the

Krotànya city. The rim of the rising sun was near the horizon.

Kahsir watched that rising from Rodja'âno's eastern wall, looked out over the vast oak forests that stretched off for leagues in all directions, and felt the enemy presence waking. Close by, Lorhaiden leaned on the parapets, sunk in moody silence, a small breeze stirring the long brown hair on his shoulders. Warriors were coming to their posts now, assuming the routine of attack and defense. Kahsir sensed the men's fatigue—he was equally exhausted. It was the fifth day of the attack. Outnumbered, they now faced the possibility of having to fight an enemy army *and* its reinforcements. The rumor had gotten to them. There was the smoke of burning on the northern horizon, which carried its own news.

Kahsir turned about, leaned back on the parapet, and looked down on the city below. Less disturbing, this view, than what he saw when he walked the deserted streets. Rodja'âno was old, this capital of the Kingdom of Tumâs—older even than Hvâlkir, the King City, capital of all Twelve Kingdoms of the Krotànya. Thousands of years had passed since Rodja'âno's building—its foundations were older than the Krotànya in the land—but it was a beautiful city whose occupants had kept time at bay by constant renovation, a city of high towers and buildings of simple lines. The broad sweep of the River Lhanic ran on the north side of the city; the ruins of the Lhanic bridge had kept Leishoranya supply wagons to the opposite bank, a tactical problem the enemy had not yet solved. Smoke from cooking fires rose over the city within the walls as some semblance of life went on despite the continued attack.

Suddenly in the dawning, Kahsir's mind was full of faces—faces of those he loved best: his grandfather, his father, brothers and sisters; his Chosen Woman. A fierce longing to see them one last time—

Dammit, no! He cut those thoughts off, blanked his mind to calmness. *You aren't going to die here! Quit acting as if you were!* Certain thoughts had ways of becoming self-fulfilling prophecies.

He shifted uneasily. Lorhaiden stood by, respecting his silence, but he could not sense what Lorhaiden was thinking. *He's probably looking forward to the fighting. Lords! If only he could forget.*

He glanced sidelong at Lorhaiden, seeing for a moment his sword-brother's face as it had been before his family had been massacred, a face free of the harsh lines that marred it now. The silver eyes had been warm then, not chips of ice. It had been an ordinary day filled with ordinary duties: Kahsir had been back in the capital, come home briefly from the war to attend Council. He had gone outside to walk in the garden by the palace, had stood leaning on the stone wall, looking at the flowers, the trees—

—the afternoon's sunlight, the three crosses of dried blood that caked Lorhaiden's cheeks and forehead, the stiffness of the face beneath those marks. The halting words as Lorhaiden spoke of what had happened. And everyone knowing, by virtue of that bloody branding, that Lorhaiden had taken the ultimate oath of vengeance, had marked himself with his family's blood and bound himself to kill and slaughter until death.

The moment he had seen Lorhaiden, Kahsir's relationship with his sword-brother had altered around that Oath. Other people might consider Lorhaiden crazy, but there was still something left of his friend and almost-kinsman. He could have turned his back on Lorhaiden, the oaths they had sworn as sword-brother and shieldman negated by this more powerful oath, but he had not. The essence within Lorhaiden had not changed—the loyalty, the love; it had only been warped, twisted by the massacre, by the oath-swearing after. If he could be patient, perhaps Lorhaiden would drift back from his cold world of revenge, closer to the warmth he had known—

Kahsir clamped his shields down: Lorhaiden was unusually moody this morning, possibly more sensitive in picking up thoughts.

He sighed quietly, looked down again at the awakening city. Years ago, centuries ago— His first sight of it: what had it looked like then? He jogged at his mind, opened inner gates, and suddenly he saw Rodja'âno through the eyes of a child, a young boy taken north by his royal grandfather. The city had stood without walls then; the war was yet to come. The centermost buildings looked much the same now, though their lines had been softened and smoothed by the touch of time.

The centuries blurred together. Over fifteen hundred years ago the enemy had found the gateway to this land, had set foot on the continent of Krusâ. Before the war had been peace, growth, eagerness for tomorrow, and unending time. But that had changed. Having achieved near-immortality, the Krotànya had become reacquainted with violent death. They had lost most of the continent in a few centuries of bloody massacre, toughened, and given up the last handful of Kingdoms over long centuries, by battle hard fought.

Kahsir straightened and unclenched his hands. The first sunrays struck the wall itself and Lorhaiden's silver-washed spiked helm flashed with cold fire. Kahsir felt a touch of sadness, a sense of having seen too much. He ran his hand along the weather-smoothed masonry of the parapet. Even the stones he stood upon had worn since last he walked them. He sighed quietly. He was five hundred years Lorhaiden's senior, and today he felt those years.

Suddenly, the sound of horns. Kahsir's heart lurched in his chest.

He spun on his heel and looked off to the east. The enemy was marching on the walls: their archers had already loosed arrows at the ramparts. Kahsir cursed, unsheathed his sword and, with Lorhaiden at his heels, ran off down the wall toward his post.

—*Archers!* His mind-sending to Vàlkir was overlaid with his visual sighting of the enemy as they surged forward, of the enemy's catapults and rams. *Get your bowmen to their posts, Vahl! Eastern wall! Fire at will!* Another quick look to the field. *Damn! Where's Nhavari?*

He looked around, but did not see the King, only felt his presence, his hurry to come to his command position. *Remàdir!* The Mind-Born's thoughts were instantly meshed with his own. *Any action elsewhere?*

—*Not much, Lord. Mainly from the east.*

Kahsir shot a sidelong glance at Lorhaiden, cursed again, and kept running.

Kahsir drew a long, deep breath and leaned against the parapets. Even Lorhaiden looked tired, though he had fought well enough despite his wounded shoulder. Carrying their scaling ladders, dragging their heavy siege engines, the enemy withdrew from out of range in the ebbing of the day, exhausted as the men who defended the walls. Kahsir removed his helm and wiped the sweat from his forehead in the chill of the wind. He blinked wearily and looked down the wall he stood on—the eastern wall, weakened by repeated assault.

Nhavari's portion of the wall was still strong but Haskon had reported more new faults elsewhere. The enemy had not only battered the wall with their catapults, they had assaulted it with their minds. Kahsir closed his eyes briefly, trying to touch his brothers, seeking them along the walls. There was chaos, the pain of the wounded. He sensed presence, nothing more.

"Lord." Lorhaiden gestured. "Remàdir's coming."

Kahsir turned. A white-robed figure walked toward them down the wall, stopping here and there to speak with the wounded.

"My Lord." Remàdir bowed in greeting. His face was

pale and shadows darkened his eyes. "May I speak with you alone?"

Kahsir glanced sidelong at his sword-brother. "Don't worry about Lorhaiden. You can trust him as you would me. What's the matter?" He got nothing from the Mind-Born. No one could. Only Remàdir's expression foretold calamity.

"It's Ssenkahdavic, Lord. He's coming south."

Kahsir stiffened. "By all the Lords of Light! Are you sure?"

"Aye, Lord. I felt his presence earlier."

"How far away is he?" Lorhaiden asked in a thin voice.

"I'm not sure. Several days, I think. But if he takes the mind-road—"

Kahsir chewed on his lower lip, turned away, and looked out over the battlefield. *No, dammit! Not now! What the Dark is he doing coming south? O Lords of Light! Could I have doomed myself by coming here? All my plans—all my hopes! Worthless now!*

"Lord?"

He turned back at Remàdir's prompting. "Have you told Nhavari yet?"

"Aye. Just moments ago. He wants to see you as soon as possible."

"All right." Kahsir rubbed his eyes with a trembling hand. *I've got to get Haskon and Alàric out of here now! Even if he doesn't come to Rodja'âno, Father has to know Ssenkahdavic's coming. The last thing we need is for Father to be trapped!* He glanced at Remàdir. "Do me a favor. Find my brothers and have them report to me immediately."

"Aye, Lord. And in the meantime—what should we do?"

"Nothing yet. I want to talk to Nhavari first. My brothers, Remàdir. Find them, please. Quickly!"

Remàdir bowed, turned, and hurried off down the wall.

"Ah, Lords!" Kahsir looked at Lorhaiden, but his sword-brother stood silent, his face closed and withdrawn. "Dammit, Lorj! You know what this means."

"Aye," Lorhaiden said slowly. "If Ssenkahdavic joins the battle—" He shrugged.

"—we don't stand a chance." Kahsir's mind filled with sights of other cities that Ssenkahdavic had destroyed. He glanced down the wall toward the steps leading to the ground. *Father may have been right after all. How could I have overlooked the chance that Ssenkahdavic would come here?* He met Lorhaiden's eyes. "Where the Void are Haskon and Alàric?"

"Kahs," Lorhaiden said. "What are we going to do now?"

"Get out of here ourselves. As orderly as we can. Father's coming down from Chailon Pass with his four thousand men. We've got the armies spread out between us and the mountains. We can try to reach them."

"What about Nhavari?"

Kahsir rubbed his jaw. "Getting him to leave his city won't be easy, but I think he'll listen to me."

"You *hope* he'll listen. All right. What next?"

"We'll have to—" Kahsir started. His two brothers came trotting up the stairs, Remàdir close behind. Alàric said something to the Mind-Born, then he and Haskon hurried down the wall.

"What's wrong, Kahs?" Alàric asked.

Kahsir drew a deep breath. "Ssenkahdavic's coming south." His brothers stiffened; Haskon opened his mouth to say something. "Not now, Kona. Listen. Remàdir sensed Ssenkahdavic. We can only assume he's coming south with more reinforcements. If the Mind-Born can help us, you're both getting out of Rodja'âno now. You've got to tell Father to stay where he is. He'll have a lot of men with him but he'll be making far too narrow a penetration into Tumâs. If Ssenkahdavic traps him when he's—"

"Now wait just a minute," Haskon said. "You're talking about *us* leaving."

"Kona—"

"Kahs, *you're* the least expendable. You're the eldest, the one Vlàdor and Father have both trained as heir, the one—"

Kahsir glared. "Then as eldest, I'm ordering you both out of the city. Now get your shieldmen and meet me back here on the wall."

"But, Kahs," Alàric said. "Have you forgotten the enemy block? How far do you expect us to get without them noticing us? We can't shield ourselves properly— they'll sense us clear. Four of us—"

"Trust the Mind-Born. If there's a way, they'll cover you."

Haskon nodded at the thought. "Aye. They can do it if conditions are right." His gaze snapped back to Kahsir. "But dammit, Kahs! To leave you behind—"

Kahsir sighed quietly. "Don't start in on it again, Kona. The subject's closed."

For a long moment, neither Haskon nor Alàric said anything; their expressions of defeat and anger spoke for them.

"I still want you to guide any refugees you find to Father's army," Kahsir said. "And make sure he understands that he's *not* to come any farther north than he must. We're going to be falling back much quicker than we ever planned."

"It's not going to be easy for Nhavari to find another place to hold," Alàric said. "Rodja'âno is too strategically important."

"If Ssenkahdavic decides to take this city, Ahri, there's not a thing we can do to stop him."

"How far back will you retreat?"

"I'm not sure. I haven't talked to Nhavari yet. But more than likely we'll retreat about fifty leagues to the southwest, toward Aigenhal. Those of us who make it will regroup there, retreat a few more leagues, then try to set up some lines of defense. Now get going. I want you both ready to leave in a quarter hour."

"Aye," Alàric said, his face curiously devoid of expression. "But keep this in mind, Kahs. Orders or no orders, I'm leaving under protest. So's Haskon. And if your staying behind gets you killed, it would be the worst blow the enemy's ever dealt us!"

"I'll be out in a moment, Lorj," Kahsir said, his hand on the door leading to Nhavari's tower rooms. "If anyone wants to see the King, tell them to wait."

Kahsir let himself in, closed the door, and faced his friend. Nhavari stared back out of shadowed eyes, his shoulders slumped.

"Well, Kahs," he said, gesturing to a chair next to the one he occupied, "this is one contingency you didn't take into consideration."

Kahsir sat down, removed his helm, and balanced it on one knee. "Don't remind me. Now everything I planned is useless. We can't fight Ssenkahdavic."

"And so Rodja'âno dies, and the north falls after." Nhavari looked out of the window at the darkening sky beyond. "Who would ever have thought Ssenkahdavic would come south?"

"Oh, dammit, Vahri, we should have suspected it. *I* should have suspected it. He's been hidden away in Fânchorion long enough now to gain back some of his strength."

Nhavari did not reply. Kahsir rubbed his eyes and stared off at the wall. *Damn, damn! Here we sit, waiting for Ssenkahdavic, being assaulted by siege engines and enemy minds! Why can't we fight back mentally? Why?* He stirred uncomfortably in his chair, hearing voices from the past—voices of the Mind-Born who taught that if one used one's mind for anything but defense, one became no better than the enemy. What you plant, you shall harvest, they said. Doing evil makes you evil . . . adds to the Darkness the enemy serves.

Dammit, I understand that, but we've got over six thousand men here, and they're depending on us to get them out of this alive. If only— He shook his head. The Mind-Born *could* be wrong. One man—one man with a very strong mind *might* be able to find a flaw in Ssenkahdavic's shielding . . . *might* be able to strike at him unawares. Of course, that man would likely die, but what was one death in the face of the thousands who could die if nothing was done to stop Ssenkahdavic?

He drew a deep breath, held it a moment, and let it go in a quiet sigh. He was Star-Born, descended in unbroken lineage from Ràthen, the first High-King to rule in Krusâ; and the Star-Born, though not to the same extent as the Mind-Born, possessed powers of mind that other men did not. It was a wild talent, in most Star-Born existing untrained, but it *did* exist.

A small shiver ran through him. He had brought the warriors and Mind-Born in Rodja'âno to this moment when they all faced death at Ssenkahdavic's hands. Should he not be the one who attempted to attack Ssenkahdavic?

Ssenkahdavic . . . Rodja'âno. Kahsir sat up straighter. Ssenkahdavic would only be coming south *if* he planned to continue on, to strike straight through Tumâs at the Kingdom of Elyâsai before the Krotànya could mount the kind of defense necessary to meet him. Ssenkahdavic likely thought the battle for Rodja'âno would be easily won, that he would not have to expend much of his strength in taking the city. A quick victory would leave him comparatively fresh for his assault on Elyâsai.

Somehow, Ssenkahdavic would have to be worn down, whether Kahsir did it himself, or used the concerted effort of the Mind-Born in Rodja'âno.

Nhavari shifted his weight in his chair. "Now what do we do, Kahs?"

"One of two things: we either try to run now, using the Mind-Born to break through the enemy's block, or we make a stand and fight until the Leishoranya *and*

Ssenkahdavic are weary. Either way, there's going to be a huge loss of life."

"Aye." Nhavari's eyes were shadows. "I've already been advised to run."

"I counsel staying. If we can tire Ssenkahdavic, it will give us more time to prepare our defenses to the south. Remember Fânchorion. If Ssenkahdavic's exhausted to the state he was in after taking Fânchorion, he *might* be so tired he'll go dormant again. This could give us another twenty years, Vahri, if we play things right . . . *and* are lucky."

"Huhn." Nhavari met Kahsir's eyes. "But Rodja'âno's lost, no matter what we do."

"True. But let's make her fall worth something. If we can gain another twenty years, we won't have fought in vain."

Nhavari nodded, coming closer, Kahsir knew, to accepting that nothing could save his city.

"We'll have to plan our retreat carefully," Kahsir said. "I want us to leave here as quickly and efficiently as we can. We'll have to fall back and reform our defenses."

"What about your father?"

Kahsir barked a laugh. "Only one thing's certain . . . if I don't die in this final engagement, he'll kill me when he sees me."

Nhavari was silent a long while; in the fading light, his face was hard to read. He bowed his head. "Kahs . . . if there was only some way to save Rodja'âno . . . to save my people, I'd—"

"I know, Vahri." Kahsir reached out and gripped the King's shoulder. "But there's not . . . not if Ssenkahdavic wants this city. The only thing we can do for your people is to tire Ssenkahdavic and get as many fighting men out of here as we can."

"You're right." The King drew a ragged breath. "Lords! I'm glad Father's not here to see this."

Nhavari's father, Sorondàr, had left the world before the war had begun. After only thirty centuries he had

grown weary of his life, had taken his ship and sailed off
into the ocean, seeking the Final Gateway to the Realm
of Light.

"I always knew Rodja'âno would fall someday. But I
never suspected it would be this soon."

Kahsir stared at his friend. "None of us did. Vahri,
how soon can you gather your commanders?"

"I can have everyone here inside an hour."

"Good. I want to tell them what I've told you. Either
way, we'll have to rethink our plans. I should be back
shortly."

"Where are you going?"

"I have an appointment with the Mind-Born. Alàric
and Haskon have got to leave the city, block or no
block. Father *has* to know what's happening here." He
tightened his grip on Nhavari's shoulder. "You'll be all
right, won't you?"

"Aye. Go, Kahs. I need a few moments to myself. I'll
have the commanders here by the time you get back."

Kahsir shook his head as he walked back down the
wall, Lorhaiden keeping pace at his side. *Lords! It's
Nhavari's city—his kingdom that will be destroyed! I
wonder if I could act so calm?*

Alàric and Haskon waited by the parapets, Remàdir
standing nearby. As Kahsir came closer, he looked closely
at his brothers. Grim-faced, they stared back in the
fading sunlight, but he sensed no further rebellion.

"Remàdir says the way is open," Alàric said. "The
enemy's not blocking as strongly. He and the other
Mind-Born will shield our going as best they can."

Kahsir nodded, then looked at his brothers again,
weighing their reactions to what he would do next. There
was no question that Haskon would fight—Alàric, too,
perhaps. A brief pang of anxiety tightened his heart:
what if Haskon refuses? He sighed quietly. *I've got to
let Father know what's happening, and take full responsibility for my actions. And I've lied to them enough.*

Get on with it. The afternoon's growing no younger.
He straightened, removed the heavy silver ring he wore
on his right hand, and extended it to Haskon. "Give
this to Father when you see him, will you?"

"The heir's ring," Haskon said, looking at it as it lay
in his palm. Alàric's brow furrowed, but he remained
silent. Haskon's eyes snapped up to Kahsir's face. "Take
it back, Kahs. You're not going to die here."

"Who spoke of dying?" Kahsir consciously kept his
voice light. He met Haskon's eyes. *It's all right, Kona,*
he Sent. *I swear it.* And then to himself, clamping
down on his already tight shields: *It's just my resignation, Kona. I don't need to die to resign.* "Get the ring
to Father," he said aloud. "It's a message he'll understand."

Haskon's jaw tightened. "Why don't you give us the
message that goes with it? We can tell him easier and
you can keep the ring."

"And what if the enemy catches you on the way there?
Eh? What then?"

Haskon looked down at his feet, then up again. "But,
Kahs—"

"For the Light's sake, Kona—take the ring and stop
arguing." He cleared his throat and turned to Remàdir.
"How far can my brothers go without drawing attention
to themselves?"

"At best, not more than twenty leagues, Lord," the
white-robed man replied. "To go farther would take so
much of their energy and ours that all secrecy would be
lost. Though the block's not as tight, the enemy's still
watching the mind-road closely; there's little chance for
greater distance."

Kahsir drew in his breath: twenty leagues would
barely put them past the village of Habaden.

"It's better than nothing, Kahs," Alàric said. "Given
luck, we'll find horses quickly enough in the steadings
farther south. With Father coming down through Chailon
Pass—"

"Aye. You shouldn't have any trouble finding him."

Haskon shifted his weight again, his face hard to read in the dim light. Weighing the silver ring in his hand, he extended the heirloom to Kahsir. "Take this back, Kahs."

"No. Stop worrying." He straightened his shoulders and turned his head at the sound of footsteps on the walkway. Two fully armed men approached—his brothers' shieldmen. Kahsir looked back: Haskon held his gaze for a moment, still rebellious, then reluctantly slid the heir's ring onto his left hand. Remàdir gestured briefly and nodded.

"Stay well," Kahsir murmured, clasping Haskon in a tight embrace. He held his middle brother a moment longer by the shoulders, then turned to Alàric. "Watch over him, Alàric. Keep him sensible if you can." A quick, fierce embrace between eldest and youngest. Though he kept his mind tightly shielded, he sensed his brothers' thoughts. *What if Kahs dies?* That from Alàric, but Haskon's thoughts were equally loud. *I don't have any right to the heir's ring, Kahs. Take it back*. Love, concern, fear: emotions intensified until he shut them away, buried his own deeper. He looked at both his brothers. "Tell Father we'll hold out here as long as we can. Don't let him come much closer than the foot of the mountains. When Rodja'âno falls, Nhavari and I will retreat toward Aigenhal. After we've got things more in hand, or if anything changes drastically, I'll try to get a message off to Father. Now go! The Light watch over you."

He stepped back as Alàric, Haskon, and their two shieldmen turned to Remàdir. The Mind-Born looked carefully at each man, and an expression of intense concentration spread over his face. Kahsir felt Remàdir's mind reach out, join with those of the other Mind-Born, then steady into a vast well of power. The shimmering arc of the gate to the mind-road solidified on the ramparts. The instant had come. It was now up to his brothers and their shieldmen to act.

The four men stepped through that gate—and only Kahsir, Remàdir, and Lorhaiden stood on the wall.

He shifted his weight, aware he had held his breath through the whole thing. The mind-link and combined shielding had been skillfully constructed. No one could have noticed the departure unless warned beforehand. As the gateway faded, he sighed in relief and the sense of loss that followed.

"Lord? Same orders?"

Kahsir glanced sidelong, saw Remàdir waiting patiently. "Aye. And bring more of your comrades to the eastern wall tomorrow. The enemy's going to come at it the hardest. And keep me advised on anything you can sense of Ssenkahdavic." He gestured to Lorhaiden and turned away. *Now, Nhavari and I must decide how long we're going to try to hold. The steadings immediately south of here have been evacuated, and we don't have enough men to form much of a defenseive line, but—* He halted suddenly in midstep; a flush of embarrassment crept over his face and he turned back to Remàdir. "For what you did, all of you, my thanks."

Remàdir bowed slightly and walked off. Kahsir watched him go and wished for a small part of his talents, but those who would ultimately take up the white spent decades in arduous training. They came from all walks of life: noblemen, farmers, merchants—their one qualification being minds of great strength and potential.

Lorhaiden cleared his throat and Kahsir came back to the present with a mental snap.

"I don't know what we'd do without them," he said, gesturing at Remàdir's retreating figure.

"We'd be in sorry straits if they hadn't chosen to remain behind," Lorhaiden agreed. "Are we going to meet with Nhavari now?"

"Aye. He's already sent for his commanders. I'll bet

he has to wake a few of them up. Lords know we should snatch as much rest as we can!" He set off down the battlements, his sword-brother matching his stride. He glanced at Lorhaiden as they walked. "Can you imagine what Nhavari's feeling, Lorj? Rodja'âno's his capital city, his home. And Ssenkahdavic's coming: there's no chance Rodja'âno will survive." He shook his head, forbidding himself other thoughts, thoughts of his own city, and of what could happen there.

CHAPTER 3

Kahsir cursed and ducked under his opponent's swordstroke. He swung his own sword up, felt it slide harmlessly off the Leishoran's shield. The warrior feinted, but Kahsir read the move, lifted his sword, and deflected the blow. A few quick steps put the afternoon sun at his back and he took advantage of the slanting light in the enemy's eyes. Suddenly, he saw an opening in his opponent's guard—he lunged, his shield held close, and felt his blade bite into the enemy's chest.

He jerked his sword away and glanced around: other Leishoranya were gaining the walls. He sensed Lorhaiden to his left, heard his sword-brother's laughter. Only Lorhaiden would laugh at a time like this. *Thank the Lords I got Kona and Ahri out yesterday. The enemy's tightened their watch over the city—no one could leave unnoticed now.*

Another Leishoran clambered through the crenel. Lorhaiden reacted first, leapt forward, and nearly beheaded the enemy warrior. Kahsir drew a deep breath, turned slightly, looking for the King of Tumâs. *Nhavari— where's Nhavari? I can't see him! What's happening to—*

"Get that damned ladder off the wall!"

Lorhaiden's voice. Kahsir swung around, faced the battle again. Several men rushed to the parapet, reached the crenel and shoved at the scaling ladder. A Leishoran had mounted to the top of it: Kahsir could easily see the enemy warrior's face, the dark perfection of its beauty.

An arrow sank into the Leishoran's neck above his chainmail. He cried out—a long, gurgling sound—and, face frozen in shocked surprise, fell backward even as the ladder toppled away from the wall.

Kahsir risked another glance to his left, to Nhavari's position, and saw Leishoranya thick on the parapets. He looked back: the wall where he and his men stood was comparatively free of the enemy.

"Lorhaiden! We've got to strengthen Nhavari's position. The Leishoranya are all over it."

"With *what*, Lord?" Lorhaiden asked. "We're running short of men ourselves."

That's truth. Kahsir turned back to the parapets. *Nhavari . . . Nhavari! Don't let the bastards break through! Hold a little longer if you can.* Another scaling ladder hit the wall, but this time Kahsir's men were quicker: they pushed the ladder away before the enemy could mount it.

"Arrows, Lord!"

Kahsir ducked behind the parapet beside Lorhaiden, heard the whine of the arrows as they passed over his head. Screams followed, cries of anger and pain.

"*Chuht!*" He turned to Lorhaiden. "We've got to get some help over here." He glanced again to his left, saw more Leishoranya on the wall. "Your brother's closest. See if he can send some of his men."

Another wave of arrows fell. Kahsir lifted his shield, heard the missiles rattle harmlessly away. He sensed Lorhaiden's mind reach out to Vàlkir and looked back to where Nhavari fought.

"It's no use, Lord," Lorhaiden cried over the noise.

"Vàlkir's been attacked again, can't spare any of his men, either. We'll have to make do with those we have."

Kahsir cursed again, glanced over his shoulder, to the west. The sun was setting but the enemy still came at the walls. *Lords of Light! They can't keep this up much longer! If we can keep the scaling ladders off the wall, perhaps—*

A roar went up from the Krotànya to his left; hatred, grief, rage—his mind was rocked by a flood of emotions. He spun on his heel, faced down the wall, his heart pounding loudly in his chest.

Nhavari! Kahsir winced beneath the broadcast pain. *The King's wounded!* Krotànya thoughts and emotions piled one upon the other, jumbled, full of despair: *Aid to us! The King's near death!*

"Lorhaiden!" He rounded on his sword-brother, gestured at the enemy. "Keep those dung-balls off the parapets! I'm taking ten men with me. Nhavari—"

"Go, Lord," Lorhaiden said. "We'll hold our own here."

Kahsir beckoned to a group of men-at-arms and sprinted off down the wall. An arrow hissed by his head, and he nearly tripped over a body, but he ran on.

To encounter a tremendous press of men by the King's position. Kahsir glanced widly around but could not guess how many of the enemy had managed to get over the parapets onto the walkway. Rage, near reckless desire for revenge swept through Krotànya minds close by. One of Kahsir's me ran ahead, shoving a way through the throng, the others at his side, ready to hold the enemy and their ladders back.

—Nhavari! Kahsir Sent, seeking a touch from the King's mind. A weak response brushed his awareness. *Lords! I can barely sense him and I'm this close—*

The Krotànya fought the enemy at the parapets, wildly unconcerned for their own safety. Kahsir paused a moment, disoriented in the rush of fighting men. A Leishoran loomed up in the confusion on the walk . . .

Kahsir lashed out with his sword, felt the blade strike flesh, pushed the warrior aside.

He reached the head of the steps that led from the wall to the ground. *Dammit! Where the bloody Void's Nhavari?* Then the crowd of Krotànya on the parapet gave back. Two men-at-arms reached the stairs, carrying the King between them. A chill ran down Kahsir's spine. *O Lords! He'll bleed to death!*

"Get him off the wall!" Kahsir yelled. "Hurry!" He looked around, seeking one of the Mind-Born. *Remàdir!* he Sent—the other would Hear. *Find us a healer! Quickly! Nhavarai's badly wounded!*

—*Aye, Lord,* came Remàdir's powerful response. *A healer's on his way!*

Kahsir motioned toward the stairway. "Be careful!" he cautioned, stepping aside as the men-at-arms began to descend. *Lords of Light! Not Nhavari! Please—not Nhavari!* He looked back at the wall: there were fewer Leishoranya on it than before. He shrugged, turned, and followed the wounded King.

Dim light, choked with shadows, filled the courtyard below the wall. Kahsir started to sheath his sword, noticed the blood caking its blade, and let the weapon dangle from his hand. Now that he had stopped fighting, he shook with weariness and stood panting in the gloom. The men-at-arms lowered the King to the ground, one wrapping another cloak around the limp body. Kahsir knelt, dropping his shield and sword, and blocked his mind from the King's pain and the rage of those close by.

"Nhavari." He swallowed heavily. Nhavari had lost his helmet; his long blond hair fell partially over his face. Pain contorted the King's fine features, his eyes stared slightly unfocused, but at the sound of his name, Nhavari struggled to full awareness. "A healer's coming," Kahsir said, touching the King's mind with thoughts of comfort, of reassurance.

Nhavari tried to speak and coughed instead: blood ran from his mouth, and his face paled even more. Kahsir shook his head, but the King was stubborn. "Quit worrying about me, Kahs," Nhavari gasped, and coughed again. "I'm done." His eyes closed, then opened, full of pain. "You've got to finish what we began. We've got to keep the enemy from overrunning the northlands." The King's mouth thinned in a grimace of pain. "Hope doesn't have to die with me."

"Don't talk like that! Help's coming." Kahsir reached out to touch the King and flinched, fully feeling the other's pain. *Dammit, Vahri! Don't let go. You've too much to live for. Lords of Light! Fight it! I know you can!* Kahsir glanced up, looking for the healer, then back. "We need you, Vahri. Your people need you! A while longer—hold on just a while longer."

Nhavari licked his lips. "I'm trying," he croaked, coughing once more. "Lords know I'm trying." An intent look crossed the King's features. He coughed again and suddenly gripped Kahsir's arm. "I'm cold—so cold," Nhavari said, forming each word with difficulty. "Stay by me."

Kahsir blinked back tears. "I'm here, Vahri. I'm here."

The King's grip relaxed somewhat, but he still held Kahsir's arm. "Is it night already? It's so dark." A shudder ran through his body. "I love them," he whispered. Kahsir leaned closer to hear. "I love them, my people." Suddenly energy lit up the pale face. "Listen to me! When Ssenkahdavic takes the city, retreat to the southwest like we planned. You'll have to regroup. Have to—" Another racking cough, followed by more blood. Tears welled up in the King's eyes, spilled down his cheeks. "Why?" Nhavari asked. "Why did . . . ?"

The hand that held Kahsir's arm tightened and then went limp.

"Nhavari!" Kahsir looked into the King's face, sensed the emptiness of death. He closed his eyes, felt his own tears come. "*Aiii*, Vahri," he whispered. His mind slid automatically into the rhythms of the death ritual. *May the Lords of Light grant you passage. May the stars welcome you home. May—*

"Lord."

He jerked his head up, gently loosened the hand from his arm. The healer stood at his shoulder, surrounded by men-at-arms and other warriors drawn by the King's death.

"I'll take him, Lord," the healer said. Mind-Born that he was, he showed his grief and loss. "He was my King, Lord. Go. The enemy's withdrawing. Your comrades will need you back on the wall."

Kahsir closed his eyes, pushed his hair back over his shoulders, then groped blindly for his shield and sword. *Back on the wall. Aye, they'll need me there. The wounded, the—* He stood, knees shaking, and those around drew back to give more space. He shivered suddenly. *I'm in command now that Nhavari's dead. And now what do I do?* He wiped his tears away, looked once more at his dead friend, then turned toward the steps leading to the parapets.

Afternoon sunlight beat down on the walls. Kahsir stood in the command position by the eastern gate, his post since Nhavari had died the day before. The enemy reinforcements had come in—another ten thousand men. The army that besieged Rodja'âno now numbered close to twenty-five thousand. He shook his head. *Maybe the Mind-Born are wrong. Maybe Ssenkahdavic's not there, and the enemy tricked the Mind-Born into thinking he is. Men we can beat . . . the Shadow we can't.*

He scratched at a cut on his forearm. *And men, only if they don't go after our minds. Damn! If we could only meet them on their own terms!*

The stillness seemed unendurable, and even the veterans shifted uneasily. Kahsir leaned on the parapets; back and shoulders tight with tension, he consciously tried to relax. Rubbing the back of his neck, he straightened and glanced around. The strain and exhaustion on his companions' faces was growing worse with the passing of every day.

Though the Leishoranya had hurled their full might against Rodja'âno's walls, those walls still stood. Great skill had gone into their making—skill and binding-words that further melded stone to stone. Kahsir looked down the length of wall he stood on. *The walls can't last forever. Sooner or later they'll be weakened beyond repair. And, Lords! If Ssenkahdavic's out there— Not a wall built can withstand him.*

For hours now, as the sun had slowly fallen into the western skies, the massive Leishoranya army had stood silent, unmoving as statues, just outside the reach of spear or bow. Some of the younger Krotànya, those with little battle experience, had guessed this the time the enemy gave over to the worship of their weapons. Not so: this was a tactic the Leishoranya used to unnerve their opponents.

"My Lord. Look. Over there."

Kahsir turned as Lorhaiden spoke, followed the line of his *baràdor*'s finger. Off to the left of the city, near the river's bend, the enemy warriors began to stir. Something cold and dark slithered across Kahsir's mind. All his worst fears, his worst expectations, were coming true. He turned to meet Lorhaiden's eyes.

"Ssenkahdavic's here," he said.

"Aye. We'll be knee deep in it soon, and we won't last very long. The walls are perilous now. They've been pounded near to rubble and repaired too many times."

Kahsir sighed, and removed his helm to run a hand through his hair. He firmly reset the helmet, tried to keep exhaustion and dread from his voice. "Even if they hadn't been weakened already, Ssenkahdavic could breach them."

Lorhaiden shrugged. "True. But it might take him longer if the walls were new."

"Huhn." Kahsir glanced at his sword-brother. *Doesn't he feel any fear?* "Argue that with the engineers another time. It won't make a damned bit of difference in the end."

Tsingar stood close to the front ranks, motionless in the afternoon's sunlight, his dark cloak and black leathers making the chill day seem warmer. The city loomed up, its walls bright in the sunshine; he was close enough to see Krotànya warriors on the parapets. He sensed his comrades nearby, the weight of the massive army behind him. Dhumaric had the honor of leading one of the first assaults against the weakened eastern wall, and as Dhumaric's second in command, Tsingar took a troop of his own, too.

Despite the sunlight, he shivered. Ssenkahdavic was coming. The Warlord had arrived only a few hours ago and had remained across the river—now, that presence permeated the field. Tsingar took a deep breath. *Gods give me strength! Don't let me fail.* He had fought with Dhumaric for centuries, but seldom under Ssenkahdavic's direct command.

He looked up at the city again, longing to stretch the stiffness from his arms and legs. *Be patient, you fool. You'll be fighting soon enough. Don't let anyone see your nervousness.*

He sensed Dhumaric's idle glance and kept his eyes trained on the city wall. *The battle—think about the battle, the joy of breaking from your position, charging toward the walls. You won't have to worry about anything when you're fighting.*

Ssenkahdavic drew nearer. Tsingar shivered again and buried his thoughts even deeper. *Ancestors! Which is worse? Dying or being noticed by the Lord?*

All around Kahsir, warriors began to stir. Some adjusted swordbelts, some loosened weapons in their sheaths, while others brought their supplies of arrows closer to hand and tested the tension of their bowstrings.

Kahsir looked out over the motionless enemy again, northeast to where Ssenkahdavic rode. Now—the time had come. His stomach tightened, his mouth filled with a bitter taste. Centuries of warfare made facing death no easier. He shifted his weight from foot to foot and looked around the wall. *I've got to talk with my commanders and discuss final instructions. Soon we won't have the time.* He reached out with his mind to contact them, reached out and found nothing—a block, an impenetrable wall: his mind lay trapped within his skull. He darted a sidelong glance at Lorhaiden and shot his sword-brother a quick thought, but Lorhaiden had been equally affected. The Dark Lord had done this; Ssenkahdavic had effectively cut off any attempts at mental sending within the city.

Lords of Light! How can I coordinate our defense if I can't mind-send? I won't know what's happening on the other walls!

"Dammit to Darkness!" He turned to Lorhaiden. "Lorj, get the commanders. Hurry! We're running out of time."

Lorhaiden nodded and ran off down the wall, shouting orders to other men for help. Kahsir looked out at the enemy again, his heart lightening. *By the Light! The power Ssenkahdavic must wield! That he can lower a mental block over an entire city— Even the Mind-Born can't equal what he can do. And I had the temerity to think of attacking him. . . .* He shook his head, fighting the dullness that lodged there, the influence of the mind-block, frowned, forced his fists to unclench, and waited for his commanders.

Eyes dark in the afternoon light, a group of grim, weary men surrounded Kahsir at his command post on the parapets: even Remàdir was there. Six of Nhavari's commanders had survived—before he died, the King had named Lorhaiden's brother Vàlkir the seventh. Each of those men commanded nearly one thousand warriors. Four of the commanders bore wounds but none, not even Vàlkir, the youngest of them present, appeared any less determined for all of that.

Kahsir turned to face these men. They sought his eyes, looking for hope, and he cringed inwardly: he could give them none. "Ssenkahdavic's coming," he said simply. "There's not a damned thing we can do to prevent him from using his powers. He's already damped our minds." A low murmur ran through the commanders, a wordless growl of anger. *Now, spin the lie out . . . tell them what you want them to hear.* "Nhavari planned to hold the city until my father could arrive with reinforcements. Then Rodja'âno would served as a base of operations to stabilize the northern border." He looked from face to face. "That hope's gone now. Nhavari's dead and Ssenkahdavic's here. If Ssenkahdavic enters the battle, we can't hope to beat him. The only thing we *can* hope to do is to tire him so he'll be in no condition to come south any time soon. When the moment comes that we can't fight him any longer, our main purpose will be to get everyone we can out of the city alive."

"But, Lord," one of the commanders said, scratching at his beard, "we're surrounded. If we try to break through—"

"I know. We'll have to fight first, make Ssenkahdavic *think* we're going to hold out until the last man. The way I see it, the enemy will come hardest at the weakened eastern wall."

The commanders murmured agreement.

"Now, if—when—Ssenkahdavic enters the battle, here's what I want you to do. Reordan." Kahsir looked at Nhavari's guard captain. All the man's polish was gone; bloodied and wounded, he still held himself proudly. "Burn the central records, the library, any place you can think of that information useful to the enemy might be kept. And bring me maps of this region."

"Aye, Lord."

"Jhovàn." Kahsir turned to a stocky red-haired fellow standing to his left. "You'll be in charge of keeping us an escape route—someplace on the southern wall."

"Aye, Lord. Durstàn's Gate. Wide and easiest."

Kahsir rubbed his chin. "Open it on my orders. And only if the enemy withdraws. Signal me with mirrors since we can't mind-send. Errehmon?" One of the veterans, a scarred man with a heavy blond beard, stepped forward. "You'll be in charge of regrouping the warriors outside the city once we've escaped." He looked at the other commanders. "Fall back around fifty leagues to the southwest. There's a small town there—"

"Aigenhal?" Errehmon guessed.

"Aigenhal. Each of you is to let his men know that's the point of gathering. Aigenhal's far enough away that we should be beyond enemy reach long enough to organize some type of defense. Also, I want you to break your companies down into bands of around fifty each—easier to slip unseen through the woods. Most of you know the land around here. Scatter. I don't think the enemy will follow you. If they do, you'll be harder to track, and they'll have to divide their forces, too. And if you run across any steadings close by that haven't been evacuated and destroyed, get those people out as soon as possible."

"And you, Lord?" asked Jhovàn.

"I'm going to try to reach my father. If my brothers were able to slip past the enemy on the mind-road, they're already there. But Father doesn't know the latest enemy positions, or that Ssenkahdavic's coming south. Once I see Father, I'll be able to give him an accurate enough overview of things."

A wiry man, his leg bound just above the knee, caught Kahsir's eye.

"How many men is your father bringing with him?"

"Four thousand at last count."

"Where is he now?" Errehmon asked.

Kahsir glanced over his shoulder to the south where the forests stretched away from Rodja'âno to the distant foothills. Farther southward lay the snow-capped peaks of the Golondai Mountains, halfway between Rodja'âno and the border between the Kingdoms of Tumâs and Elyâsai. He gestured to the southeast. "He's coming down through Chailon Pass."

"And if Ssenkahdavic merely watches and doesn't fight?" asked a heavyset men to Kahsir's left, a tinge of hope in his voice.

"Why else would Ssenkahdavic be here other than to fight? If we don't draw him into battle, he'll go right over us, over the mountains, into Elyâsai. We *must* hold long enough to get him involved. Whatever the case, the major enemy assault will still be here," Kahsir replied, slapping the parapet for emphasis. "Against the eastern wall. I want our best warriors stationed here. When Ssenkahdavic brings the Shadow down upon us, we've got the hope he'll withdraw pressure from those other walls while he's doing it. We go for the south wall when it happens. Tell your men to bring several days' rations with them—anything they'll need to make a forest journey. And—listen to me! This is important. Do *not* take wounded with you."

The commanders stirred uneasily, a few muttering beneath their breaths.

"I know, but we don't have a choice. Arm them, give them the best chance you can to go out fighting. You've got to concentrate on the ones you *can* save. Anyone who can't carry his own weight has to be left behind."

"But, Lord . . . my cousin—"

"You heard me," Kahsir said, each word evenly spaced and precise. "*Anyone.*"

"But, Lord . . . that's—" The man waved his hands. "We might as well kill them now. And I'll be damned if I let my cousin wait for—"

"No more argument, Bevàdyr," Kahsir snapped. The commander glared, his face gone white and hard. "*I'll* take responsibility. And leave your positions only at my order. The northern, western, and southern commands will withdraw first, and in that sequence. We'll stay a while here on the eastern wall to give you cover as long as you need it."

"What of the Mind-Born, Lord?" another man asked.

Kahsir gestured toward Remàdir: the white-robed man took a step forward.

"We'll be in our usual positions," Remàdir said, "scattered throughout the city. We've kept the enemy from taking the mind-road across the walls and that's what we'll continue to do. But even combined we can't *defeat* the Shadow. We can only try to deflect its Power long enough to tire Ssenkahdavic and give everyone a chance to get out."

A heavy silence fell, heavier because of the enemy's silence. Several men shifted their weight uneasily, their eyes lowered.

"Fight fiercely—I charge you with that," Kahsir said at last. "But remember, we've got to get as many possible out of Rodja'âno alive."

All eyes were on him now—eyes set in determined faces. His commanders' thoughts were easy enough to sense: no one flinched before what they all knew was coming.

"Go, then," he said. "Good luck!"

The commanders saluted, and one by one returned down the walls to their posts—all save Lorhaiden's brother.

"Should we concentrate more archers to the left of the gate?" Vàlkir asked, watching Ssenkahdavic's slow progress toward the city. Kahsir looked in the same direction: the Leishoranya warlord was riding toward the top of a small hill by the river. "It looks like he'll set himself up on that hill to direct this battle," Vàlkir said, "and if so, archery support toward the north end of the wall would be valuable."

"Aye," Kahsir replied. "Do that. But remember what

I said. Be ready to get out of the city on my order. And come with Lorhaiden and me. Our maps may not be current, and none of us is familiar enough with the land around here to be much help in regrouping the city's warriors. All we can do is get ourselves south and join up with Father."

Vàlkir nodded his understanding. He looked at his brother and grinned: blue-eyed to Lorhaiden's silver-grey; younger; but they were taken often enough for twins. "Lorj. I'll see you later."

The brothers touched hands in farewell, then Vàlkir turned and walked off down the wall to his place among the bowmen. Kahsir watched him go, a warm feeling spreading through his heart. Friends were precious; old friends beyond price.

He flexed his shoulders, loosening tight muscles, and looked down at the enemy again. Beautiful of face and form, they stood silent all around the city, thousands of them, rank upon rank, their handsomeness a mockery of their nature.

Beautiful—they were that, but cruel, and cruelty had produced that beauty. Only infants of a certain cast of features, of height, of coloring, were allowed to survive. Patterned and bred for handsomeness, the only attributes they valued more were savagery and cunning.

Damn! There still must be close to twenty thousand men out there! He looked away—looked at anything but the enemy: the time-worn stones of the walkway, the warriors who waited tensely by the parapets. Resistance seemed useless against a foe that grew stronger every year. If it had only been Leishoranya against Krotànya, things would stand differently. But in Ssenkahdavic, the enemy possessed a weapon that was, so far, unbeatable: a channel through which the Powers of Darkness could flow.

There came a sudden roar from the hillside beyond. Kahsir tensed as the enemy broke from their positions and ran toward the walls, late afternoon sunlight glinting on sword and spear. Arrows hissed past his head; he and the other Krotànya stood by the parapets ducked quickly behind their protection. The order to return fire rang out down the walls. Groups of attackers carried scaling ladders but held back, waiting for their archers to clear the parapets. Kahsir turned to Lorhaiden: their eyes met and Lorhaiden grinned savagely. Kahsir tried to match the smile, but his lips were too stiff to do more than grimace.

His assessment of the enemy had been correct: their major assault was aimed at the eastern wall. He looked anxiously up and down the length of that wall, unable to sense any new flaws—the recent repairs still held. Small difference now: the end result would be the same.

"Look, Lord!" Lorhaiden pointed. "They're bringing a battering ram up to the gate!"

Kahsir glanced down, his mouth gone suddenly dry: Leishoranya warriors swarmed below. Protected by comrades bearing shields, a large group of the enemy ran forward with the battering ram. The men around Kahsir threw spears down from the parapets—too few to be effective. A shuddering boom rose from the gate as the heavy iron end of the ram swung out and made contact.

O Lords! Is Ssenkahdavic playing with us? Why is he wasting his men like this? Why isn't he fighting? His heart sank. *Could he have guessed what we're going to try? Could he sense the trap?*

"Dammit, Lorj! We've got to stop them! Where are the bowmen?"

"Most are with Vàlkir." Lorhaiden peered down the wall, then glanced back. "From the looks of things down there, he can't help us much."

Kahsir cursed. More Leishoranya ran forward carrying scaling ladders. The enemy's use of ladders so soon indicated how weakened Rodja'âno's defenses had become.

"Lord!" A messenger darted up to Kahsir's side, breath-

lessly waving behind. "We need more bowmen! We're
having trouble keeping the Leishoranya off the parapets."

"Go to Vàlkir," Kahsir said. He glanced back to the
area the man had come from, saw brief skirmishes
taking place. "And spread the word. All further requests for archers go to Vàlkir."

The man nodded and raced off down the wall.

"Send us some bowmen, too!" Kahsir yelled after.
"We've got a battering ram coming down our throats!"

He turned and looked out over the field again, at the
attacking enemy, his heart sinking. *Lords of Light! Is
there no end to them?* The warriors that hemmed
Rodja'âno's walls seemed uncountable: for every one
cut down, another was there to take his place.

A heavy thud on the walkway behind, followed by
another, then another: Kahsir glanced over his shoulder
and drew a quick breath.

There, eyes glassily reflecting the afternoon's sunlight, lay the heads of men, women, and children—
Krotànya refugees fallen into Leishoranya hands. Expressions of horror and agony were etched on those
faces; some had been mutilated.

Kahsir clenched his teeth in sickened rage. *It's nothing new. They've done this before—you've seen such
things countless times. The battle, fool! Concentrate on
the battle!*

"By the Light!" Lorhaiden swore, pounding on the
parapet with his fists. "Give me a chance at those
bastards!"

"You'll get it, *baràdor*," Kahsir said in a thin voice.
"You'll get it."

Lorhaiden stiffened and looked out over the battlefield again. He pointed off to the left.

"He's coming, my Lord."

Kahsir swung around: Ssenkahdavic had begun to
ride down the hill toward the city. A rush of frustration
and fear tightened his heart. *Our moment's come.* He
shivered suddenly. *Ah, Lords!*

A scaling ladder hit the parapet and the men close by rushed forward to push it back. Kahsir drew his sword.

Ssenkahdavic must want Rodja'âno badly, or he'd not be willing to spend his strength here. Come, Dark Lord! Tire yourself . . . fight us and our walls!

"Lorhaiden. Go spread the word Ssenkahdavic's coming. I want everyone ready."

Lorhaiden hesitated, wavering, Kahsir knew, between his shieldman's oath and the urgent need to spread the message to the other commanders.

"Dammit, Lorj!" Kahsir snapped, jerking his eyes back to the battle. "Go do it! *Now!*"

"Aye, Lord." Lorhaiden's voice shook with emotion. Kahsir heard him turn away.

"I'll stand by you, Lord," said someone at Kahsir's left. "Hairon dàn Cwechan's my name." Kahsir glanced down into the craggy face of a simple man-at-arms. Clad in rough leather and homespun, the shorter man indicated his shield with the flat of his sword. "I can't take his place," he said, nodding after Lorhaiden's retreating figure, "but I'll stand right here till he comes back."

"Thanks, Hairon," Kahsir said. "I'll probably need you."

"Them scum." The man-at-arms pointed with bearded chin to the Leishoranya below the walls. "Them commanders stay out of trouble, most of 'em. Then they send this here dog meat forward to be slaughtered. Not like us at all."

No, not like us at all. If the legends are true, we were once one people. But the Dark possessed them—they live for death, we fight for life. Huhn. That distinction hasn't helped us. It's true what the Mind-Born say: it's always easier to destroy than to build. Kahsir glanced off in the direction Lorhaiden had taken. *Lords! Not being able to mind-send is like fighting blind in one eye!*

Anther scaling ladder hit the wall. This time, several Leishoranya managed to clamber over the parapets be-

fore the defenders shoved the ladder away. Setting his
shield, Kashir lifted his sword and met the attack of one
of the enemy; his companion fought off another Leishoran
with artless but effective swordstrokes.

The fighting doubled in intensity. Kahsir faced an
unending succession of enemy warriors, stopped thinking of what he was doing, and let his sword arm take
over his body. Everywhere he looked he saw enemy
faces. Howling their battle cries, the Leishoranya raised
more scaling ladders against the wall and renewed their
deadly barrage of arrows. Then suddenly, the assault on
his area of the parapets ceased. Kahsir glanced hastily
up and down the wall. Large numbers of the enemy
had scrambled onto the walkway now, making it difficult for Krotànya archers to shoot in the press of fighting.

*O Lords! If this doesn't work. . . . I may have made
the biggest mistake in my life by coming here—could
have led these men to death by my lies!*

Lorhaiden appeared with startling suddenness at
Kahsir's side, his sword streaked red with blood. Before
he could react to another man standing in his place,
Hairon moved from that position to Kahsir's right.

"The commanders have the message," Lorhaiden
shouted over the din. "They know Ssenkahdavic's coming." He bared his teeth in a feral grin. "They'd have to
be dead not to have noticed."

The battle dissolved into a weary haze of fighting.
Kahsir glanced to his left: Vàlkir and his bowmen had
been forced back from the northeastern end of the wall.
That position lost, he now directed his archers' fire
against the scaling ladders. Then Kahsir sensed a subtle
shift in the intensity of the attack—knew others had
sensed the same. What he had hoped for was happening: the enemy was withdrawing from their other positions around Rodja'âno and gathering below the weakened
eastern wall.

Confirmation! Dammit, I need confirmation! I can't

*act on what I sense with any surety. That mind-block's
too* fihrkken *strong!*

He glanced to his right to the far end of the eastern
wall. *There! Could that have been—?* Again, three
distinct flashes of light, evenly spaced and precise:
Jhovàn's message relayed by mirrors. The enemy was
withdrawing from the other walls.

Kahsir spun around, looking for one of the Mind-
Born. A tall, white-robed figure stood close by the
stairway leading to the ground.

"Lorhaiden! Hold my position. I'll be back in a
moment."

He turned and ran to Remàdir. The Mind-Born's face
was drawn in concentration, but he seemed totally aware
of what was going on.

"Remàdir! You've got to help me. Is there any way
you can mind-send?"

"No, Lord. I'd have to be joined by at least one other
Mind-Born, and we'd have to take our concentration
away from our defense."

"Huhn. If you *do* that, can the rest of you keep the
enemy from transporting inside the walls?"

Remàdir frowned. "Debatable, Lord. Possibly."

"Possibly. We *have* to do it. Find someone and mind-
send to Jhovàn. Tell him I received his message. *He's
to wait for my orders.* And Send to the northern and
western walls. Everyone get down. Be ready to leave
once the gate's open."

"Aye, Lord." Remàdir turned quickly away.

Kahsir watched him go. There. It was done. If
Errehmon got in position by the southern wall, ready to
coordinate the retreat— He shook his head. Errehmon,
of all the commanders, he could trust to be exactly
where he was supposed to be.

The noise of fighting intensified; Kahsir ran back to
his position. He saw fewer enemy warriors on the parapets now, but those who had gained the walls fought
with increased ferocity. A Leishoran rushed forward

and Kahsir met the man's swordstroke with his own, parried, twisted to his left, and slashed out at the warrior's unprotected side. Then Lorhaiden was at Kahsir's left hand and moments later the fighting ground to a halt.

Suddenly, the sunset glow dimmed: the light around the city deepened to a color thicker than blood. For one timeless moment, everything hung suspended and immobile. Then the stones of the walkway began to tremble beneath Kahsir's feet. His heart jumped—he sprang to the parapets and looked down.

The sky had deepened to a black far from normal night; the sun was a feeble light to his back. A wind colder than any he had felt in winter tore the cloak back from his shoulders. Below, the Leishoranya were abandoning their assault on the eastern wall, scrambling back to their lines. And there, just beyond arrow-shot— Ssenkahdavic, the Dark Lord. Legs spread wide to brace himself, the Leishoranya warlord stood with arms upraised and called down the Shadow's Power.

My Dogor, *my Doom,* Kahsir thought of a sudden. Fragments—brief glimpses into the futures flashed through his mind. *Ssenkahdavic and I are bound in this Doom together.*

He whirled around, looking for Remàdir. The Mind-Born's leader and another of his companions waited close by.

"Send to Jhovàn!" Kahsir called. "Tell him to open the gate! The battle's done! Retreat to Aigenhal!"

Kahsir turned back to the parapets and looked down at Ssenkahdavic. *Dammit, If only I could fight back— keep the bastard from using his powers! Give him back as good as he's giving us!* Everything he had been taught since childhood forbade such thoughts; mental powers could not be used save for defense. Only Hjshraiel, The King to Come, would use his mind as an offensive weapon. When he came. Kahsir's shoulders straightened. He was of the House of dàn Ahzur, one of the Star-Born, and as such, his powers of mind were greater than most people's.

Drawing a deep breath, he gripped the crenel, and sent out a heavily cloaked thought toward the warlord, seeking the slightest flaw in Ssenkahdavic's shielding. He shuddered at what his mind sensed—cold, dark, the utter commitment to destruction and death. He was sweating now, nauseated, and yet he must try . . . try to make up in some small way for dooming the defenders of Rodja'âno.

Again, he sent out a tendril of thought, seeking some way he could divide Ssenkahdavic's attention between this unforeseen attack and the resistance maintained by the Mind-Born. His mind was suddenly filled with impressions: monumental Power, Darkness that was age-old and hungry beyond description . . . a mountain of Power as seen by an ant. . . .

And then, with a strangled oath, Kahsir leapt back from the parapet, sickened by what small contact he had made with Ssenkahdavic. The stones of the battlements were glowing with a weird light and slowly, imperceptibly at first, the mortar binding them began to disintegrate.

"Fall back!" he cried. "The wall won't stand! Get out of here! Now! Everyone to safety!"

The warriors grabbed up their weapons and began to descend the wall in as orderly a fashion as possible. All along the eastern wall men relayed Kahsir's command to those who could not hear. Most obeyed. A few still hesitated.

"Go! Go!" Kahsir shouted from his position near the head of the main stairway that led down from the parapets. He waved broadly at the stairs. "Dammit, go! Get out of here before it's too late!"

One by one, small chunks of the wall began falling downward, while the remaining stones shone brighter with a baleful red light. Kahsir glanced around, his heart hammering. A small force of Krotànya still stood at the parapets, rear guard for those who fled. He swallowed heavily. The margin of safety was quickly running out.

Someone grabbed his arm, pulling him toward the stairs. He whirled around and stared into Lorhaiden's pale face.

"Come with me!" Lorhaiden cried. "Let's get out of here!"

Kahsir blinked. *Lorhaiden? Urging retreat? What of his Oath? Or is it me he's concerned for? What—*

"Lord! Please! We've got to get down off this wall."

Kahsir jerked his arm loose and gestured a few remaining warriors down the steps. "Maps!" he shouted at Lorhaiden. "Where's Reordan and the maps?"

"We'll find him," Lorhaiden yelled back. "Now let's get out of here."

"Not yet! Just a while longer! There are more men to come!"

"But, Lord. . . ."

A figure loomed up unexpectedly out of the gloom: Remàdir again. Face darkened by exhaustion, his eyes shadows in the gathering darkness, the Mind-Born stood swaying slightly on his feet.

"Go, my Lord!" he said, his voice raw with weariness. "Now! While there's time left and we've strength to maintain these walls at all."

Kahsir started to speak, but Remàdir sensed his question.

"We're draining Ssenkahdavic . . . he's spending more energy than he counted on! Go! Jhovàn's got Durstàn's Gate open. The rest of your men are retreating. It's over, Lord. Done. We can't hold out much longer."

Kahsir glanced from Remàdir to Lorhaiden, then back. "I'm going," he said. "And you, Remàdir. Don't you and your companions die here. We need you."

A brief smile touched Remàdir's drawn face. "We'll get out, Lord. But this wall's going to go quicker than we thought. Don't worry about us. Now, go, Lord. Please go."

Remàdir . . . if I've condemned you and the other Mind-Born to death by making you face Ssenkahdavic, I'll never be able to make up for it. And you'll die, man . . . you and your companions, unless you're stronger than I think you are.

Kahsir nodded and, reaching out with his left hand, gripped Remàdir's shoulder in thanks and farewell. The Mind-Born smiled again at the gesture, then turned and disappeared back into the flickering light and shadow.

Lorhaiden's hand again. Stumbling a bit at first, Kahsir let him lead the way to the steps. Vàlkir waited on the ground below with Hairon, the man-at-arms who had taken Lorhaiden's place. Kahsir glanced around, trying to gauge their chances for escape. If they could get out of the city, they could make a run to the southeast, toward Chailon Pass and his father.

Then the entire wall rocked—Kahsir was nearly thrown to his knees. Lorhaiden shoved from behind and Kahsir ran headlong down the stairway. A great explosion of mental force stunned his mind and slowly, with impossible stateliness, the wall began to fall in upon itself.

"Run, Lord!" Vàlkir cried over the tumult, pointing down a crowded street. "Nearly everyone's out of the city!"

All pretense of orderly retreat vanished. The warriors last to leave the eastern wall ran wildly through the darkened streets, certain death waiting just behind. Heart pounding in his chest, Kahsir ran with them, Lorhaiden and Vàlkir pacing him, Hairon coming behind.

Through the evacuated city they ran, and at last the opened gateway loomed up ahead. Frightened horses, dogs, and other animals mixed with fleeing warriors. Chickens and geese darted in and out among them, their terrified squawks nearly lost in the noise. An orange cat streaked by Kahsir, sprang up on a warrior's shoulder, and leapt into the shadows on the wall's other side. The remaining Krotànya poured through that gate in such numbers that if any Leishoranya had been outside the wall, they would have been swept away.

A thunderous roar of falling stone boomed out across the city. Kahsir's heart leapt to his throat. There was no need to ask: the eastern wall had broken at last. The Legions of Darkness were now free to sweep into the dying city.

Vàlkir reached the gateway first. Kahsir pushed to his side, helped shove a way forward. He heard Lorhaiden cursing behind, heard Hairon's rough words of encouragement. He risked a look up: the southern wall was beginning to crumble like the rest.

He glanced over at Lorhaiden, who was now at his side. Suddenly, Kahsir heard a loud noise above, looked up, and saw the falling stone. He jerked to one side— too late. Pain—unendurable, consuming pain; the side of his head melted in agony. Things around him snapped into preternatural clarity, edged as sharp as knife blades. Faces: the flash of faces, places he had never seen, of events yet to come. Overwhelmed, swept away, Kahsir saw everything at once: death, darkness, a void of starless night; and in that blackness, hope.

Lorhaiden called his name; he caught a glimpse of his sword-brother lunging toward him. He tried to answer, then pitched forward, dimly aware he still carried his sword. He wanted to laugh at the absurdity of raising steel against the Shadow, but unconsciousness claimed his mind.

CHAPTER 4

Hidden in the bushes, Alàric closed his eyes and
drew a long, sobbing breath. Since the Mind-Born had
shielded him, his brother Haskon, and their shieldmen
on their way from Rodja'âno, they had run from the
enemy. Leaving the deserted village of Habaden behind, they had taken to the woods, unable to use the
mind-road for fear of alerting the enemy to their position.

Habaden lay twenty leagues southeast of Rodja'âno;
the next village they had approached had been equally
deserted. Finding no horses, they had run again, still
keeping their course set to the southeast where the
forest would allow. All day long they had traveled, and
part of the night, the thickness of the woods slowing
them.

The next morning, they had stumbled onto a small
squad of Leishoranya.

In the brief fight that followed, Alàric had taken a
sword cut to his shoulder, but he, Haskon, and their
shieldmen had managed to escape into the thick undergrowth. Now they ran again, the enemy in pursuit, and
this time it was for their lives.

Burrowed beneath his bush, Alàric drew another

long breath. Though only two days had passed since he and the other three men had escaped Rodja'âno, it seemed much longer. His throat tightened. This close to the city, he had been able to sense Kahsir's presence. But suddenly, not more than three hours past, his link to his eldest brother had broken. He shut his eyes tighter. *He's not dead, dammit! I'd have known it if he'd been killed!*

A small voice mocked him. *Would you?* it whispered. *Would you really?*

And Rodja'âno? Rodja'âno was gone.

He shook his head, drew another long breath, then peered out between the branches of the bush. It was dark enough in the forest that he could see no more than a pace or two in any direction. His legs ached from running, stung from where the brush had torn at his trousers. A thin rivulet of sweat ran down his face despite the nighttime chill. He felt Haskon's nearness in the darkness, the warmth of his brother's body next to his. Their two shieldmen hid close by; he could sense them, but only because he knew where they had taken cover.

A twig snapped to his right. His breath caught in his throat at the sound. For an agonizing moment he lay there in the darkness, certain that at any instant one of the pursuing Leishoranya warriors would discover his hiding place. He heard Haskon swallow heavily, the small rustle of change in position. Time dragged by; the woods were still.

"Ahri. . . ."

Haskon's whisper was nearly inaudible in the quiet. Alàric slowly turned his head toward his brother, new leaves brushing across his face.

"We've got to get out of here, Ahri," Haskon whispered. "We've lost them—we *must* have lost them. At least several hills back."

"Huhn." Alàric shrugged, winced at the pain in his left shoulder where he had been cut. "Convince me,

Kona," he whispered. "Convince me they're not just waiting for us to break cover."

"Dammit, we can't stay here all night! Got to keep moving. Keep *them* moving. Can't give them a chance to rest."

Another quick snap of something: Alàric clenched his teeth, waiting for a second sound. Haskon let his breath out, and nudged him again.

"Is that sword cut still bothering you?"

Alàric flexed his shoulder and flinched. "It's better."

The trees rustled overhead in a slight breeze. It was chilly already and would be even colder before night was done. Alàric closed his eyes, trying to reconstruct a visual overview of the land they had traveled through since the enemy had started chasing them. *Damn! What the Void are the Leishoranya doing this far south?*

He subtly reached out his mind, trying to Read the land about. He could sense no others in the brush. Then the touch of something cold slithered across his mind.

"They're coming this way," he whispered to Haskon. "Can you sense them?"

His brother was slow to reply. "Aye. But have they sensed *us?*"

Alàric shrugged his cloak up closer around his neck. A twig bit into his thigh. He moved his leg slightly, but only encountered another.

"Let's get out of here," Haskon murmured. "They'll find us for sure."

"Shush!" Alàric reached out again, sensing what lay close by. He extended his mental search, thinning it to near nothing. Suddenly, he felt that coldness again and hurriedly withdrew his mind. "I don't know which way to go, Kona. The enemy's behind us, I'd guess about a league away. But I can't tell what they're doing."

Haskon turned slightly in the darkness. "Whatever we do, it's got to be now," he whispered. "They'll be on top of us before we know it."

Alàric frantically sought around for a clear way through the forest. "*Chuht!*" he swore. The hot flush of fear followed. "I think they've swung around to either side of us, too."

Haskon reached out and grabbed Alàric's right arm. "Get out of here, Ahri," he hissed. "You're hurt, likely worse than you'll admit. Take the mind-road back to the capital."

"Me? You should go. Now that we can't sense Kahs, he could be—"

"He's not dead," Haskon stated flatly. "Quit thinking about it."

"Kona—*you* could be heir now. If anyone should get to safety—"

"Stop it, Ahri!" Kahs isn't dead and you're going back to the capital. You've got to tell Grandfather what's happened. He probably doesn't know."

"But—"

"Listen to me. If we're surrounded, we've got to risk the mind-road. The enemy knows where we are, so we don't need to worry that the energy surge will give us away. If the four of us go in opposite directions, it will make it harder for them to track us."

Alàric drew a deep breath, struggling to calm his heart. *Haskon? Thinking ahead? He's always running into things half-blind.* "True," he allowed. "Then you're going on to Father?"

"Aye," Haskon whispered. "Someone's got to take Kahsir's message to him. You're in no condition to go anywhere but home. And Grandfather may well know what the heir's ring means to Father. This way, if one of us shouldn't make it—"

"But do you know where Father is?"

"Clear enough to get there." Haskon nodded toward the hidden shieldmen. "Pavhel and Chorvàl, too."

Alàric considered Haskon's plan, trying to find a weakness in it. The growing closeness of the Leishoranya made it easy to overlook any objections.

"All right. But let's wait a little while longer. If the enemy gets close enough to be involved in setting their ambush, they might not sense what we're going to do. They won't be expecting us to go for the mind-road. They probably think we're too exhausted."

He felt Haskon's mind brush his own.

"Are you?" Haskon asked. "Too exhausted?"

Alàric shivered in the darkness. Two thousand leagues of travel by the mind-road? "I'll make it," he said thinly.

"Take it in stages, then," Haskon said. "At least get out of *here*. If any of us stands a chance of making it back to the capital, it's you."

"I'll have to go alone," Alàric said. "Chorvàl doesn't have the strength to make it in less than several jumps, and I'm not strong enough now to help him." He frowned. "He's not going to like being left."

"I'll deal with him. Get ready, Ahri. I'm going to tell Pavhel and Chorvàl what we're going to do."

Alàric nodded and sensed Haskon's mind reach out on a hidden level to the two shieldmen. He closed his eyes and sank deep within the core of his mind, calming his breathing, his heart, his frayed nerves. If he planned to travel all those leagues by the mind-road, he would have to summon greater energy than he suspected he possessed.

The enemy's coldness touched his mind again. *Lords! They're moving quickly, too quickly! That was a jump they made!*

He turned toward Haskon. "It's going to be close, Kona. We've got to do it now!"

Haskon nodded. "You go first. We'll leave immediately after."

Alàric reached out in the darkness for his brother's shoulder. "For the Light's sake, take care of yourself. You're sure you know where Father is?"

"Aye. Now move, Ahri, before it's too late!"

Alàric licked his lips with a suddenly dry tongue. He

closed his eyes, concentrated on his destination—his grandfather's study—calling it up visually in his mind's eye . . . remembering every detail of the room and what it *felt* like to be in it. Then, his shields held tightly, he began to construct the gateway, fear lending the strength he had been afraid he did not have. If the enemy was close at all, he would have to make the edges to the gate invisible or the Leishoranya could not only sense but see the mode of escape.

And, if one hint of thought strayed from behind his shields, the enemy would know the exact location of the High-King's study.

Brush rattled on the hillside not more than twenty paces off. Startled, Alàric nearly lost his concentration.

"Go, dammit!"

He jumped slightly at Haskon's hissed order, jolted into action. Opening his eyes, he sensed the gateway close by in the darkness, the enemy coming through the woods in the night. Drawing a deep breath, he gathered his strength and leapt through the gate, leaving muffled shouts of anger and dismay behind.

"Alàric!"

Darkness lapped at the edges of Alàric's vision. The voice spoke again, calling his name. Suddenly, he could think clearly, could recognize who was speaking. It was Kahsir's Chosen Woman, his beloved: Eltàrim.

Alàric lifted his head from his arms and looked up. He was lying on the floor, sprawled out on the yielding thickness of a carpet. Lamplight showed a large room, its simplicity softened by feminine touches. A small desk sat off to one side, and a doorway opened into another room, darker than the one he was in. He blinked, disoriented. Eltàrim knelt by his side, her face touched by the lamplight, her long, dark hair falling about her shoulders. The light and shadows of the room emphasized her high cheekbones, the firmness of her mouth, the strong jaw beneath. He shook his head and tried to gather his knees under his body to stand. The effort was too much: he sank back down on the floor.

"Lords of Light, Alàric," Eltàrim murmured. "What happened to you?"

He swallowed heavily—his surroundings were still unstable. "Where are we?" he asked.

"In my sitting room."

He closed his eyes in exasperation. He had been aiming for Vlàdor, but had missed the High-King altogether. He heard Eltàrim stand, the rustle of her skirts on the floor.

"Do you think you could drink some wine?"

He nodded: anything sounded good at this stage. He hitched up on his elbows but even that was enough to make his head spin. Eltàrim walked across the room. He heard the sound of liquid being poured into a glass and realized just how thirsty he was. The footsteps returned.

"Here, Ahri."

Alàric drew a deep breath, struggled for a moment, but this time he managed to sit up. He looked around, still disoriented, from his position close by the doorway. Eltàrim knelt at his side, one hand out to steady his shoulder, and the other extending the glass.

He reached out, took the wine in a hand that shook noticeably.

"Don't drink it too fast," she cautioned.

He nodded, took several good swallows, then leaned back against the wall. The liquid burned in his empty stomach. She had put something in the wine, something that would provide temporary strength. He lifted the glass and drank again.

"Now, tell me slowly. What's happened?"

Alàric looked up at Eltàrim and wiped his mouth with the back of his hand. "Rodja'âno. . . . The day after I was supposed to leave, Kahs showed up—"

"Kahs?" Eltàrim drew a quick breath. "O Lords of Light! What was he—? Never mind, Ahri. Go on."

He closed his eyes wearily. "We lost Rodja'âno—Kahs was in it."

Eltàrim was silent. Alàric opened his eyes again and looked at her face. There were grim lines of worry etched on it; her eyes glinted at the lamplight.

"Kahs?" Her voice trembled slightly. "Do you know where he is?"

Alàric shook his head. *How can I tell her what Haskon and I both sensed?* "I don't know," he said, finishing his wine and handing the glass to her. His strength was beginning to return and he felt his mind and the room steady at the same time. "Rodja'âno fell about sunset. I sensed it. So did Haskon." He met her eyes. "We lost all contact with Kahs. *All* contact. I don't even know if he's—"

"Don't say it!" Eltàrim snapped. She stood and muttered something that went unheard. Her fear for Kahsir's safety permeated the room. "Don't even *think* such things!"

He stared at her.

"Do you think you can stand up now?" she asked, her voice steady again.

He nodded, took her hand, felt its reassuring strength, and staggered to his feet. She was very tall; the top of her head was on a level with his eyes. His knees shook for a moment, then steadied. She gestured toward one of the chairs by the window.

"Where did Haskon go?"

"He and our shieldmen took the mind-road to Father's army." He sat down and leaned back in the chair. "Even though Father told me to join him, Haskon thought I should come back to the capital since I was hurt. It's important Grandfather knows what's going on, too."

"Smart move, that." She set the glass on the edge of her desk and came back to stand at his side. "Why did you come here and not go to Vlàdor?"

His face went hot. "I was trying to get to him. I guess I'm tired enough that my aim's off."

"Huhn." She turned away and stared at the wall. When she spoke again, her voice was muffled. "Did Kahs give you any reason for his being there?"

"Father sent him to take my place." His heart gave an odd twinge. "Didn't he?"

She drew a deep breath and turned back, ignoring his question.

Alàric felt her mind touch his, asking questions, and opened all his memories of the battle for Rodja'âno and his escape afterward.

"So," she said. "Rodja'âno's fallen. No one knows where Kahsir is. And Ssenkahdavic's sent troops south of the city." She walked across the room to where her desk stood and looked down at the map spread on it. "Ah, Lords! I should have known they were moving! Where the Dark are my spies?"

Alàric kept silent for a moment. "Maybe you have some idea how we can get help there. Kahs could—"

"When we don't know where he is?" She turned, one eyebrow lifted. "I don't know what you expect *me* to do about it."

He sensed the exasperation in her voice. "Your bush-fighters and spies are based at Chilufka, aren't they? Maybe you could get a message to—"

"With Rodja'âno fallen? Now that the city's gone and the enemy's thick in the north, I don't imagine anyone's mind-sending. That's probably why I haven't heard from my spies. If I Send to Chilufka, the enemy might intercept the message."

Her frustration echoed his own. "But we've got to do something."

"What? Run off ourselves to rescue him from what-ever trouble he's in?" Her mouth thinned to a frown and she looked back at the map. "We can't do anything if we don't know where he is."

He looked away. *She refuses to see the possibility*

that Kahs could be dead. He glanced back at her, caught a brief glimpse of something dark flit across her face. *Or does she?* Whatever the case, she was right: he could only guess which way his brother had gone after the city fell. And guessing would hardly lead them to Kahsir's position.

"He talked about falling back to the southwest if Rodja'âno did fall. Even so, I'll bet he set out for Chilufka. He knows you stay in contact with the Lady Genlàvyn and others in that steading. And Father's coming down from Chailon Pass, nearly due south of there."

She nodded slowly. "That would be his best line of escape." Her eyes snapped back to his face. "But I still can't risk a Sending. If you and Haskon ran into one enemy band south of Rodja'âno even before the city fell, how many others has Ssenkahdavic sent south? And the enemy might guess which way Kahs is headed even if they don't know about Chilufka."

He held her eyes but could find no answers. She looked away and began to pace the length of the room. He watched her, seeing again why Kahsir loved her so. There was no indecision in this woman, only prudent hesitation.

"I think we'd better find Vlàdor," she said, stopping before his chair. "Are you strong enough to walk unaided?"

"Aye."

"That shoulder wound—you'll need to get it dressed."

He stood, waited for his knees to waver, felt relieved when they did not. "I've lasted this long," he said, "and it's not deep. Let's find Grandfather first."

She stared a moment; he sensed her turning something over in her mind. "Iowyn's home from Vharcwal." The hint of a smile erased some of the harsh lines from her face. "You know your sister better than I do. If you don't want to chase back north after her, you won't even *think* about Kahsir's predicament in her presence."

*　　*　　*

Alàric leaned against the wall as Eltàrim knocked on one of the double doors leading to Vlàdor's study. He felt considerably better but would not be able to go much longer without sleep. He heard his grandfather's light step, set one hand against the wall for support, and turned to face the opening doors.

"Alàric!" The High-King's face tightened in the lamp-light. "What the Void are you doing here? You're supposed to be with Xeredir. What's going on up there? And what happened to your shoulder?"

Alàric embraced his grandfather and closed his eyes, amazed at the feeling of comfort and safety that came with that embrace. He lifted his head, having to look up slightly to meet Vlàdor's eyes.

"Rodja'âno's gone. Late this afternoon. Ssenkahdavic destroyed the city."

He felt Vlàdor start. A look of pain and loss etched harsh lines on Vlàdor's darkly bearded face, a look that made him appear decades older.

Vlàdor dropped his hands. His broad shoulders slumped slightly, then he motioned into the room. "Sit, Ahri. Sit."

Alàric nodded and walked in. His knees were shaking again: he sank slowly into the nearest chair and closed his eyes. He heard Eltàrim take a chair at his side, and his grandfather draw up another. He opened his eyes again.

"Now," Vlàdor said, "tell me the whole story, from the point when you were recalled."

"It's simple enough. I got Father's message that he wanted me out of the city, but I didn't want to go. I don't think he was right about Rodja'âno. He should have come quicker with reinforcements to—"

"We'll argue that later." Vlàdor's face was a blank: Alàric could read nothing on it. "Go on."

"Anyway, I delayed leaving until the last moment, trying to help Nhavari as much as I could. He wasn't any too happy to find out I was leaving. Then, the day

after I was supposed to have left, Kahs turned up."
Alàric paused, stared at his grandfather, at the sudden
paleness of Vlàdor's face. "Grandfather . . . what . . . ?"

"Keep going. I want the *whole* story, Ahri . . .
everything!"

Alàric swallowed. *Something's wrong here. Something's* terribly *wrong.* "Well, Kahs told me he'd been
sent to Rodja'âno to take my place. I didn't believe him
because Father hadn't said anything about it. We were
arguing about what I was to do when Haskon showed
up."

"Haskon?" The High-King's voice sounded tightly
controlled; his hands were clenched into fists. "What
the Dark was *he* doing there?"

Alàric shrugged helplessly. A cold feeling crept up
his spine as he finished his tale, of how—on Kahsir's
orders—the Mind-Born had helped him, his brother,
and their two shieldmen leave Rodja'âno unnoticed by
the enemy, of the run that followed. Vlàdor never said
another word, but his expression spoke for him. "Any-
how," Alàric concluded, gesturing to his shoulder, "I
got this when the enemy found us. We ran from them
all day and finally got cornered in the woods. Haskon
ordered me home, then he and the shieldmen took the
mind-road on to Father."

Vlàdor's thick fall of dark hair made his face seem paler
than it was. The grey eyes glinted like ice in the lamplight. Alàric sensed the rage boiling beneath his grandfather's tight control.

"So. Kahs stayed behind. Do you know where he is?"

The tension in his grandfather's voice was nearly
tangible. He glanced at Eltàrim. "I lost contact with
him," he said, meeting Vlàdor's eyes. "About the same
time the city fell."

"All contact?"

He nodded numbly.

"By all the Lords of Light!" Vlàdor slammed one fist
down on the arm of his chair. "That stubborn, ox-

headed idiot! What the Void does he think he's doing? He's put our entire northern defense in jeopardy!"

Alàric shrank back in his chair. "But—"

"Did *you* know he was going to do this, Eltàrim?" Vlàdor said, turning to her. "Did you?"

She shook her head. "No, Lord. He didn't say anything to me. I assumed he was going to catch up to Xeredir, so he could try one last time to change Xeredir's mind."

Vlàdor's other fist hit the chair arm. "Damn, damn, damn! Now what the Dark do I do?"

"Grandfather." Alàric licked his lips and tried to meet Vlàdor's eyes. "What's going on? Kahs *was* ordered to Rodja'âno, wasn't he? To take my place? He wasn't lying . . . was he?"

"You're damned right he was lying." Vlàdor's voice had risen to a shout. "Lying like few of us ever can! He was *ordered* to stay away!" The High-King lifted one hand and rubbed at his forehead. "Oh, Kahs . . . Kahs! What *have* you done?"

"O Lords." Alàric glanced away, kept from looking at Eltàrim, and instead stared at the wall behind his grandfather. "I accused him of lying . . . but he denied it. Even challenged me to ask Father about it." He met his grandfather's eyes again. "Why? Why would he do something like that?"

"I can guess," Eltàrim said. She rubbed her hands together in a rare nervous gesture. "He believed very strongly that Nhavari was being abandoned, that Rodja'âno should not be given up to the enemy because of its strategic location."

"Nhavari was advised to withdraw?" Alàric asked.

"I *told* him we couldn't support him," Vlàdor shouted. "Told him that!"

"But he never said anything to me about—"

"That's because he refused," Eltàrim said, keeping her voice very calm. "He insisted Rodja'âno was too important to be given up to the enemy. Kahs thought

the same. He and your father fought about that for
days, Ahri. At last, your father turned to Vlàdor, pressed
his case that the north was becoming too dangerous for
his son, and got permission to withdraw you."

"Leaving Nhavari to fend for himself?" Alàric made
an effort to keep his own voice under control. "But
that's . . ."

"I tried to tell him, Ahri," Vlàdor said, his voice
somewhat quieter. "I tried. He wouldn't listen. And
when Kahs turned up at Rodja'âno, I suppose that
made Nhavari all the more determined to hold out."

"Grandfather." Alàric took a deep breath. "Can't you
see what Kahs was talking about? How important
Rodja'âno was?"

"Ahri, the city was going to fall eventually, and with
a great loss of life. We wanted to get Nhavari and his
men out of there, to add them to the men Xeredir was
bringing north. Our idea was to draw the enemy farther
south, into the woods and hills on the north side of the
Golondai Mountains. Xeredir wanted to fortify the passes,
bog the enemy down into a war of hit and run in the
forests. We could have kept them busy up there for
decades, possibly centuries."

"But—" Alàric gestured sharply. "Why give up a
point of strategic importance before we have to?"

Vlàdor stared, then shook his head. "Xeredir knows
me well—*too* well—and sometimes he's able to bend
me when I think of family." He drew a hand across his
eyes, and when he looked up again, the anger was
back. "But that's no bloody excuse for Kahs to totally
disobey me! Dammit! He could be *dead!*"

"Kahs isn't dead," Eltàrim said, her voice trembling
slightly. "Ahri thinks he is, but I don't believe it."

Alàric looked down at his knees. "I never said I think
he's dead. I just don't *know* he's alive."

The room was very silent for a long moment.

"So Kahs disobeyed you . . . took things into his own
hands," Alàric murmured. "I *knew* he was upset about

Nhavari, but I didn't know why. But to lie to Kona and me like that—there's no reason for him—"

"I suppose he thought there was one," Eltàrim interrupted, her eyes shadows in the lamplight. "But what's done is done. Now we're faced with what to do about helping him."

"But he could be—"

"He *isn't* dead, Alàric."

"We'll presume he's alive," Vlàdor said. He straightened in his chair, squared his shoulders, and turned to Eltàrim. "You know the country around Rodja'âno better than anyone here. Where do you think Kahs might be?"

"I could only guess," she replied. "Alàric suggested it, too. If Kahs had his wits about him when he escaped the city, he would have headed to the southeast, to Chilufka. He knows that's where my bush-fighters are."

Alàric watched his grandfather's expression, trying to sense what Vlàdor was thinking. Behind the anger, he read the emotions of confusion and loss.

After another long moment of silence, Vlàdor nodded. "That would have been the most sensible thing to do. Ahri, what are the enemy positions now?"

"I can only tell you the way things stood when I left. Their main strength was massed directly to the east of the city. The eastern wall had taken the worst beating. They probably brought it down first when they took the city. We managed to destroy the bridge across the River Lhanic. The enemy will have trouble getting supplies through unless they take the mind-road."

"How large was their army when you left?"

"Fifteen thousand, or close to it. We got a report that another Leishoranya army was marching south with reinforcements. Later that day, we learned Ssenkahdavic was leading it."

"The Mind-Born got a message out he was coming," Vlàdor said. "It was the last message we received from Rodja'âno. Ssenkahdavic! Damn him . . . damn him to

Darkness! We had no indication he would wake for another decade or two. He fought *fihrkken* hard to take Fânchorion." Vlàdor took a deep breath and pulled at his short beard. "This means he's headed south again, with nothing less than taking Elyâsai as his final goal." Another deep breath. "What did Kahs plan to do?"

"When Haskon and I left, his plans weren't firm. He said something about falling back quicker than anyone expected, likely to the southwest. I'll wager that's where anyone who got out of Rodja'âno retreated to after the city fell."

Vlàdor chewed on his mustache. For a long while he was silent. Alàric easily sensed his thoughts, but they spilled out in a torrent, too intermingled and tinged with emotion to read clearly.

"There's not much more to tell," Alàric said, rubbing his forehead. His shoulder was beginning to hurt again.

"So far what you say makes sense," Vlàdor said. "Except this. Why the Dark didn't you leave when ordered?"

Alàric stirred uncomfortably in his chair. "I don't know," he admitted. "I guess I didn't think things were as serious as they turned out to be. There was no way anyone could have known that Ssenkahdavic—"

"Dammit, Ahri!" Vlàdor's voice was soft but clipped. "We're losing every time we put an army to field whether Ssenkahdavic's there or not. Don't tell me you weren't aware of the situation. The enemy's advancing on all three fronts. The war's going just as badly to the south and east as it is to the north."

Alàric nodded slowly. "I know. But something seemed —I didn't think it right to leave Nhavari there without someone from the Royal House at his side. He's an old family friend and . . ."

"Huhn. Do you understand, Ahri . . . *truly* understand what Kahs has done? He's totally altered our strategy in the northlands! Everything we'd planned has to be changed now to fit around what he's done."

Alàric kept silent. *Damn . . . he's going to lose his temper again. Keep quiet . . . don't say anything.*

"You say Haskon and your shieldmen took the mind-road on to Xeredir's army?"

"Aye. We all had a good idea where Father was. Haskon sent me home to tell you what happened."

Vlàdor rose from his chair and walked over to his desk. Alàric started to follow, but Eltàrim motioned sharply and he settled back in his chair. For a long moment, Vlàdor stood silent. Alàric sensed his anger and frustration, the effort it took to bring that under control.

"We knew something terrible was going on at Rodja'âno," Vlàdor said, turning around and leaning back on his desk. "We've been trying to mind-send for six days now and gotten nothing. Even the Mind-Born haven't been able to break through the enemy's block. You're the first fresh news we've had. What can you tell me about Nhavari?"

Alàric tensed, tried to keep his eyes from wavering. "Not much. He was as tired as the rest of us the last time I saw him." He bit down on his lower lip. *Lords of Light! He's had enough bad news. He's bound to hear about Nhavari soon.*

"Ahri—"

There was an edge to Vlàdor's voice; Alàric sat up straighter and swallowed heavily.

"He's dead, Grandfather. I felt his death a day after Haskon and I left the city."

He flinched before Vlàdor's agony. Eltàrim's thoughts brushed his: shock, grief, and anger at the loss.

Vlàdor straightened, walked to his chair, and sat down. "You're certain, aren't you?"

Alàric nodded.

"O Lords! Nhavari!" Vlàdor's voice was hushed. He brought his fist down on one knee. "Damn, damn, damn! He always *was* too stubborn for his own good. We warned him to get out of Rodja'âno. If he'd done what we'd told him to, he'd still be alive and Tumâs would still have a chance!"

Alàric rubbed at the tension in his neck. "I don't suppose Tumâs stood much of a chance after Fânchorion fell."

"You don't have to tell me about it," Vlàdor said with an angry look. "I nearly had your hide for staying there so long at the end."

Alàric's temper rose; he tried to force the anger away. "What do you want us to do? Run?"

"Ahri." Eltàrim reached out and touched his hand. "Don't push."

"I'm sorry." He looked down at his knees again. "It's so damned frustrating. *Nothing* we've tried during the last fifteen hundred years has held off the enemy. Not one damned thing!" He took a deep breath and shifted his weight in the chair. "What about Kahs?"

Vlàdor shook his head. "There's not much we can do. We don't know where he is, or if he even escaped."

"If he had died, you would have sensed it," Eltàrim said, her voice level. "He escaped. I may not know where he is, but I know he didn't die."

Alàric watched his grandfather closely, but Vlâdor kept silent. *Do something*, he prodded himself. *Anything! Make Grandfather take some action.* He turned to Eltàrim.

"You could send more fighters into the countryside north to Chilufka."

Vlàdor stirred in his chair, his forehead furrowed in thought. "That's about all we can do. If Kahs ordered a retreat to the southwest and Xeredir's coming down from the mountains to the southeast, we'll need more help coordinating the two forces. From the sound of things, saving southern Tumâs is about all we can hope for." He squared his shoulders. "Eltàrim. Take care of this for me. And keep your people out of the villages and in the countryside. They may be the only source of information we have up there."

"Consider it done. I'll send them north tonight."

"And, Grandfather," Alàric said, "don't let Iowyn know what's happening. If she finds out—"

Vlàdor smiled wryly. "You don't need to warn me. She'd be off before we knew what happened."

Alàric blinked suddenly in the lamplight. The strength he had found in Eltàrim's wine was fading. His legs still ached and his shoulder was beginning to stiffen. He closed his eyes and fought a longing to sleep.

"You're staying here for a few days, aren't you?" Vlàdor asked.

Alàric opened his eyes again: the room swam for a moment, then settled. "No. I'll be going back north tomorrow. Now that Rodja'âno's gone, Father will need me more than ever."

Vlàdor frowned. "He doesn't need you dead. You're staying here until you're better. That's an order, Ahri."

"I'll be all right. A night's sleep in my own bed will help more than anything. I've suffered worse wounds and fought."

"Huhn. That may be true. But not this time. And before you go back to your room, I'm sending for a healer."

"Now, that I *could* use."

Eltàrim stood and walked to the door. "I'll get the healer. I'm going out anyway. I've got to find men to send to Chilufka." She looked over her shoulder. "I can see you back to your room if you want, Alàric."

"I'll be fine," he said, forcing a smile. "Go on ahead."

He looked back to his grandfather, waiting until the door shut behind Eltàrim.

"What is it, Ahri?" Vlàdor asked. "You've more to tell."

"It's about Kahs." He shifted his weight again in the chair, wincing at a stab of pain from his shoulder. "Perhaps this will make more sense to you than me. The heir's ring that Kahs wears—is there any secret message connected with it that you know of?"

Vlàdor frowned. "No. Not to my knowledge. Why?"

"Kahs has always been honorable to a fault. This is the first time he's disobeyed orders. He sent the ring back to Father. I think it's his admission that he was mistaken about Rodja'âno, *and* his resignation as an acting commander."

Vlàdor's nodded slowly. "You're probably right. It sounds like something he'd do." A sudden flash of emotion lit Vlàdor's eyes. "Maybe things aren't as bad as I think. Ahri, if Kahs managed to hold Rodja'âno long enough, he *might* have bought us valuable time. He had a lot of Mind-Born with him up there. It's possible they might have put up enough resistance to make Ssenkahdavic go dormant again."

"Aye. It's possible." Alàric sat silent, then cursed softly. "Damn! I wish we could do *something* more than retreat! Now that Ssenkahdavic's on the move—"

"You know we can't do any more than we already are. We can't fight the enemy with our minds, except defensively."

"And if we did?" Alàric matched his grandfather's stare. "What then? The Leishoranya are so used to us *not* attacking them mentally, we'd take them by surprise."

"And damn ourselves in the process. If we used our minds that way, we'd only be adding to the Shadow's power."

"But—" Alàric scratched at his beard. "Damning a few of us *might* be worth saving our people."

Vlàdor shook his head. "It would never work, Ahri. We're too outnumbered to destroy them all. And all of us together couldn't defeat Ssenkahdavic."

Alàric's vision blurred. "Perhaps not. But we might drive him dormant for a century or so, and in that time we could. . . ."

"Could what?" Vlàdor's voice was gentle. "Find somewhere else to escape to? Ahri, we either fight this war as the people we are, with everything we believe and hold right, or we give in to the Shadow. And that would strengthen the Darkness so much that when the universe is born again, the Shadow could defeat the Light forever." He reached out and touched Alàric's knee.

"Get some rest, Ahri. I'm afraid it's gone beyond the stage of talking. We can only be true to ourselves and what we believe. And if we die, it will be so the Light can live again."

"Huhn." Alaric wavered in his chair. *Can't faint now . . . got to get back to my room. . . .*

A knock sounded at the door. Vlàdor glanced up.

"Come!"

Alàric slowly turned his head as one of the Mind-Born healers entered the room. Darkness lapped at the edges of his vision.

"Help Alàric back to his room." Vlàdor's voice seemed muffled to Alàric, coming from far away. "Alleviate as much of his pain as possible. He's going to need a clear head in a few hours."

Alàric felt the healer's arms help him stand. *A clear head?* His legs automatically carried him toward the door to Vlàdor's study. He stumbled, but the healer kept him upright. *What's happening in a few hours that I need to be alert for?* The world began to turn darker, and Alàric saved all thought for the walk to his room.

Vlàdor stood in the center of the room, stared at the closed doors, and cursed softly. Rodja'âno gone. Ssenkahdavic in control of the city and the northern half of Tumâs. And Kahsir. . . .

He slammed one fist into an open hand. What had ever possessed Kahsir to disobey orders? And, having disobeyed, to have set into motion events the outcome of which was hard to predict?

His son and his grandson? Who could he trust . . . who *should* he trust? The steady or the swift? Xeredir and Kahsir had seldom fought on the same front during all the centuries of the war. Now, their contrasting styles of command were glaringly clear.

Known for his conservatism, Xeredir *was* flexible, a trait some of the younger warriors overlooked. He was steady, sure, and had an eye for the country, using the land as an ally. But, truth being known, Xeredir would take the safe, conservative course first.

And Kahsir? At times, Vlàdor himself hardly knew how to react to his grandson's style of warfare. On one hand, Kahsir was as steady and conservative as Xeredir, but Kahsir operated by instinct, taking chances that made other commanders' blood run cold. And he was right more often than he should be. His was a brilliance that dazzled, that spoke of real genius.

What Kahsir had done at Rodja'âno—disobeying direct orders aside—might have been the correct action to have taken in that situation. Vlàdor shook his head. *That's only one more example of what Kahsir can do . . . and he does it so often, you wonder if he really is that intelligent.*

"Damn." The soft curse sounded loud to Vlàdor's ears. He walked to his desk, ran his hands across the papers on it, and sighed. He would have to send for Tebehrren immediately, and the other counselors. They would have to know what had happened. By now, if Haskon had gotten through to Xeredir, Xeredir would know what Kahsir had done. The enormity of it all was staggering. All the plans, all the strategies. . . . *Everything* would have to be rethought, reordered, in light of what Kahsir had set into motion.

Why? The question rang in Vlàdor's mind. Why had he agreed with Xeredir in the first place? He had known how important Rodja'âno was. His own style of fighting more often than not coincided with Kahsir's, or at least echoed it. The defense of the northlands . . . whose ideas were right—Kahsir's or Xeredir's? Vlàdor pulled the chair out from behind his desk and sat down. Neither his son nor his grandson was wrong. But which one of them saw things the clearer?

To have adopted Kahsir's plan instead of Xeredir's would have meant ignoring the Crown Prince in favor of Kahsir, second in line to the throne. The army would have known this: known it, and reacted accordingly.

Putting Kahsir in command in place of Xeredir would have thrown the northern army into confusion.

Excuses! Excuses!

Vlàdor flinched from what his heart told him, though the excuses were true. He had been afraid of losing his heirs, both of them, in a fight he saw as being ultimately hopeless. For the first time in all the centuries of leading his people, he had made a military decision based solely on concern for family.

"O Lords," he whispered, propping his bearded chin on one hand. "What have I done by agreeing with Xeredir?"

He stared across the room at the closed doors. He could not go back and redo anything . . . remake any decision, unsay any order. Now, he must deal with what *was*, not things as he wished them to be.

The defense of the northlands thrown into shambles, and Kahsir, second in line to the throne, possibly dead.

Vlàdor sat up straighter in the chair, cursed, and stood. Tebehrren. He must send for Tebehrren first. Questions needed to be answered. If Tebehrren and the other Mind-Born had known Ssenkahdavic had awakened *before* they knew the warlord had marched south, why had they not said anything? It chilled him to think the Mind-Born could have missed something that important.

But those questions could wait. The Mind-Born Advisor would want to talk with Alàric, to sort through all of Alàric's memories of what had happened. Then the counselors; meetings; orders sent north to Xeredir and other commanders. . . .

And Kahsir?

There was no easy answer to that question.

CHAPTER 5

Lorhaiden lunged toward Kahsir but was not quick enough: the falling stone had struck Kahsir's helmet from his head—knocked him unconscious. Grabbing Kahsir's body, Lorhaiden staggered a moment in the gateway. The noise around them was deafening: the roar of men's voices, the grating of stone against stone as the southern wall began to collapse. Lorhaiden looked up from Kahsir's empty face, frantically seeking escape from the mayhem outside Durstàn's Gate. In the baleful light of the disintegrating wall, he had trouble seeing what was going on. Huge numbers of men ran off toward the southwest, toward the forest and some hope of protection. Lorhaiden snarled as someone jostled him from behind—the last of the warriors escaping the doomed city.

"Vahl!" Lorhaiden found his brother in the mass of fleeing men. "Kahsir's sword!" He had both arms under the Throne Prince's armpits, hands locked, balancing Kahsir's greater height on his chest—had his back turned to the open gate as protection from anyone running into them. "Hairon! The helm!"

Vàlkir snatched up Kahsir's sword, while Hairon scrab-

100

bled for the helmet. Smaller stones fell from above. Lorhaiden cursed, dragged Kahsir farther off to one side of the gate, out of the way of fleeing warriors and crumbling masonry. Standing wide-legged, braced against Kahsir's weight, he looked off into the unnatural darkness, toward the forest to the southwest.

"O Lords." The whisper tore at his throat. Horses! Those were not Krotànya mounts, nor were the riders Krotànya, but the enemy. Guessing the defenders of Rodja'âno would try to escape, Ssenkahdavic must have stationed cavalry by the walls. Now, those horsemen attacked the running Krotànya, sword blades glinting in the light of the falling walls.

Lorhaiden watched the thousands of men run across the fields toward the woods: the ground was alive with them. The block Ssenkahdavic had lowered over the city prevented anyone but the strongest from taking the mind-road to escape. The Leishoranya rode at the escaping warriors from all sides, cutting away at the edges of the surging mob. Lorhaiden could not guess at the enemy's numbers, but their effectiveness was easy to see. When the Leishoranya withdrew for another charge, they left the fields behind them littered with bodies.

"Vahl!" Lorhaiden jerked his eyes away from the slaughter. "We've got to get away from here. Can you jump us into the woods?"

"Not far. Not with the enemy interference." Vàlkir's eyes narrowed. "Where?"

Lorhaiden looked back at the cavalry riding down fleeing Krotànya. With Kahsir unconscious and wounded Lords knew how bad, without maps. . . . He hissed a curse. Even if he *had* wanted to go southwest, the Leishoranya cavalry made that escape route impossible. Kahsir's plan had been to go southeast, toward Chailon Pass, in an attempt to join his father. "Southeast!" Lorhaiden shouted above the noise. "Can you do it, Vahl?"

"I'll have to." Vàlkir's face tightened in concentration. "Shield us, Lorj. Hairon . . . give me help."

The man-at-arms nodded. Lorhaiden felt Hairon's mind link with Vàlkir's, a reservoir of additional strength. In the chancy light, he sensed more than saw the gateway form. His mind linked with his brother's, *seeing* what Vàlkir saw, Lorhaiden hefted Kahsir to a more erect position and dragged the Throne Prince the few steps toward the gate.

"Enemy, Lord!"

Hairon's voice. Lorhaiden glanced up: a detachment of Leishoranya cavalry galloped away from the fleeing Krotànya toward the wall. His heart jumped, and a cold sweat started on his forehead. Trusting in Vàlkir's skill, he threw himself backward through the gate.

A moment of disorientation, followed by intense chill— Lorhaiden fell over onto his back in a thick stand of undergrowth, Vàlkir and Hairon appearing instants later at his side.

The gateway disappeared, and for a long while no one moved or even seemed to breathe. Lorhaiden cradled Kahsir's head against his chest, branches and leaves all around him. Stilling his mind, he sought the darkened woods about, but sensed no enemy following.

"We made it," Vàlkir said quietly. "Lords . . . that wasn't the easiest thing I've ever done."

Lorhaiden touched his brother's mind with the heartfelt emotion of thanks. "Help me," he said out loud, levering himself up into a half-sitting position.

A rustle of leaves: Vàlkir and Hairon reached out and gently lifted Kahsir away. Lorhaiden caught at a branch, felt it give under his weight, and scrambled quickly onto his knees. He wiped his forehead, gone clammy with drying sweat, and looked through the darkness at his sword-brother's face.

And looked away. Kahsir lay utterly still, his shallow breathing the only indication of life. Lorhaiden cursed again, gathered the cloak closer around his sword-brother's body, and hunkered back on his heels.

Now what? Rodja'âno was gone. Six to seven thousand men had fled the walls and run into the enemy's cavalry charge. Casualties in the escape to the forest would be heavy: a quarter to one third of the Krotànya warriors lost seemed reasonable. Lorhaiden lifted his head and stared off through the undergrowth. Damn. He, Vàlkir, and Hairon would have to move quickly now; the enemy would assuredly send squads into the woods around Rodja'âno, hunting down survivors. With Kahsir unconscious, they would have to carry him, and the loss of time—

"Lorj!" Vàlkir's touch on Lorhaiden's shoulder brought him out of his thoughts. "Someone's coming this way."

O Lords of Light! Not the enemy! Not this soon! Lorhaiden loosened his longsword in its sheath and stared off in the direction his brother had indicated.

"Enemy?"

"No . . . ours, I think. They're shielded."

"See if you can find out. If they're ours, I don't want them thinking we're Leishoranya."

"Huhn." Vàlkir was silent a moment, a shadow in the darkness. He stirred and turned toward Lorhaiden. "Ours. Over twenty. Wounded, mostly."

"How badly?"

"Can't tell . . . I don't think anyone's hurt beyond walking."

"Have they sensed us?"

"No."

Lorhaiden rubbed his chin, at a scratch that ran along it. *Damn! We'll have to let them know we're here, or they'll attack us in the dark. O Lords! We don't need any more with us if we hope for speed.*

"Lorj, if they get much closer, they *will* sense us."

"Dammit." Lorhaiden sighed. "Let them know we're here, Vahl. They'll slow us down, but with Kahsir wounded, we can always use the extra protection."

* * *

Lorhaiden glanced over his shoulder as he trotted through the unnatural darkness. Vàlkir and Hairon came behind, carrying Kahsir between them—coming slower than he liked, but faster than he expected.

His throat tightened. *Dammit, Kahsir! You've got to come around! I've seen people with worse injuries shake them off.* He flinched inwardly. *And with lesser ones, die.*

He frowned. How far had he and the others come from Rodja'âno? The distant sounds of its death came at his back on a fitful wind. The sky stretched abnormally dark above; there would be no sunset today. He looked down toward the horizon, saw angry red light flickering between the branches. His eyes watered as a gust of smoke seeped through the trees. He clenched his teeth in anger: *Lords! They've fired the city! Those bastards! They've—*

Another fire burned suddenly in his mind's eye. . . .

He jerked awake; his father said the barn was burning. The shouts and cries of the retainers who fought the blaze jarred his mother and sisters from their sleep. A panicked flight down the front steps of the house; the surge of fear when he saw the barn aflame. He and his father rushed to aid the retainers. Squeals and loud thuds came from the barn as horses tried to break free from their stalls. The hired men had led most of them out. He hunched his shoulders against the heat, looked to his father for orders.

The first enemy arrows cut down men next to him. He whirled, heard cries of anguish, the yells of the attacking Leishoranya. A trap! The fire—a trap! Unarmed, he, his father, and the retainers stood surrounded by mounted Leishoranya, with no hope of fighting back.

Desperate, some of the retainers ran straight at the enemy; the few who got that far dragged the Leishoranya from their horses. Lorhaiden stumbled over one of the enemy and snatched up the Leishoran's longsword, threw it to his father, then grabbed the enemy's shortsword and retreated to his father's side. The last of the retainers had fallen; somehow, he and his father remained untouched.

Then his father cried out in agonized rage. He turned, looked where his father pointed, and his heart stopped. The great house was aflame! His mother, his sisters—he sensed their panic, their fear, their pain. Vàlkir! Where was— No. Vàlkir was away visiting kin. His father yelled something and rushed toward the enemy leader: an arrow thudded into his chest. Another arrow and another. He stumbled: the fourth arrow caught him in the neck.

"Father!" Lorhaiden ran toward the war band's leader. A Leishoran spurred forward and swung his sword down. The blade caught the side of Lorhaiden's head: he twisted around into a fall.

For a long moment he lay there in the flickering light of the burning barn. Hot blood rushed down his face, and flashes of light burst inside his skull. He struggled to get up but lacked the strength. Blackness lapped at the edge of his vision. The enemy's leader sat mounted a few paces away, the flames of the great house behind— sat there, bloody sword balanced across his horse's neck, laughing . . . laughing . . . laughing. . . .

Lorhaiden tripped over something in the dark. The forest, Rodja'âno, Kahsir. His heart pounded in his chest. He drew a deep breath and concentrated on the way ahead. There had to be somewhere close by that he and his companions could stop for the night.

He glanced behind. "Watch your footing," he hissed. *Damn! We're going to have to stop soon! Anywhere!*

"Lord!"

A hissed whisper came from ahead. Lorhaiden halted; the men behind him stopped and stood panting in the darkness.

"Found us a clearing," the voice said. Lorhaiden

recognized him as one of the men he had sent out as scouts.

"Defensible?"

"Got a few rocks at its center. There's a stream close by."

"Huhn." *Damned surly fellow! Some gratitude for us letting him come along. If we didn't have Kahsir with us, I don't think he or his comrades would have followed my orders.* Lorhaiden turned back to his brother and Hairon. "Kahsir?" he asked, his voice rough. "Has he regained consciousness?"

Vàlkir shook his head. "The sooner we stop, the better. He's never going to come around if we keep running."

Lorhaiden drew a deep breath, turned forward to the all but unseen scout. The Leishoranya were probably not in pursuit . . . yet.

Kahsir came back to consciousness in darkness, surrounded by the rustle of leaves. He lay stretched out on his back, on the earth, in low undergrowth. He blinked his eyes, winced, and slowly raised a hand to touch the knot on the side of his head.

"Lord."

Lorhaiden's voice. Carefully, Kahsir turned his head and heard the creak of leather clothing as his sword-brother edged closer.

"You're conscious," Lorhaiden said in a tone of vast relief. "Thank the Light for that. We thought we'd lost you there for a while."

A second shadow knelt, joining the first. Vàlkir—a shadow of equal bulk. Kahsir struggled to sit up; his head spun wildly but he finally succeeded.

"Where are we?" he asked then, tentatively fingering the side of his head.

"Several leagues south of Rodja'âno," Lorhaiden said. "We carried you."

"With your shoulder wound? Lorhaiden—"

"Ah, not me. Vàlkir and Hairon did the carrying."

"Hairon?"

"The man-at-arms. The one who stood as your shieldman on the wall."

"Ah, Hairon." Kahsir shifted and winced, twisting to see what lay around. "The rest? Do you know who many got out of the city?"

"More than two-thirds of us, I'd guess—between four and five thousand. The enemy had cavalry waiting. They attacked the men headed southeast."

"O Lords. Was Errehmon able to organize the retreat?"

"I don't know." Lorhaiden moved closer. "I didn't see him."

"As far as I can tell, we were among the last out," Vàlkir said. "We've got twenty-eight other men with us. They'd seen the cavalry attack and headed to the southeast. We traveled as far as we could before nightfall."

"Carrying me."

Lorhaiden shrugged, a rustle in the dark.

Kahsir pushed his hair back and looked around again. He could not see the other men for the brush about them, but sensed their presence, their thoughts within the dark. Wounded, most of them, but none so seriously that they could not have made good time on their own.

Damn! If I hadn't been unconscious, we could be leagues farther away by now!

He drew a long breath and looked back from the brush to Lorhaiden and Vàlkir. "Help me up."

They lifted. At first his knees threatened to fold, but then they steadied. He stood unaided and looked about again. He and the other men were hidden in the thick brushiness of the oaks that grew far and wide about Rodja'âno and gave the city its name. He thrust aside a branch, fending off offered hands. A distant light glowed among the trees, where the brush was thinnest. He walked through the trees to the height and stopped.

Rodja'âno lay burning in the darkness to the north. Tears sprang to his eyes, accompanied by a wave of vertigo.

He shivered, turned, and walked slowly back through the brush. He was still light-headed, and the lump on his skull hurt abominably. The others were waiting: some had already stretched out under the bushes, seeking badly needed sleep. Lorhaiden gestured toward a place to sit; Kahsir tried to sense his sword-brother's thoughts but got nothing. He sank to his knees, then lay down on his side. Even though he had been carried, he was as tired as if he had been running with the rest.

He looked up at Lorhaiden's shadowed face, burning Rodja'âno still fresh in his mind. "Wake me at dawn," he said.

The fires had been mostly contained now and only a few buildings burned out of control. Tsingar stood next to his commander, Dhumaric, and shifted uneasily from foot to foot, tired, yet set on edge by the day's events. One of the lucky ones, he had escaped the long battle unscathed. Dhumaric, of course, as one of the Great Lords, never really did all that much hand-to-hand fighting. That he left to the lower ranks.

Tsingar scratched at his ear, drew several deep breaths, and glanced uneasily at the rubble that remained of the eastern wall and its gate. Ssenkahdavic himself would be entering the city, presenting his compliments to his commanders. Tsingar's mouth twisted and he drew his shields tighter, for those commanders, Dhumaric included, had been unable to break the Krotànya: only Ssenkahdavic's intervention had brought the city down.

A sudden stirring rippled through the throng of darkly clad officers: Tsingar's stomach knotted. Ssenkahdavic— Ssenkahdavic was coming.

He closed his eyes. Ssenkahdavic—seen from a close position. The cold chill of apprehension; the awareness of instant death; the fear—above all, the fear.

Another deep breath—another. He opened his eyes. As Dhumaric's second in command, he was required to be present at Ssenkahdavic's triumphal entry into this broken city. He licked his lips. Danger and death walked by Ssenkahdavic's side: the warlord's moods were as unpredictable as the wind.

And there he was, riding his horse through the rubble, the highest of the Great Lords bending before him like grass in the wind. Tsingar knelt, lowered his head to the ground, and raised his hands as if bound over his head. He heard the creak of leather clothing beside him: Dhumaric—proud, powerful Dhumaric—had assumed the same position.

The hoofbeats stopped, and Tsingar sensed the warlord's mind sweep over the assembled commanders. He shuddered involuntarily, reduced to null before Ssenkahdavic's gaze.

"Rise." The warlord's voice was quiet, but it carried and echoed off the shattered wall.

Tsingar licked his lips again and stood, moving slightly behind Dhumaric. Ssenkahdavic sat his horse not more than three paces away. He was taller than any of the Great Lords, and more beautiful. The flickering light of burning buildings highlighted that perfect face, the long black hair, the deadly smile. Tsingar blinked, swallowed heavily, and kept his face expressionless.

The black eyes turned, focused on Dhumaric, and Tsingar nearly stepped backward at the flood of cold power. He kept motionless and fixed his gaze straight ahead. The warlord gestured: Dhumaric stepped forward, walked slowly to the Dark Lord's side. Ssenkahdavic bent in the saddle and said something quick and unheard. Dhumaric bowed deeply, murmured inaudible words in reply, then walked back to his place. Ssenkahdavic's eyes flicked to Tsingar for a brief instant: everything he had ever thought and done lay open before the warlord's mind. He shivered and trembled with the urge to run from the square, but there was nowhere to run and no place to hide.

Ssenkahdavic moved on. Tsingar shivered again; the oppressive weight lifted from his heart. He glanced at Dhumaric and shuddered at the commander's look of predatory intent. *Gods! What's he agreed to do now?*

"Your helm," Lorhaiden said, as they gathered themselves up in the first light. Kahsir took it to carry, not to wear, for his head still hurt. Then he stopped, turned the helm to the light, and ran a fingernail down the deep crease that scored its length. Again, he saw the dying city, the crumbling southern wall, the falling chunk of masonry. He shifted uneasily and looked up at Lorhaiden: this helm had saved his life.

He glanced at the men who stood gathered by, some still favoring their wounds. "Are any of you from this area?" he asked. No one answered, though a few men shook their heads slightly. "We'll need someone to guide us through the forests."

"Lord," said one of the men-at-arms, bobbing his head in a short bow, "I know some of these men. We be mostly farmers, Lord, from up 'round Mordunvih, north of Rodja'âno." The man-at-arms glanced at his companions. "Some be from even farther west. When the enemy come down on our lands, we ran. Those who could save their families did. Now, we be fighting Leishoranya, Lord. But we be ignorant of these lands here."

"I be from east of Rodja'âno, Lord," Hairon offered, stepping forward. "I been hereabouts only once or twice myself, but I think I can guide you. Where d'you want to go?"

Kahsir chewed on his lower lip for a moment. Unanswered questions rioted in his mind. Two-thirds of the army defending Rodja'âno had escaped, if he could believe Lorhaiden's estimate. But was Errehmon among those men? If he had managed to elude the enemy cavalry, the retreat to Aigenhal was in good hands—few men were as capable of coordinating such a maneuver as Errehmon.

"We need to find my father's army as soon as we can, and he's coming down through Chailon Pass. If I've got my directions straight, there's a steading I'd like to reach that will put us directly in his path." He looked down at Hairon. "Chilufka," he said. "Have you heard of it?"

Hairon paused before nodding. "Aye, Lord, but I never been there. I think it be close to a hundred leagues away, to the southeast."

"Huhn." Kahsir frowned. *A hundred leagues. Father's coming down from Chailon Pass and that's nearly due south of Chilufka, about two hundred leagues from there.* "Well, then, you'll lead us, Hairon. Do you know anything of the land between here and there?"

"A bit, Lord. Woods thins out to the east. You want cover, I reckon I can lead you near straight to Chilufka."

"We'll need all the cover we can get," Vàlkir said. "The Leishoranya will likely be on our trail. They're probably fanning out from Rodja'âno now, hunting survivors."

"Then let's go." Kahsir looked at his companions. "And try to hold a good pace. I don't want those bastards coming up on our backs."

Aeschu rode out of the mind-road into a courtyard that looked much like the one she had left behind in Fânchorion. Gentling her horse with a steady hand, she looked around, assessing this new city with more than her eyes. Her mind sifted through the thoughts of the men around her, weighing their hopes, their fears.

"My Lady."

Dhumaric's voice: clad in black leathers and mail, the commander strode across the courtyard toward her.

"My Lord." She allowed him to help her dismount and, as a slave led her horse away, gathered her cloak closer in the chill morning wind. Glancing sidelong, she noted the particularly eager expression on Dhumaric's face. "My congratulations on taking Rodja'âno, my Lord."

He bowed slightly, gestured that she should precede him to the stairs leading to what must have served the Krotànya King as his palace. She squared her shoulders and walked up those steps and into the echoing main hall, giving the guards that stood on either side of the great wooden doors no notice.

"My husband?" she asked over her shoulder of Dhumaric.

"He's waiting for you, Lady. I'll show you the way."

"That's unnecessary," she said, stopping to confront Dhumaric, and allowed a slight smile to touch her lips. *Games again, my Lord? Trying to put me at a disadvantage because you've been here longer than I?* "My husband knows I'm here."

"As you wish, Lady." His face now expressionless, he bowed, turned, and left her.

Drawing a deep breath, Aeschu ascended the wide stairs to the second floor, turned down a hallway still resplendent in simple richness. A set of double doors stood open at the end of the hall: the honor guard saluted her as she passed them into the chamber beyond.

Shadows clung to the room. She sensed windows to one side, but they had been covered with dark hangings. Though the rest of the palace was full of morning sunlight, here was only night.

And presence . . . and Power.

Ssenkahdavic sat enthroned at the end of the room, in a high-backed chair on a raised dais. No longer clad for war, he wore again his familiar tunic of black and gold. She felt his eyes, though she could not see them in the dim light shed by the lamps: she saw only shadows and the hint of the Shadow he served.

She stopped at the foot of the dais and bowed deeply. "My Lord husband."

He smiled slightly and gestured her to his side. "Fânchorion?" he asked.

"As you wished, my Lord. Left in Mehdaiy's hands."

She sensed a subtle change in attitude: he relaxed somewhat, leaned back in the chair.

"And now you're here," he said. "Again, you haven't disappointed me."

She bowed her head, warmed with pleasure at his praise. "Let me know what you want me to know, Lord."

His mind touched hers and she nearly cried aloud at the power she sensed. They had communed in this fashion for centuries, yet the experience terrified her now as much as it had the first time.

It was quickly over. Released, she fought down the usual dizziness that followed such speaking. She now knew all he wanted her to know about Rodja'âno—everything she needed to rule in his stead: the land about, the resistance mounted by the Krotànya, the commanders he had set up to administer the city—and the fact that he had sent Dhumaric south at the head of a select company of five hundred men. She recalled the eager expression on Dhumaric's face as he had met her in the courtyard, and eager it should be: his quarry was none other than the Krotànya Throne Prince Kahsir dor Xeredir dàn Ahzur—Kahsir, old enemy, old nemesis, who had unaccountably been present in Rodja'âno at its fall.

She met Ssenkahdavic's eyes, stilled the fear that shook her heart, and smiled.

He reached out for her hand, took it in his own, and pulled her down so she knelt at his feet. "The end is beginning, Aeschu." She had a brief impression of yawning, hungry Darkness, shot through with terror and despair—a Shadow so mighty it dwarfed all the stars. Ssenkahdavic smiled once more, as death might smile. "When I wake again, you'll see it."

*   *   *

Whenever he could as he walked, Kahsir watched the men who set out from the clearing. They were indeed a motley crew. He and the Hrudharic brothers, Lorhaiden and Vàlkir, were the only noblemen. The rest were simple men-at-arms or farmers who had taken arms in defense of their capital. But they moved well enough as a band, and he took comfort in that.

Taking the mind-road was out of the question: the surge of energy would draw enemy attention. He had no choice but to lead his men by the world's roads until they were far enough away from Rodja'âno to attempt a jump. He led the way through the woods at a fast trot. He sensed the men's discomfort, endured their furtive and sidelong glances. He awed them, yet they were even more uncomfortable around Lorhaiden. The High-King's grandson; the sword-brother with his lethal oath—he had felt the like before. Impressions spilled from behind their shields, half-raveled. He ignored the stares and the thoughts he sensed.

Lorhaiden seemed oblivious to the scrutiny. He was a blank, well guarded; Vàlkir—troubled, but with his mind to the forest about, and to the chance of ambush.

Kahsir reached the crest of a small hill and paused, shading his eyes in the noon sunlight. The land ran on, forest-clad, but something seemed different. He glanced at Lorhaiden to see if his sword-brother had noticed the same thing.

"There should be a river down in that valley," Kahsir said, pointing. "I can't even see the trace of one."

"There been a rock slide 'round fifty leagues east," one of the men-at-arms said. "The river been forced farther south."

"How long ago was that?"

"A hundred, maybe a hundred and twenty years ago."

Vàlkir stiffened. "We're being followed."

"Ah, *chuht!*" Kahsir swung around and looked behind. His shoulders tensed. "How far are they? And how many?"

"I'm not sure," said Vàlkir: most sensitive of them all, Vàlkir. "They're well shielded."

"Vahl," Kahsir said, and then motioned one of the men-at-arms forward. "We'll keep on to the southeast. The two of you fall back and see if you can Read them. Don't get any closer than you have to."

Vàlkir, the man-at-arms at his heels, disappeared over the hill. Kahsir traded a look with Lorhaiden, and led the others down toward the valley. The dry riverbed ran near to the course Hairon had set, so he turned his men and set off down it at an easy lope, his fellows falling in behind. With every other stride, his head ached. He tried a different pace, but it only made the pain worse.

So the river's moved. And if that happened only over a hundred years ago, how many more changes in the land? Damn! Damn! I thought I was somewhat familiar with the countryside around Rodja'âno. And now I find I'm not. Lords! Everything I remember could be wrong! The land's surely changed in all the centuries since I've been here in the northlands.

"They're coming back," Lorhaiden said.

Kahsir stopped, held up his hand to signal a halt, and turned to face the two that ran down the riverbed.

"Five hundred," Vàlkir said, his breath heavy. The man-at-arms stood bent, hands on his knees, fighting for air. "I sensed them clear this time. They're about ten leagues behind us. They're horsed."

"Did they sense you?"

"No."

"Who's leading them? Could you tell?"

Vàlkir took a deep breath. "Dhumaric."

"Dhumaric?"

Kahsir whirled around at the sound of Lorhaiden's voice and grabbed him by the shoulders, struggling against the mental flare of hatred and anguish that

poured from Lorhaiden's mind. *Lorj! Dammit! Don't!*
Get your shields up, man! Now! Do you want to get us
all killed? Desperately, he sought those portions of
Lorhaiden's mind still open to reason. At last, Lorhaiden's
shields came up.

"By all the Lords of Light!" Kahsir dropped his hands,
releasing Lorhaiden's shoulders. He was surrounded by
a ring of white faces, silent and observing. "You might
as well have stood on the ridge back there and yelled
'Here we are! Come get us!' Where's your caution,
Lorj?"

Lorhaiden swallowed heavily. "It's Dhumaric," he
whispered. "Dhumaric! That *fihrkken* bastard butch-
ered my family . . . he—"

"I know, Lorj. But that was then, now is now. They'll
know where we are for sure."

"And that you're with us, Lord," added Vàlkir, only
now having fully caught his breath. "That information
was there, and more."

Dammit, Lorj. You've done it!

Lorhaiden turned away, fits clenched, his shoulders
set in both anger and humiliation.

"Watch your shields, *baràdor*," Kahsir said, "or we'll
all die."

The men-at-arms and farmers murmured to themselves, several even stepping farther back from where
Lorhaiden stood. Lorhaiden turned slowly, his eyes
begging forgiveness.

"I'm sorry, Lord," he said. "Let me go back. I can
kill Dhumaric from ambush. He's—"

"No, Lorj. We've got to stay together."

"Why shouldn't I go back? I'm the one who gave us
away. I won't take anyone with me. You don't need to
worry about splitting the main group. It makes sense,
Lord. If you'd—"

Kahsir locked eyes with his sword-brother. "How
many times do I have to say it? You're not going back.
Are you sure Dhumaric's leading the only company out

there? What if he isn't? If you kill Dhumaric, that won't keep his men off us, and his death would draw any other enemy patrols close. We're outnumbered enough as it is. Let's not make it any worse."

Lorhaiden set his jaw. "Lord . . . they're going to catch up to us eventually . . . we've got wounded with us. Even if I don't go back after Dhumaric, some of us will *have* to. We've got to slow them down."

Kahsir stared at his sword-brother: Lorhaiden was right. Five hundred horsed enemy rode not ten leagues away and neither he nor any of his companions, save Hairon, had ever been in this region before. *Damn! I wish I had those maps! The roads I know, but we're far from any traveled ways.*

"Lord . . . please." Lorhaiden's voice was hoarse with emotion. "It's *Dhumaric!*"

Dhumaric. Kahsir rubbed the knot on his head, winced, and looked back down the riverbed. Lords! If he could only get his hands on Dhumaric. There were few enemy commanders he hated and feared as much as *that* bastard. He chewed on his lower lip. Unlike Lorhaiden, his desire to strike at Dhumaric was not personal—he could not abandon his men for selfish revenge. Yet what Lorhaiden said about someone eventually having to turn back to slow down Dhumaric rang true.

"Lord?"

Kahsir silenced Lorhaiden with a gesture, then looked at the men around him. Most of them came from steadings close to Rodja'âno and, untrained as warriors, carried the bow as their chosen weapon. Of his twenty-eight comrades, only four had wounds severe enough to hamper their fighting.

"Hairon." The stocky man-at-arms stepped forward. "Continue down the riverbed. Make the best time you can. Leave us signs we can follow." Kahsir motioned to the four wounded men. "I'll need two bows and all the arrows you can spare."

"You're going back, Lord?" Vàlkir asked.

"Aye. You, Lorj, and I." He looked at his men again. "Are any of you fellows woodsmen?"

Tsingar ranged just far enough ahead of Dhumaric's five hundred men that he could still reach his commander quickly. Since early morning, unable to take the mind-road because no one was familiar with the wooded countryside, Dhumaric had driven the company south by the world's roads in pursuit of a fleeing group of Krotànya. Obviously this chase had come from Ssenkahdavic's conversation with Dhumaric when the warlord had entered Rodja'âno. At any other time, Dhumaric would have delegated this task to some junior officer, possibly one more familiar with the land.

Tsingar frowned, sensing more to this chase than was obvious. He glanced around the forest: the trees and brush had grown thicker. His horse balked at something and he rocked forward in the saddle. Cursing their inability to use the mind-road, he reined around and started back.

Suddenly, his mind filled with light. Then the momentary brilliance faded, leaving— A dry riverbed to the south, more than twenty Krotànya, most of them hurt, and . . . *and* the faces of men he recognized from past battles: Kahsir and Vàlkir. Their hopes, their fears and despairs; and hatred, overwhelming hatred.

Tsingar's heart lurched: the mind that had let loose this Sending, that was so full of seething hate—he recognized its touch as well. Lorhaiden!

Then, as quickly as it had come, the Sending was cut off.

For a long moment Tsingar sat frozen. The fleeing Krotànya were led by none other than Kahsir, the Krotànya Throne Prince. And Lorhaiden, the Prince of Hrudharic whom he and Dhumaric had nearly slain all those long decades ago.

Tsingar grinned, lifted the reins, and whipped his horse back through the brush.

Kahsir pushed his way through the thickets and brambles, his mind momentarily linked to Hairon's as the man-at-arms led the other warriors away down the riverbed. Assured that the link was fixed, that he would always know Hairon's position and be able to *see* through Hairon's eyes, Kahsir turned his attention northward to where the enemy rode.

He went heavily shielded, his companions also, their greatest concern keeping the Leishoranya from sensing them. As they pushed farther northward, the enemy presence grew stronger with each step. The unstrung bow at his back caught at a sapling; he pulled the bow free and plunged deeper into the undergrowth. He was not an archer by preference, but he *had* to be better than average after fifteen hundred years of using the bow.

Though the forest was near impassable, the new spring leaves lent barely enough cover. When he sensed the enemy not more than five leagues beyond his position, Kahsir lifted his hand and brought his companions to a halt.

"Read the land for me, Vahl. And be careful."

Vàlkir nodded. Kahsir felt the younger man's mind brush past his, then thin out to next to nothing.

"Done, Lord," Vàlkir said.

"Share what you Saw."

Kahsir's mind was immediately filled with an overview of the forest, the lay of the land, the possible places to set ambushes, the false trails he could use. Touching his companions' minds, Kahsir transferred this knowledge.

"Ready?" he asked.

Nods answerd him. He grinned at his men in assurance, turned around, and set off through the forest at a trot.

*   *   *

Tsingar reined in his horse within the undergrowth, for a moment spying on the warriors who followed. Though his mind was shielded tightly, he clamped those defenses even tighter. *Chaagut. Riding with Dhumaric. What's he doing back so soon? I sent him out before me.* His back stiffened. *Damned bastard! Wants my position, does he? Well, he'll have to take it!*

Squaring his shoulders, he rode forward out of the brush.

"Well, Tsingar?" Dhumaric's voice was frightening—so deep it was virtually a rumble. "What did you find?"

Tsingar gestured behind. "The Krotànya we're following, Dread Lord—it's Kahsir and Lorhaiden."

For a long moment nothing happened. Dhumaric sat motionless on his horse; Chaagut's face showed hastily hidden surprise. Tsingar sighed quietly in relief: Chaagut had not known.

"Kahsir," Dhumaric said.

Tsingar trembled at the expression in Dhumaric's eyes. He had seen the like before when other men had died for Dhumaric's amusement, for some petty wrong punished.

"How far ahead?" asked Dhumaric.

"About ten leagues or so, Master." He kept his eyes averted: Dhumaric's voice was frightening enough. "Nearly thirty of them, on foot, in a dry riverbed, heading southeast."

Dhumaric laughed and Tsingar's stomach tightened.

"They'll be easy prey for us, Master," he said, looking up at last.

"Easy prey?" snarled Dhumaric. "Not with those two leading them, especially Kahsir!"

Tsingar flinched, barely controlling his rage at the sly expression that slid across Chaagut's face.

"Have you forgotten everything, Tsingar?" Dhumaric's voice was cold. "We've faced Kahsir and Lorhaiden centuries past, you and I. Easy prey is the *last* thing they'll be."

Tsingar chose the relative safety of silence.

—*Move out!* Dhumaric mind-sent, turning away and gesturing to the warriors who followed. *And be wary of traps. We're following one of the chief strategists of the Krotànya.*

Riding before the company again, his scouts fanning out ahead just within sight, Tsingar tried to locate the fleeing Krotànya. He cursed: they had shielded themselves beyond finding.

The woods thickened. Tsingar slowed his horse to a walk, reined the animal around a fallen tree, and took up his course again. Staying out of Dhumaric's reach when the Great Lord brooded was his main concern now. Not for the first time did Tsingar count himself fortunate to be riding with the scouts.

Scouts. He looked off to his left but could not see the man who should have been riding there. A quick glance to his right: that scout had also disappeared. The trees were thick here, the undergrowth dense, but the scouts should have been easy to see.

He tried a Sending, heavily cloaked, but got nothing. No answer, no sign of the scouts acknowledging the call. Tsingar halted. A few birds sang off in the trees, the branches stirred in a brief wind, but all else was silent.

He cursed again, lifted the reins, and set off at a slow walk through the undergrowth, his eyes raking the forest about.

Something touched his mind briefly and was gone. Tsingar jerked his horse to a stop, sat motionless, tracing the direction of that touch. He nudged his horse forward again, angling off to his left. A cold chill ran up his spine. He loosened both swords in their sheaths and kept a wary eye to the forest.

And pushed through a screen of brush to face the swaying body.

The scout hung upside down from a bent sapling, a noose made of vine around his ankles. Blood still dripped from his slashed throat.

"Gods." Tsingar drew his longsword and looked hastily around. A quick probe of the forest revealed no enemy close by. He glanced back at the body. The man had died recently—the enemy could *not* be far.

Reining his horse around, Tsingar trotted back the way he had come, then turned to the right of the path he had originally taken. His heart thudded in his chest as he rode through the trees, trying to make as little noise as possible.

A rustle of something heavy in the brush ahead. Tsingar reined in, listening for a repeat of the sound. A branch cracked loudly, then another snapped even closer. Tsingar cursed, lifted his sword, and kneed his horse off to one side of the noise.

The undergrowth rattled and a horse blundered through it, eyes wild, reins looped high on its neck. A body lay slumped forward in the saddle, arms dangling on either side of the horse's neck: the second scout—an arrow protruding from the ruin of one eye.

Tsingar jerked his horse around, kicked the animal to a fast trot, and rode back toward Dhumaric's company. This could be the work of resistance fighters, tricks Tsingar had seen to the north of Rodja'âno. Or— A sense of panic: Kahsir was out there somewhere— somewhere very close.

After a patient search, several of Kahsir's men had dug up enough poisonous bulbs to yield a coating for fifty or sixty arrowheads. A pot was needed now to boil those bulbs in—a pot the enemy cooks would surely be carrying. So, minds carefully shielded, Lorhaiden and the other men had followed Kahsir through the forest, hunting the enemy column.

Now, hidden by the thick undergrowth, Lorhaiden looked through the brush as the Leishoranya worked their way through the woods. His hand tightened on his bow, but he suppressed the longing for combat, pleased enough by all he had done today. Of the fifteen enemy warriors killed by traps or stealth, he alone had accounted for six.

He glanced to his left to where his brother knelt hidden. Vàlkir, the best bowman among them all, would try this tricky shot. He had cut the fletching from an arrow, removed its head, and coated the bare shaft with dirt; now he knelt closer than any of Kahsir's men to the passing enemy column.

Lorhaiden looked back at the Leishoranya. Five hundred warriors took considerasble time to ride through the forest. Horsed, the Leishoranya would have held an unbeatable advantage on open ground; afoot in the woods, Kahsir and his band had the upper hand.

As long as they stayed a safe distance from the enemy.

The end of the enemy column came into sight. Heavily laden pack horses, each led by one man, stumbled along through the brush. The cooks. Lorhaiden held himself absolutely still, sensed the concentration of the men around him. If Vàlkir missed his shot, they would have to mind-road it out of here quickly enough to keep the enemy from tracing their path.

The last pack horse passed. Lorhaiden craned his head, saw Vàlkir straighten and take careful aim.

A thin sound—a subtle *whush*: Vàlkir had released his arrow. Lords keep any of the Leishoranya from noticing over their own noise in the brush.

The pack horse neighed in pain as the headless arrow bounced off the sensitive area between its hind legs. Rearing and throwing the man who led it off his feet, it lunged off into the undergrowth, spilling food, cooking utensils, and whatnot as it ran.

Several of the Leishoranya who led the other pack animals ran off after the horse, but it would be long gone by now. After the loss of fifteen men, the enemy officers would be more concerned with keeping the column tight than the loss of a horse and supplies.

As Lorhaiden settled back in the undergrowth to wait, he caught the brief glint of light reflecting from something that had rolled off to one side in the woods. He hoped it was a pot.

Keeping up with the enemy column had not been difficult: Dhumaric and his officers could keep five hundred men, their mounts, and the pack animals only so quiet. Kahsir glanced up, to as much of the sky as he could see, and judged it sundown. He shifted his cloak closer in the chill, and pushed on through the brush. Less than a quarter league separated him from Dhumaric's five hundred, but he and the two men who followed him must approach closer.

He took a quick look over his shoulder. Vàlkir nodded: the enemy remained unaware. The man-at-arms who walked behind Vàlkir held his bow strung, an arrow nocked, his eyes moving in a constant scan of the forest.

—*Lord*, Vàlkir Sent. *We'd better stop here. The enemy's just now beginning to fix their dinner.*

Kahsir nodded. *How far?* he Sent back, trusting to Vàlkir's ability to See the land and all in it without enemy detection.

—*Over the next two rises.*

—*Pickets?*

—*Five on our side of the camp, a like number on the other sides. They're stationed about twenty paces from the company.*

Kahsir knelt, motioning Vàlkir to his side. The man-at-arms remained standing, careful to place himself so that no back-lighting would reveal his position.

—*Can you do this without the enemy knowing, Vahl?*

—*I've got the strength for it, and you'll be helping*

me. Given luck, it'll be over so quickly no one will notice.

Vàlkir opened a leather pouch and shook out a handful of small white mushrooms: *ulv'den*, little-death, they were called. Only a few of them could bring quick death to many men: Kahsir and his companions had gathered enough to fell hundreds.

Stilling his mind for what would follow, Kahsir glanced one last time at the man-at-arms who stood guard close beside them, leaning against the trunk of a low-hanging pine tree.

—*Now?* he Sent.

Vàlkir nodded.

Kahsir extended his shielding so it enveloped himself and Vàlkir. Once he felt the shields lock in place, he tightened them, overlaying them with impressions of not-being, of mental invisibility. Then, carefully, he lay a hand on Vàlkir's shoulder—

—and Saw what Vàlkir Saw, sensed what Vàlkir sensed.

The enemy cooks had fired the traveling cauldrons they carried on the pack horses. Pointed ends buried in the fire pits, the cauldrons now contained dried meat, greens, potatoes, and other vegetables, along with water the cooks had brought in from a nearby stream.

Kahsir felt a subtle draining of his mental strength. Vàlkir drew on it to add to his own, and sat motionless, staring at an invisible point before him.

A slight shimmer in the air, the merest suggestion of a hole in space, and the gateway formed.

It was small, that gate, only large enough to admit two hands. Kahsir increased his concentration, willing the gate to invisibility, and waited. Part of his mind focused on the gateway, the other part kept watch on the enemy. The cook turned away from the fire, going back for something else to add to the cauldron.

—*Now!* Kahsir Sent.

Vàlkir carefully thrust a hand through the tiny gate, and dropped the mushrooms into the stew.

His divided vision showed Kahsir the cook coming back with a handful of carrots. *Quickly, Vahl!*

His other hand steady, Vàlkir dumped the last of the mushrooms, then jerked his hand back through the gate.

Kahsir immediately shut down his support, Vàlkir cancelled the gateway, and the two of them sat panting in the twilight.

—Did they sense you? Kahsir asked.

—No, thank the Lords.

Kahsir grinned slightly, scrambled to his feet, and tottered a moment, weaker than he expected. What he and Vàlkir had done was considered next to impossible. Not only had they created a gate and sustained it without the enemy noticing, but they had *used* that gate, which required an even greater expenditure of energy.

You're damned good, Vahl, you know that? Let's get out of here.

Tsingar sat by his fire, not far from Dhumaric's tent, and patted his meal cake into firmness, reached out and dropped it on the hot stone he had dragged out of the fire. Settling back on his heels, he looked across the darkened camp.

Dhumaric had divided his company of five hundred in two. As second in command, Tsingar should have been with the other group as their commanding officer, but Dhumaric had ordered him to stay, assigning Chaagut to that duty. Tsingar reached out with a twig and moved his sizzling cake on the stone. Chaagut. A problem in the making.

A junior officer sat down across Tsingar's small fire, his steaming traveling cup in his hands.

"Stew's ready," the fellow said. "You'd better get some or it'll be gone."

"Ssst." Tsingar glanced off toward the crowd of men who had lined up to be served the rest of their dinner. "I know who's cooking tonight. I'll pass."

"Huhn." The officer had his mouth full now. "That's because you got what was left over from Dhumaric's meal."

Leftovers, indeed, but leftover venison, a deer recently shot, and far better than anything that ever came out of the stewpots. Tsingar glanced down at the fire, hurriedly reached out with his boot dagger, and turned the meal cake.

"So what do you think about the men we've lost?" the officer asked.

Tsingar withdrew behind his shields—one did not lightly ask that question, innocently or not. Fifteen men dead, victims of ingenious traps. As the day had progressed, the company had moved forward at an increasingly slower pace, wary of further surprises.

The officer's eyes glittered in the firelight. "Do you think it's resistance fighters, or Kahsir?"

Tsingar set his meal cake to cool on another flat stone at his side. "I don't know. Could be either. But I'll bet those traps are Kahsir's. They're set too damn well. That's experience."

"Huhn." The officer finished his stew, licked his lips, stood, and set off to the stream to wash his cup.

Tsingar took up his meal cake, burned his fingers, and let it fall back on the rock. He glanced at Dhumaric's tent: the doorflaps were shut, forbidding entrance. Dhumaric was in a foul mood so, taking care to select men he could trust, Tsingar had set up the pickets, five men to each side of the clearing. Now he looked forward to getting as much sleep as he could. Past experience told him he would need it.

The sound of someone being violently ill jarred Tsingar awake. He sat up, blinked groggily, and looked around: contorted forms of men writhed on the ground. Tsingar scrambled out of his blankets, stood, and tried to force his fogged mind to work.

"Tsingar!"

He turned around. Dhumaric stood outside his tent, face and body highlighted by the dim light of the dying fires.

"What the Void's going on?" Dhumaric demanded.

"I—Lord, I don't know." Tsingar caught up to Dhumaric, who had stalked off toward a group of convulsing warriors.

The clearing reeked of vomit and feces, but Tsingar could not look away from the nightmarish scene. Dhumaric paused by several still bodies and shoved at them with his foot.

"By the Gods! They're dead!" Dhumaric whirled on Tsingar. "Where are the pickets? Get those men in here immediately!"

Tsingar saw several other men standing, faces blank in the firelight. "You . . . you and you! Get seven more men and replace the pickets! Send them to me! Move!"

The warriors snatched up their weapons and trotted off to the perimeter of camp. More and more of the vomiting men had fallen silent now, slipping down from their contorted crouches to lie still in their own filth.

The pickets appeared one by one out of the woods, hesitated, then loped across the clearing to stand before Dhumaric.

"Has anyone crossed your lines?" Dhumaric rapped.

The pickets shook their heads, casting nervous sidelong glances at each other.

"No, Master," one of the men said, bobbing his head deeply in a bow. "We've seen and sensed no one."

Tsingar cringed as he felt Dhumaric reach out into each of the pickets' minds, to rummage there, seeking the smallest detail of memory any of the men might have forgotten.

One of the warriors whimpered as Dhumaric released them all.

"Damn!" Dhumaric turned on Tsingar. "They're right. No one's broken through."

Bodies lay everywhere. The smell of burning flesh where men had rolled into their own fires mingled with the odors of vomit and excrement. Tsingar drew a shallow breath: well over a hundred men had died.

"Cooks!" Dhumaric's eyes bored into Tsingar's soul, leaving behind the impression of instant and violent death. "Get me the damned cooks! Now!"

Tsingar ran across the clearing. The cooks were awake now, and stood in shocked silence by their fireside. Tsingar motioned curtly for them to follow and returned to Dhumaric.

Dhumaric's right ... it's got to be something the men ate. And only some of them, or we'd all be dead. And if it is something we ate, where did we get it? Did we bring it with us, or did it come from outside? The pickets swear no one crossed their lines. Gods! We won't be able to trust anything we eat now.

Dhumaric was questioning the cooks. Tsingar shivered suddenly. If whatever had poisoned the men had come from outside the camp, then where was the enemy? How many of them were out there? And how had something poisonous gotten into the food supply?

"Tsingar!" Dhumaric snapped. "Talk to the men who aren't sick. I want to know what each of them ate tonight."

Tsingar hurried off across the clearing. A chill sweat dampened his forehead. He had escaped hidden death this night, but how or why he could not guess.

Kahsir leaned forward as one of the men-at-arms stirred the viscous liquid in the stolen Leishoranya pot, and found it hard to keep a smile from his face.

Earlier, Vàlkir had reported that the enemy had eaten the poisoned stew, and that as far as he could tell over one hundred thirty-five men had died. Dhumaric was even now questioning the cooks, who swore no one had tampered with their provisions.

They would isolate the stew eventually, but now they

could not trust any of the dried meat or vegetables the cooks brought with them. That meant having to depend on what each man carried in his saddlebags. A forced march demanded energy that meal was not likely to give.

The man-at-arms stopped stirring the poison, which now clung in a thick paste to the end of the stick he used.

"It be good now, Lord," he said. "Good and deadly."

Kahsir looked at his waiting companions. "We've got enough poison for sixty applications—five arrows each. Unless you're damned sure of your shots, don't make them."

He leaned forward on his knees, and carefully dipped his arrows in the mucky paste. Holding them away from his body, he sank back in his place, drew out his boot knife, and notched each arrow just above the fletching so he could tell which were poisoned and which were not.

"Now listen to me," Kahsir said, as his companions dipped their arrows into the pot. "We'll go after the enemy tomorrow morning, just as they're getting ready to ride out. They'll have their pickets in by then and the camp will be in a general state of turmoil. We'll get as many as we can, then mind-road it out of there."

"Them bastards be able to trace our going, Lord," a man-at-arms pointed out.

"Not if we make quick multiple jumps. Vahl will give us our jump points before we attack and the two of us will take turns making the gates when we run. Questions?"

Fourteen intense faces stared back at him through the firelight. Not a question was asked.

Tsingar stood by his horse in the early morning light, tying his saddle bags behind the heavy war saddle. The smell of death was all around. No one had dragged the bodies of the poisoned men off into the woods, afraid that lurking Krotànya might strike from out of the dark. Though Dhumaric had isolated the stew as source of the poison, even now men kept a wary eye to the forest about.

The remaining men of Dhumaric's company, reduced—Tsingar estimated—to less than three hundred fifty, had formed their column. Dhumaric stood in the center of that column, surrounded by his junior officers. Though Tsingar could not hear what his commander was saying, he knew the words well enough: move slowly, move steadily, use your *minds* to see as well as your eyes. Suspect everything, trust nothing, not even what you think is safe.

Tsingar scratched at his ear, reached for his reins—

—And fell flat on the ground at the noise of passing arrows.

Two men close to him staggered backward, shot in their legs just below their chain mail—minor wounds, ones that. . . .

The men staggered again and wheezed, their faces turning a mottled purple, and toppled forward to lie without moving on the forest floor.

More arrows! Tsingar hugged the ground, not sure where the enemy shot from. Cries of agony rose around him, not only from men but from their horses. Tsingar's blood ran cold—poison again, only this time on the arrow tips.

"Return fire!"

Dhumaric's voice boomed out above the shrieks of dying men and animals. Tsingar buried his head, imagined an arrow tearing into his body at any moment.

Kahsir again . . . this time he was sure of it, as he was sure that somehow, some way, Kahsir had poisoned their provisions.

"Follow their trail, you dung-headed idiots!" Dhumaric bellowed. "They're taking the mind-road!"

Tsingar sensed the energy flare that accompanied a jump, and sought after the invisible enemy.

* * *

—Get out of there! Kahsir Sent, lowering his bow. *Link minds and follow me!*

With one last look at the milling enemy, he leapt through the gate he had made. Darkness, chill . . . a small stream at his feet and another gate forming. His companions at his back, he threw himself through the gate, the coldness biting at him, the darkness, the void tearing at his mind—

—another clearing, another coalescing gate. He sensed some of the men-at-arms tiring, shot a quick thought to Vàlkir for additional help, ran to the gate and leapt through it—

—into a thick stand of trees. His head felt like someone was driving a knife into it. He stood, wavered on his feet. Dimly aware of his men around him, he constructed the last gate, jumped through—

—to stand by the edge of a dry riverbed, Hairon and the other men waiting hidden in the brush close by.

Kahsir sank to his knees, rubbed his eyes, and looked around at the white faces of his comrades. Two of the men-at-arms had lost consciousness, and even Vàlkir seemed shaken, but all of them had made it through the jumps without the enemy following.

CHAPTER 6

Morning sunlight angled down on the riverbed. Birds sang from the trees above, leaving all else silent. Kahsir looked at his gathered warriors, satisfied that the men who had turned back with him to annoy the enemy had regained enough of their strength to continue on.

Hairon and his companion had left behind traps of their own in the riverbed. Now, there was little left to do but run, to make the best time possible on foot.

Cursing their lack of horses to carry the more seriously wounded men, Kahsir started forward, keeping his mind spread out like a net behind and before them. Vàlkir had spent more energy than he should have, and Kahsir sought to lend him help.

The riverbed curved on, its general course heading southeast. Remembering all the traps Hairon's men and his own had left behind, Kahsir thought of Dhumaric, and wondered if it was enough.

Standing closest to Dhumaric, Tsingar glanced sidelong at the other officers who had gathered at the commander's order. His shoulder ached from where he had thrown himself to the ground when the Krotànya had attacked with poisoned arrows, but he was alive. At least fifty other men were not.

"Listen to me," Dhumaric growled. "In the space of one night, we've lost nearly two hundred men. Two hundred! That should tell you what kind of man we're following."

Tsingar listened to Dhumaric's words with one ear—he had heard the like before. Anyone who took Kahsir lightly was lucky to live to change his mind. The way ahead would be full of traps, and Dhumaric's progress slowed to a crawl, but the Great Lord had decided to keep going, even though he had lost nearly half his men.

"Now move out," Dhumaric said, "and warn your warriors of what I've told you. We're on horseback and the Krotànya on foot. That will ultimately make the difference."

In the cloud-mottled sunlight of late morning, Kahsir ran down the riverbed, searching the far side for a way up into the forest's cover. The rocky banks were high— the pebbles loose and no good for climbing. Despite all the traps they had left behind, he and his men could still be caught, trapped by the pursuing Leishoranya.

A heavy thud from behind made him jerk to a halt and turn. One of the men-at-arms, a big fellow who hailed from north of Rodja'âno, had fallen—his wounded leg had given way at last.

"I'm finished, Lord." The man's face was white with pain. "Can't run no longer."

Kahsir touched his companions' minds, seeking the strongest. "You, Gherric. And Lhars, Weoric, and Adhanil. Carry him." He looked back the way they had come. *The river's moved, dammit! Over a hundred years before.*

"We got to climb them banks," Hairon said, his hand nervous on his sword hilt. "Could get steeper a ways on."

Kahsir shut his eyes and waved Hairon silent. *Think! It's there! In the older memories!* Forests, trees, rivers—centuries of walking and riding through them. But *which* forest? Damn the loss of the maps! He sought a landmark! Lords . . . *any* landmark! *Maybe the river's been forced out of its bed, but the old path it took will still look the same. Remember, man! Remember how the river used to run, its twists, the fords, the forest about—*

"Keep going!" he cried. His mind fixed on a still, bright memory. "There's an old ford about a league away. Move!" The four men he had chosen picked up the man-at-arms and started off at a lope, the rest following. Kahsir turned to Vàlkir and Lorhaiden. "We've about run out of traps, and Dhumaric will be expecting them. Vahl, if Lorhaiden and I help, can you set down a false impression for the enemy to Read?"

After a moment's hesitation, Vàlkir nodded.

"Good. Dhumaric knows we're hurt, most of us, and exhausted from our attacks on his men; he won't expect us to head for the forest." Kahsir looked back down the dry riverbed. "Vahl, lay down the impression that we entered the forest here. He'll doubt that, and rightly so. To confuse things further, lay down that we kept to the riverbed, then went into the woods. Faced with three overlapping possibilities, he might choose the wrong one."

"And when we reach the ford?" Vàlkir asked.

"We'll create a barrier of some kind, Lords know what. Something he'll believe we'd try to keep him off our backs. When we're done with that, weave an impression we went off into the forest, which is actually what we'll do." Vàlkir nodded slowly, falling into the rhythm of things. "By then, we'll have thrown him so many lies he may disbelieve the truth."

It was nearly midday when Tsingar rode up on the edge of the riverbed where he had Seen Kahsir and the others running. Behind, Dhumaric's men held their places, exhausted, tempers near to breaking, but relieved to be out of the forest and all the deadly traps it held.

"Now we'll make some time," Dhumaric said. "We aren't done with Kahsir's traps, but he'll have left fewer of them. He knows we'll be moving faster than he can."

Chaagut rode forward, to rein in behind Dhumaric. "Could we take the mind-road, Master?"

Dhumaric did not look around. "We don't know the land. If we probed ahead, the Krotànya would sense our position and be off before we could trace them."

"Do you know how far ahead Kahsir might be?" Tsingar asked, ignoring Chaagut as if the other man had never spoken.

Dhumaric rose in his stirrups, waved his following men forward, and started down the steep incline to the riverbed. "Not far enough," he said.

The enemy followed closer behind. Kahsir sensed them coming: a cold spot between his shoulder blades. But for Dhumaric to attempt the mind-road—that needed an exact location, and any probe Dhumaric made could not be hidden well enough.

The riverbed below lay blocked by a loose rockslide he and his companions had called down. Vàlkir had just finished leaving another false impression of their course, and stood by Lorhaiden's side. And now—now, they must run again.

"Let's go," Kahsir said to the others, who had sunk down in their tracks, and now lifted weary faces and listened. "The Leishoranya are mounted and we're not. Once we're in the forest, that should turn in our favor again. They're exhausted, wary of traps, and riding hard. They can't carry their horses on the mind-road any more than we can take our wounded. So we're even. A while longer, friends. Then we'll rest."

No one answered. Kahsir gestured, and led the way

into the forest, avoiding the pathway that led from the ford.

The rockslide that blocked the riverbed lay fresh and easy to read—perhaps too easy after the further traps that had lurked in the riverbed. Another seven men dead, several horses left behind, lamed beyond riding, and more time lost.

"Tsingar," Dhumaric said. "Which way do you think the Krotànya went?"

"East, Master. They left the impression they went into the woods here. But I think they kept to the riverbed. They've got wounded with them and can make better time."

"And you?" Dhumaric asked Chaagut.

Chaagut paled slightly, and lowered his head. "My opinion's nothing, Dread Lord," he said, voice as oily as yesterday's poisonous stew.

"He's damned clever, that Kahsir," Dhumaric murmured. "Listen and learn. He wants us to think he continued up the riverbed, but with his wounded, he'll do the exact opposite of what we'd expect."

Tsingar curled his lip in Chaagut's direction, but forced his face blank when Dhumaric turned back.

"We'll enter the forest here," said Dhumaric, pointing up the steep bank. "And send out more scouts, Tsingar. We haven't much time to lose."

Kahsir and his men traveled all afternoon, keeping to as fast a pace as the trees would allow. He kept his mind open to the fullest, but had not sensed the enemy again. *Do you honestly think you* could *sense them? It's Dhumaric back there, fool.*

Though the forest had not grown thicker, the light dimmed well before it should. Kahsir cocked his head at a faint sound from behind: it came again—the distant rumble of thunder. The first heavy raindrops fell on the

new leaves above. Kahsir gestured the men behind
closer, drew his cloak up about his neck and shoulders,
and increased his pace.

In a short while, the rain had turned into a downpour. He slowed to a walk in the blinding gusts, kept
his eyes on the ground, alert for exposed roots. Rain
like this would hold his band to a crawl, but it would do
the same to the enemy. He frowned, blinked the rain
from his eyes. "Go last," he said to Lorhaiden and
Vàlkir. "Keep us from straggling."

The two brothers nodded and fell back to the rear.
Kahsir pushed back the drooping tree branches, slipped
once on the muddy ground, and fought for balance.
Someone cursed loudly from behind. The rain slack-
ened momentarily, then fell again in sheets. Holding
his forearm above his eyes, Kahsir squinted ahead.
There was no path, nor would there likely be one.
Then, even through the rain, he heard another, deeper
sound—the sound of rushing water.

*O Lords! It's probably the river that was forced
south!*

He rounded the tree ahead and the sound of water
grew louder. At last, he saw the river through the
trees and rain, and his mouth went dry. Wide, though
probably not deep, the water swept by, full of debris
from the mountain run-off.

His men stood around him, each of them staring at
the river.

"We can't cross that," Lorhaiden said loudly.

A wordless growl of assent followed Lorhaiden's words.
Even though the men-at-arms distrusted Lorhaiden and
tolerated his presence only for Kahsir's sake, they knew
truth no matter who spoke it.

"Let's go farther east," Vàlkir suggested.

Kahsir looked ahead through the rain. "Are you picking up anything?"

"Possibly. It's too unfocused yet. The enemy's behind us—east or west. One way's as good as the other."

Kahsir nodded and turned eastward, trudging along through the rain. His head still hurt; he was hungry and had forgotten when he had eaten last.

The light grew dimmer. Thunder rumbled overhead and the rain fell straight down now with no wind to blow it about. Kahsir shivered in the chill. *Damn! Dhumaric could trap us against that* fihrkken *river in the dark.*

"Lord! Look!" Lorhaiden stopped and pointed off to their right through the trees.

"It's a bridge!" Vàlkir said, coming closer. "That's what I might have been sensing. But it looks near to falling down."

Kahsir smiled wearily. "All the better for us. If we can make it to the other side and destroy that bridge behind us, the Leishoranya won't have a way across."

No one spoke. The rain fell in sheets, a continuous hiss through the new leaves. Kahsir drew a deep breath.

"Let's move," he said, "before the storm gets worse!"

The first light of morning woke Kahsir, and for a long moment he lay silent, listening to his companions, who slept nearby. The storm had gone, but water still dripped down from the leaves. He rolled over onto his side, hitched up on one elbow, and looked out across the clearing.

The night before, having crossed the river and destroyed the dilapidated bridge, he had pushed his men near to dropping until they had reached this place. Drenched, exhausted, everyone had fallen asleep the moment they had stretched out in the wet undergrowth. Everyone, that is, save the men chosen by lot to stand picket.

He stirred uneasily. Something was wrong—the sense of it gnawed at the edge of his awareness. Nothing seemed out of the ordinary. Save for the rustle of leaves above and birdsong from the trees, the clearing stood silent. He closed his eyes and sought mentally— again, nothing.

"*Chuht!*" He rose to his feet. His limbs protested, stiff from yesterday's running and from having spent the night in a puddle. He hastily checked his weapons, but their wrappings had kept them dry.

Lorhaiden and Vàlkir slept close by. He shook them both by the shoulder and sat back on his heels between them.

"Wake the others," he said as they sat up. He stood, attached longsword and shortsword to his weapons belt, and peered off into the forest. "I want us to be ready to move out at a moment's notice."

"Trouble?" asked Lorhaiden, smoothing down his tangled hair and setting his helm in place.

"I'm not sure. Just wake them. I'm going to check on the pickets. And Vahl, keep your mind open to its fullest."

Kahsir walked off into the forest, unable to shake the growing sense of unease. The woods about lay silent, too silent—even the birdsong had gone. He jerked to a stop. Everything around reeked of danger. He turned immediately and trotted back through the dense growth of trees to the clearing. *Lords! We've got to get out of here! Now!* He relaxed somewhat: his comrades had awakened. Armed and silent, they sat in the clearing's center, ready to set out.

DANGER!

Kahsir's mind shrieked a warning. He dropped flat to the ground and rolled away from the tree he stood by. At the same instant, a knife thudded into the tree trunk not a finger's width from where his head had been.

Suddenly, the clearing filled with Leishoranya warriors, crashing in through the trees and underbrush. But they had lost the advantage of surprise, and now faced fully armed Krotànya warriors who leapt up to meet their coming.

Kahsir ripped out his sword, cut down a Leishoran who loomed up in his path, and fought his way toward his companions to close the battle ring. *Dammit! This shouldn't be happening! Ambushed in broad daylight! Where the Dark are the pickets?*

Shieldless, he fought with two hands now, his long-sword in his right and shortsword in his left. One opponent he missed altogether; the second he managed to hit. He had been the only one of his band standing apart when the attack began. Thank the Lords—the battle ring was forming quickly. He dropped his last opponent and swiftly spun into his place, Lorhaiden at his left and Vàlkir at his right.

Twenty-six Krotànya stood against about thirty of the enemy. Someone had kicked Kahsir's shield over to his feet. Hastily sheathing his shortsword left-handed, trusting to Lorhaiden for protection, Kahsir bent and snatched up his shield barely in time to turn the downward slash of a Leishoran's sword.

From that instant on, the entire battle became a blur, remembered only here and there by moments when death seemed inescapable. Kahsir fought on in blind intensity, and only when no new foe came before his sword did he realize it was over and that he and his companions had won.

"Kahs!"

He jerked back to full awareness at the sound of Vàlkir's voice. His heart pounding raggedly, he leaned on his sword and drew a long, deep breath. His shield arm ached; he let it drop, and looked around to see who lived and who had died.

Lords! What had happened to the pickets? How could they have missed the enemy's approach? He looked to left and right. Only nine men alive of the twenty-six who had stood at the onset of the ambush, and over half of them had been hurt in the fighting. A chill ran down his spine. He looked closely at the fallen Leishoranya. *Was this part of Dhumaric's company? And if it wasn't, how many other enemy forces are beyond us to the south? We could be walking into another ambush.*

"By the Light!" Vàlkir whispered, looking around at the contorted bodies. "They nearly got us all!"

Kahsir nodded and glanced at the enemy warriors again. The majority had been slain outright, and those who still lived would die soon enough.

"Hairon," he said, and the stocky farmer turned around. "See if you and Lorhaiden can find out where these warriors came from. If they're not Dhumaric's, we could be facing big trouble."

Lorhaiden set down his shield and sheathed all but his shortsword. "Unless they're babbling in their death throes, we won't learn anything."

"Huhn. Take a look anyway." As Lorhaiden and Hairon walked off, Kahsir turned his attention to the surviving members of his band. The worst hurt sat binding their wounds, but everyone appeared able to travel. And his own dead? There was little time to give them anything but a mass grave, or to say more than a few words of parting. *Forgive me. I don't have a choice.*

He turned away from the dead and scratched at the stubble on his chin. *Where the Void is Dhumaric? If he tracked us, the Light grant he didn't take the mind-road across that river. Lords! If I'm wrong, he might be anywhere—even ahead of us!*

"Lord!" Hairon's voice.

Kahsir sheathed his sword. Vàlkir at his side, he knelt down by Lorhaiden and Hairon. The wounded Leishoran who lay between them gazed up. Instant recognition flickered behind void-colored eyes that looked out of a face too beautiful to be human. But cold—so very cold. Like ice, like death.

"Vahl," Kahsir said, glancing away from those eyes. "You're the best of us at this. Try to sense what he's thinking, if you can." He swallowed heavily, sickened at the thought of touching even the edges of a Leishoran's mind. "He's dying. His shields should be down."

Vàlkir lifted one eyebrow and turned back to the dying man.

Kahsir shook his head. *Vahl can't force his mind. That's forbidden. But if he can pick up something—anything. We've nothing to lose and information to gain.*

Vàlkir moved closer to the dying Leishoran. The warrior glanced quickly around and then, gathering himself, turned his head and spat directly into Lorhaiden's face.

Kahsir leapt toward his sword-brother an instant too late. With a wild cry, Lorhaiden buried his shortsword in the warrior's chest. At the moment of his death, the Leishoran sent out a message of surprising strength and complexity—a message no one could have blocked in time. Kahsir's shoulders slumped, and he rocked back on his heels.

Lorhaiden! Rage built up; he struggled to remain calm.

Lorhaiden knelt opposite, staring down at his short-sword, which stood in the Leishoran's heart. Slowly shaking his head, he looked first to his brother, then to Kahsir.

"Lord. . . ." Tentative, shaking, Lorhaiden's voice was a mere whisper. He wiped the spittle from his face. "I—"

"Go away, Lorj," Kahsir said, amazed at the quietness of his own voice. "Go. I can't be responsible for what I might say."

Lorhaiden hesitated, stood, then backed away, disappearing into the brush on the edge of the clearing.

"*Aìi'k'vah!*" Kahsir smashed his fist down on the ground at his side. *When will he learn? Ah, Lords of Light! When will he learn?* "Vahl?"

"This man was the last of the enemy alive," Vàlkir said. "And the others erased their memories as they died. Even if I try, I won't be able to read anything."

"The warrior Lorhaiden killed . . . did you catch all of his Sending?"

"Not all of it." Vàlkir rocked back on his heels and

crossed his arms on his knees. "I know it was directed
at Dhumaric and that it informed him you and Lorhaiden
were here." He gestured at the dead warrior. "He also
managed to give a good impression of our position."

"*Chuht!* I was afraid of that." Kahsir looked around
the clearing. Lorhaiden had come back, to stand uncer-
tainly at the edge of the woods, his face expressionless.
"We don't have time to bury our dead now. We'll have
to let the forest have them. I know. I don't like it
either. But now that Dhumaric's got a sense of where
we are, he won't be far behind, even with that river to
slow him down."

CHAPTER 7

Dawn broke cold this morning. Tsingar shivered, came back to camp from relieving himself in the forest, and rubbed his eyes.

"Tsingar."

Dhumaric's voice seemed to come from all directions, though he stood at Tsingar's shoulder. "Wake the officers. We should be only two days behind Kahsir, and I want that distance cut in half."

"Aye, Master."

A group of men slept a few paces away—the officers; featureless lumps, they lay huddled together for warmth. Tsingar's bones ached with weariness, though he was no more exhausted than the rest of Dhumaric's company. Dhumaric had set a pace next to impossible to keep.

He shivered, remembering the ruined bridge, the river crossing that followed—the swollen water, the noise, the death that waited in the flood. A day was spent waiting to gain sufficient strength for the company to take the mind-road across that river. Dhumaric had sent thirty of the most rested men ahead on foot to ambush Kahsir; but Kahsir had escaped the ambush, had killed the men sent after him. The river crossing had left Dhumaric's company too exhausted to take the mind-road a second time. If they stopped to rest again, the Krotànya would have an even greater lead.

Tsingar still kept to the right tack. One of those thirty men had lived long enough to Send Tsingar the approximate Krotànya position. That death message had been surprisingly clear—clear enough to make the death of thirty men small price to pay for such information. Dolts and witlings, they had served their purpose . . . had been totally expendable, their sole purpose to be thrown against the enemy and, in the next life, to come back a few steps higher in rank, doomed to repeat the process again.

Tsingar shook his head and stopped by the sleeping officers.

"Wake up!" he yelled. Seeing Chaagut's face, he jabbed his junior officer in the side with his boot toe. *He's getting a little too big for his boots and had better learn to keep his place.* Tsingar curled his lip. *And, by the Gods, I'll be glad to teach him.*

Light-headed from hunger and near the edge of exhaustion, Kahsir walked through the forest. His men followed behind, some stumbling as they came; he sensed their misery, their longing for rest. It had been three days since the ambush and two since they had hunted.

And they were too exhausted to turn back and harass the enemy.

He glanced up as he walked. Late afternoon sunlight slanted through the trees, and in a few hours darkness would fall. He looked around and swore softly. *Lords of Light! It's all familiar, but it's not!* The forest looked wrong—different somehow, less thick. He frowned and chewed on his lower lip. His memory of the land about proved faulty, for this land too had changed.

Kahsir shook his head, drew a deep breath, and

forced himself onward. A tree loomed up in his path: he skirted it, and then caught a glimpse of something odd. He stopped suddenly, and for a long moment stood frozen, staring.

A road.

"Hairon?" Kahsir looked around again, seeking landmarks. "Are we close to the steading?"

"Close enough, Lord."

"We'll make better time if we keep to that road, Lord," said one of the men-at-arms. He leaned back against a tree, arms hanging limp at his sides. "I'm sick to death of fighting trees."

"So am I," replied Kahsir, "but I don't like the idea of walking in the open. At least the forest gave us cover."

"Ah, take it, Lord." Lorhaiden spoke for the first time in hours. "With the Leishoranya trailing us, we need speed now more than cover."

Kahsir glanced at Lorhaiden but, as had been the case since the scene in the clearing, Lorhaiden avoided his gaze. *Dammit, Lorj. I don't need you fighting me— not now. Forget your pride, man. I need your help, not your temper.* He looked at the men who stood grouped close by. "Lorhaiden's right. Let's take the road. But keep an eye to the forest, all of you, and at the least sign of the enemy coming, scatter into the woods. Vahl?"

"Aye, Lord?"

"Can you sense Dhumaric or his men? How far away they are?"

"No, Lord. They've shielded themselves tightly." Vàlkir's laugh was rough. "And I'm not in any condition to tell for sure."

"Huhn. Try to keep mental watch behind us. If Dhumaric finds this road, we're dead."

Hand resting on swordhilt, Kahsir cautiously led the way onto the narrow road he guessed led to the steading of Chilufka. *Lords! If only I could Remember— recognize where I am. It's been well over a hundred*

*fifty years since I was at Chilufka. Not a damned thing
looks the same!* It took all his concentration to keep his
feet moving. He glanced down as he walked, noted the
ruts worn in the packed earth, and felt a faint jolt of
recognition.

The forest beyond the river had grown increasingly
dense—thick enough so that Tsingar had to walk his
horse through the worst parts of it. The other men in
Dhumaric's company had fared no better—their cursing
became so constant that Tsingar no longer noticed it.

The delay had not sweetened Dhumaric's mood—
everyone was short tempered and on edge. Suspecting
traps and ambushes waiting behind every tree, each
man moved as cautiously as he might, continual vigi-
lance sapping strength as much as the fight against the
forest.

Back in his rightful place at Dhumaric's side, Tsingar
no longer rode as scout. His numerous subordinates
ranged out before the company, reporting directly what
lay ahead, so he felt confident in his knowledge of the
land. And, tired of contending with Chaagut, he kept
his junior officer riding with the advance scouts.

But Chaagut was back for the moment. There was
little he could do until Chaagut provided an opening,
and so far, aside from subtle actions and even more
subtle words, Chaagut had acted in every way the
diligent officer he was supposed to be. Tsingar cursed
silently, led his horse around a clump of brush. There
was such a thing as being *too* clever.

The light dimmed and the road became shadowed,
but Kahsir kept his pace as brisk as he could. *How far
have we come since finding the road? We must have
followed it for close to an hour. There's got to be some
place close to stop for the night. We're all but done for.*

Suddenly, not more than ten paces ahead, a small
band of warriors stepped out of the woods into the

road. Kahsir's heart leapt to his throat. He grabbed for his sword, and then his knees weakened with relief as he recognized the warriors as Krotànya. Even in the fading sunset, their nationality was apparent; they were hard men, clad in homespun and leather, bearing simple weapons of high quality—weapons that held the sheen of constant use.

Kahsir drew a long breath and stepped forward, his hand raised open-palmed in the sign of peace. "I'm Kahsir dor Xeredir," he said. "Are we close to the steading of Chilufka?"

A murmur ran through the men he faced. They shifted their weight and lowered their weapons.

"Lord," said one of them—their leader, from the looks of him. A silver brooch held his cloak back from his shoulders and his garments were of finer quality than his companions'.

"Rothàr!" Kahsir said. "I didn't recognize you!" March warden of the steading of Chilufka, Rothàr worked closely with Eltàrim in mounting resistance against the Leishoranya in the northlands.

Rothàr stepped closer. "You fought at Rodja'âno, Lord?"

"Aye," Kahsir said. "We barely got out alive."

The warriors who stood behind Rothàr murmured among themselves again, only this time there was an undercurrent of rage in that murmuring.

"Have you seen anyone else?" Kahsir asked, his mind suddenly filled with images of Haskon and Alàric. "Any other survivors?"

"No, Lord, but people who know this country would have passed west of us—" Rothàr pointed to his left and behind. "—for the ford lies there."

"Huhn." Kahsir swayed on his feet a moment, locked his knees, and met Rothàr's eyes. "We're being followed. Leishoranya. About three hundred of them." The steading men stiffened, and Rothàr took a step closer. "We don't know how far back they are, but they're horsed. Maybe a day or two behind us. How many men can you draw in from the land around us?"

"On no notice, maybe one hundred fifty."

"Dhumaric's going to find the road sooner or later," Vàlkir said, "and make up for lost time."

"Can you send men north to slow him?" Kahsir asked.

Rothàr nodded. "Aye."

"We've got to warn the steading," one of Rothàr's men said.

"I'll take care of that." Rothàr faced his men. "Alfdyr . . . Todhya. Gather as many warriors as you can. I want you a day's march north of here before dawn. Warn the other steadings close by, and try to keep in contact with me."

The two warriors nodded and, gesturing to the other men, slipped back into the forest with practiced ease.

"You're exhausted, Lord," Rothàr said to Kahsir. "Can you make it to the steading? It's another half hour's walk."

Kahsir looked over his shoulder at his companions. "I think we can make it."

Rothàr turned and set off at a slow walk down the roadway.

No one spoke. Kahsir listened to his companions' footsteps on the road, their labored breathing from behind him. The air had grown chilly, and the sharp scent of pine trees filled the air. Now that rest was near, each step seemed slower than the last.

After walking at least another half hour, Rothàr led the way around a bend in the road. The great house of Chilufka stood atop a gently swelling rise, surrounded on all sides by pine trees. Several smaller wooden dwellings lay clustered farther back in the shadows. From somewhere behind the house, Kahsir heard the noise of the river Rothàr had alluded to earlier.

He followed Rothàr to the front porch of the mansion, torch-lit against the night. Another group of people materialized out of the dusk, mounted and silent as the shadows they rode through. A woman's voice drifted through the darkness, instructing the riders to seek rest and food, and Kahsir started at the familiar tones. The armed company rode off into the twilight. The woman dismounted, handed her reins to a retainer, and turned toward Kahsir and his companions. Torchlight caught the gold of her hair, revealing a face worn and tired beneath its beauty.

"My Lady Genlàvyn," Kahsir said.

She walked to his side and bowed slightly in greeting; her leather riding dress was mud-splattered and her boots caked. "This is an unexpected surprise, my Lord. It's a long time since you've been to this steading."

Kahsir's heart jumped. *Maybe she's had news of Alàric and Haskon.*

Genlàvyn had turned to his companions, who waited behind. "I'm Genlàvyn dàn Sherrev u Perrahdic," she said with a smile. "Welcome, all of you, to Chilufka."

Kahsir luxuriated in the hot, soapy water, his head propped up on the edge of the tub. He felt like he could sleep for days, but the worst of his exhaustion had gone. Chilufka might well be off any of the traveled ways, but its lady knew how to entertain. He had not seen such a tub since leaving the capital.

He rubbed at the knot on his head: it had nearly vanished, though he winced in pain at the gentle probing. He shifted in the water, scratched at a healing bug bite. *Take your time about this bath—it may be the last one you see for a while.*

Relaxed, he leaned his head back again, his eyes threatening to close. Suddenly, he stiffened. *Where the Dark is Dhumaric? Across the river by now. And the warrior Lorhaiden killed? The message aimed at Dhumaric? Those men must have been part of Dhumaric's war band. Now Dhumaric knows where we were, and the direction we'd likely take.* He shifted uneasily again, for he brought death to Chilufka on his heels.

And the steading of Chilufka itself? How many people lived on the steading? Eltàrim had never mentioned that particular, being more interested in the fighters that operated from Chilufka. He scratched at his bearded chin. The steading would have to be evacuated with Dhumaric this close behind, and that operation would take time. The quickness of the evacuation would depend on how ready Genlàvyn and her people were to leave their lands on short notice. And, once away, the only direction to take would be toward Chailon Pass, in the hopes of meeting outriders of his father's army.

Haskon? Alàric? Where were they? He could trust Alàric to think before acting, but Haskon—? Rothàr had said that no one had seen either of them. His throat tightened. Lords! Let them be all right! He had not been able to sense anything of his brothers after they had left the walls of Rodja'âno and, while in the forest, had kept his mind so shielded that it would have taken one of the Mind-Born to reach him. Perhaps his brothers had managed to take the mind-road to his father's army. He dared not think of the alternatives.

And his father Xeredir—where was he? Holding his place at the foot of the Golondai Mountains, or coming north? If Alàric and Haskon had won through to Xeredir, Xeredir would know enough to hold his position.

And know of his eldest son's disobedience.

But the Mind-Born had more than likely spread that news already, what few of them had lived through the fall of Rodja'âno.

Xeredir knew. He *had* to know.

Kahsir grimaced. He dreaded meeting his father . . . dreaded explaining *why* he had disobeyed. Yet he could hardly put that meeting off. And now, surrounded by the relative protection of the steading, he might be able to Send to Xeredir without the risk of alerting Dhumaric.

No. Even that was far too dangerous. Word must

have reached Xeredir of Rodja'âno's fall—if not through Alàric and Haskon or the Mind-Born, then from the refugees who had fled southward.

Should he try to hold here, to wait until Xeredir and the army arrived? Though Dhumaric had lost nearly half his men, he could always gather reinforcements. And, it was always possible that Dhumaric was not the only Leishoranya commander operating this far south of Rodja'âno. Xeredir needed to make a broad advance into Tumâs, not a narrow one. Setting out from Chailon Pass directly and rapidly to Chilufka would put him in danger of attack. Besides, Chilufka was thickly wooded and too low-lying to defend.

As Kahsir stepped out of the tub, his legs wavered, then steadied. He grabbed a towel, rubbed himself dry, and wrung as much water as he could out of his hair. A razor had been set out for his use. He glanced at himself in the mirror, grimaced at the shadowed, thinner face that looked back, and carefully shaved the new beard away.

Running a hand over his now-smooth chin, he walked from the bath into his room next door, and began dressing. His clothes stank. He wrinkled his nose at the smell but decided Genlàvyn would understand.

"Lord?"

He turned. Lorhaiden stood just inside the doorway, bathed, shaved, and already dressed.

"Lord, I want to talk to you before we go down to dinner."

A twinge of warning. *What's on his mind now?*

"Can't it wait, Lorj?"

Lorhaiden shifted from one foot to the other. "No. I want to go back, Lord."

Kahsir stared. "Go back where? What are you talking about?"

"Dhumaric." Lorhaiden's worn face was expressionless, but his eyes glinted in the lamplight with a familiar fire. "I want to go back."

"You're out of your mind!" He turned away, sat down on the end of his bed, and pulled on his boots. "You're so tired you're not thinking straight."

"Lord—"

"No. You are *not* going back after Dhumaric. This entire steading's going to be evacuated in short order if I have anything to say about it. I'll need your help to do that."

"But, Dhumaric—"

Kahsir closed his eyes, drew a deep breath, and stood. *Don't push, Lorj. Don't.* He looked at Lorhaiden and his shoulders tensed. "No. Didn't you hear me the first time? We'll have time to fall back and strike at him *after* we've evacuated the steading. Now drop it, Lorj. Let's go eat."

Lorhaiden kept silent, but his hands clenched into fists at his sides.

"Lord, I'm oathed to you as sword-brother and shieldman, but my other Oath is stronger. I've sworn on the blood of my family to kill every Leishoran I can get my hands on. And now . . . now Dhumaric's within my reach. Can't you see? I *have* to go back."

Kahsir held Lorhaiden's eyes. *He's not going to give it up. He can't. Not with those ever-present memories of how Dhumaric massacred his family.* "Lorj," he said aloud, "I've told you once, and I'll say it again. I don't care *what* you do after we get out of this. You can chase Dhumaric from one end of the world to the next for all I care. But right now we have other things far more important to consider than your vengeance. We've got to help Genlàvyn and her people get out of here before Dhumaric finds the steading. Now, for the Lords' sakes, drop the subject. I'm too tired to argue any more about it."

A retainer led Kahsir and Lorhaiden down the stairs. The odor of food cooking grew stronger. Kahsir's mouth watered and the dull pain of hunger sharpened. His knees feeling stronger, he slowly followed the retainer down a long hallway toward the back of the great house where light spilled into the dimness from a large room.

The huge kitchen was brilliant with light and abuzz with voices. For a moment, Kahsir stood in the doorway, watching the seeming disorder of the room. A long wooden table ran nearly the entire length of the kitchen. People were already seated along the table, some finishing their meals, others only just beginning. Men, women, and children came in and out of the room in a steady stream. The high voices of the children mixed with the deeper ones of the menfolk, the softer tones of the women. A large white cat sat in a windowsill. One of the men on his way out of the kitchen tossed the cat a piece of meat.

Kahsir looked around for Genlàvyn and finally saw her at the far end of the kitchen. She still wore her leather riding clothes, but the mud had been cleaned from her skirts and boots; the leather was nearly black where the water had dampened it. Nodding for Lorhaiden to follow, Kahsir carefully threaded his way toward her through the crowded room. He caught the looks of recognition as he passed by Genlàvyn's people; there was a general bowing and murmur of greeting. He sensed the questions they longed to ask, the comparative mental silence he left behind as he crossed the room.

"There you are, my Lord," Genlàvyn said. She gestured behind to a fellow standing by a large stewpot. "Cook here will serve your dinner."

Kahsir sniffed: the smell of stew sent a surge of energy through his body. "My companions? Where are they?"

"Some of them were too tired to eat. We gave them a little soup and let them sleep. The rest of your men have already eaten and gone off to bed." She smiled slightly. "You *were* a long time in your bath."

"Huhn." Kahsir took his plate, waiting as the cook

poured a cup of what appeared to be ale. The thick stew did not run on the plate, and large flour dumplings were scattered throughout. "I could have used another hour in that tub, though I'm afraid I would have fallen asleep in the water."

Lorhaiden stepped up to the cook next; even his normally expressionless face showed eagerness. Genlàvyn motioned to the empty end of the table and Kahsir followed her. He set his plate down, took his place, and reached out for a knife and fork that lay close by.

The first bite of the stew was delicious beyond description. He tried to eat slowly. Lorhaiden sat at his side, across the table from the Lady Genlàvyn, his cheeks stuffed with food. Kahsir grinned at his sword-brother, took a long swallow of ale, and mopped up the last of his stew with a final bite of dumpling.

"You can have more, Lord," Genlàvyn said, "if you're still hungry."

"Just a little. I'll fall asleep at the table if I eat too much."

Genlàvyn smiled and gestured. A tall, blond-haired woman had just entered the kitchen. She came to Genlàvyn's side, curiosity evident on her face.

"My cousin, Maiwyn dora Lazhyr dàn Iofharsen," Genlàvyn said. "Kahsir dor Xeredir dàn Ahzur."

He nodded a greeting and the young woman bowed, her grey eyes fixed on his face.

"Maiwyn," Genlàvyn said, "please refill Kahsir's plate when you get your own. Join us, will you?"

Kahsir looked back at Genlàvyn as Maiwyn took his plate. Lorhaiden had finished eating and sat silent, staring off into nothing. *Damn! He's still angry.* He frowned in Lorhaiden's direction but his sword-brother ignored the look. *If you start anything here, Lorj, I swear I'll—*

"I've got good news for you, Lord," Genlàvyn said. "When you arrived, I'd just come back from meeting with some of my bush-fighters. Word got through to them that your brother Alàric was safe in the capital."

Kahsir straightened on the bench. *In the capital? What the Dark is Ahri doing there? He and Haskon were supposed to go to Father.* He shivered slightly. "What happened? Is Alàric all right? Have you heard anything about Haskon?"

"I don't have much more news than that Alàric's wounded. No, Lord. It's nothing serious. He and Haskon were chased by the enemy and Alàric took the mind-road back to the capital. According to him, Haskon and their shieldmen were going on to your father."

Kahsir drew a deep breath. *They're all right. They've got to be all right.*

Maiwyn returned with his plate half-filled with stew, balancing it alongside her own. He smiled at her, took the plate, and set it down on the table. "How did your people get word of my brothers, Genlàvyn? Is anyone mind-sending now that Rodja'âno's fallen?"

Genlàvyn moved over on the bench so that Maiwyn could sit down. "No. We're too close to Rodja'âno for that. Eltàrim sent some more bush-fighters north the other night. It seems that Alàric had only then arrived in the capital."

"Huhn." He briefly closed his eyes. Eltàrim. His heart ached at the mere mention of her name. He sighed quietly. Alàric's and Haskon's faces filled his mind. *Ahri's hurt, Haskon's supposedly with Father—* He picked up his fork and ate a few bites of stew and dumpling to hide his expression.

"Was the battle at Rodja'âno as bad as messages tell?" Genlàvyn asked.

"Probably worse." Kahsir reached for his cup. He noticed the kitchen had lost most of its occupants. Soon, with fewer ears to hear, he could speak to Genlàvyn about the evacuation of her people.

"Chilufka lies close enough to Rodja'âno that we're in danger," Genlàvyn said. "In the past, we could expect some protection from the city, but now that's gone. I'm afraid Eltàrim will have to find another place to send her fighters."

He lifted one eyebrow. So she *was* aware that she and her people would have to leave the steading. That was one less thing he dreaded having to tell her. He finished his stew, shoved the plate to one side, picked up his ale, then set it down again. He verged near to falling asleep as it was—more ale would only make it worse. Maiwyn had finished her own meal and was staring in his direction, while Lorhaiden still gazed off into nothing. Kahsir stirred uneasily on the bench and looked at Genlàvyn. "I assume Rothàr told you that we were followed on our way here."

Genlàvyn met his eyes, her face gone hard. "Aye, he did. By whom?"

"Dhumaric."

Lorhaiden scowled. Kahsir turned slightly and glared at his sword-brother, daring him to say anything.

"Dhumaric?" Maiwyn spoke for the first time. "All the way from Rodja'âno?"

"It's a long story." Kahsir glanced away from Lorhaiden to Maiwyn. "We're old, old enemies and besides, he knows Lorhaiden's with me. He'd like nothing better than to get his hands on us both."

Genlàvyn sat poised on the edge of the bench. "Is he close behind you?" she asked.

He nodded and quickly explained the situation, all the while sensing Lorhaiden's anger. "The way things stand now," he said, looking steadily at her, "you and your people should get ready to leave this steading."

For a long moment she sat silent. "You're right, Lord, but to give up this home—even more, this base of operations. . . . I don't know where I can relocate to continue helping the resistance. We can't abandon our positions too quickly. If we do, the enemy can just walk in and take over a great portion of the northlands. Few though we are, we steaders are dangerous in our own woods." She paused, her forehead furrowed in thought. "I'll also have to get word to the other folk who live close by. We depend on each other here in the back country."

Kahsir nodded. Nearly all the steading people had left the kitchen now. Those who still remained listened to the conversation, all the while trying to appear they were not. "Then you'd better get the news to them quickly, Genlàvyn. If Dhumaric's as close behind us as I think he is, we'll have to be out of here tomorrow morning."

Genlàvyn stared. "Tomorrow?"

"Aye." There was a hiss of indrawn breaths; the steading's people leaned closer to hear. "We tried to wear Ssenkahdavic down at Rodja'âno, but I'm not sure we succeeded. *He* could be on the march as well as his commanders. I've told you Dhumaric's on our trail. We don't know how far away he is, but I've fought him enough in the past to know him. Now that he has an idea which way we were headed—" He let his voice drift off. "Our only choice is to run."

"We're likely the last of Rodja'âno's defenders this close to the city," Lorhaiden said. "We left the walls long after most had fled. Even if we weren't being followed, the Leishoranya will spread out from Rodja'âno to hunt down any of its defenders who survived."

"Tomorrow." Genlàvyn looked at her cousin Maiwyn, then back. "I'm not sure that—" Her eyes sought Kahsir's. "There might be something you could do to give us a bit more time. You said your father was several days' march to the south. Couldn't you contact him and have him send men north to give us aid?"

"Father's just come down from Chailon Pass. His men are exhausted and—as far as Dhumaric following us is concerned—I'm afraid it would take Father and his men too long to get here, even if they tried. As I remember it, Chilufka lies nearly two hundred leagues from the mountains. I'm sure you can see the problem." He blinked away his yearning to sleep and rubbed his newly shaven jaw. "As for Sending to my father—I don't want to do that for the same reason I didn't in the forest. Dhumaric's hard on our heels, and that bastard has a mind strong as some Mind-Born. As of now, we hope he only has a *general* idea of which way we went. We don't want to give him any help."

Genlàvyn straightened in her chair: Kahsir sensed her anger and frustration. For a long while she sat silent, hard lines appearing on her face. "So much to do in so little time," she said at last. Her eyes glittered in the lamplight. "One thing's for sure: I'm not going off without leaving warriors behind. We may not be able to defeat the Leishoranya on the open field, but, as I said, these woods are ours." A small, cold smile touched her lips. "Even Dhumaric doesn't know the hidden ways."

Kahsir bowed his head slightly to her. "I've never known you to shrink from danger, Genlàvyn, and you won't start now."

Her laugh was as hard as her eyes. "No, I won't start now." She stirred on the bench. "You're falling asleep on your feet, Lord, and a good night's rest will do you wonders. From what you tell me, I think you've got the time."

"Huhn." Kahsir snorted a laugh. "None of us would be any good in a fight now, if it came to that. Or escaping, for that matter."

"Then sleep, Lord. If we're going to leave tomorrow, I have a great deal to do before *I* can rest."

Ever since Chaagut had tricked him into going the wrong way, Tsingar had been overly attentive to his duties. That had been hours ago, a backtracking that had enraged Dhumaric and put Tsingar in fear for his life. Time lost, the Krotànya farther away: Chaagut had made Tsingar look the fool.

The thickness of the forest and the darkness made it hard to walk without running into trees. Tsingar heard the other men close by. Dressed in black leathers and dark cloaks, his comrades were all but invisible in the night. Leading his reluctant horse, he felt his way forward, using his mind more than his eyes. He tripped, caught at a tree, and cursed softly. If Dhumaric did not stop them soon—

"Halt!" Dhumaric's voice rang through the stillness. "Make camp!"

Make camp? Tsingar kept his thoughts buried beneath his strongest shields. *Better to turn around and go back to Rodja'âno, my Lord. We've already lost half our men. And I'll bet you've gone long past the point you were ordered to, haven't you? Your obsession may get us all killed.*

Tsingar held the bridle of Dhumaric's horse while the other warriors tethered their mounts to trees. He heard the quiet voices of officers setting pickets, the rustle of brush as men sought places to sleep. But before he could put out a hand to help Dhumaric dismount, Chaagut was there.

"Tsingar," Dhumaric said, his voice a rumble in the darkness. "Walk on a bit and see what lies ahead."

"Aye, Master." Tsingar hastily clamped down on his already tightened shields. *Why me? Why not one of the lesser officers?* He was so tired he could scarcely keep awake, while Chaagut stood at Dhumaric's side, ready to answer any requests. *I'll send Chaagut, since he looks so damned alert.* He caught sight of Dhumaric's face in the darkness and sensed the expression on it. "Aye, master," he said again, bowing deeply. "I'll go at once."

Tsingar nearly fell onto the road before he saw it in the dark. His heart skipped a beat and then thumped loudly in his chest. He glanced up at the sky to get his bearings, but the trees were so thick above the roadway he could see no stars. Still, he sensed the road led south, or close enough to that direction that it would serve Dhumaric's purposes.

He turned and walked quickly back through the trees to where Dhumaric waited.

"A road, Master," he said quietly. "It leads south."

"Ah?" Dhumaric's bulk was a darker shadow in the night. "Have Kahsir and his men been down it?"

Tsingar swallowed heavily. "I didn't check, Dread Lord, but—" Dhumaric's mind touched his and he flinched before the slightly controlled rage that yearned to reach out and kill.

"Idiot!" Dhumaric swore, his voice very soft and tinged with threat. "Lead me to this road, *if* you can find it again."

Tsingar walked off into the forest, his knees trembling. The amused thoughts of the men still awake who had overheard spilled to him in the darknss. He heard Dhumaric's heavy tread behind, sensed Chaagut following. He fought down his rage, fully shielded his mind, and concentrated on the way ahead. When he reached the break in the forest, he stepped back and let his commander walk out of the woods to stand on the road.

For a long moment Dhumaric stood silent, facing south. Then, he knelt on the roadway and laid both palms down on the ground. Tsingar shifted nervously at the edge of the forest and glanced sidelong at Chaagut. From what he could see of the other man's face it was expressionless, impossible to read in the night.

"This is it," Dhumaric growled, standing and turning to Tsingar.

He instinctively flinched back a step. "Dread Lord?"

"This is the road," Dhumaric repeated, satisfaction in his voice. "Kahsir and his men may not have been down this section of it; no one has for some time. But they're there." He pointed south. "I *know* they're there."

Tsingar's heart fell. A trek down the road in the night? "Shall I rouse the others, Master?"

"That's an excellent idea, Dread Lord." Tsingar stiffened at Chaagut's suggestion. "We'll be able to gain ground on the Krotanya if we march all night."

Tsingar cursed silently. Chaagut was exhausted, too, like the rest of the company. Tsingar sensed the trap and kept silent.

"No," said Dhumaric, and Tsingar released his pent-up breath. "Though we haven't run into any more traps, we can't assume there aren't any. And if we caught up to Kahsir, the men we left back in the woods wouldn't be in any shape to fight. Let them rest tonight: tomorrow we'll make up for it." He turned back toward the road and stared southward. "We'll leave before dawn, Tsingar. See that it's not a moment later."

Kahsir awoke with a jerk, startled out of his sleep by a touch on his shoulder.

"Lord?" It was Lorhaiden. "Genlàvyn's people have started to gather."

"Already?" Kahsir rolled over, rubbed his eyes, and sat up. "What time is it?"

"An hour past dawn, Lord."

"*Aii!*" He swung out of bed and stretched, wincing at the stiffness in his legs. The window had been left open overnight and the room was chill. "You should have waked me sooner."

"I just got up myself. I think the Lady allowed us some extra sleep. Light knows we needed it."

"Huhn." Kahsir picked up his clothes. "Lorj! Look at this, will you? They've been cleaned and mended."

"Aye. Everyone found the same."

Kahsir pulled on his pants and then his shirt. "Lords! It feels good to be in clean clothing again. We must have been a sight when we arrived. And our smell—faugh!" He reached for his mail and its undershirt. "How are the wounded? Better?"

Lorhaiden nodded briefly. "Sleep helped them more than anything." He walked to the window and looked out. "When do we leave, Lord?"

"The sooner the better. We don't know where Dhumaric is, but I'm afraid he's closer than any of us would like." He pulled his leather jerkin down over the mail shirt and stared at Lorhaiden, at the tenseness hidden behind the stony face. "And don't even start in on it, Lorj. You're not going back after him. I need you here."

Lorhaiden's shoulders stiffened and he turned away.

Kahsir frowned and sat down to put on his boots. "I want you to help the Lady's people. They're going to need it."

"As you command, Lord." Lorhaiden bowed and started toward the door.

"And don't go all stiff and formal on me," Kahsir called after his sword-brother. "I need you to help me, not fight me."

Lorhaiden nodded slightly and left the room. Kahsir shook his head. *Ah, Lorj. You make it so damned hard on yourself. How draining it must be to hate all the time.*

A large number of people had gathered by the front porch of the great house. Kahsir glanced at the sun and began to pace up and down behind Genlàvyn's motion-less figure.

"How many more are coming?" he asked, stopping by her side.

She looked at the people gathered in the yard before her. "Not many more. But Chilufka's a large steading, and those who live farthest away probably won't be here for a while."

He nodded and looked out over the clearing. Frantic activity centered now around the grain bins. Men stood in those bins and dumped bag after bag of grain into the wagons that had been driven up alongside. Much of the grain was already gone, taken away to be dumped into the tannery vats. Drovers had driven the livestock off into the woods and fields farther east. Now men were tossing salt licks into the well to poison its water.

Genlàvyn gestured to a woman who stood close by. "Destroy the dried fruits next, Timmah. Lye should do the trick, don't you think?"

The woman nodded grimly and turned away. Another wagon rumbled off toward the tannery. Young children stood, bewildered, close to their mothers, their older siblings hard at work with the adults. Several men worked at caging the steading's cats and dogs. The large white cat Kahsir had seen in the kitchen last night yowled unhappily from one of the nearest cages.

A group of women came out from one of the sidehouses carrying bottles and jugs of wine and ale. They walked to a corner of the clearing and one by one broke the bottles and jugs on the ground. The faint morning breeze blew the mixed scents to Kahsir across the clearing. He sneezed and glanced down at Genlàvyn.

She's being thorough, that's for sure. He fidgeted, aware of the passing time. "How long do you expect this to take?" he asked, gesturing at the scene of destruction.

She turned, pushed a strand of hair back behind one ear. "Not that much longer, Lord. We started last night and should be ready to leave before midday."

"Huhn." Kahsir started pacing again. "The sooner we're on our way, the better. We're cutting this a little finer than I'd hoped."

Genlàvyn turned around, the leather of her riding dress creaking softly. Her eyes were brilliant blue in the sunlight, her face drawn and pale. "We're moving as fast as we can," she said, weariness and frustration tinging her voice. "I refuse to leave the enemy anything they can use, and—"

"I'm sorry," he said, lifting a hand. *Did she sleep at all last night?* "I shouldn't question your methods. You've been one of our greatest aids in the north for years

now, and I trust your experience. But the enemy's
getting closer. I'm worried, that's all."

"You have a right to be." A small smile softened her
face. "Dhumaric's enough to make anyone uneasy."

"Add to that: he has a longstanding grudge against
me. As for Lorhaiden and Vàlkir, Dhumaric was the
one who slaughtered their family. He knows they're
here, too. He'll make an extra effort to catch us if he
can. Around three hundred men ride with him, and I
wouldn't want to face him with only the warriors you're
taking with you and the men I lead."

"I understand. Rothàr has sent every warrior we can
spare north. We've even drawn on some of the steadings to the east and west. King Nhavari made sure that
every one of us who ruled a steading knew what to do
in time of need."

"Is Rothàr staying with them?"

"No. He's delegated that position to a lieutenant he
trusts above all others. Rothàr will come with us."

"They *do* know they're facing Dhumaric, don't they?"
Kahsir asked. "He's damned good."

"Aye. They know. They'll be careful." She stared off
at her people again, a thin frown crossing her face. "As
for leaving—we'll be ready by midday, I can assure
you of that."

"I hope so." He started pacing again, hands locked
behind his back. The white cat yowled again. "Lords
only know if that will be time enough."

The midday sunlight poured into the clearing by the
great house; new leaves and pine trees swayed gently
before a slight wind. Kahsir carefully settled his helm
on his head, rubbed his horse's neck, and drew several
long, deep breaths. He glanced around: everyone leaving for the south had gathered in the clearing. They
were quiet now. Faces drawn with fatigue, they waited
mounted, small clusters of them, but even the children
kept still. A large number of pack horses stood close by,

bearing necessary staples for the journey: flour, oil, and a few quarters of meat. Genlàvyn's people also had packed mementos and personal possessions, things they thought too precious to be left behind. Now, in the clearing's silence, the steading folk waited for word to ride out.

Women and children made up the bulk of the people; the men who would be coming along were farmers and craftsmen, not warrior-trained. Kahsir frowned: *We're all but dead if Dhumaric wins past the warriors Rothàr left behind and overtakes us. If we have to fight with only my men and the warriors Genlàvyn's taking—*

Genlàvyn gestured to a group of twenty armed men who stood close by, members of the rear guard she was leaving stationed close to the steading.

"If you sense the enemy coming, if they've managed to elude the men Rothàr sent north, fire the great house. You'll get a message from Rothàr's men, I'm sure . . . Dhumaric can't kill *everyone* we've left behind. Set fire to the barns, the wagons, the storage sheds, anything the enemy might use. Then join your comrades."

One of the men stepped forward. "If we set fire to the woods, Lady, that would be quicker."

"No." Another of the men spoke. "It rained hard the other day and the woods are too wet. Besides, we'll need the trees and brush for cover ourselves."

"He's right," Genlàvyn said. "Just set the buildings on fire. But make sure you wait until you get word that Dhumaric's on his way. The fires will draw him like a beacon. Do you understand?" The men nodded slowly, their eyes glinting in the sunlight. "We're depending on you and Rothàr's men to slow Dhumaric down. Don't fail us." Her voice trembled slightly. She straightened her shoulders and looked around at her mounted people. "Ride," she commanded them. "Follow me."

She turned her horse and led the way out of the clearing; her cousin Maiwyn and the wives and children

of her retainers followed close behind. Several of her
warriors had already gone ahead to serve as scouts.
Kahsir caught up to Genlàvyn and the Lady Maiwyn,
Lorhaiden and Vàlkir coming just behind. Their nine
comrades from Rodja'âno dropped back to ride with
Rothàr and the other warriors at the rear.

Kahsir watched Genlàvyn closely. There had been no
hesitation in any of her actions: what she had done, she
had done quickly and thoroughly. But to leave her
steading, her home, her lands, all the centuries of
memory—to order them destroyed behind her— He
saw Genlàvyn look over her shoulder only once at the
house she was leaving forever. The falling sunlight struck
the tears on her cheeks, and then the forest shadows
hid them from his sight.

Tsingar rode warily down the roadway, his eyes
flicking from side to side, scanning the forest as well as
he could. Under normal circumstances, he trusted the
scouts he sent out before the company, but that assurance had fled. Dhumaric had been right when he had
spoken of more traps waiting: ambushed time after time
from the thick undergrowth and dense stands of trees
by the roadway, Dhumaric's company stood reduced by
another hundred and forty-one men. Krotànya lurked
behind every tree, around every curve in the road—
how many of them, Tsingar could not guess. He estimated their number at well over a hundred. After each
new ambush, Tsingar withdrew as far from Dhumaric as
possible: the commander's anger grew more deadly with
each man who fell to the Krotanya.

The last enemy strike had pushed Dhumaric near a
killing rage. Tsingar sensed just enough of Dhumaric's
thoughts to know that soon the Great Lord would snap
. . . that soon he would take some sort of retaliatory
action. Why he had waited so long remained a mystery.
Dhumaric had chosen to move south in utter secret—
possibly instructed to do so by Ssenkahdavic himself—

but there seemed no reason to continue that secrecy now. The Krotànya knew more about Dhumaric's whereabouts than he did theirs.

"Tsingar!"

Tsingar looked down from the forest. Dhumaric had thrown up a hand and halted the column in the roadway. Turned so that he faced the rear of his company, Dhumaric waited for Tsingar to ride forward.

"Dread Lord?"

"There are Krotànya hidden ahead. I was able to break through their shielding and See where they're waiting. They're going to try another ambush, and this time I don't mean to let them get away with it. Hold my horse."

Tsingar slid down from the saddle, looped his reins around his left arm, and took his commander's horse, holding it by its bridle. Dhumaric dismounted heavily, stood motionless in the road, then turned south. Tsingar watched for a moment, then slowly backed away, leading his horse and Dhumaric's toward the waiting men behind.

He sensed Dhumaric gathering Power, sensed the subtle darkening of the light that filled the roadway where the commander stood. Tsingar's mouth went dry: he had enough strength of mind himself to know what Dhumaric attempted.

A darkening cloud seemed to hang around Dhumaric now, seething with shadows cast by no living thing. Tsingar sensed the unease of the men who waited just behind him, and tried to subdue his own fears. Linkage with the Gods of one's Clan remained a deed for only the strongest.

And suddenly Tsingar felt that Power unleashed, portions of it breaking off and going straight to the points where Dhumaric aimed it. Tsingar flinched as the backlash of that released Power lapped at the edge of his mind. Behind him, one of the men whimpered.

Dhumaric staggered, caught himself, and straightened. When he turned to face Tsingar, his face was the face of death.

Tsingar walked slowly forward, still wary of what his commander might do. Dhumaric's eyes lost some of their blindness and focused over Tsingar's shoulder.

"You!" Dhumaric rasped, pointing a finger at someone behind Tsingar's back. "Come here."

Tsingar heard a sharp cry of fear. He stopped, led the two horses off to the side of the road, and turned around. One of the warriors had dismounted. The man walked stiff-legged toward Dhumaric, his face gone suddenly blank. Tsingar shuddered, but could not look away.

Swaying in the weakness that followed such use of Power, Dhumaric caught the warrior by the shoulders, gripping the man so hard his knuckles turned white. The warrior struggled for a moment, twitched, and began to moan. The moan grew louder, then turned into a shriek of utter terror.

The scream shut off abruptly: the man convulsed one last time, and went limp.

Dhumaric let his hands fall to his sides. Released, the warrior crumpled to the ground, his ravaged face turned in Tsingar's direction. Tsingar swallowed heavily and looked up at his commander, his heart thumping against his ribs.

"Drag this carrion off," Dhumaric said, gesturing sharply toward the forest. His voice rang with strength again and his black eyes glittered in the sunlight. "We'll continue on immediately. We don't have to fear ambush for a while."

Tsingar nodded, tethered both horses to a sapling, and returned to Dhumaric's side. Grasping the dead man under the arms, Tsingar dragged the body off into the brush. He had seen Dhumaric borrow strength hundreds of times, but it still unnerved him.

Not only had Dhumaric reached out with the Power he had summoned and killed every Krotàn hidden within reach—killed them mind-to-mind, as surely as if they had had their throats slit— but he had smothered their mental death-cries to prevent any other Krotànya from knowing what had happened.

Tsingar dropped the body behind a stand of pines, wiped his hands several times on his pants, and walked back to the road. With fingers that shook only slightly, he untethered the horses and returned to Dhumaric's side.

Dhumaric took the reins, spared Tsingar not the slightest glance, and mounted. As Tsingar swung up into his saddle, Dhumaric motioned forward. "Ride!" he called. "At a canter. We're getting closer!"

Kahsir followed the Lady Genlàvyn as she led the way through the steading's lands, keeping to a westerly trail when possible. He felt the enemy behind. How far away they were he could not guess, but they were closer than he had hoped. He did his best to increase his pace, forcing the other riders to do the same, but even so, the pack horses were heavily laden and held the company back.

The land fell away in the late afternoon light as they drew nearer to the river; its sound grew even louder in his ears. Directly behind the great house, the rocky bottom threw water up into swift rapids, but the river calmed at the ford and straightened out. Genlàvyn had said here the water was no deeper than a horse's chest. Still, recent rains and melting mountain snows would, she cautioned, make the crossing perilous.

Kahsir finally caught a good glimpse of the river through the trees and his heart tightened in fear. The river flowed by in a rage of brown water, and even when the trail led down the bank, the ford looked far too turbulent for his liking.

He saw himself as a young man again, barely to his majority. Once there had been a time when he had faced death in just such a crossing. Water—rushing water— Swept away, he could not breathe for far too long a time. . . .

He blinked, rubbed his head, firmly back in the present, and looked across the ford.

Three of the steading men urged their balking horses into the river to guide those who followed. They stationed themselves evenly in the riverbed, indicating by gestures that everyone should cross just downstream of them. The businesslike approach these men had toward the crossing made it seem so *fihrkken* simple.

Kahsir looked across to the opposite side where a steep trail led up the rocky bank through tumbled boulders. He calculated its angle and its width, frowned, and glanced at Lorhaiden.

"The trail's narrow over there," he called over the river's noise. "We'll have to go up it single file, and that leaves us open to attack."

Lorhaiden's hand caressed his sword hilt. "Dhumaric?"

"Aye." Kahsir glanced back the way they had come. "I feel him behind us and not all that far away." He ignored Lorhaiden's ready surge of anger and turned to Vàlkir. "Vahl—you, Hairon, and Rothàr stay here with me as rear guard. Lorhaiden," he gestured across the river, "go with Genlàvyn and her people. Don't let them go any farther once they've crossed. I want all of us to travel together."

Lorhaiden's jaw tightened but he nodded and rode slowly down the trail. Gesturing across the river, his mouth moving in unheard words, he explained what everyone was to do. Kahsir turned his horse back up the trail.

Tsingar kept his horse at a canter directly behind Dhumaric. Armed now, shield held at his side and sword grasped firmly in his other hand, he looked ahead as he rode, toward the steading where Dhumaric sensed Kahsir had fled.

After Dhumaric had killed at least seventy-five of the

waiting Krotanya he sensed lying in ambush, there had been no further enemy attacks. The price paid to regain some of his strength would bother Dhumaric, for even the Great Lords did not attempt to leach another man's vitality too often . . . the strain on body and mind was considerable.

But the time gained by eliminating possible ambushes seemed to have been worth the trouble. The Krotànya were closer now—Tsingar could sense that without needing to be told.

Dhumaric had divided his remaining one hundred men, sending thirty each to the left and right through the forest in a flanking maneuver, and now led the way toward the steading, followed by the remaining forty warriors. Fully expecting resistance, Dhumaric planned to meet it head-on, helped by the two bands he had sent ahead.

The roadway curved sharply. Tsingar kicked his horse into a gallop, only to haul back on the reins to avoid colliding with Dhumaric. The commander had halted at the edge of the clearing. Before him, flames leaping skyward burned what was most likely the great house of the steading. Not only was that building afire, but other smaller ones behind it.

"Damn him!" Dhumaric bellowed, bringing his fist down on one knee. "Damn him! Damn him!" He reined his horse around in a tight circle, backlit by the burning house. "Tsingar! Get the men together! Kahsir can't be far ahead!"

Tsingar sent out a sharp mental summons to the leaders of the two groups of thirty who rode flank. He glanced back at Dhumaric: the Great Lord's face had darkened with rage. Once again, Kahsir seemed to have eluded him.

The two bands came crashing in through the brush, some having trouble with their horses as the animals shied away from the fire. No one had noticed the smoke because of the thickness of the trees overhead, and the fact that they rode in from upwind of the steading.

Dhumaric wheeled his horse around and pointed to the southeast. "Ride! The Krotànya aren't far ahead! After me, fools!"

Tsingar glanced over his shoulder at the burning house, kicked his horse to a fast trot, and followed Dhumaric down the winding trail.

Time crawled by as Kahsir waited. Now and again he glanced through the trees to watch the river crossing. One by one, Genlàvyn's people set out across the ford, the guides always near in case of trouble. The pack horses balked at the edge of the water, but splashed on to the opposite bank, encouraged by the men who led them. Genlàvyn's white cat huddled motionless in one of the cages atop a pack horse, too terrified even to howl. Kahsir turned away from the river, shifted nervously in the saddle, looked back to the north again. *There are so many of Genlàvyn's people, and so few who can fight. If Dhumaric catches us here, at the ford. . . .*

"Lord." Vàlkir gestured toward the river. "Everyone's across."

Kahsir looked one last time to the north, then turned back to the ford. His mouth went dry and his hands started trembling. Cursing his fear, he rode out into the surging river. His horse balked not more than three steps into the water, shook its head, and then continued on. Kahsir held his cloak and weapons above his head, knees gripped tightly to the saddle. The water was bitingly chill: he gasped softly as it crept up higher on his legs. He consciously slowed his breathing, bit his lip, and forced his eyes away from the water to the waiting shore. His horse slid on an unseen rock. His heart leapt to his throat, then calmed as the horse caught itself in a desperate scramble and continued on.

The last few steps to the pebbly bank seemed to take

forever. The instant his horse reached that shore, it shook itself dry with a violence that made his teeth chatter. Kahsir closed his eyes briefly in relief, then looked over his shoulder. Vàlkir, Hairon, and Rothàr splashed to his side—more water spattered from their horses.

Genlàvyn, her cousin, and Lorhaiden waited at the foot of the narrow trail. Kahsir gestured upward.

"You go ahead, Lady," he called over the rush of water. "We'll be right behind."

She nodded, turned, and rode up the bank, Maiwyn following immediately after. Kahsir reined his horse around and stared back across the river.

"Dhumaric's closer, isn't he?" Vàlkir asked.

"Aye." He shivered slightly in the chill, wrapped his dry cloak close, and reattached his swords to his weapons belt, shoving his knife back into his boot. "And if we—"

"Lord!" Lorhaiden said, and pointed across the river. "Look!"

A mounted company of Genlàvyn's men thundered down the trail to the ford, as fast as their horses would go. Reaching the water, they drove the horses into it, obviously familiar with the ford and able to take it at what seemed a dangerous pace. The man who rode at the fore waved his hand above his head, pointing back toward the steading.

"O Lords," Kahsir breathed. He nudged his horse close to the edge of the river and reached out to the approaching man's mind.

—*Dhumaric!* the fellow Sent. *He's at the steading!*

Kahsir's heart contracted. "Vahl, Lorj, Rothàr . . . get Genlàvyn's people moving down that trail! Send at least twenty warriors with them."

"But that only leaves us with thirty—"

"Lorj, dammit, don't argue with me. Do it!"

Lorhaiden jerked his horse around and, followed by Vàlkir, scrambled up the steep trail.

When the first of the steading men reached the pebbly bank, Kahsir waved him up the trail. His seventeen companions followed, drenched and cursing, trying to reattach their weapons as they rode.

"Rothàr," Kahsir said, turning to Genlàvyn's march warden, and lifting his voice to be heard over the rush of water. "How much longer do we have to ride through this forest before we reach the meadowlands beyond?"

"A good half day, Lord. Beyond lies a long expanse of fields that runs up to the high forests in the foothills."

"Where's Chailon Pass from here?"

"Almost due south. Burdened as we are, nearly ten days if we keep to the world's roads."

"*Chuht!*" Kahsir turned his horse and ascended the steep trail, Rothàr following behind. There, on their horses on the edge of the trail, waited Lorhaiden, Vàlkir, Hairon, the nine warriors who had escaped from Rodja'âno, and twenty of the steading warriors.

"Genlàvyn and her people are gone, Lord," Vàlkir said. "We sent them off at a canter, along with twenty warriors. They should have enough strength to take the mind-road once out of the woods."

Kahsir drew a deep breath and looked at the leader of the men who had ridden from the steading. "Do you know how many men Dhumaric has with him?"

"Not precisely, Lord," the man replied. "I'd say 'bout a hundred."

"Damn!" Hairon wiped the end of his nose. "We whittled that bastard down a bit, didn't we?"

Kahsir felt some of the knots in his stomach loosen. Better one hundred than the two to three hundred Dhumaric *might* have had. "Rothàr. What kind of a chance do we stand if we take this side of the ford and try to hold it?"

Genlàvyn's march warden chewed on his lower lip, then glanced up. "Fairly good. We're badly outnumbered, but we hold the better ground."

"Huhn. We don't have much of a choice. If we don't

hold them at the ford, they'll be all over us in the woods." Kahsir looked around, assessing the natural defenses he could use. "All right," he said loudly, turning his horse so he faced the warriors who had stayed behind. "In what time we've got left, let's destroy this trail and get ourselves set up in those boulders over there. And for the Lords' sakes, I hope some of you fellows are handy with the bow."

CHAPTER 8

Alàric left the mind-road on the gentle slope of a hillside above his father's camp. For a moment he sat silent, cursing the dull pain in his shoulder. The healers had helped as much as they could in the short time he had been at home and he could hardly expect more.

Below him stretched a sea of tents. Various divisional banners flew above the individual commanders' tents and, if Alàric squinted into the early morning sunlight, he could just make out his father's banner at the center of camp.

Sudden movement down the hillside caught his attention and he recognized Haskon. When Alàric had Sent ahead that he would be coming in from the City, Haskon had said he would be waiting. Now Haskon rode up the hill, shoulders set in tight lines of anger.

"Ahri!" Haskon reined in his horse close beside. "Your wound?"

"It's better. Lords of Light, I'm glad to see you. I didn't know if you'd made it to Father's camp or not."

"We had all the reason in the world to make it. None of us wanted to die. Pavhel was hit in the leg by a lucky shot, an arrow in the dark. No—it's not serious, just painful."

"Huhn."

Haskon kneed his horse closer; when he spoke, his voice trembled. "Remember how Kahs told me to take the heir's ring to Father, that it was a message he would understand? Well, Father understood all right. Kahs was telling him that he'd made a mistake at Rodja'âno and that he was resigning his command."

Alàric nodded. "I know all about it, Kona. I walked right into the middle of things back home . . . started making my report to Grandfather without the slightest notion he knew nothing about Kahs being at Rodja'âno."

Haskon stared. "How did Grandfather take *that* news?"

"How do you think he took it? I haven't seen him that angry in decades, Kona. I thought he was going to hit me."

"Huhn. You should have seen Father when *he* found out. I don't think I'd like to be in Kahs' boots right now."

"I still can't believe he lied to us," Alàric said. "That's damned hard to do to a sibling."

"Well, he's obviously got a stronger mind than we know about. And as for lying to us, I think he wanted to get us out of the city."

"I'll bet he did. But where the Dark *is* he?"

"I don't know. No one does." Haskon frowned. "Lords, Ahri . . . he *could* be—"

"When we were hiding in the bushes, you were the one who kept telling me he was alive. What's happened?"

"Nothing. I've just had more time to think about it."

"Well, I agree with Grandfather." Alàric nudged his horse into a slow walk down the hillside; Haskon quickly caught up. "We'd have known if something had happened."

"But if he's alive—"

"I know, I know. He's in danger. Both Grandfather

and Eltàrim agreed about that, too. They also said we can't do much until we know where he is. But I think I might know."

"His exact location?"

Alàric reined in his horse and Haskon stopped beside. "Possibly. If *you* were Kahs, where would you go after getting out of the city?"

"He said something about falling back to the southwest."

"All right. But other commanders could have taken charge of the retreat. I think Kahs would try to get to some place he knew."

"Lords, Ahri! He hasn't been in the north for over a century! Where—"

"He'd also be carrying news of the enemy's most recent positions," Alàric interrupted. "I think he would have tried to get to Chilufka."

Haskon rubbed his clean-shaven chin. "Where Eltàrim sends her resistance fighters. Huhn. You're probably right."

"When I talked to Eltàrim she said it was his best line of action."

"Why haven't we heard from him if he went to Chilufka? What's taking him so *fihrkken* long?"

"He could be wounded, and lack the strength. He could have some other plan that prevents him. Or the enemy could be keeping him from taking the mind-road."

"All right. Let's assume he hasn't taken the mind-road because he can't. We still don't know where he might be headed."

"I'm betting it's Chilufka."

"Where's that from here? Northwest, isn't it?"

Alàric nodded. "Several days northwest, if I remember correctly."

"Lords! If he isn't there, finding him will be like hunting for a button in a gravel pile."

"He'll come this direction—if he can."

"Huhn." Haskon started off toward the camp. "Don't

bring the subject up around Father," he cautioned as Alàric caught up.

"I wouldn't count Kahs out yet. He's damned resourceful." He frowned, gestured an ending to the conversation as he and Haskon entered camp.

Tents spread out in all directions, neat even lines in the sunlight. His view of the camp from the hillside had shown Alàric a thick stand of trees that grew to the east; the horses were pastured in the high meadows to the south. Now that Alàric had come down from the hill, the size of the camp seemed overwhelming. The tents of the four thousand men who had come with Xeredir to the north seemed to stretch on to the horizon.

Xeredir's tent lay in the center of the encampment, the banners of the House of dàn Ahzur fluttering slightly in the morning breeze. Alàric slid down from the saddle, tethered his horse to one of the wagons drawn up nearby, and waited for Haskon to dismount.

People had begun to stir now in this daybreak; smoke from cooking fires and the scent of food hung in the chill air. There was increased activity at the far end of the camp: in that direction stood the gathered wagons, horses, and tents of refugees from Rodja'âno. Dogs barked in the distance and the calls of children floated on the crisp air. He shook his head and turned to Haskon.

"Lords—the refugees! There are so many of them! Look at the size of their camp."

Haskon nodded grimly. "Aye. And there are more to come, I'll bet on that."

"But what the Dark are we going to do with all of them? They can't stay with the army."

"Let Father worry about that," Haskon said. "I'm sure he has a plan."

"I'd better," said a voice from behind, "or we're all in trouble."

Alàric turned around, his heart leaping. "Father!" He

embraced Xeredir, closed his eyes, and for a moment rested his head on his father's shoulder.

"By the Light, it's good to see you." Xeredir stepped back. "From what Kona tells me, you both had a close call in the forest."

"Aye, but we were lucky." Alàric looked closely at his father: Xeredir and Vlàdor shared the same appearance— the same dark hair, height, and build. Only their eyes were different: Vlàdor's grey as sea at dawn, Xeredir's touched with blue. Now his father's bearded face was drawn tight with anger and worry, etched with lines of tension.

"Sit, both of you." Xeredir gestured to the grass before the tent, sat down cross-legged. "Your shoulder's better?"

Alàric took his place at his father's side, glanced quickly at Haskon, who sat down opposite. "Much. A few days' rest and Grandfather's healers helped."

"Huhn." Xeredir looked down at his left hand and touched the heavy silver heir's ring he now wore. Alàric cringed inwardly at the expression that crossed his father's face. "So, Ahri. What news from home?"

"Grandfather sends his love. So do Eltàrim and Iowyn. Eltàrim sent more fighters north to Chilufka. That's about it. I wasn't out of bed long enough to catch up on the local gossip."

His father touched the heir's ring once again, absently, yet the touch lingered. When he spoke, his voice sounded tightly controlled. "They haven't heard anything from Kahs, have they?"

Alàric swallowed heavily. "No, Father. Not a thing."

Xeredir closed his eyes and rubbed the bridge of his nose between forefinger and thumb. "I suppose I would have heard by now if they had."

Alàric looked away.

"Tell Father what you and told me on the hillside," Haskon said.

Alàric froze, turned, and shot his brother a startled look. *And you warned me to watch what I said.*

"What?" Xeredir sat very still. Alàric stared at anything else, at the sunlight winking off Xeredir's chainmail, the texture of the cloak around his father's shoulders. "What is it, Ahri? If it has to do with Kahs, I want to know about it."

"I think I know where he might be," Alàric said.

Xeredir's eyes narrowed. "If he knows what's good for him, he won't come here."

Alàric stared at his father, searching for some kind of lightness behind the words. There was none.

"Father—"

"I suppose you know what he's done," Xeredir said.

"Grandfather told me."

Xeredir lifted one eyebrow. "That's all? 'Grandfather told me'?"

Alàric stirred uncomfortably. "What do you want me to say?"

"Huhn." Xeredir looked away. "I suppose *you* agree with him, too."

"I don't think my opinion one way or the other makes much difference, does it?" Alàric said.

"He *did* slow Ssenkahdavic down," Haskon interjected.

"And threw all our plans into total disarray!" Xeredir snapped. "Add to that: disobeyed orders, assumed a command that wasn't his—"

"You'd rather be fighting Ssenkahdavic yourself?" Alàric asked, meeting his father's eyes and holding them. "If Rodja'âno hadn't stood as long as it did, you might be facing just that."

Xeredir stiffened, took a long, deep breath, and when he spoke, his voice was icy. "Kahs didn't know Ssenkahdavic was coming south when he went to Rodja'âno," he said, holding up one finger. The second finger joined the first. "He rode a streak of luck which—" The third finger lifted. "—just ran out. Now you tell me, Alàric

. . . what's he going to do, eh? Damned fool could get himself killed running around in the woods."

Alàric bristled. "You think I enjoy being pushed in the middle between you and Kahs . . . between you and Grandfather? I don't think Kona's any fonder of the experience than I am. But I can see what *has* happened— what we're left to deal with. And I'll tell you, Father . . . I'd much rather take the field knowing Ssenkahda-vic's been slowed down, possibly forced dormant, than to walk right into his arms."

For an endless moment, he locked gazes with Xeredir, determined that he would not be the first to look away.

"Ahri thinks Kahs might be trying to get to Chilufka," Haskon said in a tone of vast discomfort. "The longer I think about it, the more sensible it seems."

Xeredir remained silent.

"I'm going after him," Alàric said, bracing himself for his father's anger. "He's got to need help about now."

"You'll do no such thing!" Xeredir grated. "I don't need *two* sons out running around in the forest. One's more than enough."

Alàric squared his shoulders. "I'm going, Father. I don't care *what* Kahs has done . . . he's my brother and, dammit, I'm going to try to help him."

"Ha!" Xeredir's laugh was bitter. "You don't have any idea where he is . . . if he tried to get to Chilufka or not."

"I'm still going. Kahs and I are close enough that I'll be able to sense him sooner or later."

"And you think your bond is closer than father and son?"

"You haven't gone far enough north," Alàric said. "I can't sense him this far away, either."

"What did Vlàdor say to you?" Xeredir asked suddenly.

Alàric blinked. "You shared a Sending with him before I got here. You know everything I do."

"What did he *really* say to you? And what did he say to Kahs?"

"I haven't any idea. I wasn't there."

"Well, you all seem to be privy to information that I'm not."

"What do you mean?"

"You all agree with Kahs. Even Vlàdor's beginning to change his mind about what to do here in the north."

Alàric shot a sidelong glance at Haskon. "I don't doubt that. Things have changed since he first laid his plans."

Xeredir sat motionless for a moment, his face totally without expression, then stood and disappeared inside his tent.

Haskon rose and motioned for Alàric to follow.

"Damn . . . he's madder than I think I've ever seen him," Alàric murmured as he and his brother walked slowly down the aisles between the tents.

"Understatement." Haskon's green eyes caught the sunlight. "If I were you, and I planned on going off to Chilufka to hunt for Kahs, I'd get out of here right now."

"Huhn. Before Father comes back out of his tent and throws me in leg irons. I understand."

"And for the Lords' sakes, Ahri, take some men with you. You don't have any idea what you could be riding into."

Alàric grimaced. "Don't worry. I won't go alone."

Haskon stopped and gripped Alàric's arm. "Bring him back," he said, his voice quiet. "Bring him back if you can."

Alàric urged his weary horse across the broad expanse of fields. Behind rode the nineteen warriors he had handpicked from his father's army; his shieldman, Chorvàl, rode at his side. Alàric stretched in the saddle, easing tired muscles: he and his band had ridden all day and taken the mind-road once since leaving camp. He flexed his shoulder: it was far less painful, and even its stiffness was fading. He looked forward again, trying to remember exactly where Chilufka lay.

Since leaving his father's camp, he had more than one impression of his eldest brother's whereabouts. He felt certain it was *not* Chilufka, but close to that steading. And those impressions had been made more vivid by the feelings of danger attached to them. Though he could not have specified the exact form of danger, he knew Kahsir had met trouble of some sort, or—in the way of such impressions—*would* face that peril soon.

He glanced to his left as he rode: the sun was several hours from setting. Time was running out. He was closer to Kahsir than before, but unless no other alternative presented itself, he did not want to make a night ride through unknown territory.

Ahead, a solid line of trees and forest stretched uninterrupted on either hand. Throwing up his hand to signal a halt, Alàric stared at this forest, closed his eyes in concentration, and opened his mind to its fullest. There were no other paths leading into the dense woods save one to the east, a second off to the west, and yet a third even farther beyond. He shifted in his saddle and probed again. *Be careful. Choose wisely. A mistake now could undo all your haste.*

Suddenly, things settled into place. There—the pathway off to the west. Thoughts—emotions: danger; darkness; the minds of many people attempting to mask terror and despair.

Alàric stared at the woods, weighing the distance he and his band had yet to ride, then reined his horse around and cantered off toward the middle trail, his men following. At the edge of the forest he slowed, looked once to the right and left, then entered the dimness of the trees.

You're running out of time, a small voice mocked. *Can you trust your guess, or are you too concerned for Kahsir's safety to judge accurately?* He silenced the voice and led on.

The trail stretched ahead, shrouded in silence and deep afternoon shadow. He held his horse to a quick trot, unsure of his path. His skin crawled and his mind shrieked danger. Clenching his teeth, he risked a quicker pace.

Damn! If there are Krotànya coming through the forest, they might think we're the enemy. Do I dare risk a Sending? he cursed again—he *had* to risk it.

—*Krotànya!* He made the Sending clear, aimed at a narrow target. *Legir! For the Light! We're coming!*

For a moment he had no answer and his heart thudded loudly in his chest. Had he made a mistake? Then another thought came back.

—*Krotànya!* a mental voice responded. *We need help!*

Alàric glanced at the warriors behind to see if they had received the same message, and dared an even faster pace down the dim trail, peering closely ahead, not trusting only to his horse's sight. The trail wound through the trees; time dragged by and the light grew steadily dimmer. Suddenly the way turned sharply left. He rounded that bend and nearly collided with a waiting horseman.

Alàric yanked back on the reins, and the other rider stared briefly in recognition.

"Thank the Light!" The rider's smile was visible even in the shadows. "Follow me, Lord."

The horseman spun his mount around and raced off into the twilight. Alàric hesitated momentarily, then, gesturing to his comrades, set off at a canter after. For a brief, mad moment, he had no sense of direction, but finally caught sight of the man ahead. The rider slowed his pace, disappeared around another bend in the trail, while Alàric followed closely. Suddenly, Alàric reined his horse to a stop.

There, clogging the shadowed trail, waited a large group of women and children, a few menfolk and warriors with them. Alàric's guide rode forward to the side of a woman who led the company. Though he strained to hear, Alàric missed most of the quickly spoken words. The woman glanced up, nodded, and rode to his side. Suddenly he recognized Genlàvyn in the forest's gloom. His throat tightened: *Kahs? Is Kahs—*

"He's here, my Lord," she said. "He got free from Rodja'âno and fled south to Chilufka. We left the steading this morning. A large Leishoranya company followed us." A quick gesture behind. "Your brother's down by the river now, along with his own men and some of my warriors. They're trying to hold the enemy at the ford."

The dread that had coiled ice-cold at the roots of Alàric's heart died away. He closed his eyes briefly: *Lords! I'm in time—if only barely so.*

He looked at his men and pointed to five of them. "Get back to my father as fast as you can. Tell him I found Kahsir and we need help." He turned back to Genlàvyn. "Keep going, lady," he said. "We may be shielded but the enemy's probably aware we're here. Father's camp is close to ten days' ride south—take the mind-road if you can."

She nodded, gestured her people back so that he and his band could pass. He motioned his men forward, and led them in single file past the women and children who waited behind.

And then—he saw the woman who had ridden at Genlàvyn's side. His eyes met hers and his mind reeled as if lightning-struck. But before he could blink, she was gone as he rode by.

He turned to look over his shoulder at her retreating figure, jolted back into reality as his horse sidestepped something in the path. The moment's peril flooded back, and his brother's face leapt to mind. He lifted the reins and kicked his horse into a canter.

The light had nearly gone from the trail now, overhung as it was by the thickly clustered trees. Alàric pushed on, his men following behind. He peered intently ahead as he rode over the unfamiliar ground, using his mind as well as his eyes to avoid any obstructions in the path. The trail began to fall away. The noise of the river sounded clear now as it swept by in a flood of water.

A feeling of oppressive darkness touched his mind—a sense of internal pressure. He threw up his shields and the tightness inside his skull lessened somewhat. Damn! The enemy must be trying some kind of mind-block, and a strong one at that if he could feel it this far from the river.

He rode on a short ways and rounded another turn. The trail abruptly left the forest ahead. He reined in his horse in that margin, then eased out of the woods as a Krotànya warrior stepped out of the brush, sword and shield held at the ready.

"Alàric dor Xeredir," Alàric said, naming himself. The man started and peered upward in the gloom. "What's going on? Where's my brother?"

"Ahri!"

Alàric turned in the saddle. Kahsir came up along the rocks on the river bank, his face full of mixed expressions: joy and anger—relief mingled with concern. Alàric dismounted and hugged his eldest brother tightly.

"What are *you* doing here?" Kahsir demanded. "You're supposed to be back in the capital."

How had he—? Alàric made the connection: Genlàvyn must have spoken with some of the men Eltàrim had sent north.

"I left this morning for Father's army." Alàric released his brother and stepped back. "Lords, Kahs! Haskon and I lost all contact with you the afternoon Rodja'âno fell. I thought you hadn't managed to get away, that you'd been captured or—" He drew a deep breath and gestured behind. "I've brought Chorvàl and fourteen warriors with me. What's happening? Have the Leishoranya attacked yet?"

Kahsir glanced over his shoulder at the river. It was

twilight out away from the darkness of the woods, but visibility was fading quickly.

"Aye, they've attacked. Now they're after us mentally. They have some good archers with them, but so do we." He grasped Alàric's arm and turned away from the others. "It's Dhumaric, Ahri. He's been on our trail all the way from Rodja'âno."

Alàric's heart lurched. "Do the other men know?"

"By now they do. I don't want to keep reminding them."

"Dhumaric." Alàric shivered. Memories filled his mind—the Leishoranya commander's brilliance on the field of battle, and his cruelty. He scratched his beard, then glanced up at his brother. "How many does he have with him?"

"Around one hundred."

"You're serious?"

"Deadly serious. He started out with five hundred." Even in the shadows, Kahsir's narrow grin shone white. "We managed to send most of his men to the Dark."

"A tale lies in that, I'm sure."

"Huhn. The enemy's only tried to cross the river once, and they found that more deadly than they liked. Besides having to face us, they'll find the ford dangerous now and footing not the best. We're at a physical stalemate. They can't cross and we can't afford to leave. I think that's why Dhumaric's started attacking our minds."

"Damn. He's good, isn't he? I felt that attack before I reached the edge of the forest."

"He's strong all right . . . near Mind-Born level, I'd say. Did you send Genlàvyn and her people on?"

"Aye." Genlàvyn. But the woman who had ridden at Genlàvyn's side— "I didn't realize Chilufka was quite so close."

"Huhn. And since you're so interested in the lady who rode with Genlàvyn, her name is Maiwyn of the House of dàn Iofharsen. She's Genlàvyn's cousin."

Alàric glanced quickly away. *By the Light! Am I shielding that poorly?*

"What do we do now, Kahs?" he asked, changing the subject. "Father's inundated with refugees from Rodja'âno and he's planning to send them south in another day or so." He peered off into the twilight, north across the river. "And now that Ssenkahdavic—"

"He's used too much of his strength," Kahsir said. "We fought him hard. He had to use a great deal of power to bring Rodja'âno down. It's going to be some time before he can move again."

"That's what I thought might have happened." Alàric turned and led his horse to where the other mounts were tethered. He smelled the biting scent of pines that grew among the other trees in the forest. It was nearly dark now. He fumbled with the reins as he tied them around a small tree, then took down his bow and arrows. Kahsir walked up to stand at his shoulder.

"What happened when the city fell, Kahs? Haskon and I thought maybe you'd been killed."

There was still enough light left to see the grim expression that hardened Kahsir's face, but Alàric was barely prepared for the touch of his brother's mind, the onslaught of incoming information, heavily layered with scenes of what had happened during the past few days. He Sent back his own hurt and anger over being lied to, his overriding love and concern despite the betrayal, and everything Xeredir had told him.

The link broke, and Alàric's mind spun as he tried to come to grips with all he had learned. Kahsir smiled grimly, turned, and gestured toward the river. Alàric stared after his brother's broad-shouldered form as Kahsir walked away. *You're so damned sure of yourself all the time. The way you carry on, you'd have people believe you never suffer doubt about anything.* He frowned and his anger ebbed away. *Jealousy doesn't solve anything. Quit acting like a child.*

Glancing behind to be certain all his men had come

out of the woods, Alàric followed Kahsir down the rocky trail, crouching low for cover from enemy arrows. His brother knelt behind a large boulder. He sank to his heels beside and looked out across the river.

Outnumbered as they were, Kahsir's men held what seemed to be the upper hand, having the advantage of height and better protection. Still, with Dhumaric commanding the enemy war band on the river's other side, anything could happen.

"Is there another ford close to us?" Alàric asked. He squinted in the fading light up and down the river, then looked at Kahsir.

"No. A half-day's ride farther west, perhaps. Dhumaric shouldn't be able to circle around behind us, if that's what you're saying. I think he's used the mind-road at least once. He's as tired as we are, but we can't hold him off forever."

"That's for sure. We can stay here only so long before our odds run out. If you were Dhumaric, wouldn't you try to jump a strike force across, especially if you were faced with this standoff?"

Kahsir nodded. "I've already considered it. Genlàvyn's march warden has taken precautions. He sent three men each to our right and left to stand sentry. They're all familiar with this land. No Leishoran will get to us unawares."

"Huhn." Alàric stared off across the river. His mind filled with images that had bled over from Kahsir's memories—the lay of the land, the way the river turned, the existence of the ford farther west, and horses the enemy seemed unwilling thus far to leave. "We still can't stay here much longer, Kahs, especially with the enemy attacking our minds. That will drain us as sure as fighting. We've given Genlàvyn and her household time enough to reach the meadows. I sent five men back to Father for help, and told Genlàvyn to take the mind-road if she and her people could. Even staying to the world's roads, if they travel all night, they should be safe sometime tomorrow morning. That's when we should leave." He glanced at his brother's all but unseen face and gestured across the river. "Dhumaric's over there, Kahs, not some thick-skull."

"Don't you think I know that?" Kahsir snapped. Alàric blinked before his brother's vehemence. "There are other reasons why he found us," Kahsir whispered, "but I won't go into them now."

A shadow loomed up in the deeper shadows and slid into place at Kahsir's side.

"Lorhaiden," Alàric said, reaching out to clasp Lorhaiden's arm in greeting. "I'm glad to see you alive."

"And you, Lord." Lorhaiden linked his arms around his knees and stared across the river, looking impatient and frustrated.

Alàric glanced away from the shadowed figure and frowned. *Moody as ever, isn't he?*

A whirring noise alerted Alàric. He and the others ducked for cover as a shower of enemy arrows passed over their heads and fell on the rocks behind.

"They missed," Kahsir muttered. Alàric shifted his bow. "Too dark," Kahsir said. "Save it."

Tsingar sat in the bushes and cursed. He cursed the river, the trees, his exhaustion, and the impossibility of crossing to the other side. Dhumaric was up against a bad situation this time. He had kept up a continual mental attack against the Krotànya, but they seemed to have linked minds and, as of now, had turned those attacks aside. And even Dhumaric needed to rest sometime. Killing the hidden Krotànya who waited in ambush had left him weakened, despite the strength he had leached afterward.

One more long look across the river. The Krotànya on the opposite bank held the better ground, had the company pinned down at the ford. Dhumaric had already lost two men who had grown bold enough to step out from cover. Tsingar snorted. *Fools! I'm surrounded*

*by fools, like those idiots who just shot off into the
dark. They can't even see what they're aiming at.*

He tried another probe: nothing—the Krotànya maintained their heavy shielding. But something had happened earlier, a subtle shift in the balance of power. He
could not read that shift, but it bothered him.

Since arriving at the ford and finding it defended by
Kahsir and the Void knew how many other Krotànya,
Tsingar had avoided Dhumaric whenever he could.
Dhumaric was still all but trembling with rage. Not
only had Kahsir escaped again, but the Kròtanya Throne
Prince had destroyed any provisions that Dhumaric
might have appropriated.

Tsingar glanced at the other men who knelt in the
trees close by and hoped they had not noticed his
unease. He chewed on his lower lip, fought down his
urge to get up and pace. Chaagut was somewhere near.
He heard his junior officer's voice and grimaced: his
position was becoming precarious, Chaagut's bid for
power more open and direct. Chaagut was clever, and
it was a cleverness he had to admire. He would have to
do something about the situation soon, or any retribu-
tion he planned would be difficult, at best.

"Tsingar."

He started at Dhumaric's voice, moved over to make
room. Dhumaric's humor had grown fouler.

"Easy prey, you said? Just when I get close, Kahsir
slides free again. If you hadn't led us off in the wrong
direction. . . ." Dhumaric laughed and cold chills ran
down Tsingar's spine. "But this time, I have a surprise
planned for him. Rest, Tsingar. Tell your men to sleep
if they can. Chaagut and I have a plan. Let Kahsir
worm his way out of this one if he can."

Dhumaric turned and stalked off into the darkness.
Tsingar drew a long, shaking breath. If he did not move
against Chaagut soon, he could lose everything. He
closed his eyes, wiped his sweaty hands on his trousers.
After a long moment, he stood and glanced around.

Keeping very quiet, he walked even farther apart from the company, and knelt behind a tree.

Carefully, with suitable reverence, he withdrew his weapons. One by one he laid them out across his knees—longsword, shortsword, boot-dagger—mutely comforting. He touched them each: a man's luck was caught up with his weapons and the Gods he served. He prayed silently to those Gods and the last of his rage subsided. *Grant me this, if nothing else. Let me be more clever than Chaagut.*

CHAPTER 9

Vlàdor stared at the large map that hung on the wall. The shadows in the corners of the room looked deeper than shadows should. Wearily, he closed his eyes and sank back into his chair, burying his face in his hands. *How much longer? Lords of Light, how much longer?*

When he opened his eyes again, the map was still there: no amount of wishing would make it go away.

He stood, sighed deeply, and took up the brush and inkpot on his desk, then walked slowly across the room. Dipping brush in ink, he carefully drew a red cross-mark through the circle on the map labeled Rodja'âno. Then, with equal care, he began making long, diagonal lines across the northern portion of the Kingdom of Tumâs. Done, he returned to his desk and cleaned the brush with slow, deliberate strokes, holding his emotions in check by the simple acts he did.

Rodja'âno, eleventh capital to fall before the Shadow: the most recent name on the list of great cities that were only memories. Now that Rodja'âno had fallen, only Hvâlkir still stood untouched by the enemy. Hvâlkir, once capital of the Twelve Kingdoms of Vyjenor, which

196

too would perish unless Hjshraiel came to the people who awaited him.

And as for Rodja'âno . . . Vlàdor still was not sure what the ramifications of Kahsir's actions would be. Had Rodja'âno been abandoned early on, as the original plan called for, Nhavari might still be alive and the loss of life suffered at Rodja'âno slight, if any. Yet Kahsir had, facing tremendous odds, managed to hold the city against Ssenkahdavic. As Alàric had pointed out, this action might have wearied Ssenkahdavic to the point that he might go dormant again, as after the fall of Fânchorion.

Kahsir. There had seldom been a commander who rode his luck to the extent Kahsir did. For someone as conservative as Xeredir, this method of waging war must be terrifying. Vlàdor shook his head: both of them—his son and his grandson—were brilliant commanders. The simple fact remained that at times Kahsir's genius made Xeredir's strategies look hesitant and plodding.

The silence in the room became unbearable. Vlàdor recapped the inkpot and stood for a moment. *I've got to get out of here before I go crazy. I've been holed up alone for hours!*

A knock came at the double doors.

Vlàdor glanced up from his desk. "Come in!"

Lord Devàn dàn Chivondeth, supreme cavalry commander, entered the room, a smile of greeting on his face. He had come directly from combat, still dressed in leathers and chain mail. Behind came Tebehrren, chief of all the Mind-Born, clad in the simple white of his kind.

"Devà!" Vlàdor clasped his friend's arm in greeting. He turned to the Mind-Born, one eyebrow lifted. "Lord Tebehrren," he said, "you honor us."

The ghost of a smile touched Tebehrren's face. "I won't be long, Lord. I used Devàn here as a passport through your closed doors."

A strange man, Tebehrren. Seeming untouched by

what went on about him, he always lived in the realm
of his mind. But he had tried to make a humorous
statement, and Vlàdor laughed softly in response.

"You're always welcome, Tebehrren . . . you know
that."

"Does Devàn know?" asked Tebehrren, then finished
silently, *About Rodja'âno?*

"No." Vlàdor glanced at Devàn, tried to think of what
he would say, *how* he would say it. "I was going to tell
him."

"Tell me what?"

Vlàdor gestured.

Devàn swung around to stare at the map. His darkly
tanned face went pale as he turned back. "Rodja'âno,"
he murmured. "She's fallen?"

"Aye, Devà."

The cavalry commander was silent for a long moment; then he walked slowly over to the map, reached
out and touched the circle labeled Rodja'âno. His shoulders slumped. "My kin?" he asked in a quiet voice.
"Have you heard anything of my kin? Many of my
House live in and around Rodja'âno."

"I know, Devà." Vlàdor struggled for the right words.
"Nhavari evacuated Rodja'âno of all but its warriors.
The refugees fled south. I don't have any idea yet who
survived the storm of the city."

Lord Devàn turned away from the map, his left hand
running over the hilt of his longsword. "Alàric was in
Rodja'âno," Devàn said, his voice steady at last. "Do
you have any news of him?"

"We recalled him, but he waited until the last moment. As you remember, Xeredir and I had planned to
abandon Rodja'âno and draw the enemy southward into
the hills and forests. At the same time, we were going
to fortify the Golondai passes." Vlàdor sighed quietly.
"To make a long story short, Kahsir disobeyed Xeredir
and me, and went to Rodja'âno. And then, for some
reason I still don't understand, Haskon showed up.

Kahs ordered both Alàric and Haskon out of the city when he learned Ssenkahdavic was coming south. In fact, Alàric was just here—he left again this morning to join Haskon with Xeredir's army."

"And Kahsir?"

"I don't know, Devà. I don't know. He didn't die at Rodja'âno, I'm certain of that. If anything does happen to him, I'll know it. We're bound too closely."

"But you haven't heard from him?"

"No. We haven't had any sendings at all from the lands around Rodja'âno."

Tebehrren shifted his weight slightly. "I have news of Kahsir," he said without preamble. "Or, I should say, lack of news." Vlàdor's heart jumped. "He *is* in considerable danger, Lord, and tightly shielded. Most of the Mind-Born who stayed at Rodja'âno died in that last defense against Ssenkahdavic, but those few who survived have been in spotty contact with me. I've searched for Kahsir myself, but I could pick up nothing more of him. I can assure you he *did* escape Rodja'âno. This is certain."

Vlàdor stared at Tebehrren's finely chiseled features. Tall, dark-haired, and elegant, the Mind-Born stood motionless, white cloak shimmering in the lamplight.

"Nothing more?"

"Dhumaric's near him."

Vlàdor's heart lurched again. "Dhumaric!" he whispered. Lord Devàn had stepped closer, listening intently. "Kahs has crossed Dhumaric so many times that he'll stop at nothing to get revenge. By the Light! If only we could go after the enemy the way they—"

"It's forbidden, Lord," Tebehrren interrupted. "You know that. We can't use our minds to kill."

"That's easy for you to say," Vlàdor said with a frown. "You and your fellow Mind-Born dwell in regions of mind far more elevated than those the rest of us inhabit. You—"

"We've got families and homes, too," Tebehrren murmured. "That doesn't change the law. What's used for destruction eventually turns back and consumes the user. It's easier to defend than attack—but harder to *truly* use the Powers of Light than those of the Shadow."

"Do we all have to die of patience?" Vlàdor asked. He turned away, walked across the room to stand by his desk. His hands shook; he took a deep breath and clasped them behind his back. "We use the same weapons as the enemy. They worship theirs; we've come to honor ours. But *they* turn their minds against us and, on that level, we can't fight back."

Tebehrren shook his head and gestured sharply. "Only Hjshraiel can do that. He will be Ssenkahdavic's bane."

"If there are any of us alive for him to fight for," Vlàdor snapped. Hands still locked behind his back, he walked across the room to Tebehrren's side. "There are times when I wonder whose side you're on, Tebehrren."

The Mind-Born's face froze. "And what do you mean by that, Lord?"

"Just what I said. Why, if you're so damned powerful, didn't you know Ssenkahdavic had awakened? And you got the message from your fellow Mind-Born he was coming south too late for us to do anything."

"What could you have done, Lord?" Tebehrren asked mildly. "What could *any* of us have done?"

"Something." Vlàdor glared. "Anything, but sit on our hands. You know what we face—I'll bet you know more about it than I do. Yet you're never able to tell me how we can overcome the enemy. Whenever we're beaten again, we hear the same damned thing. 'Hjshraiel will come to save you.' When, Tebehrren? When?"

Tebehrren closed his eyes briefly. "Not even the Mind-Born know that."

"Huhn." Vlàdor hunched his shoulders and let his hands fall back to his sides. "That's surprising. I often wonder just how ignorant you *are*." He sought Tebehrren's eyes. "Tell me honestly: do you know something I don't? And if you do, are you simply leading me along—playing a gambling game with prophecy, with the blood of our people as coin?"

"My Lord!" Tebehrren's voice shook. "How can you—"

"We all know the prophecy," Vlàdor interrupted, close to shouting. "Hjshraiel will come out of the Krotànya people, born to face Ssenkahdavic, born to be a channel for the Powers of Light, to restore the balance between Light and Shadow. He-Who-Is-To-Come." He barked a laugh. "And come when? What good's a prophecy or a rescue if there's no one left alive to see it?"

Tebehrren's eyes were steady. "If you remember, Lord, the Mind-Born didn't make this prophecy. We've had to learn to deal with it like everyone else. He'll come in his own time. And remember this also: the harder we fight against the Darkness, the more we weaken that Power. Nothing ever dies—not people, not worlds, not stars. And when the universe is born again, everything we've done to help the Light will be taken into account."

"Huhn." Vlàdor gestured briefly. "Tell that to the men dying on the battlefield. Tell that to their widows, to their children, to all the rest of my people who—"

"My Lord . . . please—" With a shrug, a gesture aside: "— can't this argument wait until another time?"

Vlàdor glanced where the Mind-Born indicated, seeing Devàn as if for the first time. His friend had backed up and, face white in the lamplight, hands clenched at his sides, was standing motionless by the map.

"Don't drag Devàn into this, Tebehrren. This is between you and me: High-King and Chief Advisor to the Throne. Matters of state." He glanced back again. "Matters of survival."

Tebehrren shrugged. "You're tired, my Lord. And you've had your fill of bad news. You wouldn't be saying these things if—"

"Wouldn't I?" Vlàdor turned his back on Tebehrren and began pacing up and down in front of his desk.

"I've asked myself these same questions before. Defense. That's the only thing you Mind-Born seem to understand. That's all you ever tell us we're allowed." He stopped, turned, and stared. "Don't you ever wonder what people think? We're tired of retreating, of defending against attack. That's all we've done in this damned war. And those tactics haven't won us anything, have they?"

"They've kept you and your people from damning yourselves to the Darkness the enemy serves."

"And I suppose that's worth the countless deaths we've suffered. It seems we Krotànya stand as an obstacle to the enemy—something that prevents them from growing stronger. What I'd like to know," he said, walking to the map and turning around, "is who elected us? *Why us*, Tebehrren?"

Tebehrren shook his head slowly. "I can't answer that, Lord. I simply don't know."

"You don't know. Hah! You seem to know everything else! Look at this map, Advisor! Look at it!" Vlàdor's hand shot out and pointed at the bloodied record of his people's history. "Shall I read off the names of the capitals that have fallen? Vlostâ, Osain, Godenikhil, Dun'ysibno, Ynodaka, Tolândan—"

"My Lord—"

"I'm not done yet!" Vlàdor shouted, his finger moving westward across the map. "Legânoi, Hyldenvlyn, Kakordicum, Fânchorion—" He drew a deep breath, lowered his voice back to normal tones. "And now Rodja'âno. Not a pretty sight, is it?" He dropped his hand. "We've got our backs to the sea and only one Kingdom out of twelve still whole. But we're not to worry, are we? *Hjshraiel* will save us from total destruction!"

Tebehrren bowed his head.

Vlàdor's eyes narrowed. "You seem damned reluctant to advise, Advisor. Even when you tell me about Hjshraiel, you tell me nothing new. Listen to me.

We're losing this war, Tebehrren. Just because the things we believe are right and true doesn't mean we'll win. By all the Lords of Light! Those of us who aren't Mind-Born live here and now, not in the futures. Hjshraiel's not come to us yet. What are we to do, then, against these uneven odds?"

"Fight, my Lord, fight," Tebehrren said softly, lifting his head. "Fight with all the strength and cunning you can muster. But don't condemn yourselves to the same darkness as the Leishoranya."

Vlàdor threw up his hands in exasperation. "We might as well try to dam up a river with a napkin!"

"If we set our minds to death and destruction, Lord, we become no better than the enemy."

"I have a people to protect. And for the near fifteen hundred years of this war, I've done a poor job of it."

"You see yourself with only your own eyes. Other folk may see you far differently."

Vlàdor shrugged and glanced away.

"I'm sorry you have doubts about us Mind-Born," Tebehrren said. "We act only as we can. If nothing else, believe that we want to win this war, too. But keep this in mind: none of us can stand up to Ssenkah-davic's powers. Not all of us combined can." Tebehrren's face softened. "And if there's anything I believe in, it's that Hjshraiel *will* come."

"Huhn." Vlàdor glanced away from Tebehrren and looked for a moment at the map on the wall. "It's a damned frail hope to die for."

Tebehrren gestured helplessly. "It's the only hope we have left." He drew a deep breath. "If I learn anything more concerning Kahsir, I'll tell you. And if you feel like continuing this conversation later, I'll be more than willing to talk to you. But I don't think you're ready for that now. Rest, Lord. If you need me, call. I'll come at once."

And, as with all his kind, the Mind-Born was there and suddenly he was not.

* * *

"I wish they wouldn't do that so often," Devàn complained. "It's hard to keep track of who's coming and who's going."

"Ah, to them it's like the flip of a hand. If it were as easy for the rest of us, I suppose we'd do it, too." Vlàdor straightened his shoulders. "Wine, Devà? I think we both could use it."

"Aye, Lord."

Vlàdor walked to the sideboard, unstopped a beaker of wine, and poured Devàn a glass, then filled his own.

"You certainly didn't solve much," Devàn said. "Tebehrren was as difficult as ever."

"Difficult? Huhn! He's—" Vlàdor gestured helplessly—and took a long swallow of wine. His mouth felt dry enough to spit dust. "I'm telling you, Devà—I wonder about the Mind-Born from time to time. They're teachers; they're healers; they're advisors—"

"And they're obnoxious," Devàn growled. "Sometimes."

Vlàdor laughed, startled by the harshness in his voice. His eyes strayed back to the map. "I'm sorry you had to find out about Rodja'âno that way. I would rather have told you at my own pace."

"It wouldn't have made any difference. Ssenkahdavic took the city, didn't he?"

"Aye." Vlàdor paused, took a deep breath and another long swallow of wine. "It looks like we've reached the end of the war, Devà. Where else can Ssenkahdavic turn now but south? The last capital."

"What of the other Leishoranya armies?"

"From what our scouts tell us, there are at least two afield of major size, though they seem to be stationary right now," Vlàdor said. "Then, of course, there's the third—the army to our north that just took Rodja'âno. The enemy's probably enlarging that army day by day. And none of these reports take into account all the many enemy forces that only number in the mid-thousands."

Lord Devn walked over to the map, reached out, and pointed to the south of Elyâsai.

"Here, Lord—the Kingdom of Bynjâlved. For decades now, the army that took that Kingdom has consolidated its strength around its base at Kakordicum." A long, sun-darkened finger moved up across the map toward the northeast. "And here's another army of the same size—near sixty thousand strong—in Hyldenvlyn, in the Kingdom of Cwaivonnel. These must be the two armies our scouts have seen mobilizing."

Vlàdor stared at the map, then nodded. "You're probably right. The other forces are too small and too far away." He turned and beckoned his friend to one of the chairs by the window. "It appears we're effectively surrounded," he said, sitting down. "How are things going on the borders?"

"As well as can be expected, Lord. You've heard all the reports." Devàn took the chair on the other side of the small table. "We're still holding our own, but that changes from day to day. The enemy has sent reconnaissance parties across the border into Elyâsai. We're facing invasion on all three fronts, and—knowing the enemy—I'll wager those invasions occur all at once."

"I don't doubt it." Vlàdor shifted in his chair and pulled at his beard.

Devàn set his cup down on the table. "So, tell me. What are you going to do now that Kahsir's ruined your plans for defense of the northlands?"

"I'm not sure 'ruined' is the proper word. He certainly spoiled any chance for us to use the plans Xeredir and I came up with at first. But none of us had foreseen Ssenkahdavic awakening so soon. We thought he'd stay dormant for a much longer time. Kahsir's being there at Rodja'âno and holding the city as long as he did might have prevented Ssenkahdavic from coming farther south."

"Then it seems to me that Kahsir did us all a favor by disobeying you."

"True. But it's not helped family relations much. You know how Xeredir and Kahs are continually arguing strategy. They fought over this one for days, Kahsir pointing out—and rightly so—that Rodja'âno was too important strategically to abandon. And, of course, it was Nhavari's capital, and you know how close Kahs and Nhavari have been. Anyway, Xeredir came to me and got me to second his order recalling Alàric." Vlàdor sought his friend's eyes. "I honestly thought Xeredir was right . . . that his stragetem had a greater chance of succeeding than Kahs'. And so I agreed. Kahs obviously couldn't abandon his friend Nhavari, or admit that Xeredir was right. So. . . ." He spread his hands. "Now I've got a son who's convinced he's been betrayed, and a grandson who's disobeyed every order he was given."

"And what are you going to do?"

"I don't have much choice. I've got to deal with what Kahs set in motion, try to dovetail it into any plans Xeredir might have."

"Huhn. Do you have any news of Nhavari?"

Vlàdor stiffened and met his friend's eyes. "Nhavari's dead, Devà."

"O Lords!" Devàn bowed his head and for a long moment remained silent. At last, he drew a deep breath and looked up. "That's one man I cared about."

"Everyone did, Devà. With him dead, the Kingdom of Tumâs is as good as gone. The only hope his people have now is for someone strong enough to take his place—to lead their resistance."

"Xeredir?"

Vlàdor nodded slowly. "Possibly. As for Kahsir, the first news any of us have had about him was what Tebehrren just told me."

"Near Dhumaric." Lord Devàn made a wry face. "He's one enemy commander to avoid at all costs. I've fought him enough myself to know that."

A long silence fell on the room. Vlàdor took another swallow of wine, looked at the late afternoon sunlight filling the study, bringing out the warm shades of the cream-colored walls and fine wood furniture. Tebehrren's voice echoed in his mind. He grimaced. To be sure, he and his people would fight against the enemy . . . they had done little else for the past fifteen hundred years. But as for Hjshraiel—another King would see that wonder, not he. If Hjshraiel ever *did* come, and was more than a comforting myth. He straightened in his chair and frowned. "Devà. I want to ask you something and I'm going to expect nothing from you but brutal honesty."

"When haven't we been honest with each other? Ask. I'll answer as best I can."

Vlàdor looked at the man who sat in the chair opposite. *Oldest and dearest of friends—close as any swordbrother. What will we do, you and I, when the light goes out of this world?*

"How long do you think we have," he asked, "before the Shadow falls on us, too?"

Devàn did not reply at once. He swung around in his chair and looked across the room at the map and its preponderance of red, then sighed quietly and turned back.

"If we last two more years against the enemy, we'll be lucky. One year, if we're not. Summer of the coming year, I'd guess."

Vlàdor held his friend's gaze, then lowered his eyes. "I agree with you. A year or two, at the most." The silence in the room grew deeper still. "We can't let the warriors know what we think," he murmured, turning his glass slowly between his hands. "They have so little hope left. I hate duplicity, but our armies must feel some confidence in themselves and the futures, or they'll be slaughtered. And most of the line soldiers could give a peddler's hoot about the universe that's to come after this one."

Devàn nodded, looked down into his cup, and finished the last of his wine. "So, my Lord, could I. Most of the time. But as much as I hate to admit it, Tebehrren's right, you know. We've got to fight the enemy with everything we have, if for nothing more than a sense of pride, you see? I'll be damned if I let someone beat me down into the muck without at least striking back." He set his cup down. "I'm going home, Lord," he said, standing. "I came straight here as soon as I arrived and I probably smell like something three days dead."

Vlàdor smiled. "You'll be back for dinner, won't you? I'd enjoy your company."

"Certainly. I'll see you then, Lord."

Devàn briefly touched Vlàdor's shoulder, turned and left. For a long time, Vlàdor sat staring at the sunlight glittering on his cup. Then he glanced over at the map: the shadows in the corners of the room had grown darker yet.

CHAPTER 10

Alàric shivered slightly and gathered his cloak closer. False dawn stole down the river, its dim grey light lending an atmosphere of unreality to the ford. He glanced sideways from where he sat: Kahsir and Lorhaiden slept deeply.

At least half the Krotànya were still awake, their linked minds a shield that protected even those asleep. Alàric sensed Vàlkir a bit farther down among the boulders—felt the strength of Vàlkir's mind, and his alertness.

Alàric looked out at the river again. The air was full of the heavy scents of damp rocks and ground. He flexed his shoulder: it had stiffened somewhat but the pain had nearly gone. Birdsong came to him even over the sounds of the river. He shifted his position, swatted at a cloud of tiny insects, and stared at the opposite bank.

The enemy still lurked there, though for the moment the intense attack Dhumaric had mounted was still. Earlier, Alàric had tried a probe, only to meet an enemy mind-block. He probed again and encountered the same resistance, though it seemed a bit thinner.

Huhn. They're tired, too. It's no easy thing to keep a block like that in place while Dhumaric goes after us.

There was a sudden sound from the river. Alàric jerked upright and for a long moment scanned the opposite bank. Nothing moved save the turbulent river current, but he kept his eyes trained on the water and the forest across it. A bug bit his ear. He slapped at it and looked away.

His backside ached from sitting so long. He rose slowly to a crouched position, keeping behind the cover of the rocks, and rubbed at his cramped legs. Darting from boulder to boulder, he crept up into the concealing trees above the ford.

The bugs were worse here. He cursed and began walking through the trees, watching the river as he went. Full dawn was still over an hour away. Then Kahsir would likely withdraw from the ford, trying to gain some distance on Dhumaric's company before they knew he was gone.

By now Genlàvyn's people should have reached the open fields on the south side of the forest. If the messengers had made it to Xeredir's camp, she and her company might have already met any men sent out to help them. Alàric stopped for a moment, leaned against a tree, and stared out at the river. A brief image of the Lady Maiwyn came to mind. *Lords! I've never met a woman who's turned my head like that! What the Dark's going on?*

He scratched at his beard, at an insect bite on his cheekbone. *You're in love, idiot—and after only seeing her once.* He snorted and flexed his shoulder, rubbing at the healing wound. *Thought you were above such things, didn't you? And after all the grief you gave Kahs when he and Eltàrim fell in love.* He started walking again, keeping his eyes trained on the woods across the river. *I suppose it can happen to anyone.*

He drew up short and held his position. The light was still deceptive, but for a brief moment the brush on the opposite bank had seemed to stir. A brief gust of wind? An animal? He licked his lips and came to the very edge of the trail leading down to the ford. The brush across the river was still again.

He started out along the edge of the trees, holding his eyes to the opposite bank. A tree branch slapped against his face and he batted it aside. Now that Ssenkahdavic had taken Rodja'âno, things in the north-lands were falling apart. Huhn. To say nothing of what Kahsir had set in motion by disobeying orders. Xeredir now faced the problem of drawing together the Krotànya who had scattered after the fall of Rodja'âno and linking them with the men he had brought across the Golondai.

Again, the brush and trees moved jerkily beyond the ford. Alàric froze, knelt by a tree trunk at the edge of the river bank. A cloud of tiny insects descended out of the leaves; he swatted at them and cursed silently. For a long moment, he stared at the enemy's position, but the forest remained still.

His bladder was full. He changed positions, but that only made the uncomfortable pressure worse. He stood slowly and looked around for a concealed spot to relieve himself. Then something touched his mind—a quick impression that left no afterimage. He paused, turned slowly, and looked out from between the trees across the river. He shivered in the damp chill. Lords! Could it be—?

He quickly walked back to the trail leading down to the ford. For a moment he stood at the edge of the forest, staring across at the river's opposite bank. He tried a mental probe. The enemy's block still held, but—

"*Fihrkken* Darkness!" His hissed curse sounded loud in his ears. "O Lords above and below! How could we have missed it?"

His heart pounding in his chest, he hurried down among the boulders to where Vàlkir sat. Again, he probed across the river. The mind-block was wrong—an empty wrongness, hollow and mocking.

Alàric's mouth went dry. He knelt by Vàlkir and touched the other man's shoulder. Vàlkir looked up, his face drawn and his eyes shadows in the dawn light.

"I've—have you felt it, too?" Alàric asked.

Vàlkir nodded. "I think so."

"Damn . . . oh, damn. Should we try to force the enemy block?"

"Don't have a choice," Vàlkir said, straightening behind his boulder. "Link with me."

Alàric drew a deep breath and settled down next to Vàlkir. Closing his eyes, he calmed his breathing, his heart, then reached out his mind and linked it with Vàlkir's. The resultant double vision made him blink. He concentrated on what his own eyes saw and let Vàlkir draw additional strength from him. Though he no longer Saw through Vàlkir's eyes, he felt what the other man felt. Gently, tentatively, Vàlkir began forcing the enemy's mind-block.

Sweat broke out on Alàric's forehead. Kahsir had warned against anyone trying this: the danger was obvious. Open as he and Vàlkir were, the enemy could breach their shields and destroy them all. *If* the enemy was still there. He felt Vàlkir force the block even more, and cringed before the attack that never came. His stomach knotted. The mental block shuddered, then dissolved as if it had never been.

Gone! The enemy was gone! And neither he, Vàlkir, nor anyone else had noticed their departure!

"Kahs! Wake up, Kahs!"

Kahsir jerked awake, blinked for a moment, and stared up at Alàric's face in the half-light. Behind him, face hidden in the shadows, knelt Vàlkir.

"The enemy—they're gone!" Alàric's whisper was raw with urgency. "And I don't know when they left!"

A cold chill stabbed through Kahsir's heart. He sat

up, steadied himself against the rock he had slept by. "Are you sure?"

Alàric licked his lips and nodded. "Without going across the river to check . . . aye, I'm sure."

Kahsir closed his eyes and rubbed them fiercely, commanding himself awake. If the enemy *had* left the ford, it could only have been in the past few hours. He and Lorhaiden had taken the first watch, maintaining the linked shielding with their comrades while Alàric, Vàlkir, and the other half of the men had slept.

And now. . . .

Lords of Light! What do we do now? He looked at his brother's tense face. "You forced their mind-block?"

"Aye. Vahl and I did. I know you told me not to, but—"

"Thank the Light you did." Kahsir looked around. Lorhaiden had awakened and was watching, his eyes pools of shadow in the near darkness. "There's no hope for it, Ahri. We're going to have to get out of here fast."

"The enemy's gone?"

Lorhaiden's whisper was all but lost in the noise of the river. Kahsir glanced sidelong and nodded. "Ahri and Vahl tried their mind-block. He says they've left their side of the ford."

"*Chuht!*" Lorhaiden's voice this time was not lost in the sound of rushing water.

Kahsir drew a long, deep breath and rubbed his eyes again. When he had gone to sleep, Dhumaric had still been pushing at the Krotànya shielding. He laughed humorlessly. Damned if Dhumaric had not pulled the trick of going at the enemy time and again, and then sneaking off when it would seem logical to think he rested. So. Dhumaric had left the ford in total darkness. But *where* had he gone? To the east or the west? Genlàvyn had said the other ford was worse than this one. And crossing the river in the dead of night? Dhumaric's men were surely as exhausted as Kahsir's own. He shuddered at the thought.

"We aren't leaving, are we?"

He turned and stared at Lorhaiden's shadowed face. "You're damned right we're leaving. We've got to keep Dhumaric from coming around behind us."

"But. . . ." Lorhaiden gestured sharply. "We still don't know for sure that he's left, Lord. It could be a trap. He could have set up a false impression for us to read and be on our backs as soon as we go into the forest."

"Huhn." Kahsir checked his swords, his boot-knife, and drew his cloak closer against the dampness. "He could also have split his force, and be coming at us from both sides. Not knowing for sure doesn't leave us any choice. We've *got* to move."

"But—"

"Lorhaiden. Don't press it."

"My Oath. . . ."

"*Damn* your Oath! You'll get your chance at Dhumaric. Don't worry about that. Vahl?"

"Lord?"

"Try another probe across the river. See if you can pick up anything that could tell us how long ago the enemy left."

Vàlkir nodded and stared off across the ford. Kahsir shifted his weight, hand on the hilt of his boot-knife. *Damn Dhumaric! Damn him, damn him! He's too full of tricks!*

"Lord." Vàlkir looked back from the river. "As best I can tell, they left sometime several hours back."

"Oh, *chuht! I* could have told you that," Lorhaiden interjected. "He was still there when Kahs and I went to sleep."

Kahsir stood, keeping a wary eye turned to the opposite bank. "Let's get out of here. Now!"

"Shall I—?"

"You're not going anywhere without the rest of us, Lorj!" Kahsir snapped. He looked around the rocks: half the men were awake and watching, their eyes dark shadows in their faces. The other warriors still lay curled

up in their cloaks, exhausted from their part in maintaining the shielding. "Wake up!" Kahsir bellowed over
the noise of the river. "On your feet! The enemy's
gone! Let's get out of here! Move!"

Sleepy groans greeted his words. Men staggered to
their feet, grabbed for their weapons and helmets; those
already awake watched him intently. Kahsir gestured
sharply up the trail.

"Hurry!" he yelled. "Mount and wait for me."

He turned back and looked across the river. *Dhumaric,
you bastard! One jump ahead of me, aren't you? How
the Dark could you have crossed the river? It's as
dangerous as it was yesterday! Unless—* His heart sank.
*The mind-road? It could be. Leave it to Dhumaric to
try that . . . the Leishoranya way.*

"Kahs?"

He turned. Alàric and Lorhaiden stood at his side.
The rest of the men, including Vàlkir, had gone up the
trail.

"Let's ride," he said, and scrambled up the steep
incline.

His men were mounted, some with eyes still puffy
from sleep. Kahsir took the reins of his horse from
Vàlkir and swung up into the saddle. He waited until
Alàric and Lorhaiden had mounted, then turned and
led the way into the forest.

It was even darker on the trail as it wound its way
through the trees. Kahsir urged his horse to a fast trot,
unsure of his path. *Lords! He needed light for a faster
pace!* They faced hours of riding before the forest opened
into the meadows.

"Rothàr!" He glanced over his shoulder at the march
warden, who rode just behind. "Send several of your
men out as scouts. I don't know where Dhumaric is,
but I'll bet he's trying to cut us off before we reach the
meadows. And tell the scouts not to get too far ahead. I
want them to contact me every quarter hour."

Rothàr nodded and fell back to make his choice.

Kahsir shook his head. He was riding blind, possibly into an ambush. *I'm an idiot . . . a bloody idiot! Why didn't I follow my instincts and leave the ford after nightfall?*

But that would have left Dhumaric free to come at our backs.

Damn him to the Darkness he serves! Give that bastard a chance and he'll turn up exactly where you don't want him!

Two scouts edged their way past the war band. Kahsir watched until they rode out of sight into the gloom. They dared not send out probes to see where Dhumaric rode, for to do so would create a small chink in their shielding. *Oh, dammit! If that dung-ball gets even a hint of where we are, we're done.*

He glanced behind: Alàric, Lorhaiden, and Vàlkir followed, the rest of his men riding in single file, close to each other in case of attack. He looked forward again and rubbed the empty finger on his right hand where the heir's ring belonged.

Alàric's anger of last night filled his memory. He *had* lied to his brothers, tricked them out of the city; their eagerness to add hidden meaning to his words had merely made it easier. Then, a further complication, everyone had thought he had died at Rodja'âno because he had lost consciousness when he had escaped. The tight shields he had maintained that night and the days after reinforced this notion. And when Haskon had reached Xeredir with the heir's ring—

Kahsir swallowed heavily. Not only had he disobeyed both his father and grandfather, he had taken a command that was not his. And then, realizing that he had failed in what he had tried to do, throwing the entire defense of the northlands into shambles in the process, he had resigned all command. He dreaded the coming meeting with his father. What *would* he say to Xeredir when he met him? *If* he met him.

Visibility gradually increased as the sun touched the

treetops. Rothàr had said a half-day's ride would bring them out into the meadows. Kahsir increased his pace, hearing the riders behind do the same. Taking the mind-road was out of the question in all but the direst circumstances. Dhumaric would be waiting for him to do that—ready to follow the telltale energy surge. Even after resting, most of his men were too tired to make a journey of any distance safely. And if they ended up having to fight after taking the mind-road, they would all be doomed.

He shrugged and lifted his reins, urging his horse to a quicker pace. Given his present alternatives, he could dare nothing faster on an unknown trail than a canter, and trust to the scouts Rothàr had sent forward.

The sun stood two hours shy of midday when Kahsir led his men out of the forest. For a long moment he sat there in the sunlight, the fresh southern breeze stirring the hair on his shoulders. Dhumaric? He glanced around, his mind held open, yet could not detect any presence of his enemy. He shook his head. Where the Dark was Dhumaric? Was his apparent absence part of a trap?

"Lord?" Rothàr had ridden to his side. "The scouts haven't found any evidence Dhumaric's been here."

One of the knots in Kahsir's stomach loosened—but only one. "Then let's ride. I want to put as much distance between us and the forest as possible."

He lifted his reins and set out across the meadows at a canter. Though Alàric and the men he had brought with him from Xeredir's camp had ridden their horses hard yesterday, they seemed to have regained some of their strength. Kahsir looked ahead, up the slope of the meadows. With luck, he and his companions could cross the fields into the high woodlands of the foothills by late afternoon. Once there, though he hoped to find Genlàvyn and her household waiting, his greatest wish was to join forces with any warriors Xeredir might have sent to help.

If Dhumaric did not catch them first.

By noon he rode silent, Alàric at his side and Lorhaiden only a few paces behind. Lorhaiden had wanted to talk, but guessing that his sword-brother still wanted to turn back after Dhumaric, Kahsir had silenced him with a look. Now, shielded tightly, he led the way out across the meadows, holding his course to the southeast.

The land rose under his horse's hooves, the grass growing shorter every time he crested a hill. The meadows were open enough to prevent an ambush, yet too uncluttered and generally flat to give protection in case of attack. The waving grass shimmered in the sunlight. Birds took to wing, their calls faint in the wind, and swept off to either side of the advancing Krotànya in erratic flight.

Kahsir glanced sidelong at his brother, and tried to catch Alàric's eyes. Alàric felt responsible for having let the enemy leave the ford undetected, even though Vàlkir had stated that he found Dhumaric's illusion one of the best and strongest he had ever encountered. Alàric kept his eyes straight forward and Kahsir gave up trying to break his brother's wall of silence.

A sudden cry from the rear guard: Kahsir swung about in his saddle and looked behind. Horses stretched out in a full run, a large number of Leishoranya galloped in utter silence across the plains toward his band of warriors.

Dhumaric!

Calculating the angle of their approach, Kahsir predicted interception unless he and his men could outdistance the enemy.

"Ride, Krotànya!" He grabbed for his shield and loosened his longsword in its sheath. "At a run!"

His men obeyed instantly, kicking their horses into a gallop. Kahsir looked around—no cover visible, no height to run for. He had no choice—he had to try to outrun Dhumaric.

Idiot, idiot, idiot! Why the Dark didn't I leave the ford sooner? He cursed aloud. *If I can get a message to Father or Haskon, maybe they can help. Maybe the men coming north to protect Genlàvyn might be near.*

Kahsir glanced at Alàric. *Ahri,* he sent, *I'm going to try to contact Father. You're surer of his position than I am. Guide my Sending.*

A look of concentration spread across Alàric's face and he nodded. Summoning as much power as he could, Kahsir sent out a message for help, loading the Sending with multiple layers of information describing what had happened and what the present situation was. For a moment the Sending wavered as if changing directions, then steadied again, and he linked minds with Haskon.

The contact broke. He glanced behind at the Leishoranya—an even hundred of them. Exactly how many was unimportant; with the thirty men he led, he dared not turn and charge them.

Alàric's mind touched his. *It's Dhumaric, isn't it?*

—Aye. It was useless to try to talk—words aloud would be torn away by the wind and the thunder of hooves. *What happened to the Sending, Ahri? You had your focus, then—*

—Father's moved his camp. Somewhere closer. I caught the impression of some of his men to the south of us.

—How many?

—Couldn't tell. Did you talk with Father?

—No. With Haskon. Kahsir glanced behind at the enemy, then forward again, and kicked his horse to a faster run.

Tsingar whipped his horse to a gallop. He glanced at the other men who rode beside him, at the eager looks on their faces. They were close and getting closer. The Krotànya could ride only so far before Dhumaric's company overtook them. Kahsir only had around thirty men riding with him, so the odds were decidedly in Dhu-maric's favor. And yet it would be close . . . very close.

At last! Tsingar bared his teeth in a fighting grin. The Krotànya were doomed and rode as if they knew it. The death Dhumaric had promised for Kahsir and Lorhaiden would be more than interesting to watch.

—*Vàlkir!* Kahsir Sent over the thunder of hooves. The answering reply from farther back in their company was clear and distinct. *Vahl, take your bowmen to the rear!*

—*Aye, Lord.*

—*And be careful.* Kahsir gripped the saddle with his knees as his horse leapt over the small rivulet of a stream. He glanced over his shoulder: Vàlkir and the other bowmen dropped back to the very rear of the galloping band. Kahsir turned his attention forward again: *Lords! Let the enemy's horses tire sooner than ours!*

And: *Dammit, Ahri!* he Sent. *When you caught that impression of Father's men, how far away were they?*

—*Not much farther.* Alàric looked ahead, eyes nar-rowed against the wind. *Those two hills up there—we'll go directly between them.*

Movement came to Kahsir's left. Lorhaiden urged his horse over until he was riding close enough to reach out and touch.

—*Lord, I have a suggestion.* Lorhaiden shifted his shield, gathered up his reins again. Kahsir caught Lorhaiden's thoughts as surely as if his sword-brother had broadcast them. *I could*—

—*No!* He glared at Lorhaiden. *No.*

He took a quick look over his shoulder: Dhumaric's company drew closer. Kahsir cursed—the small valley that parted the hills lay ahead. He started up it, his horse beginning to labor and stumble now, not only from the steeper terrain but from exhaustion. The ground grew rougher, the rocks more numerous. Without looking around again, he sensed his men hard on his heels, and the end of the valley closer.

Suddenly, shielded from the pursuing Leishoranya, on a level of communication difficult for any but family to read, a clear voice echoed in Kahsir's mind.

—*Ride on*, it instructed. *Be ready to turn and fight*.

Kahsir's heart lurched. He glanced at Alàric. His brother and the other men had Heard the words, too: he could tell that from the looks on their faces.

—*Father!* exclaimed Alàric. *What's he doing—?*

—*Don't worry about that now.* Kahsir unsheathed his sword. He glanced over his shoulder: the last of his warriors had ridden out from the valley into the open fields.

—*Vahl*, he Sent. *You and your archers turn first. Lorhaiden, you and Rothàr take the left and right flanks. Alàric and I will handle the center. For the Light's sake, don't let any of those bastards get too close to you. Engage and disengage as quick as you can. Be ready to turn, on my signal.*

Screaming their war cries, Dhumaric's company burst out of the valley into the meadows.

—*Now!* came Xeredir's mental command.

—*Turn, brothers!* Kahsir sent. *Turn and fight!*

He wheeled his horse about, his men turning at the same instant. And down the slopes of the hills behind the enemy, fanning out to strike not only at the rear but envelop the flanks, rode three full Krotànya companies— three hundred men—sword blades catching the sunlight.

A roar of startled anger rose from the enemy as they recognized the trap.

"*Legir!*" Kahsir lifted his sword above his head, shouted the battle cry of the Kingdoms. "*Legir! For the Light! Legir! Legir!*"

He kicked his horse into a gallop, aimed directly at the enemy. But as quickly as he had moved, Lorhaiden responded first, howling his own battle cry. Kahsir glanced at Alàric and followed Lorhaiden, their thirty companions rushing forward on either side. He drew his shield closer to his side, near enough now to the three Krotànya companies that he could see the glitter of stars on his father's banner.

Hold off! he Sent to his men. *Strike and get out of the way until Father's warriors hit the enemy's rear!*

He kneed his horse toward one of Dhumaric's warriors, darted in, exchanged a few furious sword strokes, then pulled back again. Vàlkir's bowmen seemed to be doing the most damage, firing from a distance into Dhumaric's confused company.

Kahsir sensed his father's men plow into the Leishoranya rear—where warriors attempted to turn from their headlong charge—and into the enemy flanks.

—Now! Kahsir Sent. *Engage at will!*

Kahsir chose one of Dhumaric's warriors at random, met the man's sword with his own, jerked to one side and slashed out behind. The Leishoran yelped shrilly and Kahsir rode on as another enemy warrior came in from the right.

This man was left-handed. Kahsir had no time to shift his own shield and sword. He twisted, took the enemy's blow square on his shield, rocked in his saddle from the sword stroke. He jerked back on the reins, spun his horse clear, and rode toward his opponent. The Leishoran was slower turning, for he had been riding faster. Kahsir kicked his horse to a gallop, and caught the Leishoran in the neck with a sidelong sword cut. Blood covered his sword now and spattered his hand. Lorhaiden fought somewhere out of sight, yelling Dhumaric's name.

Xeredir's men had started pressing inward: the field behind them was littered with bodies. Dhumaric's warriors hesitated, broke and tried to run, but Kahsir saw only a few slip between his men and his father's. The Krotànya sensed victory, cheered, and gave chase. Dhumaric had not stood a chance, caught between Kahsir's men and the three companies Xeredir led.

Kahsir saw his father riding toward the center of the

battlefield. He looked around again. No enemy was close enough to engage, and the other Leishoranya seemed well in hand.

And now, the time had come when he must face his father, and take responsibility for what he had done.

His stomach tightened.

Lifting the reins, Kahsir drew a long, deep breath and turned his horse toward mid-field, where his father waited.

CHAPTER 11

Kahsir reined in his horse so he faced his father. Xeredir sat waiting, motionless in the saddle, his eyes gone steel grey, and his face held carefully blank.

Well aware of the attention he and his father received from the Krotànya warriors around them, Kahsir forced a wide smile, leaned over, and embraced Xeredir.

"Father," he said, loud enough so that he knew himself heard. "By the Light! You couldn't have timed that better!"

He felt the stiffness in his father's arms, and a small part of him went cold inside. But Xeredir also knew the importance of public greetings; he leaned back from Kahsir's embrace and grinned.

"I kept thinking about you after Alàric left," Xeredir said. "Finally, I couldn't restrain myself any longer. So here I am."

"Fortunately for us." Alàric had ridden up beside: he nudged his horse closer. "You left Haskon back at camp?"

Kahsir noticed a slight tightening of his father's shoulders.

"Aye." A hint of that same stiffness lurked in the words spoken. "I'll be damned if I have all *three* of my sons on the same battlefield at once. He wasn't happy about being left, but he's so busy with the refugees he won't have a chance to pity himself." Xeredir glanced at Kahsir. "Is that deep, Kahs?"

Kahsir looked down at his leg, at the blood he had not felt, and ran his fingertips across the oozing cut. "No. I didn't even know I'd been hit." He looked up at his father. A stranger would have noticed nothing but relief and subdued happiness on Xeredir's face, but a son— He glanced sidelong at Alàric, saw the tightness of his brother's mouth, and knew Alàric had read the anger, the hurt, that Xeredir hid so well from other eyes. "How many wounded?" Kahsir asked.

"Only a few." Xeredir looked around at the other Krotànya on the field. "And I don't think we lost a man."

"I'm short a shieldman now," Alàric said. "Chorvàl took a slash in the shoulder, and he's not going to be riding anywhere for a while. Where's Lorhaiden?"

Kahsir glanced around. "I don't know." *When did I see him last? Surely he's not—*

"Isn't that him over there?" Xeredir pointed to the north, to the distant edge of the meadows.

Kahsir squinted in the same direction, trying to make out the tall figure walking among the enemy dead. "It could be."

Xeredir turned his horse and started off at a walk toward the far end of the meadow; Kahsir exchanged a long look with Alàric and followed. Nearly all the enemy had been killed. Their contorted bodies lay scattered on the field, and the wounded groaned softly as Kahsir rode by. The death birds had already gathered, crying from above.

Kahsir looked ahead, close enough now to see Lorhaiden clearly. Bloodied longsword in one hand, Lorhaiden walked slowly from body to body, turned each over with his booted foot, stooped to look, then

moved on again. *What the Dark is the idiot doing now?*
Kahsir frowned and rode closer.

"Lorhaiden!" he called, but received no answer. "Lorj!"
he called again, louder this time. He glanced at his
father and Alàric, then looked back at Lorhaiden. "I'll
go talk to him."

He dismounted, his knees trembling slightly, handed
his reins to Alàric, and walked toward Lorhaiden.
' "Lorj!" he said loudly. Lorhaiden muttered something he could not make out. "What's wrong?"

Lorhaiden swung around, kicked at the dead Leishoran
who lay before him. His face was white and his pale
eyes nearly expressionless. Kahsir's heart jerked. *Lords!*
He's in one of those moods again. It's been so long since
the last one— Damn! Just what I don't need with Fa-
ther set off.

"He's gone," Lorhaiden said, his words slow and
disconnected. "I've looked at all the dead. He's not
among them. He's gone, escaped. . . ."

"Who, Lorj?" *I've got to stay calm—keep my voice as*
level as possible. Anything I do now might make things
worse. "Who's gone?"

Lorhaiden's mouth drew back in a snarl of feral hatred. He threw his sword at his feet, his body stiff with
barely controlled anger.

"Dhumaric!" he whispered in a raw voice. "*Dhumaric!*
Misbegotten, slime-bred, murderous perversion of life!"
Lorhaiden's voice had risen. He bent, snatched up his
sword, and started off toward the valley's far end. His
voice rose to a howl. "DHUMARIC!"

Kahsir glanced quickly over his shoulder at his father
and brother; their white faces stared back. "Get Vahl,"
he said. "Hurry! I'll try to keep him here."

He heard a horse gallop off. His attention had fixed
totally on Lorhaiden, who began muttering again. "Lorj,"
he said, and allowed a chill to enter his voice. "Leave
it, Lorj. You'll get another chance at him." He caught
up to his sword-brother, snatched at Lorhaiden's sleeve,

braced against the big man's strength. *Insult him. Maybe that will make him mad enough to forget Dhumaric.* "You brainless fool! Can't you see he's not here? Are you blind?" Lorhaiden pulled away. Kahsir's heart sank. He bit his lip and followed. "Come back to camp with us. You're all right, Lorj. You're alive. You can always catch him again."

There was a sound of hooves behind, of more than one returning horse, and Vàlkir's voice mixed in with Alàric's.

"Lorj," Kahsir said, finally getting a grip on his sword-brother's shoulders. He stepped in front of Lorhaiden, looked down into his eyes, into the witless stare. "Vahl's here. Aren't you going to greet him?"

Vàlkir appeared on Lorhaiden's other side. His face was pale but he seemed calm enough. "I've got him, Lord," he said and took Lorhaiden's arm.

"Dhumaric!" Lorhaiden cried once more. He appeared to focus slightly on Vàlkir, and some measure of reason crept into his expression.

Vàlkir put an arm around his brother's shoulders and turned him away. Kahsir could not hear what Vàlkir said as he led Lorhaiden off across the meadow, but the sound of Lorhaiden's sobs tore his heart in two.

"Kahs?"

Alàric's voice came from just behind. Kahsir turned around. His brother had dismounted and held the reins of both his horse and Kahsir's.

"Will he be all right?" Alàric asked, gesturing with his chin.

Kahsir glanced over his shoulder once more at Lorhaiden and Vàlkir, then looked back at Alàric.

"I think so. If anyone can talk him to reason, it's Vahl." He looked up as Xeredir rode to his side, jolted out of his concern for Lorhaiden. Now that he, his brother, and Xeredir had ridden away from the other warriors, the anger Xeredir had suppressed glittered in his eyes. Kahsir sought for something to say, something ordinary. "Father. Did Genlàvyn and her people reach you?"

"Aye. They're safe."

"Thank the Light for that." Kahsir took the reins from Alàric, swung up into the saddle, and looked once more at the now distant figures of Lorhaiden and Vàlkir. *If Vahl can't talk some reason into him, I don't know what we'll do.* He waited until his brother was mounted, then rode back toward where the Krotànya were gathering, his father and Alàric on either side.

"I haven't seen Genlàvyn in decades," Xeredir said, his voice near a conversational tone. "Her cousin Maiwyn certainly is beautiful."

"Maiwyn?" Kahsir gave his brother a sidelong glance. "Alàric seems to think so."

Alàric's face flushed slightly. "Now, wait a moment, Kahs. Just because—"

"I commend you on your taste, Ahri," Xeredir said with a smile.

Kahsir lifted an eyebrow at Alàric's expression and rode on.

The Krotànya warriors had gathered in fair order at the south end of the meadow. Few had been seriously hurt. Kahsir took off his helmet and wearily rubbed his forehead. A battle had been won here and, small that it was, any victory came as a welcome surprise to the Krotànya these days. Even though Dhumaric had somehow managed to escape.

Yet when he looked back at his father, Kahsir sensed another battle waiting, and one he dreaded more.

Xeredir dismounted and stretched the stiffness from his back and shoulders. Twilight had fallen, and the cooking fires of his camp shone welcome. He heard Haskon's voice, turned, and watched his three sons greet each other.

His hands clenched and he fought down a tightness

in his chest. *Dammit . . . I can't go off like this in front of everyone. But Kahs and I are going to have this out before night's over.*

"Haskon, Alàric!" They turned around. "Go tell my commanders we'll be having council after evening meal." Those two nodded and walked off into the fading light, Alàric recounting the battle in the meadows, his hands moving as he talked. Drawing a deep breath, Xeredir looked at Kahsir. "Let's sit down," he said, motioning behind at his tent.

His eldest son preceded him silently, then stood back, waiting to be the second to go inside. Xeredir's jaw clenched: *Does he truly not trust me to let him go first?*

The interior of the tent was lit by two hanging lamps. Xeredir gestured his son to one of the camp chairs and hooked the other one closer with his boot toe.

"So," Xeredir said, lowering himself into the chair and removing his helmet. "I think it's time you and I had a talk, Kahs. A deadly serious talk." He swallowed—his voice had risen in volume. He tried again, consciously keeping his tone quiet. "Do you have any idea what you've done, Kahs?"

Kahsir's eyes were level in a face that seemed made of stone. "Disobeyed you."

"Worse than that. You've set a precedent. Now, any time someone thinks they know better than their commanding officer, they'll— "

"Ah, *chuht*, Father!" Kahsir's voice was clipped and cold. "Are we Leishoranya or Krotànya? What happened to our freedom to question?"

"Freedom to question be damned! I'm talking about disobeying orders!"

"I see. And all orders must be obeyed, even if they're—" Kahsir glanced away. "—stupid."

"Dammit! Look at me, Kahs!" Xeredir made a conscious effort to unclench his hands. "You question my orders? Who the *firhkken* Dark do you think you are?"

Kahsir turned back, his eyes catching the light from the lamps. "Your equal on the field, Father. Your fellow commander. There are times you forget that."

Xeredir sat silent a moment. His heart gave an absurd little lurch in his chest. "Aye," he said, "I suppose I do. But, dammit, Kahs. What you did—"

"No one outside the family knows I disobeyed you."

"That's beside the point. The point is: you've totally destroyed all the plans your grandfather and I had laid for defense of the northlands."

"Defense?" Kahsir lifted one eyebrow. "Seems to me more like a retreat."

Xeredir stared, fought for breath, for words: breath came first. "If I didn't honor your mother, I'd swear she betrayed me and your father was a—"

"But she didn't," Kahsir said, and leaned back in his chair. "And I'm *your* son, and we've got to learn to live with each other."

"Dammit, Kahs! You're not infallible! You had no idea when you left for Rodja'âno that Ssenkahdavic was coming south!"

"And *you* didn't know it, either, did you, when you and Grandfather made your battle plans!"

"You listen to me," Xeredir grated. "Not only did you disobey me, disobey your grandfather, and take a command that wasn't yours, *but* you very likely brought Nhavari to his death!"

The look that crossed Kahsir's face made Xeredir flinch.

"Think it over, Kahs," he said, trying to sound reasonable. "Nhavari had been ordered to withdraw from Rodja'âno . . . no, not ordered, exactly, but the action was *strongly* suggested to him by both your grandfather and me. If—"

"That suggestion—"

"I'm not about to argue that now," Xeredir shouted,

"so save it and listen, will you? You're no idiot. Think it through. If you had stayed away from Rodja'âno, like you were ordered to, Nhavari would have seen the futility of staying to defend his city. But, oh no . . . you show up with some half-assed lie about me coming north with reinforcements. Of course he's going to stay. Why shouldn't he? He loved his city, his people, and he saw in your lie a chance to save them."

Kahsir leaned forward in his chair, his eyes ice in the lamplight. Before he could speak, Xeredir plunged on.

"Don't you see it, Kahs? He would have abandoned Rodja'âno, withdrawn his troops, and we'd be left with an army that hadn't been torn apart by the Leishoranya when the city fell."

"*And*, facing Ssenkahdavic, Father . . . a Ssenkahdavic fresh and in full possession of his Power. Even *you* have to admit that."

For a long moment, it seemed to Xeredir that neither he nor Kahsir moved. The tent grew so quiet that the sounds of the camp outside were clear. Xeredir drew a long breath.

"That's true. But you didn't know that, I didn't know that . . . for the Lords' sakes, even the Mind-Born didn't know!"

Kahsir's jaw tightened. "Then, thank the Light *one* of us in this family is lucky."

"That's the point exactly! You depend on your luck more than any commander I know. And I'll admit it, Kahs . . . sometimes it scares me spitless."

"Why? Because you can't write it down somewhere . . . order it up with a wave of the hand? What's so damned foul about being lucky?"

"You—"

Kahsir leaned forward and rested his arms on his knees. Xeredir could feel his son's tension. "There's no doubt you and I differ on tactics and on strategy. I can see virtue in many of your maneuvers. But we've *got* to make a stand sometime, or we'll find the enemy in the capital before winter."

Xeredir sighed quietly. "Kahs, Kahs. The north's all but gone now. Rodja'âno would have fallen anyway. Can't you see—"

"I see all too well. You expected me to leave a friend I've known nearly all my life to defend a city without any help from us, granted that he chose to stay despite your suggestions to pull out. You expected me to ignore the fact that we could have used Rodja'âno as a supply base, a center of operations in the north. If you had taken your four thousand men to Rodja'âno, we could have held the enemy longer."

"You're forgetting Ssenkahdavic," Xeredir said.

"No, I'm not. I'm talking about what we all did . . . you, Grandfather, me . . . *before* we knew Ssenkahdavic was coming south. What I'm trying to tell you is *why* I did what I did. You asked me to listen to you. Dammit! Listen to me!"

Xeredir held his son's gaze, then dropped his eyes to his clenched hands. "You realize we're going to have to come to some kind of understanding, or our entire command structure could fall apart. There can't be two opposing strategies here in the north."

Kahsir's shoulders stiffened. "I resigned my command," he said softly. "I sent you my ring as my word."

Xeredir saw the quick glitter of emotion in Kahsir's eyes. He pulled the heavy silver heir's ring from his left hand and extended it. *Lords, Kahs! Don't fight me so! We'll work it out. We have in the past.*

"Here's your ring back. I hope you never send it to me again." He watched Kahsir slip the heirloom on but was unable to read his son's shielded thoughts. "We're going to face each other at the council meeting, Kahs," he said, "and I know we're going to disagree. At least do me the favor of respecting my position as supreme commander here in the north."

"I will, Father." Again, that glitter of emotion in

Kahsir's eyes. "After all, I'll just be sitting in as an interested bystander."

Xeredir winced, hoped his son had not seen it. "You still have your command, Kahs . . . but it's where it's always been: the *southern* border. And for the Light's sake, don't ever fight in the same city with your two brothers again. Promise me that."

"You know none of us were aware the others were there. Besides, we made it out alive, didn't we?"

"Huhn. Be more careful of yourself, then."

"I'm not your only heir. There's Haskon, or Alàric, to say nothing of Iowyn."

"You know Haskon could never be King," Xeredir stated flatly. "He doesn't have the temperament for it. Alàric, perhaps. And Iowyn—well, she's less than steady. None of them were born to it like you. We're entering a new phase of this war and we need all the cool heads among us we can find. Now's not the time to take chances."

Kahsir smiled, a tired, gentle smile. "As you would expect, I disagree. There are times when we've got to take chances—great chances—if we're to win anything at all."

"Maybe. But I don't like to risk much for small reward."

And what did you do this very morning, if not that?

Xeredir flinched away from the inner voice. Kahsir sat staring at something only he could see on the tent wall, idly playing with the heir's ring on his right hand. *Aye . . . there are times when all men must take chances. And I've always fought conservatively. Kahs certainly isn't a hothead, but he's able to make intuitive leaps in judgment, to see things in a new light, to have vivid glimpses into alternate futures. And I don't find that easy. Am I jealous . . . jealous of my own son?*

He glanced at Kahsir, not really sure of the answer.

Things are changing: more young warriors fight with the armies and few of those men have cultivated pa-

tience. Soon, my way will become outmoded, and where will I be then? Xeredir shifted in his place by the fire, and buried himself deeper behind his shields. *For that matter, where will any of us be?*

Night was not far off. Tsingar longed to stop at the next place that offered protective cover, but Dhumaric would make that decision, not he. His minor wound had become a dull pain which sharpened whenever his horse stumbled. He dared a look behind at the other warriors who had survived the Krotànya surprise attack. There were around thirty of them, and most bore wounds as well.

And among them, the Gods of Chance be cursed, was Chaagut.

Tsingar looked back at Dhumaric, who rode stiff-shouldered a few paces ahead; even *he* had been wounded. It was a small slash across his sword arm, yet the fact that he had been touched by any of the Krotànya seemed a greater pain than the sword cut itself.

Dhumaric had led the way north all day, toward the abandoned steading Kahsir had fled from, and territory where other Leishoranya war bands might be waiting. Too weakened by battle and all the maneuvering beforehand, they had been held to the world's roads and so had made terrible time. No one had spoken during the journey: a tense, grim silence gripped them all.

By all the Gods, I've seen Dhumaric fail! He blundered and blundered badly. He hates Kahsir so much it distracted him, kept him from acting with a clear mind. He kept going long after he should have, considering the number of men he lost. I hate Kahsir too, but— Tsingar shifted uncomfortably in the saddle, wiped the end of his nose, and peered at Dhumaric's broad back. *The chance to capture not only Kahsir but Lorhaiden must have been a lure too strong to resist.*

His horse stumbled again. He cursed silently and burrowed deeper behind his shields. *Gods! What's*

Ssenkahdavic going to say about this? Or the Queen?
He grimaced. *Perhaps we'd all be better off if Dhumaric was kept from going after Kahsir.*

Dhumaric turned around, glanced over his shoulder, his face expressionless in the dusk. Tsingar's heart thudded unevenly.

"Tsingar. Scout ahead and find a campsite. We'll rest tonight. We've far to go before we find any of our people."

Tsingar bowed low in the saddle. He drew a deep breath, rode off, and began the search for a place to stop.

Kahsir sat on the ground next to his father's chair and watched the commanders take their places for the council meeting. He shifted to one side and looked for Lorhaiden. *Where the Dark is he? I haven't seen him or Vàlkir since leaving the battlefield. If Vahl's not making some progress—*

He shrugged and glanced at the commanders again. They were all so young. Most of them probably had not been born when the war had begun. Though it was difficult to guess ages, one of the men who sat opposite looked no more than a hundred years old. Kahsir snorted softly. *It's so hard to talk to them sometimes. They're too damned impatient! So many of us older ones, the veterans, are dead.*

He frowned again. *Don't think of dying! You'll see the end of this war.* The high walls of Rodja'âno stood again in his memory; brief scatters of future events, of faces and places yet unseen, flashed in his mind. And behind them, Ssenkahdavic's figure loomed, waiting in the darkness.

Kahsir looked up: his father had risen from his camp chair and was facing the assembled commanders.

"Now that Rodja'âno's fallen, we're in danger of losing the northlands." Xeredir paused and looked slowly around. "The enemy already controls the northern part of Tumâs. The territory south of Rodja'âno is the only buffer we have now between Ssenkahdavic and the Kingdom of Elyâsai. Four thousand men rode down from the Golondai with us. That's a large force, but compared to the army that took Rodja'âno, it's nothing."

Kahsir caught movement to one side: Lorhaiden and Vàlkir. Other commanders had noticed the late arrival, too; as the brothers joined the seated semicircle of warriors that surrounded Xeredir, men whispered quietly to each other, some drawing back from Lorhaiden, eyeing him with distrust. Kahsir tried to catch his sword-brother's eyes.

Lords! The story of Lorhaiden's fit must be all over camp. Who the dark besides Father and Alàric was there to see it? He looked carefully at Lorhaiden in the firelight. His face was calm now and his eyes had lost their feverish glitter. Vàlkir must have been able to talk him back to reason. Kahsir sighed quietly. *Damn you, Lorj! How do I convince everyone you're still not stark raving mad?*

"We've got another problem besides trying to stop the enemy," Xeredir was saying. "The refugees. We damned well can't take them into battle with us, but we're going to have to move north quickly to shore up our defensive lines. Errehmon and the other commanders at Rodja'âno retreated southwest to Aigenhal. We've got to join forces with them. And the fighters who fled Chilufka are going to need help. That takes us back to the refugees."

One of the hundred-commanders looked up. "It would take fewer warriors to ride back to safety with them, Lord, than to protect them here."

"That's true." Xeredir was silent for a moment, and Kahsir craned his head to see who had spoken. "But the way's long. Many of the refugees are physically exhausted, in a state of shock. They've got children with them, and their wagons aren't made for that kind of travel."

"I agree with Denahr, Lord," said Vàlkir. "The refugees won't be traveling into danger. As far as we know, no Leishoranya have penetrated south of here. The refugees only need few warriors to guide them, a few talented to help them make that speed. The rest of us could march north and set up our defensive lines."

"We can make a stand here," Lorhaiden inserted, gesturing behind at where the snow-covered mountains stood hidden in the night. "If we're successful, the enemy won't have any choice but to go west around the mountains instead of straight south."

No one spoke for a long moment. The commanders looked at Lorhaiden as if only now acknowledging his presence.

"That's the direction they plan to take anyway, Lorj," Kahsir said, turning to look at Lorhaiden. "Nothing much lies south of the Golondai that other Leishoranya armies haven't taken or won't take soon. Oh, they'll try for the mountains; it's the most direct way south. But I'll bet they send the great bulk of their army to the southwest, *around* the Golondai. They're after the Kingdom of Elyâsai now, *baràdor*, and the capital." He glanced sidelong at his father, remembering what Xeredir's original plans had been. "We should make these mountains our allies. There are only a few passes open this early in the year: we can destroy all the ways in."

"Destroy?" This from the young hundred-commander Kahsir had stared at, a man obviously new to his post.

"Aye," Kahsir nodded. "Grandfather destroyed nearly all the passes across the Mountains of Shadow. Why can't we do the same here?"

He felt his father's stare and looked up.

"It could be done," Xeredir admitted. "The refugees could set off as soon as possible to the southwest. We could leave our engineers and some of the Mind-Born behind to fortify the approaches to any pass the enemy might find attractive. Then we could march north, and throw up our defensive lines there and to the west after we've destroyed the passes."

Haskon snorted something and dug in the ground between his feet with a stray piece of kindling. "We don't have enough men to even give Ssenkahdavic much of a pause," he said bitterly, "especially if his army turns south all at once."

"Ssenkahdavic won't leave Rodja'âno for some time yet," Vàlkir said. Most of the men gathered around the fire nodded in agreement. "Take it from one who was there when the city fell: he used too much energy destroying it. Even *he* has his limits."

"He won't leave soon, aye, that's sure," Kahsir said. "But his armies are going to come southward much faster than any of the Leishoranya high command had thought at first."

He saw a few puzzled looks from the men around him. "Look," he said, and reached out to sketch an imaginary map before them. "They've already set up a fairly narrow corridor to Rodja'âno, which I'm sure they're filling as rapidly as they can with men from their other armies. Now we were chased even farther south of Rodja'âno by Dhumaric. Though we defeated him, I'll bet he's not given up the chase yet. Behind him, he left another narrow corridor, which is going to be more difficult to fill than the one leading *to* Rodja'âno. For a while, both these corridors will be empty, to a certain extent."

Kahsir paused, feeling his father's stare.

"If we're able to make contact with the four to five thousand men who survived the fall of Rodja'âno, plus any fighters we can draw in from the forests, we'll have a force close to ten thousand. Granted, that's not much compared to the twenty thousand that took Rodja'âno, but it's enough."

"We could always send for reinforcements," another of the younger men suggested.

Kahsir frowned, leaned forward, and rested his arms on his knees. "That's an attractive idea. Where the Dark are we going to get them? The enemy's moving west now from the old capital of Legânoi; they're coming north from Kakordicum. We're facing action on three fronts. We can't draw warriors off the other two."

"You said close to ten thousand men are enough," Xeredir said. "I think I see what you're after. Explain."

"If we can make ourselves mobile enough, we can strike at both sides of these corridors."

"With only ten thousand men? That won't hold the enemy."

Kahsir looked up at his father. "True. But it will slow them down."

Vàlkir nodded emphatically.

"We've done it before, Lord," another commander said to Xeredir. "Of course, we can't hold the enemy, but picking away at those corridors won't help them."

"I agree with what Vahl said," Lorhaiden stated. "Ssenkahdavic won't be leaving Rodja'âno for a while—not until summer, if then. If we can attack the enemy *before* they can consolidate their armies, we'll have a chance to do some real damage."

Kahsir glanced back at his father.

Xeredir shifted his weight uneasily. "What about our defensive lines? What you've proposed means dividing our forces—"

"You've just said we can't hold Ssenkahdavic back." Kahsir caught his father's eye. *Quit looking for excuses, Father. Follow our reasoning, will you?* "Why should it matter if we divide our forces or not? Besides, it will make it a lot easier for Errehmon and the other men who escaped Rodja'âno. They won't have to wait for us to link a defensive line to theirs."

Silence fell on the assembly. Kahsir held his father's gaze, daring him to speak.

"Kahsir's right, Lord," Vàlkir said. "If we split our army into smaller units, we'll be more mobile. We know this country; the enemy doesn't. We could use that to our advantage."

"If we can keep Ssenkahdavic from marching westward," added another hundred-commander, "he'll turn south and try to cross the Golondai. And with the passes destroyed, *and* fortified, that's going to take some time."

Kahsir watched his father closely. Xeredir had earned the reputation for being a brilliant commander—brilliant, but conservative. And now that conservatism was holding him back.

Look beyond the small maneuvers, Father! See what could happen several jumps away. Think, Father—think! Trust your intuition. You've chosen the offensive position in the past. Do it again!

"Aye," Xeredir said at last. "It's a good plan . . . a plan that should work. Besides, we don't have much choice."

Kahsir let loose his breath, only then aware he had been holding it, waiting to see if his father would agree with him.

"First, we'll gather what Mind-Born we have among us and talk to them about destroying the passes. If they refuse—" Xeredir shrugged wearily. "Kahs, I want you in charge of the refugees. You, Lorhaiden, Vàlkir, and Alàric. See that those folk reach safety. Haskon, you and I will work with the other commanders on our strategy. Let's all meet here again tomorrow morning. We've got a lot to do and little time to waste."

Tsingar sat in the darkness, a cold trickle of sweat running down the side of his face. He was exhausted by the ride from the Krotànya ambush, and his wound hurt abominably, but he used what little of his strength was left to hide behind his shields. As long as Dhumaric did not notice him, he felt safe.

Another long, wailing moan filled the clearing where Dhumaric had chosen to stop. Tsingar winced. Four men had died already at Dhumaric's hands, and now the fifth was nearly spent, his mental and physical strength leached from him by Dhumaric's need.

For Dhumaric planned to take the mind-road to Rodja'âno, to ask for reinforcements to go after Kahsir. To do so, exhausted as the Great Lord was, he needed strength he did not have.

Tsingar shuddered and thanked the Gods that he had not been the only one to survive the Krotànya ambush in the meadows.

The candle flames danced and wavered as Aeschu leaned back in the chair at the end of the small room outside her husband's chambers. She looked at Dhumaric, who stood before her, white-faced, smelling like something dead and too long unburied.

You fool! You go after Kahsir as my husband ordered, lose men to traps and ambushes, but keep on, beyond your ordered point of disengagement. And then you lose all your men but thirty. You've got nerve, my lord, haven't you, to come back here, begging for more.

"And how many men would you need, my Lord?" she said aloud, leaning her chin in an opened hand, her elbow propped up by the chair arm. "Another five hundred? A thousand?"

"Lady, please keep in mind that the men I'm asking for are not only for me. I have an open corridor behind me, leading from Rodja'âno to the steading by the river. If I'm to go after Kahsir, I can't afford to have Krotànya coming at my back."

"And you think they will?"

Dhumaric snorted a laugh. "Oh, aye, lady. And with a vengeance. I found that out the hard way."

"And why should I let you set out again after Kahsir? He's escaped you once, twice . . . how many more times, my Lord? Five or six?" Dhumaric's face went very stiff. "We'll track him down someday. We've got all the time in the world to do it. Why now, my Lord? What's the rush?"

"Lady, please remember that not only do we have a chance to go after Kahsir, but Haskon, Alàric, *and* Xeredir. *All* the heirs of the Krotànya High-King. Their deaths would be one of the greatest blows we could strike against the Krotànya. I think this merits more attention than you're giving."

Aeschu stared at Dhumaric, allowing no expression to cross her face. "You may be right, my Lord. But I can't give you men without being answerable to my husband, so if I do, you had best be sure you win." She let a small smile touch her lips. "You do understand, don't you . . . *you* would be responsible to him for those men . . . not I."

Dhumaric kept silent, but she sensed his unease, despite his heavy shielding.

"Again, my Lord . . . how many men do you require?"

"Fifty thousand, Lady."

"Fifty thousand? You seem to expect heavy fighting."

"Not necessarily. The corridor must be stabilized. We must have our supply lines. . . ." He waved one hand. "You know all this, Lady. I, personally, won't need that many men to follow me."

"And what of Xeredir? How many warriors does he lead? Still the four thousand that my husband sensed ride with him?"

"I think so."

Aeschu sat silent for a moment. Fifty thousand men. Dhumaric was correct that he had forced a corridor into Krotànya territory that must either be strengthened or abandoned. And fifty thousand might not be enough. Double that number, and the corridor could not only be maintained, but widened.

And Dhumaric? She watched him as he stood before her, full of his stolen strength. Dangerous, this one . . . very dangerous. Why should he get the glory for taking Kahsir and his family? That was a pleasure she would rather give to her husband. Besides, it was only a matter of time before the Krotànya would be utterly beaten.

She smiled again.

"All right, my Lord. I give you five thousand men to go after Kahsir and—" She waved a hand southward. "—any of his family you can find." *If you're so good, you won't need more, will you?* "I'll also send warriors behind you to stabilize the corridor. Who did you leave behind with what was left of your men?"

"My second in command, Tsingar lur Totuhofka chi Higulen."

"You have his exact location?"

"Aye, lady."

"Very well. Rest here this evening. Tomorrow, I'll need that location so I can transfer it to the minds of the troops who will be under your command. You can expect these men within several days. I'll have to call them in from units already in the field."

Dhumaric bowed slightly.

"If you don't have anything else to say, my Lord," Aeschu said, leaning back in her chair, watching Dhumaric with hooded eyes, "you may go."

He bowed again, deeper this time, and left the room. For a long while, Aeschu stared at the door Dhumaric had walked through.

And win or die, my Lord. It's all up to you.

The last of the commanders walked off from the fire. Kahsir glanced at Lorhaiden and Vàlkir, at his brothers, and then at his father.

"When should the refugees leave?" he asked.

"Tomorrow, if they can." Xeredir lowered himself back into his camp chair, and rubbed at the bridge of his nose. "At the latest, the day after. We've got to get those people out of here quickly. If we divide our forces, we'll need all the maneuverability possible."

"And after we've seen the refugees to safety?" Alàric asked.

"Continue on south to the capital." Kahsir jerked his eyes up to his father's face. "And don't give me that look, Kahs. You've all been out here too long now as it is. It's time you rested."

"But, Lord." Lorhaiden leaned forward from his sitting position, his hands moving in nervous gestures. "You've been fighting for a long time, too. You'll need help here. We could always come back."

"No. I'll have enough commanders. Kahs is right. There's war to the south and east. And the weather is a lot better than here in the north—which means a push there if it follows pattern."

Kahsir felt anger build up inside. His chest tightened with it and he struggled to keep the words he wanted to say from tumbling out. *Adopt my ideas, and then send me home like some whipped dog? Damn you, father! Can't you let me help you?* He drew a long breath, and looked away.

"I want you all to take at least a ten-day's rest in the capital," Xeredir said, and his mouth thinned into a frown. "And I expect you to stay that long and not rush off. I'll talk to Vlàdor about it."

Alàric yawned. "We'd better let the refugees know they're moving."

"Aye. And early, too, if they can." Xeredir moved closer to the fire and its warmth. "They've got to understand how quickly they must move. You do it, Ahri. You'll have an excuse to visit Genlàvyn and her cousin."

Kahsir glanced at Alàric: his youngest brother had never been as taken by a woman as he had by this cousin of Genlàvyn's. Caught between weariness and Xeredir's baiting, Alàric merely shrugged.

"Who knows, Ahri," Kahsir said. "Since I'm in charge of this, I could have you ride with those two ladies all the way back to Hvâlkir."

"I'll *fihrkken* ride by myself if you don't leave me alone."

"Everyone's ready for bed," Xeredir said. "Go, Ahri. I'll talk to you all tomorrow."

Kahsir watched Alàric, Lorhaiden, and Vàlkir leave the fire. Lorhaiden was always moody and depressed when kept from battle, but he needed rest as much as any other warrior. Kahsir smiled. A few days in the capital certainly would be welcome. The only problem he could foresee would be handling Lorhaiden.

"Kahs."

He looked up from the fire. Everyone else had gone—he and his father were alone.

"I saw that look you threw me when I said you were going back to the capital. Do you understand why?"

Kahsir held his father's gaze. "You want me out of your sight. That's obvious, isn't it?"

"Don't, Kahs. I want you to return to your own command—"

"Which I don't have right now."

"It's yours to take. I told you that."

"Can't you see that I want to stay here?" Kahsir asked. "This isn't exactly your type of fighting—no, no . . . I didn't mean for it to sound that way. It's just. . . ." He shrugged. "I'm good at what you plan to do, that's all. And I owe it to Nhavari to help his people."

"You have helped his people," Xeredir said, and Kahsir was startled at the gentleness of his father's voice. "Now help me by going back to your army and leaving me to mine."

For a long moment Kahsir stared at his father, then looked away.

"And Kahs . . . I'm worried about Lorhaiden. You saw how the other men looked at him when he and Vahl came to council. I'll tell you, what I saw today makes me nervous. Watch him closely, will you?"

"When haven't I watched him?" Kahsir asked. "He's always difficult between actions."

"Huhn. Seems to me he was more than just difficult this time," Xeredir said.

Kahsir shifted uncomfortably. He grasped for an excuse. "Dhumaric's escape drove him to the brink."

"And not over it? No, no. Don't answer. It's that damned Oath of his." Xeredir spoke with genuine vehemence, anger and frustration in his voice. "It's destroying him. He could be a good commander if he wasn't so caught up in revenge."

"Aye. But he's rational enough to hold himself back from sheer idiocy. I think."

"You hope. He'd better be, or he'll never command anything, not even himself. And what I saw today doesn't give him much credit for sanity."

You don't know Lorhaiden like I do, Father. There's still something worth loving in him. "Maybe. But he hasn't let me down yet."

"The Light forbid there's a first time. He behaves because you ride him close. You told me that yourself. And he needs his rest, too. Make sure he gets it, even if you have to hit him over the head to ensure it."

Kahsir grinned at the thought. "I think now that Hairon's elected himself Lorhaiden's shieldman, I won't have to watch Lorj that closely."

"He's that good, then?"

"Hairon? I'm not sure 'good' would describe it. They're total opposites, the two of them. I think Hairon will hold Lorhaiden in check when I'm not around." He glanced down at his feet. "There are times when Hairon thinks Lorhaiden's a bit mad."

"Well, he's not the only one." Xeredir scratched at his beard. "How can Lorhaiden be an effective commander if his own men think he's crazy?"

Kahsir shook his head. "He's handled things well enough. He took orders. He saved my life, dammit, at Rodja'âno. He's not as unbalanced as everyone thinks."

"Well, then, he'd better start learning to act like it."

"I'll talk to him," Kahsir said. *And how, when any*

mention of the Oath sets him off? "But not now. Dhumaric's escape is still too fresh in his mind. Maybe after we get back to the capital."

"And what about Dhumaric, Kahs? Having him loose in the northlands bothers me."

"It should." A log on the fire cracked loudly. Kahsir flinched and glanced out beyond the firelight at the clustered shadows before he looked back at his father. "While Dhumaric was chasing me through the forest, I kept asking myself why out of all the Leishoranya to be on my tail it had to be him. And he *will* be back. He doesn't like to lose, that one."

CHAPTER 12

Alàric left Xeredir's fire behind and walked off toward his tent. At least his father and Kahsir had not come to blows yet, but he sensed that the two of them had exchanged more than civil words. Not for the first time did he thank the Lords he was not in Kahsir's place.

What the two of them planned to do about their differences was anyone's guess. Alàric had seen the look Kahsir had shot Xeredir when told he was being sent back to the capital. It was a delicate situation: neither Xeredir nor Kahsir was willing to move from his position, yet each seemed to have reached the conclusion that further fighting between them would make things worse.

The refugees had gathered at the west end of his father's camp—far enough away that he would have to ride to them. He frowned, looked back over his shoulder at his father and eldest brother, remembered their words, and felt his ears burn. *Can't leave me alone, can you? So I'm behaving like I'm love-struck. Huhn.* Everything he had said, every pointed remark made when Kahsir had fallen in love with Eltàrim, came back to him. *I suppose Kahs has every right to go after me. I didn't show him much pity then.*

His horse stood tethered behind his tent; Alàric sighed quietly and bent to pick up his saddle. Maiwyn's face had frequently been in his mind since the meeting on the trail south of Chilufka. He drew the cinch tight, let the stirrup fall back in place, and reached down for his bridle. *Now what do I do? No one's ever affected me like this. Does she feel the same toward me? And if she does, will she acknowledge it?* He frowned: the House of dàn Iofharsen, though old, was only of minor nobility. And he was the High-King's grandson.

Alàric swung up into the saddle and rode off into the darkness, his grey horse still worn out from battle. He rubbed his chin and sat back in the saddle. *I'd better let things take their course. If I rush in, I could spoil everything. I'll know soon if she was as affected as I was.*

The refugees had settled down into an orderly collection of tents and wagons grouped around large fires. Each of these individual fires represented some head of House or some spontaneously elected leader. Xeredir had given the refugees whatever help he could, so they might have been far worse off than they were.

The sights and smells of each camp Alàric visited sank into his memory. Firelight flickered on the sides of wagons and tents, on the anxious faces of the people he passed. No one spoke loudly save the younger children, who likely did not understand what had happened. The attitude of most of the refugees vacillated between stunned disbelief and a growing rage over the loss of their kin, their homes, their way of life, and their hope.

Alàric grew hungry from smelling the odors of cooking food, though he had eaten before council. After a while, he lost count of the number of people he talked to. The refugees were a mixed lot—minor nobility, farmers, traders, landholders, and Rodja'âno townsfolk. Young children cried in the distance as their mothers put them to bed, while the older ones stood wide-eyed in the firelight to watch as he rode by. Not one of the refugees had complained about leaving in the morning. They seemed anxious to put as much distance possible between themselves and the nightmare of Rodja'âno.

And I'm going away, too. Alàric reined in his horse between two wagons and rubbed his eyes. *Father's right. We need to rest. At least I know I'm coming back north . . . though without Nhavari, things won't be the same.*

He straightened in the saddle. Only one fire was left to visit—Genlàvyn's. He turned his horse, lifted the reins, and trotted off through the darkness toward the Chilufka camp. Eager hands helped as he dismounted, and several warriors he had met at the ford called his name in greeting. He waved at those men and then turned from his horse to face Genlàvyn.

"My Lord Alàric," she said, bowing. "Welcome to our fire. What are you doing here?"

Maiwyn—where was she? He glanced around but did not see her. "Father thought it best if all the refugees leave for the south. Can you and your people be ready by tomorrow morning?"

"I'm sure we can. Are you staying here, Lord?"

"No. Father chose Kahsir, Lorhaiden, Vàlkir, and me to ride with you to safety."

"That's good news, Lord. I'll feel more protected now."

The voice came from behind, low-pitched and melodious. Alàric's heart skipped a beat and he slowly turned around. She stood quietly in the firelight, her white-blond hair aflame.

"My Lady Maiwyn," he said, bowing slightly.

"I'm glad you're riding with us," Genlàvyn said. "We couldn't be in better hands. And since I never had the chance to thank you, I'll do it now. Your arrival at the ford turned things in our favor. And your father came to help us, though I was surprised that he came himself."

"So was I," Alàric admitted. He felt Maiwyn's stare. "We'll be gathering in the fields to the west after morning meal. If you need anything else, let me or my father know."

Genlàvyn nodded. "Would you care for something to drink? We managed to bring some wine with us from Chilufka."

Alàric hesitated—Maiwyn was still staring. "That sounds good. I'm a bit parched after all the talking I've done."

"Has everyone agreed to leave tomorrow morning?" Genlàvyn asked.

"Aye." He followed her and Maiwyn toward their tent. "Everyone I've talked to is anxious to go."

"I'm not surprised." Genlàvyn's rage and loss spilled out from behind her shields. "I'd like to be out of here as soon as possible myself. Too many bad memories."

Maiwyn walked alongside her cousin's guest and could not keep from looking at him. He was even taller than she remembered. Not as tall as his brother, Kahsir, but few men could equal that height. Alàric was also a rarity among the Star-Born: he had been born blond, which was unusual for one of the Royal House (though his forefather, Ràthen, had been nearly as blond). A short beard broadened his already prominent jaw, and his level, grey-blue eyes were set deep beneath straight brows. He was a handsome man, but she had not been affected merely by his good looks; it was something deeper and more powerful than outward appearance.

Many legends existed concerning the royal family: and since the enemy invasion, those legends had increased. Vlàdor, the High-King; his son, Xeredir; Xeredir's three sons and his daughter . . . Maiwyn frowned slightly. Legends were only people, flesh and blood like any others; yet she knew so little but tales about the person she walked beside.

Genlàvyn gestured to several folding chairs in front of

her tent. As Alàric sat down, Genlàvyn took her place beside him, and Maiwyn hastily sat down in her own chair. One of her cousin's retainers brought wine. The expression on Alàric's face as he drank showed just how thirsty he had been. He glanced in her direction, their eyes met, and she looked away, down into her cup.

Lords! What's the matter with me? Why am I so totally confused? It's as if—

"I'll be staying in the capital for at least a ten-day after we arrive," Alàric was saying. Maiwyn glanced up, her heart skipping a beat. She and her cousin were headed to Hvâlkir, to stay with kinfolk of Genlàvyn's late husband. "Father wants my brothers and me to rest before we go back to war again."

"You're probably looking forward to that," said Genlàvyn. "Has it been a while since you've been away from the fighting?"

"Aye. Still, I'm not aching to lie around doing nothing."

"We're going to Hvâlkir ourselves, though most of my people will stop north of there to stay with kin. Some of my husband's House live in the capital—the dàn Ahrmendha—and until I've relocated myself and reestablished my network of fighters, we'll be staying with them. I'd like to invite you to dinner some night. It's small payment for the help you've given us."

Maiwyn's heart skipped a beat. *Lords of Light! What's Vynni doing? Doesn't she know that—*

"Thanks," Alàric said. "I'll remember that." He turned slightly. "Have you ever been to Hvâlkir before, Maiwyn?"

She started and hoped he had not seen. "No, Lord. I've heard the city is beautiful."

"It is. And large. I'm glad you have kin there. They can help you find your way around at first. Have you lived in the north all your life?"

She nodded. "I was born in Fânchorion and left just before the city fell."

"Ah? I was in Fânchorion, too, at the end."

"I know, Lord. I saw you once from a great distance when you stood on the walls. My father and brothers stayed behind to defend the city and sent me away before the siege began. They all died there. My mother was killed in an accident years before, so I've been living with my cousin."

"I'm sorry," Alàric said. "I didn't mean to remind you of such things."

"There's no need to apologize, Lord. I've lived with those memories for the past nineteen years. My father and brothers died where they wanted to, doing what they thought best."

For another brief instant, his eyes met hers. She glanced away, and for a long moment sat silent while Alàric and Genlàvyn discussed the order of riding for tomorrow. Camp sounds flooded back: the crackling of the fire in front of the tent, dogs barking in the distance, the low murmur of voices close by.

Alàric set his empty cup down beside his chair. "I've got to be going," he said and stood. "Morning will be here sooner than we think. All of us should try to get a good night's sleep."

Maiwyn rose from her chair only a moment after Genlàvyn stood.

"Again, my thanks for all your help," Genlàvyn said.

Alàric bowed slightly. Maiwyn's heart leapt to her throat as he turned in her direction.

"I'll look forward to seeing you tomorrow," he said, smiling. It was a smile that made him appear a much younger man. "We can ride together for a while and you can tell me of your life in Fânchorion."

Maiwyn nodded, not trusting her voice. A man-at-arms held the horse for Alàric as he mounted, and Maiwyn looked around just in time to see him ride out of the firelight into the darkness.

"Wynna."

Maiwyn looked at her cousin.

"What's going on between you two?" Genlàvyn asked, gesturing after Alàric.

"What do you mean?"

"Ah, you don't even know—or do you?"

"Know what?"

"He's utterly captivated by you. You'd have to be blind to miss it."

Maiwyn glanced away, trying to hide the expression on her face.

"And you," Genlàvyn pushed on, "you're just as taken with him."

"I wasn't sure if that was true." Maiwyn looked back at her cousin. "I don't know what happened. I've never felt this way before."

"Lords, Wynna! You're a beautiful woman. You had suitors in Fânchorion when you were growing up."

"Too many of them. They were all so—so ordinary. None of them made me feel the way Alàric does."

"This whole thing began back on the trail, didn't it?"

"Aye." She groped for words, anything to say what she felt. "When I met him there, my whole world seemed to change. One moment I was myself, and the next. . . . I never thought anyone could affect me so."

"Maybe the two of you are bound by your *Dogor*. Perhaps it was fated that you meet on that trail."

Maiwyn gestured helplessly. "Maybe. I'm so confused right now I can't think straight."

"I understand," Genlàvyn said with a small laugh. "I felt much the same when I met Tomasàr before we were married."

Maiwyn nodded. *We can ride together*, Alàric had said. Her heart suddenly soared. Maybe Genlàvyn was right—it could be that she and Alàric shared a common *Dogor* that had led them to that shadowy trail.

Both hands clasped around the wine cup she carried, Maiwyn walked a short distance away from the fire. She closed her eyes, lifted the cup, and rested her chin on its edge. *My fate? What is my fate? And tonight—?*

Who would ever have thought this could be happening to me?

Alàric rode through the darkness to his own tent, everything he passed blending into a solid blur. *It's certain! I'm as affected seeing her the second time as the first. And, if I'm not mistaken, she's been touched by the same feelings.* It was a strange emotion. Love: not *uvelo*, the love of family, kin, places, and things, but true *uvaiah*, the love of a man for a woman. *Uvaiah*—a three-pronged love of soul, sex, and mind.

Tomorrow. He would see her tomorrow and for a long while after: the journey to Hvâlkir would take many days if the refugees kept mainly to the world's roads. He smiled. *I've never felt like this before. And after all I said to Kahs when he fell in love with Eltàrim— If only I'd understood then what I know now. And Haskon? Lords! If he starts in—*

His tent loomed up. He looked around, briefly disoriented, then sat up straighter in the saddle. Both Kahsir and his father sat waiting beside the fire. From their stillness, he could tell they had been there for some time.

"Kahs. Father." He dismounted and let the reins drop. "I thought you'd be asleep by now. Where's Haskon?"

"He's asleep," Xeredir said. "We wanted to hear what you found out when you visited the refugees. Are they willing to leave come morning?"

"Aye. No one complained. A few people want to leave nearer mid-morning than right after sunrise."

"I don't see why not. At least they'll go tomorrow and not the day after."

"It's over two thousand leagues from here to Hvâlkir, and that's a long ride," Kahsir said. "Since any steadings we pass the first few days may be abandoned and destroyed, we'll have to hunt on our way south."

"I expected as much." Alàric sat down beside his

brother and father. He sighed, leaned back on his elbows, and stretched his feet out toward the warmth of the fire.

"I can't see you going all the way by the world's roads," Xeredir said. "Trained warriors and scouts could make that ride in thirty days if they had remounts and pressed themselves. It would probably take unskilled riders around a hundred days. The military situation's bad enough that you'll have to make it sooner. We need you back at your commands."

Alàric saw his eldest brother stiffen, and cleared his throat. "Two thousand leagues? If we alternate between the mind-road and normal travel, we can cut the journey near in half."

Kahsir nodded. "We'll have to start out by jumping short distances. Maybe the refugees who aren't used to traveling long distances will get better at it."

Alàric shifted position. It would not be easy shepherding the refugees south, wagons and livestock and all. At least Kahsir would be there to help. And Vàlkir. Alàric smiled. He had always been close to the youngest of the Hrudharic brothers. But Lorhaiden? He looked from his father to Kahsir. "How's Lorhaiden taking being sent back to Hvâlkir?"

Kahsir shrugged. "You saw him when he left council. He'll be difficult to handle, but I think I can do it."

Better you than me. "Good luck, Kahs. I think you're going to need it."

"How was Genlàvyn?" asked Xeredir. Alàric glanced up at his father, but the question was serious. "Does she have everything she needs?"

Alàric nodded, then glanced at his brother. "No, Kahs. Don't you start in on me again. I've had about all I can take for one day."

Kahsir raised an eyebrow in mock dismay. "Touchy, aren't you? I was going to ask how the Lady Maiwyn was, that's all."

"Huhn," Alàric grunted and looked away. *I'll just bet you were.*

"I'll let the subject drop. For now." Kahsir grinned. "Of course, I can't speak for Haskon. He's—"

"Come, Kahs." Xeredir stood and motioned his eldest son to his feet. "You two could go on all night like this. Remember, Ahri. We still have council tomorrow before you leave."

"Aye, Father. I'll see you then."

Alàric sat his horse in the morning sunlight, his reins held loosely in one hand. The first of the refugee wagons had started on its way out of camp, the others jostling behind to get in line. Alàric had a fair idea of how many wagons would be making the trip south. When he added in those who, like Chilufka's folk, had horses aplenty but no wagons, the size of the column was greater than he liked. *Strung out like this, we're an easy target. We'll have to be damned careful.*

"They're in fair order, Ahri," his father said. "They'll make it all right."

"Lords, I hope so." Alàric had to speak loudly over the noise. People called to one another, horses neighed, and dogs barked from within the wagons. The rumble of wheels on the ground grew louder as more wagons began to roll. Alàric glanced sidelong at Xeredir, who had nudged his horse closer. "I don't foresee any problems, but—"

"You've got a hundred warriors with you, and you're headed south, away from any enemy we know of."

"Look." Kahsir sat to Alàric's right. "Genlàvyn must have found a wagon for herself. That's her white cat over there."

Alàric followed the line of his brother's pointing finger. A wagon not far back in the line was starting forward; the woman sitting in front had a caged cat on the seat beside her. Alàric looked for Maiwyn but did not see her.

"Kahs, Ahri—you'd better be going," Xeredir said. "Try to make the best time you can without pushing the refugees to exhaustion. Take the mind-road more often than you would normally, and for shorter distances at first. I don't think you'll have to worry much about the enemy, but don't go lightly on your watch."

Alàric glanced away from the refugees to his father's face. The hurt and anger still showed to his family eye, but evidently some of the conversation Xeredir and Kahsir had shared last night had helped the situation. He looked at his brother. Kahsir sat a bit stiffly in the saddle, and when he spoke it was terse—he was obviously still upset about being sent away from the northern fighting.

"Take care, Kahs," Xeredir said, touching his eldest son's shoulder. "And you, Ahri. Keep in touch on your way."

"I'll be back, Father," Alàric said, "to join you and Haskon."

Xeredir motioned toward his camp. "We should be here, but if not, we'll leave signs."

Kahsir reined his horse around and set off toward the wagons. For a long moment, Alàric held his father's eyes, then turned and rode after his brother.

CHAPTER 13

Morning sunlight slanted down through the trees around the campsite and warmed the clearing somewhat. From where Tsingar sat, he could see nearly all the men who had escaped with Dhumaric from the Krotànya ambush. They had made camp in a large clearing on the south side of the river that bordered the destroyed steading. A few other stragglers had come in after Dhumaric had taken the mind-road back to Rodja'âno, bringing the total number of warriors to thirty-eight.

Tsingar shivered and shifted position. Only Dhumaric and a few of the other Great Lords would dare bother Ssenkahdavic or his Queen with requests—especially after blundering as badly as had Dhumaric. But now the Great Lord was back, bearing news that the Queen herself had promised him five thousand men, *and* would send thousands more to fill the empty corridor to the south of Rodja'âno.

Drawing a deep breath, Tsingar glanced around the clearing once more. Within several days, Dhumaric would have enough men to form an army, and would then follow any trail or hint that would lead him to

Kahsir. Tsingar had ordered several scouts south, but none had returned yet. He stretched and looked around the clearing. Chaagut sat with several others a few paces away. They were gambling and, from the sound of things, Chaagut was winning hugely.

One day that luck of his will run out. Tsingar stood and walked off into the woods. *And, Gods willing, I'll be the one who brings it to an end.*

It was quieter here in the forest, away from the warriors. Inactivity sat badly with them: they quarreled and scrapped with each other, making the best they could of their boredom. A bird sang out somewhere off to Tsingar's right as he walked, and he glanced in that direction. Then he heard something else—a snapping of the undergrowth. He froze, hand on his swordhilt.

The sound came again, closer this time. It was not a man walking through the forest, nor a horse, for that matter. The noise came in fits and spurts: a loud rustling, silence, then the cracking of brush again. Tsingar drew his sword and angled off to one side of the sounds. He found a concealed spot behind a tree, sank to his heels, and waited.

A man limped forward between the trees only a few paces away. Head bowed, trailing a leg behind, he halted for a moment in the dappled sunlight, then staggered on.

Tsingar hissed in exasperation, sheathed his sword, and stood. The wounded man was one of the scouts he had sent south to keep watch on the Krotànya encampment. Tsingar stepped out from behind the tree and into the man's path. The scout halted, tottered a moment, then regained his balance. One frantic eye came into focus; the other had been ruined by a swordstroke. Sudden recognition sharpened the bloody face. The scout croaked something in a fading voice, then toppled forward.

Tsingar caught the man as he fell, and the warrior

repeated what he had said. This time Tsingar understood. Before he could reply, the scout was dead.

He lowered the body to the ground and hunkered down on his heels. For a long moment he sat there, staring off into the woods. He looked down: an ant crawled up from the leaves and walked across the dead man's face. Tsingar watched in rapt fascination as the ant reached the scout's staring eye and, after a slight hesitation, crawled off across it.

"Gods!" Tsingar breathed. He repressed the urge to laugh out loud. "Gods." He glanced around, made sure he was not seen, grabbed the scout's body under the armpits and dragged it off into the deeper brush. The prevailing winds—which way did they blow at this time of year? He struggled onward, seeking somewhere to leave the dead man so his stink did not reach the camp.

Xeredir looked at the gathered Mind-Born. Six of them had come from the ranks of the refugees; their nine companions had come from the capital, sent here by his father. All fifteen of them stared back, their faces, usually remote and calm, set in hard lines of determination. Xeredir sighed quietly. This was not going to be easy, even though Vlàdor had spoken with the Mind-Born he had sent north.

"I know what I'm asking goes against our beliefs—" Xeredir looked from face to face. "—but it's necessary. We've got to keep the Leishoranya from the southlands as long as possible. I'm not asking you to turn your minds against the enemy, only to use them as a defense." He kept using the word: defense sat well with the Mind-Born—at least as well as any tactic might that involved destruction.

A tall woman, whose blond hair sat braided high on her head, nodded. This was the Lady Chitàna and, as far as he could tell, the rest of the Mind-Born had chosen her as their leader.

"We know," Chitàna said. "But we'll need time, Lord, to turn our minds to what you'd have us do."

Xeredir sighed. This was not their first conversation—they had gone over the situation before. What had his father said about the Mind-Born's refusal to act? He frowned slightly. "Lady," he reminded her, "time may be the one thing we're short of. For the sake of our people, please keep this in mind."

"Tsingar!" Dhumaric's voice was raised in irritation.

Tsingar leapt to his feet and hurried to Dhumaric's tent; only his commander slept in relative comfort. He paused before the opened doorway. "Aye, Dread Lord?"

Dhumaric stuck his head out from his tent; his huge bulk followed. His face was set in anger, his eyes only narrow slits in the sunlight. "Where are those dung-eating scouts of yours? They should have been back two days ago!"

Tsingar kept all expression from his face, his shields shut tighter than ever. "I don't know, Dread Lord. Perhaps they ran into more Krotànya."

"Huhn." Dhumaric snorted in disgust. "That I doubt. As far as I can tell, they're far to the south of us." He glared. "*You* chose those men, Tsingar. Were they stupid enough to let themselves be caught?"

Tsingar stiffened at the accusation. "No, Master," he said, keeping his head bowed. "They've served you well before."

"Then where are they?" Dhumaric slapped his thigh in vexation. "I can't do anything until I know what's going on to the south. And those damned Krotànya are so shielded, no one can Read them."

"They're probably consolidating their forces, Dread Lord," Tsingar said. "Scouting the land. Or maybe they're resting after battle."

"Not if I know Kahsir. He's with his father now, and those two can make trouble for us."

Tsingar kept silent, stepping back as Dhumaric began

to pace. Heart beating raggedly in his chest, he watched his commander prowl up and down before the tent. *I am nothing. I am less than nothing. My mind doesn't exist. There is only a blank, a void, nothing at all.* His knees were shaking. He drew a quiet breath, gaining strength from the inner litany. Still, when Dhumaric turned around, he flinched back a step.

"Find those scouts for me, Tsingar," Dhumaric hissed. "And find them soon!"

Tsingar swallowed convulsively. "I'll send out more, Dread Lord," he said, keeping his eyes lowered. "If any of the first group returns, I'll let you know immediately."

Silence. He dared a quick look up. Dhumaric's stare was sharp and intent, though his mind appeared to be elsewhere.

"I don't care what you do, or how you do it," Dhumaric growled, waving his hand in dismissal. "I'm interested in the results, not the method."

"I exist only to serve you, Lord." Tsingar quoted the ancient phrase of submission. Dhumaric snorted again and went back into the tent.

For a long moment, Tsingar stood by the tent door until his knees stopped shaking. Then, smiling briefly, he went off across the clearing to where the other warriors sat.

"Lord?"

Xeredir turned away from watching the setting sun as the two warriors approached. They were members of the sentry-band he had sent north to guard against any Leishoranya advance, and had likely ridden for two days to reach camp. Both were weary, but the man they carried was nearly dead. Xeredir's heart jumped. It was a Leishoran.

"We found him crawling through the brush," one of the sentries said, answering Xeredir's unspoken question. "We were lucky to catch him before he killed himself."

Xeredir left the front of his tent and looked at the man who hung from the ropes held by the two sentries. The Leishoran had indeed come close to killing himself, but not quite.

"Is he conscious?"

"Sometimes, Lord." The other sentry shrugged. "When he is, he's too weak to go after us with his mind. And we haven't been able to get anything out of him, if I Read your thoughts right."

"Huhn. Haskon," Xeredir called. His son came out of the tent, his face settling into grim lines when he saw the Leishoran. "Go get Lady Chitàna. Hurry!" Haskon went off at a run and Xeredir looked back.

"Where do you want us to put him?" asked the first sentry, nodding down at the unconscious Leishoran.

"Behind my tent," Xeredir replied. "And find someone to guard him. More than one man. Warn them to keep tightly shielded at all times. Unconscious or not, I don't trust any Leishoran."

The two sentries carried their captive off. Xeredir watched them go and frowned—if there was one enemy scout to the north, there were twenty. Trust to Dhumaric to send them out. The Leishoranya commander would want to know what lay south of him before he came himself.

Damn! He began to pace up and down before his tent. *How many men has Dhumaric gathered by now? Kahs told me Dhumaric would come after him with a single-mindedness that bordered on fixation.* He scratched at his beard. *At least Lorhaiden's gone now. We'd never have any rest if he was still here.*

He sighed quietly. Dhumaric was one of the worst enemies he could have drawn to fight against. It would take all his skill and cunning to match the Leishoranya commander's strategies. He and Dhumaric had fought in the past—more than once. He shook his head; Kahsir's words echoed in his mind. *Of all the Leishoranya to come after me*, Kahsir had said, *why did it have to be Dhumaric?*

Aside from any information Chitàna might find, another benefit came from catching this enemy scout. Perhaps now that the Mind-Born had actual evidence of how close the enemy was, they would take action sooner.

Tsingar frowned nervously as he walked to the edge of the clearing. Squinting in the falling sunlight, he glanced quickly over his shoulder at Dhumaric's tent: the door flaps remained shut—he could feel no probings in his mind. He kept his movements slow and unhurried. This was a dangerous game he played, possibly the most dangerous of his life.

The six men he had chosen to send out as scouts waited at the edge of the forest. Chaagut stood among them, talking to his companions in a manner above his rank and station. Tsingar snarled silently. *He thinks he's so damned clever. We'll see about that.*

He waited until he had the scouts' undivided attention, even Chaagut's. They were all uneasy at having been chosen to go south: word had spread that the first group of scouts had not returned. Tsingar glanced sidelong at Chaagut; Chaagut was certainly aware of his hatred. Everyone in camp kept their minds tightly shielded, but some emotions were nearly impossible to hide.

"Listen to me," he said, pitching his voice so his scorn was obvious. He looked at Chaagut, daring him to respond, but Chaagut kept silent, his face a neutral blank. "Dhumaric wants news from the south. The other scouts I sent out haven't come back. They were either caught or killed. I hope you'll be more careful."

The six men shifted from foot to foot. Chaagut started to say something, but decided against it.

"Find out everything you can about the Krotànya," Tsingar said. "We know where they are, what they're doing, and who's leading them. But none of the other scouts have been able to tell us any more than that Xeredir is still in camp. That's not important now. Dhumaric wants to know where Kahsir is—Kahsir *and* Lorhaiden."

Chaagut glanced up from his feet. "Which direction should we take?"

"I'm not leading this group, Chaagut. You are. By all the Gods, you've led scouting expeditions before! What's so different about *this* one?" For a terrifying moment, Chaagut looked like he would reply. "I *do* know this: don't approach the Krotànya from the north. That way's heavily guarded. The other scouts must have been killed or captured there. From what I can tell, the best way to take is from the west. When Xeredir came down from the mountains, he came from the southeast."

Chaagut's face became totally expressionless. Tsingar glanced away, cleared his throat, and looked back.

"Now get out of here," he said. "And don't come back unless you've got news of Kahsir, or a fresh report about the Krotànya army."

Hands clasped behind his back, Xeredir looked down at the Leishoran, then darted a sidelong glance at the Lady Chitàna. She stood utterly still. Though observing the captive intently, her face was as composed as if she had been sitting in meditation. Xeredir clamped his shields down out of habit—around the Mind-Born little could be hidden. He looked at Chitàna again. *Aren't they ever touched by what's happening? They care. I know they do. But they damned well could show a little more emotion.*

Chitàna turned and he met her eyes steadily. If she had Heard his thoughts, there was nothing he could do about it.

"He's near death," she said, her voice cool and controlled. "We won't learn much from him without forcing his mind, and that's forbidden. But touching the edges of it—" She shrugged. "I'll see what I can do."

"Is it safe to—?"

She lifted one eyebrow. "He's in no condition to hurt anyone right now, Lord. I'll be all right."

Her white cloak fell about her as she knelt by the unconscious scout. Xeredir frowned slightly and hunkered down beside. She reached out, held her hands close to the dying man's head, and closed her eyes, her face settling into the calm that so marked any of the Mind-Born. Xeredir opened his mind totally now: anything she learned might spill over so he would not have to ask questions later.

The moments crawled by. Chitàna seemed to be taking a long time at what she was doing, longer than Xeredir would have expected. Finally, she looked up from the dying Leishoran, her eyes slightly unfocused.

"He has a strong mind, Lord," she said. "Quite strong. And—different." She shuddered briefly. "This is the first Leishoran mind I've touched even the edges of, and I hope it's the last. What do you want to know?"

Xeredir glanced down at the unconscious man. "Is he from Dhumaric?"

"Aye." She volunteered further information. "He was sent south along with several others. They split up once they crossed into the high meadowlands. I couldn't tell if he knew what happened to his comrades. When he was caught, he tried to kill himself as ordered, but botched the job." She shuddered again, distaste for what she had done visible on her face.

"How far away is Dhumaric?" Xeredir asked. "Do you know where he is?"

"Several days' ride to the north, Lord. Somewhere just south of the steading of Chilufka."

Xeredir pulled at his beard and stood, fighting the impulse to pace. *South of Chilufka? He must have fallen back and gathered more men. And, knowing*

Dhumaric, he's sent out an appeal to Ssenkahdavic for more warriors.

"Which side of the river is he on?"

"The south side, Lord."

"Huhn. Is there anything else? Reinforcements sent south by Ssenkahdavic? Anything at all?"

She nodded slowly. "The rest of his memories were jumbled, possibly on purpose, either by this man or others who set some seal on his memories. But I'm certain of this: Dhumaric either went to Rodja'âno himself, or sent a messenger, asking for reinforcements. He's calling all the men he can to his side."

Xeredir turned and looked away, out across the fields by the camp. *You don't need to tell me why. He's still after Kahs and Lorhaiden. He obviously doesn't know they left for the south several days ago. That's a stroke of luck. If I can keep my sentries tight enough so that no other scouts break through, I might be able to keep that news from Dhumaric even longer.* He smiled grimly. *Maybe I'll be able to use his fixation to my own advantage.*

He turned back to Chitàna. "You see, Lady," he said, looking directly into her eyes, "how short of time we are. If Dhumaric comes south, other Leishoranya armies will surely be close behind. We've got to destroy those passes, and quickly."

For a long moment she remained utterly still, her face expressionless. Then she nodded, slowly and with obvious reluctance.

"You're right, of course. I'll talk to my companions."

She stood, bowed, and went quietly off into the dusk. When Xeredir looked down from her retreating figure, the Leishoran was dead.

It had rained earlier during the day. Tsingar pulled his cloak closer and tried to find a comfortable position. The night air felt chilly and damp, and the grass was wet where he lay. He longed for a place to stay indoors, out of the evening's chill, but since suffering the repeated ambushes Kahsir had sprung on them on the way to the steading, and the defeat in the meadowlands, Dhumaric had grown wary of spending the night anywhere but in the open.

Tsingar shifted position again, tightened his mental shields. *By the Void! Dhumaric's got the bit in his mouth again. If Kahsir and Lorhaiden have escaped, it won't be anything new.* Time and again, one or either of those two men had been in such a position that Dhumaric had been assured of capturing them. Then, as had been the case in the meadows, the Krotànya Princes had managed to escape.

Sleep would not come, not just yet. Everyone else lay still, breathing heavily in sleep, even Dhumaric in his tent. The crickets and other night insects sang loud in the brush close by. Only the pickets were awake: one had just passed on the clearing's edge, weapons glinting in the firelight.

A brief rustle came from Dhumaric's tent, followed by silence. Tsingar rose slowly to his feet, gathered his cloak tighter, and slipped off to the edge of the clearing. He stopped, leaned against a tree, and scratched at a bug bite on his ear.

Events of the past few days made things perfectly clear: Dhumaric should give up the chase. He was so consumed by catching Kahsir and Lorhaiden he was not thinking logically. There would always be other chances to capture them. The Krotànya were losing ground rapidly now, and though they did not show it, they must know they were beaten. How could they not know it? They were outnumbered, the next to last of their capital cities had been taken, and Ssenkahdavic had set three great armies in motion, poised for the final kill.

But Queen Aeschu had promised Dhumaric five thousand men, a force of sufficient strength to meet Xeredir's four thousand head-on in battle. Tsingar chewed on his lower lip: this granting of Dhumaric's request could mean more than it showed on the surface. As Ssenkahdavic's wife, the Queen ruled in his name, and knew strategy as well as, or better, than most generals. Was she throwing Dhumaric to the south knowing he would destroy the Krotanya . . . or, was she sending him out to be defeated?

One thing Tsingar *did* know: there was no love lost between his commander and Ssenkahdavic's wife.

The brush close by rustled, and one of the pickets came through the forest, slouched and carrying his spear loosely in one hand. Tsingar snarled at the man, raised his fist threateningly, and the fellow snapped to immediate attention. Stiff-backed, carrying his spear ready in both hands, the warrior walked off into the darkness.

Tsingar stared after the picket for a long moment, then turned back toward Dhumaric's tent. *It's about time something went my way tonight.* He threaded his way in between sleeping warriors to his own place at Dhumaric's feet, wrapped up in his cloak, lay down, and slept.

Xeredir looked into Haskon's eyes and saw no wavering in them. He leaned back in his camp chair, rubbed his forehead with one hand, and sighed.

"So, Haskon. You still think we should divide our forces? Even after what we found out from that enemy scout?"

Haskon nodded slowly. "Aye. If Dhumaric gets his reinforcements, and *if* he ends up with an army the size of ours, we don't dare meet him on the field of battle. That's not demeaning your skill, or anyone else's. It's just a fact. Our strategy is to strike at the flanks of the enemy forces coming south to fill the corridor Dhumaric made. Taking Rodja'âno wasn't easy, and there's still a lot of territory for the Leishoranya to take in hand. We've got them guessing now. From what Kahs said,

Dhumaric can't be sure we aren't all over these woods, waiting to strike at him."

"Huhn." Xeredir looked out of the tent and off into the distance. "That doesn't make me feel better about it, Haskon."

His son shrugged. "Dhumaric's only one of the commanders we'll face. There will be others, along with their armies."

Xeredir reached for his cup, drank deeply, then set it back down on the table at his side. "But Dhumaric's specifically after us. He doesn't know Kahs and Lorhaiden have left for the south."

"He wouldn't be too unhappy if he got a chance at you," Haskon observed dryly.

"True. But that doesn't change things. He's determined to come south at the head of all the men he can find. I wouldn't want to face him with only two hundred men at my back."

Haskon was silent. He shifted his weight in the chair, his fingers nervously tapping on his knee.

"Let's think it through, Haskon. We've caught three more of his scouts. That's the second lot he sent out. They've all given us the same information. Once Dhumaric feels he has enough men, he'll come south." Again, Haskon refused to reply. "Surely you have *some* ideas. After dividing our forces, what should we do about Dhumaric?"

Haskon looked up from his hands, his mouth quirked in a half-smile.

"Stay out of his way, I suppose."

Tsingar wandered aimlessly around the clearing, swatting at the late afternoon midges. Over three thousand men had gathered in the past few days, with more to come from Rodja'âno. Soon Dhumaric would command a force near five thousand strong, an army that would probably be larger than the one Xeredir led.

Only Dhumaric's officers and their lieutenants could

hold a place in the clearing. The rest of the warriors, the lowly ones, had to fend for themselves in the forest and other smaller clearings nearby. Tsingar looked at the other officers who shared Dhumaric's clearing. They fought and argued among themselves as much as the warriors who had been here before. But the camp, for all of that, was far more orderly. Some officers had even come with their mind-slaves, and those broken-minded, witless dregs of his people's birth failures at least kept the campsite tidy.

"Tsingar!"

He turned, saw Dhumaric beckon, and hurried across the clearing.

"Aye, Master?"

"One of the scouts you sent south has returned," Dhumaric said, gesturing behind. Tsingar waited, all his senses screaming danger. "It's Chaagut."

Tsingar's heart lurched to a stop. "What's he found out, Master?"

He felt a sudden wave of dizziness. For a brief instant, he was caught up by Dhumaric's mind, weighed, appraised, then dismissed.

"He's in little condition to talk." Dhumaric's deep voice drifted over his shoulder as he turned away. "Wounded, badly. He's your subordinate, Tsingar. You question him."

Struggling to keep his face as empty as his thoughts, Tsingar bowed his head and followed. There, slumped up against a tree close to Dhumaric's tent, his face drained of all color and a gaping slash down his side, lay Chaagut.

Tsingar hunkered down on his heels. "Chaagut," he said. Chaagut stirred feebly, looked up and licked his lips. "What's your news, Chaagut?"

Chaagut licked his lips again, motioned weakly toward a water bottle hanging at the front of the tent.

"Do it," Dhumaric snapped.

Tsingar leapt up, caught at the water bottle, and

returned. Chaagut drank greedily, his throat working. At a gesture from Dhumaric, Tsingar grabbed the bottle away.

"What's your news?" he asked again, kneeling so he looked directly into Chaagut's eyes.

"Xeredir." Chaagut spoke through clenched teeth. "I . . . I couldn't get close enough. There were too . . . too many sentries." Tsingar shifted uneasily. "We came in from the east . . . were ambushed." A shudder of agony ran through Chaagut. "But it's . . . it's Xeredir who leads them."

"Dammit, we know that! How many, fool?" demanded Dhumaric from behind. "How many exactly does he lead?"

Chaagut swallowed heavily. He closed his eyes, grew paler yet. "I don't know, Dread Lord," he said faintly. "I couldn't . . . couldn't get close enough to tell. Many, Dread Lord . . . many."

"The four thousand we suspect?"

"Aye. . . ."

"What about Kahsir?" Dhumaric asked, his voice deceptively soft. "We think he's with his father. Did you find out where he is?"

"Nothing . . . Dread Lord." Chaagut gasped softly in pain. "We . . . found out nothing. . . ."

"By all the Gods!" Tsingar swore, allowing real frustration to enter his voice. "I told you to come in from the west! What the Void did you think you'd prove by—"

"Tsingar. Shut up."

Dhumaric stepped closer and, careful to keep his face and mind hidden, Tsingar moved aside. For a long moment, Dhumaric stared at the dying scout. Suddenly, Chaagut whimpered several times, eyes shut in both pain and something else Tsingar shrank from: Dhumaric had forced Chaagut's mind open. Then, with a convulsive shudder, Chaagut stiffened and slowly fell on his side.

"Dead?" Tsingar whispered.

Dhumaric shrugged, a creak of leather clothing. "Aye."

Tsingar closed his eyes as Dhumaric moved back from the body.

"That's what you wanted, isn't it?" Dhumaric's words were colder than death, than ice.

"Master?" Tsingar's voice shook; he made no effort to control it.

"You knew he'd think you were sending him into a trap, so you told him to do the right thing, to approach the Krotànya from the west." Dhumaric barked a laugh. "And he disbelieved you! That's rich, Tsingar. Rich, indeed."

Tsingar flinched, bowed his head to his knees, and waited for whatever judgment would follow.

"No matter." Dhumaric shrugged. "I've got what I wanted." Tsingar looked up—Dhumaric was staring off to the south. "By the Gods of Darkness!" Dhumaric whispered. "I've got them all—Vlàdor's heirs! All possibly in one spot! Xeredir, Kahsir, Haskon, and Alàric!" His terrible voice went softer yet. "And Lorhaiden." He laughed. "When the rest of the men sent from Rodja'âno reach us, we'll set off. Listen to me, Tsingar."

"Aye, Dread Lord?"

"The third time pays for all. Send another group of scouts to the south. I want to know exactly how many warriors Xeredir has with him, and if he's expecting reinforcements." Dhumaric's lips thinned. "And tell them, Tsingar, *stress* to them that I don't want to see any of them again, alive or dying, unless they can give me the information I need!"

CHAPTER 14

Kahsir stretched in the saddle and looked around as he rode. Pine forests lay on either side of the roadway, breaking once in a while to highland meadows. The first signs of spring were everywhere: birds sang out from the trees and early blooming flowers thrust up from beneath winter-brown grass. He had ridden this way centuries ago, and the land was as beautiful as ever.

Already, only five days from the base of the Golondai Mountains, the weather was warmer. He had led the refugees down the mind-road twice, so they were much farther west than if they had come only by the world's roads. They had met bad weather twice so far, but the storms, while soaking, had not lasted long.

He turned in his saddle and looked behind at the long column that followed. Despite warnings that it was only a matter of time before enemy armies penetrated this region, some of the refugees had already left, heading off toward lands their kin farmed. The number of people who remained had grown steadily smaller, with the journey not even a third done.

Kahsir snorted and turned around. In one way, that was a good thing. Though Hvâlkir was the largest city his people had ever built, it would not hold its own population, plus the other refugees who gathered there.

Yet, one day, all the Krotànya would seek Hvâlkir, the last bastion of the dying Kingdoms.

He glanced behind once more as he started around a long, wide bend in the road. Genlàvyn rode not all that far back in the column; Kahsir squinted and made out his brother's figure. Since leaving Xeredir's camp, Alàric had ridden with Genlàvyn and her cousin, Maiwyn. Kahsir smiled slightly. Maiwyn and Alàric had grown closer during the past five days, though Alàric had been tight-lipped about what had gone on between the two of them.

The sun was beginning to set; in another hour, the time would come to halt. Kahsir glanced to his left, to the peaks of the Golondai Mountains, aflame now in the setting sunlight. The tallest of those peaks, Sijei Mountain, had been his landmark. From that point on, the mountains angled off to the southwest. The refugees would skirt them and then turn south.

It still hurt, his father sending him off like this. *Dammit! It would have been one thing if he'd refused to implement any of my strategies. But to take nearly every suggestion I made, dovetail the plans into his own, and* then *send me packing like a misbehaving child.* . . . Kahsir drew a deep breath. Perhaps it was better. He doubted that he and Xeredir could co-command after what had happened at Rodja'âno.

The question remained: could he and his father *ever* truly trust each other again?

Kahsir rode over the crest of a small rise: a stream cut through the valley below. This far south, the rivers were less full than those to the north, the mountain run-off having started earlier. He reached the edge of the narrow bridge and urged his horse across. Looking down at the stream running below, he saw the water glitter in the sunlight as it danced over the rocky bottom—a shower of vanishing jewels. Once he reached the other side of the stream, he rode off to his right, reined in, and watched as the refugees began to cross.

He looked down the long column of people again and saw Lorhaiden's distant figure. When not riding at Kahsir's side, Lorhaiden fell back to ride with his brother. Kahsir frowned and rubbed his chin. Lorhaiden had been unusually silent; his moodiness after leaving combat was present, but there was an undercurrent of something else. Kahsir shook his head and looked back to the stream. He had not been able to read Lorhaiden's thoughts for several days now, and Lorhaiden had grown gloomier and more withdrawn the farther away from battle he went.

Though far from his father's camp, Kahsir still felt a sense of danger. He lifted his reins. There were far more pressing things than Lorhaiden's moodiness to worry about.

"Father?"

Xeredir turned as Haskon came to the tent door.

"One of the northern sentries has returned," Haskon said. "I think you'd better come with me."

Xeredir tried to read his son's expression, shrugged, and followed Haskon across the campground to its outer edge. Haskon was grim and moody on the way and Xeredir did not try to talk to him. Men sat cleaning weapons or telling stories and waved as he and Haskon passed. On the edge of camp, Haskon stopped and pointed.

A warrior waited at the campground's edge, near to a stand of trees. Xeredir glanced at him as he and Haskon walked closer, but saw nothing unusual. Then, the sentry's abnormal stance became obvious.

"Wait, Father." Haskon held out his hand in a signal to stop. "Look at him closely."

Xeredir stopped, and his heart tightened. The sentry's eyes were vacant, staring, in a face unnaturally pale.

"When did it happen?"

Haskon shook his head.

Xeredir glanced sidelong at his son. "Mind-broken?"

"Likely." Haskon's mouth was twisted into a grimace. He gestured at the unresponsive man. "He only had wit enough to find his way here when the enemy was through with him."

Xeredir looked carefully around at the trees and the meadowlands to the north. "Was he followed?"

"Not that I can tell. I sent out a squadron to retrace his steps: the way he came is clear enough. The men should be back by nightfall."

"*Chuht!*" Xeredir faced the sentry again. "Have you tried to touch what mind he has left?"

Haskon grimaced again. "Aye. There's not much. What he still has shrinks from me. Perhaps Chitàna can help us."

"Perhaps." Xeredir frowned and rubbed the bridge of his nose. "I've taxed her patience frequently enough lately. One more time won't make a difference." He paused for a moment and Sent out a call for her, warning her ahead of time what she would face.

Haskon walked a bit closer to the motionless sentry. "I wonder how it happened?"

"I can guess." Xeredir heard a sound from behind and turned. It was Chitàna, arrived in the abrupt fashion of the Mind-Born. She bowed slightly, her attention fixed on the sentry.

"When did he come in?" she asked Haskon, already seeming to know more than Xeredir had told her.

"Not a quarter hour ago, Lady."

She murmured something. Her eyes narrowed, her shoulders tensed, and her mouth curled in disgust.

"Can you tell what happened?" Xeredir asked.

She stared for a brief moment, nodded, then turned away. He followed her the few steps to the sentry's side, Haskon trailing along behind. The sentry still stood motionless, nothing showing he was aware he was in the presence of others. Haskon made a disgusted noise and Xeredir hushed him with a gesture.

Chitàna reached out and set her hands on the sentry's forehead. Xeredir winced at the look of revulsion that crossed her face, but did not call her back. For a long while she stood silent, hands held to the sentry's head, her lips moving in soundless words. Finally, a shudder ran through her. She let her hands drop, shook them as if she had touched something distasteful, and turned around. Xeredir involuntarily stepped back from the force held in her eyes.

"The enemy got most of his memories, Lord; much you wouldn't want them to have. He wasn't privy to major council decisions, but he *did* know Kahsir, Alàric, and the Hrudharic brothers headed south with the refugees. He was also aware of the camp rumors that you're thinking of dividing your forces. He didn't know much more than that—or more of what they wanted to know. They broke his mind and left him."

Xeredir clenched his fists. *Damn! Damn! Now Dhumaric will know for sure where Kahs is! Or at least where he isn't! We'll have to make speed at everything we do now. Our timing's got to be perfect.*

He sighed quietly, and looked from the sentry's face to Chitàna. "What can we do for him?" he asked.

She shrugged helplessly. "Not much, Lord. He doesn't have any chance of recovery."

Xeredir turned quickly away. "Do what you have to," he said, "but don't let him suffer."

She reached out and touched his arm, a gesture unusual for one of the Mind-Born to make. "I'm sorry, Lord. He was a good man, and he'll be missed. Trust me. I'll try to make it as easy for him as I can."

"Thanks, Lady." Xeredir started back to his tent, motioned for Haskon to follow. The mind-broken sentry, Chitàna's task . . . he shivered though the sun was warm.

*   *   *

Smoke from the cooking fires hung over the clearing, stirred by a faint breeze. Tsingar dismounted, threw the reins to a warrior who stood nearby, and stretched the stiffness from his legs. He glanced off across the clearing, squinting in the sunlight: more officers had arrived since he had ridden out in the morning. The last of the promised warriors from Rodja'âno must have ridden in. Tsingar had no firm idea of exactly how many had gathered around Dhumaric's standard, but judged the number close to five thousand.

Dhumaric's mind touched his, a cold tendril that whispered through his brain, commanding instant attendance.

Tsingar turned from his horse, walked across the clearing to Dhumaric's tent. As he neared it, the tent flap was drawn back and Dhumaric stepped outside. Another man followed. There was something familiar about the stranger but Tsingar could not place him.

"We've got news at last," Dhumaric said without preamble. "Two of your men ran into a Krotànya sentry. They surprised him so thoroughly that they were able to break his mind and bring me the information I need."

Tsingar watched Dhumaric's face, alert for the slightest change in expression. He glanced sidelong at the newcomer—where had he seen the man before?

"Kahsir and Lorhaiden have headed south," Dhumaric said, "leading a band of refugees from Rodja'âno. The army Xeredir led north through the Golondai Mountains only numbers four thousand."

"Four thousand?" Tsingar shifted his weight uneasily. "Dread Lord, that's not much less than—"

Dhumaric sneered. "There's a rumor in the Krotànya camp he's going to split his forces, probably into companies of five hundred each. I'd tend to believe that. They've patterned their armies after ours, so such a breakdown would be reasonable."

A division of forces—four thousand into five hun-

dreds. That would give Xeredir eight highly mobile companies. "But, Master—won't that make trouble for us? They'll be able to move faster than—"

"Perhaps. But five hundred stands little chance against five thousand. And that's how many men I'll have by tomorrow morning."

"Ah? The last of those sent from Rodja'âno are here?"

"Aye." Dhumaric gestured at the man who had been standing silent at his side. "Tsingar lur Totuhofka chi Higulen, this is Girdun lur Adhogar chi Dyntu. He came south as war leader of the largest company Queen Aeschu sent us. The two of you will be working together."

Tsingar's back stiffened. "Master?"

"You'll both report to me, but beyond that, all scouts will be under your joint control. I want to be constantly informed of what's going on in the Krotànya camp. I don't want anyone entering or leaving it without my knowledge. Even if your scouts have to make a sending to me, have them do so. I want to know what's happening—*everything* that's happening. Do you understand?"

"Aye, Master." Tsingar bowed his head. "And when we leave, where will we be going?"

"After Kahsir, you fool. Now that he's this close, you don't think I'd let him escape again, do you? Xeredir's four thousand we'll leave our army. If he divides his forces, we'll do the same—it should be easy to match his numbers with our own. We'll take the five hundred I've handpicked after Kahsir. If we move in haste and in secret, Xeredir won't know we're gone. He'll be kept busy enough trying to figure out what we're doing and trying to counter our moves with his own." Dhumaric turned toward the south, hands opening and closing into fists. "Xeredir's right. To be mobile you must have fewer men." He turned back. "Tell me, Tsingar—what chance do you think Kahsir and Lorhaiden have against our five hundred, weighed down by the refugees they lead?"

"Not much, Dread Lord," Tsingar replied, his head still lowered.

"Report to me after you've sent off the scouts," said Dhumaric.

Tsingar bowed deeply. When he glanced up again, Dhumaric had entered his tent. The lowered door-flap forbade intrusion.

He looked closer at his fellow officer's all-too-familiar face. If he was going to work with the man, he had best get to know him.

"Have you eaten yet?" The officer shook his head and Tsingar gestured across the clearing. "We're served down at that end of camp. I've already had my meal, but I'll join you in conversation." He set his pace to match Girdun's as he started off. Girdun's face, his voice—both were hauntingly familiar, but the Clan name chi Dyntu was not. "Haven't I seen you somewhere before?" he asked.

Girdun shrugged. "Perhaps in Rodja'âno. Before being sent to serve Dhumaric, I was attached to Ssenkahdavic's honor guard. Or it could be a family resemblance. I had a cousin who fought with this company."

"Ah? And who was that? I probably knew him."

"I'm sure you did," Girdun said mildly, his eyes flat black pools. "His name was Chaagut."

The Golondai Mountains stood mist-wrapped and foreboding, their massive bulk overpowering in immensity. Xeredir stood on the rocky slopes of one of those mountains and drew his cloak tighter. The air was close and clammy, the chill mist clinging. The sound of boot soles on stone came from behind. He turned and met Haskon's eyes.

"How many passes are left to destroy?" he asked, looking back up at the mountains.

"Three, I think. The rest are nearly impossible to cross, even in the best weather. And once we've built our fortresses, it shouldn't take that many men to defend them."

"Huhn." Xeredir glanced to the west: Kahsir and the refugees were ten days gone. Xeredir knew how things went on that journey, since Kahsir made reports by a brief, heavily cloaked Sending each night.

Haskon stirred uneasily. "We're doing a terrible thing, Father," he said, gesturing at the mountains. "All that beauty, destroyed in a moment."

"Think how the Mind-Born must feel," Xeredir said, looking back at his son. "You know how they fought this. But they recognized necessity when they saw it."

"Took their own damned time doing so," Haskon muttered. "They awe me," he said a few moments later. "Truly awe me." His memories spilled out from behind his shields, as strongly as if he had Sent them: vast slides of rock, entire faces of mountains plummeting downward, forests ruined in those slides. "To be able to join minds and bring mountains down—" Haskon shrugged and shook his head. "I still find it hard to comprehend."

Xeredir smiled slightly. Haskon in a meditative mood was a rare sight.

"Have you sent men north to start destroying the Rodja'âno Road yet?" Haskon asked.

"Aye." Xeredir tore his eyes away from the mountains. The Rodja'âno Road lay close to three hundred leagues west of his camp. Since Kahsir and the refugees had taken the mind-road, they had already reached it. Destroying that road behind Kahsir by stages as he went south would make Ssenkahdavic's march even harder when he chose to lead his armies from Rodja'âno.

The Krotànya had built few major highways; the Rodja'âno Road remained the longest. It ran southwest through the Kingdom of Tumâs, around the end of the Golondai, to the River Abhlin, where ferries waited to take travelers across into Elyâsai. From there, the highway continued in its southwesterly direction, straight toward the capital of capitals, Hvâlkir.

And now, after serving its purpose for thousands of years, Xeredir had ordered the destruction of the Rodja'âno Road to prevent the enemy from using it.

He closed his eyes and took a deep breath. The smell of pine trees, of the mist clinging to their branches, was strong. A brief flash of Kahsir's face came to mind. Xeredir held that face in his mind's eye for a moment: part of him wished that he had not sent Kahsir away, that he had shared his command with his eldest son. If events proved as he foresaw, Kahsir's luck might be an asset.

Xeredir shivered slightly in the chill, and looked up the mountainside again. Three more passes awaited destruction, and then he would have to face deploying his forces across the northlands.

Land of ours, forgive us. What we do, we do from necessity. And if we fail, all the mountains and forests and valleys won't count for a damned thing against the enemy's might.

A sudden deep, booming roar rolled down through the trees and mist. Xeredir jumped, startled, as the ground trembled under his feet. As he looked off into the mist up the mountainside, the loss of beauty ran like a knife through his heart.

"Only two passes left," Haskon said.

The midday sun shone hot on Tsingar's shoulders, but he dared not show his discomfort—the lesser officers must not think him bothered by such trifles. He turned around slowly, looking over the clearing. Only a few men were left. Dhumaric had already sent most of them off to their various units to await further reports from the scouts as to what Xeredir chose to do next. If the Krotànya Crown Prince *did* divide his four thousand, Dhumaric's men would do likewise; if not, they would try to lure him northward, to ground more of their own choosing.

As for Tsingar, he would ride with Dhumaric, who was taking a strike force of five hundred warriors west after Kahsir.

Tsingar took off his helmet, ran a hand through his hair. He poked absently at the interior padding of the helm, satisfied that it was in good condition. He looked up: Girdun stood watching from across the clearing.

Heart beginning to thump raggedly, Tsingar allowed no sign of unease to cross his face. He reset his helmet, nodded in Girdun's direction, turned, and went back to his business. Breaking camp was always a tedious job, and today was no exception.

He picked up his saddlebags and walked to his tethered horse, conscious of Girdun's following stare. For a moment he stood still, chewing on his lower lip. *Why? Why Girdun? Chaagut's cousin. Gods!* He threw the saddlebags across the horse's back behind the heavy war saddle, cursed when the animal shied beneath the unwelcome weight. *How much does Girdun know about Chaagut's death? How much did Dhumaric tell him? All? Part of it? Nothing?* He caught hold of the horse's mind, stilled it, and began securing the saddlebags.

There came a sudden scuff of boot leather on the ground behind. Taking a deep breath, he slowly turned around.

"I've sent the last of my advance scouts out, Tsingar," Girdun said, his face unreadable in the sunlight. "Have yours left yet?"

"Aye." Tsingar fought control into his voice and expression, forced his eyes to meet Girdun's. "Around a half an hour ago."

Girdun nodded. "Then Dhumaric will want to talk to us. You look busy."

"I am. Tell him I'll be there soon as I can. We'll get our orders for—"

The sound of scuffling came from behind; Tsingar

whirled to look. Two junior officers were quarreling over something, but broke off when they noticed he was watching. He leered at them and turned back around. Girdun had gone. He sighed quietly in vast relief and finished tying down his saddlebags.

Girdun's a problem. I've got to watch him. I'm finally rid of Chaagut and his bid for power, and the last thing I want is more trouble. He shifted from foot to foot, glanced up at the sunlight in the trees. *Gods! If Girdun knows how Chaagut died—*

He turned from his horse and walked toward Dhumaric's tent. Several warriors were busy pulling it down while Dhumaric and Girdun talked together at the edge of the clearing. He winced at Girdun's laugh.

Patience . . . patience. Everyone makes mistakes, and Girdun's no different.

Tsingar looked off into the woods, taking the time to still his face to a blank, then looked back. Girdun glanced up and Tsingar flinched inside. *Danger!* a voice cried out in his mind. He took a deep breath, acknowledging his peril. One did not toy lightly with Ssenkahdavic's honor guard.

CHAPTER 15

Kahsir jerked awake in the pre-dawn darkness, for a moment unsure what had wakened him. He felt it again—the subtle pressure of a Sending so deep and hidden only one of his family could have made it. Xeredir!

—*Kahs! This must be quick. Dhumaric knows you, Alàric, Vàlkir, and Lorhaiden are riding south with the refugees. For the Lords' sakes, be careful.*

Kahsir sat silent, his blanket wrapped close, shivering for a moment in the chill morning air. *Damn! You're sure?*

—*Sure as I need to be to contact you like this. He caught one of my northern sentries, broke the fellow's mind, and. . . . You can guess the rest.*

—*How long ago was that?*

—*Two days. I said nothing to you about it, because I wasn't sure Dhumaric would follow you. But one of the Mind-Born I've got with me just said she sensed Dhumaric had left his camp—that he was headed after you.*

—*Lord! If Lorhaiden—*

—*I know. Keep him ignorant of this, Kahs. You don't*

*need any more trouble than you've got already. Some-
one's coming after you, to give you reinforcements.*

—*How many men do you think Dhumaric has with
him?*

—*I'd guess five hundred. The Mind-Born wasn't sure.*
The tone of Xeredir's Sending darkened. *For the Light's
sake, increase your pace! Take the mind-road more
often if the refugees can manage!*

—*We'll try.*

—*I'll let you know if anything changes. And be careful, Kahs.*

Xeredir's Sending broke off. For a moment, Kahsir
sat staring into the dawn light. Dhumaric. That bastard
was worse than a dog worrying a bone. Kahsir sighed,
all desire for sleep vanished. He gathered his blanket,
stood, and stretched the night stiffness from his body.
Increase your pace, Xeredir had said. He grimaced.
The refugees were exhausted as it was, but he might be
able to push them a bit more.

He sought Lorhaiden's mind and felt briefly com-
forted to find his sword-brother still wrapped in sleep.

The rugged peaks of the Golondai Mountains, their
snows brilliant in the sunlight, lay to Kahsir's left as he
rode. The sight of those mountains was comforting, as
well as beautiful. The mountains were far older than
the Krotànya on this continent: only the land had changed
since Kahsir had ridden this way before—the land and
the forests.

He remembered legends of the far past . . . of days
when his people had only just come to the continent,
escaping the enemy and certain death that lay behind
them. *Then* a man would count himself fortunate to see
over a hundred years before dying; and to die of old
age, rather than choosing to go from the world, undi-
minished in mind or physical strength. Kahsir tried to
envision such a brief life span but gave up. *How odd to
live at a faster pace than the land.* He shook his head.

At least then one could count on landmarks to guide one.

He glanced away from the mountains and looked behind at the following refugees, hunting for Lorhaiden. His sword-brother's mood had grown darker the farther he went from the fighting in the northlands. *That damned Oath of his is going to get him killed yet.*

At last he spotted Lorhaiden riding with his head bowed, wrapped in silence, off to one side of the column of refugees. Lately, not even Vàlkir had been able to bring Lorhaiden out of his moods. Hairon gave his shield-master a wide berth—always there if needed, but never pushing Lorhaiden into one of his familiar rages.

In a way Kahsir found it a stroke of good fortune that Lorhaiden had been keeping to himself: hiding his mind from Lorhaiden had never been an easy thing. And in this instance, after the Sending his father had made this morning, it was imperative.

Kahsir looked forward again, straightened in the saddle, and rubbed at the lower part of his back, easing the tense muscles. Every night since leaving Xeredir's camp, he had made a heavily cloaked Sending to his father. Each of those Sendings had been short and to the point: Xeredir imparting details of the military situation, and Kahsir telling of the refugees' progress.

And each of those Sendings had contained nothing in them that he could not repeat.

Until this morning.

Kahsir took his feet from the stirrups and let them dangle. *Damn! I'm trapped! I can't let anyone know about Dhumaric for fear of Lorhaiden finding out. And I can't increase our pace without some kind of explanation.* He clenched his fist around the reins. Dhumaric would likely take the mind-road in pursuit and, even though those jumps would be shortened by lack of knowledge of what lay before him, Dhumaric would be cutting the distance between himself and the refugees

dangerously thin. Yet there were limits as to how close
Dhumaric could come without being noticed, which
would allow the refugees to take the mind-road in escape. Riding this deep into unsecured Krotànya territory, Dhumaric might be more cautious than usual. If
nothing else, the ambushes and traps the Leishoranya
commander had suffered north of Chilufka might have
made him wary.

Kahsir looked up at the Golondai again. He stood no
chance against Dhumaric if he had to fight before
Xeredir's reinforcements reached him. Weighed down
by the refugees, with only one hundred warriors at his
side, he would face destruction. He lifted the reins,
urged his horse into a faster pace, and hoped no one
would question the slight increase in speed they took
henceforward.

The fire crackled loudly in the silence as Xeredir
looked at the faces of the men who had come to the
council meeting. Noises from the camp behind intruded
on this stillness: men called back and forth to each
other, horses neighed and stamped in anticipation.

He cleared his throat and shifted his weight from foot
to foot: the commanders turned his way again.

"What you'll be facing is a war of wits. I doubt very
much that Dhumaric's men will strike out in any one
direction: they'll probably sit right where they are for a
while, letting their scouts give them some notion of the
land around them. Go ahead and divide our four thousand into companies of five hundred, but I don't want
any of you to leave camp until you know the enemy's in
motion. Let them make the first move."

"How will we know that, Lord, if we don't send men
north to spy on the enemy?"

Xeredir glanced at the man who had spoken. "I'm
leaving the Mind-Born with you—they'll know what's
going on. Dhumaric's officers can't shield their entire
army." He took a deep breath. "From here on out,

you'll be operating on your own. Keep in mind that five hundred men is still a very mobile force. *Use* that mobility: there's no way of knowing how many of the enemy you might meet at one time. The corridor Dhumaric's forced from Rodja'âno southward will likely be strengthened *after* the corridor that leads from Fânchorion to Rodja'âno, but be wary. Lords know the enemy has the manpower to fill both corridors at fairly short notice."

Once again, he looked from commander to commander. He had their total attention now—every eye was trained on his face.

"The men who escaped the enemy at Rodja'âno will be trying to move toward you. A conservative estimate of four thousand men would give Errehmon eight companies of five hundred each. Adding our eight companies, we'll have sixteen highly mobile forces spread out up and down the enemy corridors. The key here is to strike and disengage before the enemy can do much damage to you. Any questions?"

The commanders were silent, some shaking their heads in the negative.

"Let me emphasize this again. Be especially wary of the enemy. You know what happened to the sentry they captured—how they broke his mind. I repeat: don't engage the enemy unless you have to, and you know you'll win. Keep at them all the time. Pick at them, raid them, but don't be lured in. Spread wide so they'll have to spread out their own attack. And if any of you or your men *are* captured—" Xeredir glanced down, chewed on his mustache for a moment, then looked up again at the men who stood clustered close by. "If you're captured," he finished, his voice very soft, "forget. Forget everything you know, beginning with your life."

The commanders muttered among themselves, some making gestures to ward off such an evil.

"And you, Lord?" one of them asked. 'Where will you be?"

"I'm going after Kahsir with reinforcements." Haskon jerked his head up, but Xeredir ignored him. "Dhumaric's striking out after Kahsir and the refugees, and Kahsir only has one hundred warriors with him. I'll leave Haskon here as your commander. He'll keep my standard with him. Since the Leishoranya are spying on this camp, they might think I'm still here." He glanced up at the sky, judging the time. "I'll be leaving around midday. If you have any questions for me, ask them now." No one spoke; the only sound was Haskon's ragged breathing. "Good. Go, friends. Luck be with you."

The commanders nodded and left the council circle, the low murmur of their conversation fading as they went. For a long moment, Xeredir avoided looking at Haskon.

"Father."

Haskon's thoughts spilled over his shields in a torrent. Shock—there was plenty of shock, coupled with concern and rebellion. Xeredir turned around.

"What do you think you're doing, Father?"

"Exactly what I said. I can't think of any better way to confuse Dhumaric than for him to think I'm here."

"But—" Haskon shook his head slowly from side to side. "You're—"

"Listen for a moment. Dhumaric's focused his vengeance on Kahs and Lorhaiden. Let him think I'm still here, far to his east, waiting to see what his army will do. He already knows we're going to divide our forces, but he'll wait until we do before he moves. Knowing we stand ready to set out in companies of five hundred, he'll worry about being attacked from behind. He'll be less single-minded on his goal."

Haskon shifted his weight uneasily. "You're right, Father, I know that. But—" He gestured helplessly. "How many men are you going to take with you?"

"Two hundred cavalry."

"Two hundred—?"

"I know . . . I've granted Dhumaric five hundred. Since he's interested in speed above all, I'm betting every last one of that five hundred is horsed. Dhumaric will likely expect to make up time when he and his men hit open ground." He waved his son silent. "I only brought five hundred cavalry north with me, Kona, not expecting to do much save fortify the Golondai passes. But what Kahs did at Rodja'âno changed all my plans."

"But two hundred against Dhumaric's five hundred—"

"I can't take *all* our cavalry with me. Leaving you with only three hundred horsemen is bad enough without taking more. If things happen as I've foreseen, the enemy's not going to move until we do. Once you've established that's true, send three hundred infantry behind me. It's vitally important that the enemy know nothing of this: use the Mind-Born to shield the men you send after me. With my two hundred cavalry and the one hundred who ride with Kahs, plus the three hundred infantry, that will give us six hundred against Dhumaric."

"Not the best of odds."

"No. But we can't spare more now. The enemy *could* move at any time, and I want you to be ready for that."

"How will they know where you are, Father? You'll be going shielded—"

"I'll be taking one of the Mind-Born with me. The Mind-Born staying here can give the infantry commander our location." He tried to smile in encouragement. "Don't worry about me. I'll be all right."

"Lords, I hope so. Be careful, will you?"

"I'll be careful." Xeredir scratched his beard, met and held his sons' eyes. "Here's where my reputation as a conservative commander will do me good, Kona. Dhumaric's underestimated me—he thinks I'll never change, and that's a terrible mistake in war. The last thing he'll expect is to see the old conservative break out of his shell and attack."

Tsingar rode in his place just behind Dhumaric, Girdun at his side and the other five hundred warriors following closely. The afternoon sun shone strong on his face and the early spring day felt warm. Birds sang in the trees and a light wind rustled the forest. Tsingar scratched the end of his nose, worrying an insect bite, and cursed softly.

He glanced sidelong at Girdun, but his fellow officer seemed unaware of this furtive scrutiny. When Dhumaric had left his army behind, Tsingar had assumed Girdun would stay with them as commander. It only made sense: Girdun was the highest ranking commander after Dhumaric, and Dhumaric hardly needed two scoutmasters and seconds in command on a quick strike like this one. He frowned, caught the grimace in time to mask the expression. Now, left in close contact with Girdun, the chance Girdun would find out what had happened to Chaagut was far greater. Tsingar shifted uneasily in his saddle. *Gods. I don't think he knows how Chaagut died. I can't be sure, but I don't think so.* A wave of terror ran through his heart. *What if he's playing with me like I played with Chaagut at the end?*

He glanced away, into the forest. Reports from the south supported Dhumaric's guess that Xeredir would divide his forces, but the Krotànya Crown Prince had not sent them out into the countryside yet. Xeredir was probably waiting for Dhumaric to make a move before he made his. Tsingar snorted. As far as Dhumaric could tell, no one had noticed when he had set out after Kahsir. Xeredir had stayed behind, also as Dhumaric had predicted: the scouts who had watched the Krotànya camp reported his banner still standing there.

Dhumaric raised a hand and gestured. Tsingar caught Girdun's eye, and trotted forward with him until they rode next to Dhumaric.

"Tell the men we're going to take the mind-road soon," Dhumaric said. "We've got a lot of ground to cover and we're not going to do it at this rate. The forest is too damned dense to allow us any speed. Tsingar, contact the advance scouts. Have them make short jumps forward until they're twenty leagues ahead of us; they're then to send back a visual impression of their position. Transfer that sighting to your half of the company. Girdun, do the same with yours. I want us at least twenty leagues farther west within the hour."

Tsingar bowed and rode forward past Dhumaric. Letting all thoughts drain from his mind, he prepared to contact the scouts. It was beginning again, the relentless pursuit of that pair Dhumaric hated the most. If any of the five hundred men who followed hoped for rest and regular meals, they hoped in vain.

Alàric shifted in his saddle as he rode and stared off across the grasslands, shading his eyes in the noon sun. Nothing disturbed the rolling plains save for an occasional tree or two and the gentle rise and fall of the land itself. He shifted his heavy cloak farther back over his shoulders. If only a wind would come from somewhere, anywhere—even the northeast, though that could bring rain. The cloak that had served so well in the early spring weather of the northlands was becoming too heavy. Yet it was not hot by any means, and if he took off his cloak, he would soon feel the chill.

For the first time in a long while, Maiwyn did not ride at his side, but in one of the wagons behind. He smiled as he thought of her—of her eyes, her hair. . . .

"Alàric!" Kahsir's voice. He jerked back to reality with a start. His brother and Hairon rode to his side, and nudged their horses closer. "Thinking of Maiwyn, brother?" Kahsir asked. "You have that special smile on your face."

"Huhn." Alàric refused to be baited; nonreaction was his best defense. He reined his horse off to one

side of the wagons, halted, and waited for his brother
and Hairon to come to his side. "What are you doing
here? And where's Lorhaiden?"

Kahsir lifted one eyebrow and exchanged a glance
with Hairon. "That's a good question. I was going to ask
you if you'd seen him."

"No, not lately. Have you asked Vàlkir?"

"I can't find him, either," Kahsir admitted, glancing
behind, up and down the column of refugees.

Alàric tugged at his beard. *Where the Dark could
Vàlkir be?* "I saw him not all that long ago," he said, a
sudden memory vivid in his mind. "He looked like he
didn't feel well, so I left him alone."

"Ah?" Kahsir's face sharpened and a sudden jolt of
wariness stiffened Alàric's back. "He's never sick.
Where'd you see him?"

Alàric shrugged, gestured at the passing refugees.
"Everywhere. About. Up and down. He's never in one
place long enough to notice. What's wrong, Kahs?"

"I don't know. I hope nothing."

"Want me to look for him, Lord?" Hairon asked.

Alàric glanced closely at Hairon. The farmer's craggy
face showed a concern that seemed far more serious
than the situation warranted.

"No." Kahsir shook his head. "We'll all go look for
him, *if*," he glanced at Alàric, "you can leave Maiwyn
long enough to come with us."

"*Aiii!* You don't see her anywhere near, do you?"

Kahsir grinned, reined his horse around, and gestured. Alàric followed him and Hairon off down the
long column of refugees, scanning those he passed, and
then looked ahead, alert for a glimpse of Vàlkir. *Something's going on here, and Kahs isn't letting me in on
half of it*. Another memory: the last time he had seen
Lorhaiden had been around the evening campfires the
night before. And Kahsir had said something in passing
about Lorhaiden's absence when the refugees had set

out this morning. Alàric touched his horse with his heels and caught up to his brother.

"What's happened to Lorhaiden?" he asked.

Kahsir's mouth was drawn in a tight line of aggravation and concern. "I don't have any idea. But I'm worried, Ahri. Something tells me he's not just off hunting."

The column of refugees seemed endless, though it had grown steadily smaller. Kahsir looked closely at each wagon he passed, at each group of people riding out beyond the wagons. Vàlkir had to be somewhere close by. Unless—

"Lord?" Hairon pointed down the line of refugees. "That be Vàlkir's horse, be'n't it?"

"Aye," Kahsir said. "It looks like his."

The horse, a big bay that Vàlkir rode, walked tied to the back of one of the wagons.

"Whose wagon is that?" Alàric asked.

"I don't know," said Kahsir, "but I mean to find out."

He nudged his horse into a canter and, followed by his brother and Hairon, rode to the wagon. The back gate was open and the wagon was full of children. And Vàlkir.

"Vahl!" Kahsir kept his horse at an easy pace behind the moving wagon. "What are you doing in there?"

Vàlkir looked up, eyes slitted against the sunlight outside the interior darkness. "Telling stories, Lord," he said. He looked away; for a moment there seemed to have been a hint of something besides greeting in his eyes. "Do you want to talk with me?"

"Aye. Where's Lorhaiden?"

Vàlkir remained silent. The children looked back and forth from Kahsir to Vàlkir, totally confused.

"Vahl," Kahsir prompted. "Where is he?"

"I can't answer you, Lord."

"Can't, or won't?"

Vàlkir's discomfort was easy to read. Kahsir jerked a

thumb away from the wagon, and turned his horse off to the side, with Hairon and Alàric following close behind. He glanced over his shoulder. Vàlkir appeared at the wagon's rear and, gathering up his reins and pulling his horse close, jumped over into the saddle. With obvious reluctance, he slowly rode to Kahsir's side.

"Well, Vahl? Why won't you answer me?" Kahsir asked as Vàlkir stopped at his side.

"I promised, Lord. I gave my word."

"To whom? Lorhaiden?"

"Aye."

Kahsir glanced briefly skyward and sighed. "Vahl," he said, his voice tight. "Tell me. Now. We've got to find him."

"Why, Lord?" Vàlkir's blue eyes were level in the sunlight. "Has he done anything wrong?"

"You tell me that."

"I'll betray his trust if I do."

"And if you don't, you'll betray the rest of us. Choose, Vahl."

"He's gone off, Lord," Vàlkir said at last, his voice so soft Kahsir nearly missed his words.

"Where?"

Vàlkir hung his head in defeat and despair. "I don't know, Lord. Truly. I asked him, but he wouldn't tell me. He made me promise I wouldn't say anything. And I couldn't Read him enough to guess. In fact, I couldn't Read him at all."

Kahsir nodded: Lorhaiden had some of the strongest shields he had ever encountered. *Gone off, but gone off where?* Suddenly, his heart lurched. *By the Light! There's only one place that fool could be going! Only one direction he could have taken.* He closed his eyes briefly, a bitter taste filling his mouth. *Why didn't I see it sooner? Lords of Light, why?*

*   *   *

Feeding five hundred men on the march had become a problem, though each had ridden out well-supplied with trail rations. Ever since the Krotànya had poisoned the stew north of Chilufka, Dhumaric had refused to take more than what each man could carry in his saddlebags. The plan, of course, was that hunting would make up for what they had left behind.

The game, however, was wary, and in the thick forest, hard to bring down.

Tsingar frowned: he could hardly tell which was worse, his hunger or his exhaustion. He glanced sidelong at Girdun, who rode seemingly untouched by the hardships of the trail. *By the Gods! If that one can stand the hunger and exhaustion, so can I!* Dhumaric was settling for no delay. Despite grumbling from the warriors, he had kept the pace at a maddening speed.

Dhumaric rode mostly silent now, gathered in upon himself, steeping himself in his hatred. His mood stood out from him like an invisible cloud, and Tsingar had avoided any unnecessary contact with him.

Now, as he rode, Tsingar called up an overview of the country round about into his mind. South, to his left, loomed the forbidding heights of the Golondai Mountains. When Ssenkahdavic chose to march his armies southward, they would go through the passes the Krotànya used—undoubtedly a hard passage, but far better than marching a force the size of the one Ssenkahdavic would lead around those mountains.

Tsingar looked off again to his left, to the Golondai. Something about passes niggled at the back of his mind, a memory from centuries past. He tried to break the partition to the old memories, to find a key to that fragmentary thought, but lost it again. Something—something he could not remember. . . . And suddenly, memory was there: the descent from the frozen heights that divided the continent, the exhaustion that had left hardened warriors weakened and drained. Icy winds howled through what passes the Krotànya had not destroyed; even Ssenkahdavic had not been able to take his entire army over those mountains by the mind-road. The Krotànya, who lay in wait, cut down warriors who were too numbed to react quickly. The losses Ssenkahdavic had suffered had been terrible.

Tsingar shivered in the sunlight, fully back in the present. With a final glance at the Golondai, he reburied his memories, finding nothing presently useful, and concentrated on the way ahead.

The sun had begun to set now. All afternoon, Xeredir had ridden at the head of his two hundred warriors, trusting his scouts to lead by the shortest way. He personally knew one of them, a fellow named Yalrhaci.

A clever man, Yalrhaci. He had once been a trader whose routes had taken him back and forth across the Kingdom of Tumâs. Even when the enemy had invaded the eastern borders of Tumâs and pushed on toward Rodja'âno, Yalrhaci had managed to keep most of his trade routes open. And, as the enemy had drawn closer to Rodja'âno, he had been instrumental in helping many people escape from the Leishoranya. Sometimes working with Eltàrim and her bush-fighters, other times by himself, he had been of incalculable aid. Only when Yalrhaci had seen he could no longer trade freely had he discarded the wagons and pack horses of his profession and taken up the sword and shield of a warrior.

Now the former trader rode back toward the company, hand uplifted to tell that no danger threatened. Satisfied, Xeredir waved in return, trusting to Yalrhaci's judgment. Yalrhaci seemed to know every hidden pathway, every dip and rise in the land, and how to take advantage of them. Even held to limited use of the mind-road to keep the enemy from guessing his position, Xeredir had made better time than he had hoped.

It's going to be a close thing, this following Dhumaric. That bastard's liable to turn up anywhere. His camp was nearly due north of mine, just south and slightly west of Chilufka. I'll bet he's heading west, waiting for the first opportunity to turn to the southwest. Xeredir had held his own course straight west, hoping to beat Dhumaric to that crucial point where the way turned southwesterly, or to be only slightly behind.

And Haskon, left behind at the command post in the meadowlands? Of all the people chosen for the task, Haskon was the most impatient; yet he was an excellent leader, having an instinctive power of command. It would do him good to learn to wait.

Kahsir and Alàric, Lorhaiden and Vàlkir. Since leaving the campsite, Xeredir had shared no more sendings with his eldest son. Kahsir had been puzzled when told not to report in the usual fashion. *Someone's coming after you,* he had reminded Kahsir, *to give you reinforcements.* What he had not said was that he would be leading that company.

Yalrhaci reined in his horse, saluting Xeredir in the open-handed greeting of warriors.

"Everything's all right?" Xeredir asked.

"We may have a problem," Yalrhaci said, his long, somewhat narrow face troubled. "There's a gorge ahead and it's too wide to cross. I know you don't want to draw the enemy's attention, but it's going to take too long to parallel the gorge to a crossing. We'll have to take the mind-road again."

Xeredir shrugged in resignation. Though another three hundred of his men followed only a day or so behind, the last thing he wanted was to face Dhumaric now. Two hundred against five hundred? He shook his head. If he was defeated before the infantry following could bring help, Dhumaric would have a free hand at Kahsir and the refugees.

Kahsir cursed silently: if only Lorhaiden had been graced with a few more brains and less bravery—or less idiocy. He was not sure which. He picked up his saddlebags and started toward his tethered horse.

"And where by all the stars do you think *you're* going?" Alàric asked, stepping into his path.

Kahsir looked at his brother—at the stubborn set of the bearded jaw, the narrowed eyes. This would not be easy—not that he had expected it to be if he met anyone, but with Alàric set off—

"Kahs?" Alàric cocked his head and refused to move. "Where are you going?"

"After Lorhaiden," he said shortly, trying to step around his brother.

"The Void you are! What's gotten into you? Don't you realize—"

Kahsir set the saddlebags at his feet, resigned to talking it out. "I'm *oathed* to him, Ahri . . . he's my *baràdor*. You know what a sword-brother's oath means. Lorhaiden's taken no one with him. In his idiocy, he's ridden off the Light knows where with no one to stand at his side."

"And what do you think *you're* doing?" Alàric asked, his voice a near whisper. "You're as crazy as he is!"

"Huhn. I'm going anyway, crazy or not. And you can't stop me, so don't try."

"What about the refugees?" Alàric gestured behind at the campsite, at the wagons and fires. "Father and Grandfather gave you this task. Are you going to let them down?"

"Now look here—I don't need you to remind me of my duty. If I was the only one with any brains who was leading this group, I'd say you're right. But I know they'll be all right with you."

"Me?" Alàric lifted his hands, then dropped them, utter helplessness in the gesture. "I'm just your aide. If Father had wanted me to take these people south, he would have—"

"Ah, stop it, Ahri! By the Lords! You've held command before—hundreds of times. Why are you so concerned now?" He locked eyes with his brother. "Is it because of Maiwyn? Is that it? Do you want to spend all your time with her, and—"

Alàric's face stiffened, but Kahsir saw the hurt in his brother's eyes.

"I'm sorry," he said, reaching out to touch Alàric's shoulder. "That was unfair of me and cruel. Cruel and untrue."

"I'm worried about you," Alàric grated, his bearded jaw set tightly. "You don't know which way Lorhaiden's gone, you don't know where Dhumaric is. . . . Ah, aye, I know about that. You thought you'd kept it a secret, but I know."

Kahsir drew a deep breath. "*Aii'ya!*" he whispered, sinking to his heels by his saddlebags. "How'd you find out?" he asked as Alàric hunkered down beside.

"Now I'm being cruel," Alàric said. "You didn't give it away. I merely suspected—suspected and drew you out. But Lorhaiden suspected it also. There's some dark bond between him and Dhumaric: something forged, perhaps, by the massacre of his family. He was convinced enough of it to go off by himself."

Ahri's right. A dark bond. And I'll bet that bond will lead Lorhaiden straight to Dhumaric. He sighed heavily, met his brother's eyes again. "You're clever," he said, "too damned clever to get out of taking over leadership of the refugees. You should be able to get them out of any trouble they meet." He stood. "I'm going. Don't fight me. I can't help how I feel about Lorhaiden, despite his multitude of idiocies."

"How many men does Dhumaric lead?" Alàric asked, standing. "Do you know?"

"Father said he suspects Dhumaric took five hundred after us."

"Five hundred?" Alàric's face went pale. "We've only got one hundred with us, and—"

"Father's sending reinforcements, Ahri."

"But if Dhumaric gets to us first. . . ."

Kahsir put both hands on Alàric's shoulders and shook

his brother gently. "For the Light's sake, get a hold of yourself. Maybe you *have* gone dull-witted on me. You certainly picked a fine time to fall head over heels in love."

Alàric's pale face reddened. "Maiwyn has nothing to do with—"

"Then stop acting like you can't think your way out of a corner! Take the mind-road, Ahri. You're not stupid. You'll know what to do."

He picked up his saddlebags and started off toward the horses. Alàric followed.

"At least take someone with you," Alàric said at last. "You don't have any idea when or where you'll catch up to Lorhaiden, or even if you will. Take someone else. I'd feel better if you did that."

"No." Kahsir shook his head. He rubbed his horse's nose in greeting; the black nickered softly, tossed its head, and then stood hipshot. Kahsir threw his saddlebags behind the saddle, began tying them down. "I'm going alone," he said, looking sidelong at his brother. "Any more than one might draw enemy attention."

"And what am I to say when you're missed?"

"Tell them I'm off hunting. That won't sound too unlikely."

"Huhn." Alàric's eyes moved slightly, his change in expression a warning that someone stood behind. Kahsir turned around.

"Lord," Vàlkir said. Hairon stood at his side, the reins to their horses in his hands. "Shall we go? If we want to catch up with Lorhaiden, we'll have to be quick about it."

Kahsir still stared, unable to say a thing.

"I'm glad Hairon's coming along," Vàlkir said brightly, ignoring Kahsir's stare. "The land's changed, but he's more familiar with it than you or I. Some of his wife's kin farmed lands not all that far away."

"Ahri!" Kahsir swung around and faced his brother. "If you—"

"Ah, no, Kahs," Alàric protested, lifting his hands in defense. "I had nothing to do with this. They came of their own accord. In fact, I tried to stop them, thinking I'd be able to talk some sense into your thick head." He laughed softly. "Since I've obviously failed in that, at least you'll ride out with the best men I could have sent with you."

CHAPTER 16

Twilight crept down on many-towered Hvâlkir, the King City. From his vantage point in the garden that sat close to the side of the palace, Vlàdor could see a good part of the city below. Starlike, lamps lit one by one, and the sea seemed to still to grey velvet cloth.

He turned his head slightly, not wishing to intrude on private thoughts, and glanced at Eltàrim. She stood motionless in the fading light. Her entire stance was calm but the worry she felt surged just beneath her shields. That worry drew them closer; it was an emotion shared not only by High-King and field commander, but by a grandfather and a grandson's beloved.

Nothing much in the way of news had come from the north in several days. Vlàdor had received a message from Errehmon, the commander who had taken charge of the retreat from Rodja'âno. Xeredir had ordered Errehmon to divide his forces; now, having done so, Errehmon commanded nine companies of five hundred each. Xeredir then ordered Errehman to take those companies and attack the enemy as they came south from Fânchorion to stabilize the corridor forced between Fânchorion and Rodja'âno. Xeredir, himself would try to prevent the Leishoranya from strengthening the corridor that ran south of Rodja'âno and the steading of Chilufka.

Vlàdor had seen his grandson's hand in these orders, though Xeredir had given them—Kahsir's style of fighting, one he had used time and again to his advantage.

But of Xeredir and his grandsons, Vlàdor had no word.

He turned as footsteps crunched on the gravel behind. It was Tebehrren, unannounced as usual. Vlàdor smiled a stiff greeting. Not even the High-King commanded the Mind-Born; they came and went according to their own will, beyond the reach of kings.

"My Lord." Tebehrren bowed. "'Lady,'" he said, bowing to Eltàrim. He straightened, his face showing no expression in the dim light save patient waiting. "You need me tonight."

"Do I?" asked Vlàdor. Then, he gestured briefly. "I'm sorry, Tebehrren. My mind was elsewhere. Please join us."

Tebehrren lifted one eyebrow, acknowledging Vlàdor's apology. "Your mind's elsewhere, King. But where?"

"And *you* don't know? Ah, damn my tongue. Everything I've said today has come out backward. Aye, my mind's elsewhere. It's in the north, with my son and my grandsons."

"That's why you need me," Tebehrren said, his voice cool and collected as always. "There's a lot happening in the northlands, things hidden from many inquiring minds." He looked at Eltàrim, then back. "Even yours, Lord."

Vlàdor sighed. Talking to the Mind-Born was like having a discussion with a bank of fog—conversations wrapped in endless riddles, words that made sense only in retrospect. Perhaps it was the way their minds worked.

"We're more highly trained," Tebehrren added, reading Vlàdor's shielded thoughts with amazing ease and skill. The hint of what might have been a smile flickered across Tebehrren's face. "But I'm interested in *your* mind tonight, Lord, not mine."

Eltàrim stood straighter. "What should we know, Lord Tebehrren?" A hint of frustration entered her voice. "We live in the here and now, in daily events, not in the ether of the mind. Don't play with us."

Tebehrren inclined his head in her direction, then looked back. "I have news of your son, Lord, and your grandsons."

Vlàdor's chest tightened. Eltàrim moved closer, her mind fixed on Kahsir.

"I'll be brief," Tebehrren said, "and as direct as I can. Dhumaric's now aware of all Xeredir has planned to do—or nearly all. Xeredir's added a few twists Dhumaric missed. What you've probably perceived, and what concerns you, is Kahsir. He and those who ride with him are in grave danger."

"Ah?" Vlàdor's shoulders tensed; he forced the muscles to relax. "Xeredir made a Sending to me a few days ago. He told me much of what you've said—even of Dhumaric's intention to go after Kahs and the refugees. But Dhumaric's many leagues behind and the refugees are protected."

Tebehrren nodded slowly. "That's true. But did Xeredir tell you that the force Dhumaric took with him after Kahsir was five hundred strong?"

Vlàdor's breath caught in his throat.

"Or," persisted Tebehrren, "that Dhumaric's taken the mind-road several times to shorten the distance between himself and your grandsons? No? I didn't think so."

"He said he *suspected* Dhumaric would take five hundred men after Kahsir. How the Void could he have known for sure? And even if he *did* know, he wouldn't risk sending that information to me. There are too many enemy minds in the northlands waiting to intercept such news."

"That's why I'm here, Lord," Tebehrren said quietly.

"I can give you additional information. You can act on it, if that's your choice."

Vlàdor turned away from Tebehrren and Eltàrim, his jaw clenched.

"Another thing, Lord." Vlàdor turned reluctantly around until he faced the Mind-Born. "Xeredir himself has gone after Kahsir to bring him reinforcements."

"Xeredir?" Vlàdor shook his head: how unlike his son to leap into the unknown, to risk— No. That was not true. He would do the same for Xeredir, for *his* son. Why should Xeredir be different? "When?" he asked, his voice rough.

"Three days ago, Lord."

Vlàdor started to speak, then looked from Tebehrren to Eltàrim and back. She stood silent, her face pale and set in the dim light.

"There's one other thing, Lord," Tebehrren said. "I'm not sure if telling you this will help or hinder what you're deciding to do. I sensed—*sensed* only—worse danger. Kahsir and Lorhaiden: they're both caught up in something I can't See."

"With the refugees?" Vlàdor rubbed his hands together. It was a nervous gesture; he forced his hands apart. "Are the refugees in danger, too?"

"Possibly, Lord."

"Tebehrren." Vlàdor looked directly into the Mind-Born's shadowed eyes. "You and I may not agree on a number of things, but you've always advised me well, and you've been a worthy friend. What can I do? Within the limits of my power, what *can* I do?"

Silence fell on the garden. Vlàdor heard the sounds of the leaves, rustling to an evening's wind—the noise of his heart beating, a slow thunder in his ears.

"You ask me to tell you what you can do," Tebehrren said at last. He gestured, at once weary and apologetic. "All I can tell you is what you *can't* do. That, of course, is to use your mind against the enemy."

Vlàdor caught back his curse before it escaped. "Time's

running out for any action I can take if all you say is true."

"Time?" The Mind-Born dismissed the word with a quick flip of his hand. "What is time, Lord? We have all that will ever be."

"You may," Vlàdor snapped, losing his patience at last, "you and the other Mind-Born. But the rest of us are running perilously short of it." He held out his hands in appeal. "I ask you as a friend, as a father. What can I do to help my kin?"

Tebehrren's expression softened in the twilight. "I'll keep you informed, Lord, as best I can, of what's happening to the north. The instant I find out anything of importance, I'll let you know. As for advice: that's cheap to give and always more than you want. But I can tell you this, temper your actions with reason. You'll have the strength to do what you have to do."

"He's an odd man," Eltàrim said as Tebehrren left the garden. Her thoughts spilled out from behind her shields. Vlàdor sensed her frustration. Though she had known the Mind-Born's leader most of her life, she still could not Read him.

"He's a pompous, puffed-up—" Vlàdor drew a deep breath. "No. I take all that back. He's an old friend, a good adviser, who's stood by me for centuries. I can't fault him for being what he is."

"Well, he certainly isn't the most helpful friend you have," she said.

"Hardly." He followed Eltàrim to a low stone bench beneath one of the melenor trees. Sitting down beside her, he sniffed the sweet scent of the budding white blossoms, and drew a long, slow breath.

"As for being helpful," he said at last, "I don't think he had much to give."

"Damn!" Her voice was soft, but he sensed the rage beneath it. "*I'd* help you if I could, but with Chilufka gone, and Genlàvyn out of touch, I don't know *what* the Dark's going on up north! I can't get in touch with my men. I don't know where they *are*—" Her voice faltered.

He nodded. "I'd send more men to the north to aid Kahs and Alàric. But I don't have them. I simply don't have them. Unless. . . ."

"Unless what?"

"Ah, no," he shrugged. "It was only an idle thought. A maybe. A might be. I can only deal with what is."

She was silent for a long moment. "I wish I could go." She looked up directly into his eyes. "Give me a sword and shield, and if not many men can be spared, then some."

He stared at her. "No, Tahra. Not that I don't think you'd be effective. But I need you here: everyone who fights in the north needs you here. You're coordinating some of the best resistance we have against the enemy, and I can't risk losing you, too."

"Then let Iowyn go. You could call her back from the south—"

"I can't do it. She's a good fighter—one of the best— but she doesn't know how to command. Lords knows she has enough trouble commanding herself."

Eltàrim's shadowed eyes never left his face. "It's so frustrating," she said, her voice trembling, "to sit here and do nothing."

"What do you think I'm feeling, if not that?" he asked. "I'm stuck here in the capital, like a spider in the center of his web. I can't leave for fear of losing sight of something on the other side."

She laughed quietly and without humor. "We're in the same web together, then. And as for not letting me go, or Iowyn—it won't be long before we're fighting. And we won't do it because we like it, or want to, but because we must."

"So, Devà." Vlàdor turned from the map in his lamp-lit study to face Lord Devàn, his after-dinner wine for-

gotten in his hand. "You can see how things are tangled."
He glanced back to the map. "From what I can tell,
Kahs and the refugees should be here." He pointed
toward the Golondai Mountains where the range turned
to the southwest. "Xeredir—" His finger moved back
east, toward a point just north of Chailon Pass. "—has
his campsite set up here."

"Dhumaric?"

"Here." Vlàdor pointed to a position north and west
of Xeredir's campsite. "At least that's where I think he
started from. The Fields of Kormâlden are here, and he
fled back northwest from them toward Chilufka after
Xeredir defeated him."

"And Xeredir?"

"He's gone after Kahsir, so he should be west of his
camp. His army's waiting at the foot of Chailon Pass,
broken down into companies of five hundred. They'll
hold their position until the army Dhumaric left behind
sets itself in motion. I haven't any idea how many men
Xeredir took with him when he went after Kahsir. But
from what Tebehrren told me, Dhumaric's force is five
hundred strong."

Devàn shook his head. "That's going to pose a problem. Five hundred men is a large and mobile enough
company to do terrible damage."

"Huhn. That's an understatement." Vlàdor stretched
the tension from his shoulders. "I wouldn't want to face
Dhumaric and his five hundred men with less than the
same number at my back."

"How many warriors rode out with the refugees?"
Devàn asked.

Vlàdor turned, walked across the room, and gestured
Devàn to one of the chairs by the window as he sat in
the other. "Xeredir told me one hundred. They volunteered to ride with the refugees before going back to
fight in the north."

"One hundred." Devàn sat down and was silent for a

moment. He shook his head. "Disaster, Lord. They wouldn't stand a chance against Dhumaric."

"Even if Xeredir *does* catch up to them before Dhumaric, that's three hundred against half a thousand." Vlàdor sighed, set his cup down on the table between the chairs, and rubbed his hands together. "And we can't spare the men to send north to aid them. The situation's too precarious in the south and east for that."

"Perhaps not," Devàn murmured. "I brought over five hundred of my own men back to the capital with me. They've fought recently and deserve their rest, but—"

Vlàdor jumped. "Are you saying—?"

"I'm offering to march north, Lord. If we take the mind-road, we could reach the northlands quickly."

"But we don't know where Dhumaric, Xeredir, *or* Kahsir are, Devà. You could blunder around up there for days before finding them."

"Ah-h-h," Devàn growled, dismissing that. "Get Tebehrren to tell you where he thinks they are. *He's* always full of news."

"I told you about our conversation this evening . . . he's not been too helpful. I honestly think he doesn't know where *anyone* is for sure. He also told me something else. Kahsir and Lorhaiden are in grave danger, somehow separate from the refugees. He didn't know any more about that, either. And he said as much, Devà, if you can believe it."

"Well, tell him to find out!" Devàn said. "By all the Lords of Light! He's your adviser, isn't he? What the Void's he doing if he can't help you in this?"

"All right. I'll talk to him. And as for you and your men—all I can ask you to do now is stay here in the capital. I can't afford to lose you, too." He drew a long breath. "I'll send for Tebehrren. But keep this in mind— unless we can get him to give us an exact location, you and your men aren't going anywhere."

Devàn nodded and stood. "If you *do* get something out of him, let me know. I'll alert my men that we could be riding out on the slightest notice.

Vlàdor nodded and watched his friend leave the study. Until he knew for certain what was going on in the north, his hands were tied, no matter how eager Devàn was to ride out. For a long moment Vlàdor sat staring at the closed doors; then he looked from them across the room. The large map hung there on the wall, bloodied with red ink in the lamplight, silently mocking all his plans.

CHAPTER 17

Xeredir looked through the steadily falling rain and shivered in the chill. He glanced up at the sky, shielding his eyes with an upraised hand, but could not tell how long the rain would last. A thin trickle of water ran down his neck and his helm dripped like the eaves of some roof. He cursed softly and turned his horse from the vantage point he had occupied on the hill crest, and rode back to where his men waited in the forest.

It was even gloomier under the drooping branches, and water fell from them in huge drops. Though the pine trees gave off a pleasant scent, Xeredir found the chill worse here than it had been in the open.

He dismounted, tethered his horse to a sapling, and tried to shake the worst of the rain from his cloak. The weather had slowed his men considerably. To preserve secrecy of movement, he had led them down the mind-road as seldom as possible, and then only for limited distances. Now, he considered taking the mind-road again, if for nothing more than to escape the rain.

"Lord."

Xeredir turned around: a man stood close by in the gloom, white cloak darkened by the wet.

"I've received word from your son, Haskon," the man said.

From the other Mind-Born with him, Xeredir amended. He and the other men who were not so highly trained trusted to the Mind-Born for information. And not knowing where—or even how close—the enemy might be, secrecy in message sending could make the difference between living and dying. "Aye, Mataihyàr? And what news?"

"Nothing of importance. He says no one's moving— not him or the enemy. From what the Mind-Born tell him, the Leishoranya have divided their forces, too. They've tried to draw Haskon north by subtle feints, but he's ignored them."

Xeredir laughed softly at the thought of Haskon sitting still for anything, then waved for Mataihyàr to continue.

"There's not much more, Lord." The Mind-Born paused. A young man, not long from his training, he had volunteered to ride west with Xeredir. "Haskon says he'll wait for your orders before he sends the companies out, unless there's real provocation by the enemy. That's all, Lord. What I shall send in return?"

"My love," Xeredir answered. "If we find anything concerning Dhumaric's whereabouts, I'll let him know."

Mataihyàr nodded and returned to his place slightly apart from the other men, hidden by the low branches of pine.

Xeredir looked out from the forest at the western horizon. The unseen sun was setting; it was foolishness to go any farther at this hour. Even Dhumaric would have been slowed by the rain; Leishoranya grew as hungry, cold, and miserable as Krotànya.

He looked back over his shoulder. "Has anyone see Yalrhaci?"

Several men shook their heads, a few murmured in the negative.

"He should be back by now, shouldn't he, Lord?" asked Elhvàn.

Xeredir glanced at his shieldman and nodded, then turned and sought somewhere dry to sit down. Elhvàn followed.

"Do you want some of us to go look for him?" Elhvàn asked.

"No." Xeredir sat down on a fallen tree trunk and rubbed his eyes wearily. "He's the last one we should worry about. Wait. He'll be back in a little while."

"Huhn."

Elhvàn wandered off. Xeredir knew he had not convinced his shieldman—his own doubts were too strong. He looked out from the forest again.

The rain was falling harder now; long lines of it obscured the fields that lay beyond the trees. Dusk was fading to night. He rubbed the back of his neck. *Lords! Let Yalrhaci be all right!* A gust of rain spattered down from the shadows in the trees. *What if something's happened to him? I haven't been this way in decades, nor have most of the scouts.* He looked back at the forest. Kahsir's observation that the land had changed was becoming persistent reality now.

His men began to make nests for themselves in the undergrowth behind; the pickets he had selected earlier left for their stations. He shrugged, stood, and walked back to the camp. Elhvàn offered two strips of dried meat. Xeredir wolfed them down, then turned and followed his shieldman.

Elhvàn had prepared a place to sleep: drier than most, it lay hidden beneath a hastily constructed shelter—pine limbs laid up against a half-fallen tree. Xeredir crawled beneath those branches and nodded a good rest to his shieldman. Trying to get as comfortable as possible, he stretched out and gathered his cloak tighter. Though he was tired, his tense muscles simply would not relax.

"Elhvàn." His shieldman moved closer, a rustle in

the darkness. "When Yalrhaci comes back, wake me. I don't care what time of night it is."

"Aye, Lord." Elhvàn was worried; Xeredir heard it in his voice. "And if he's not here by morning?"

"Morning will come soon enough. Sleep now, while we have the chance."

Tsingar knelt in the dark by the dying man, Dhumaric and Girdun standing just out of view behind him. The Krotàn was seriously wounded, and it was impossible to guess how long he would live.

"Where'd you catch this one?" Dhumaric asked.

"Ten leagues or so from here, Master." Tsingar blinked the rain from his eyes, peered at the Krotàn again. "A trader, Dread Lord, by his looks. We've caught several of them before. They all tend to dress the same: no armor, leather clothing, soft-soled boots."

"By the Dark! What's a trader doing out here? Who's he trading with—the dead?"

Tsingar laughed; it was expected. "He was headed westward. Probably escaping Rodja'âno, or territory near it."

"Huhn." Dhumaric and Girdun came closer. One of the warriors who stood nearby lifted a torch so Dhumaric could see.

"He does have the look of a trader," Girdun said. "Yet there's something I don't like about him. He's too well armed, don't you think?"

"For a trader?" Tsingar looked back down at the dying man. Lately, Girdun had questioned everything he had said. Time and again he ended up taking the defensive, skillfully maneuvered there by Girdun's seemingly innocent words. He ignored Girdun and eyed the dying man's weapons: longsword and shortsword, boot-knife and small axe carried at the belt. "Aye," he said, "he's well-armed. But I'd expect any of the Krotànya to go armed to the teeth these days. In fact, I'm surprised we found him at all." He glanced up at Dhumaric, then down again. "Word's gone out among the Krotànya, and most have fled. They know they're beaten here in the north."

"Has anyone tried his mind?" Dhumaric asked.

Tsingar stiffened. "Not yet, Dread Lord. We just brought him in. If you wish, we'll do it now."

"I think I would have done that first," Girdun said, his voice mild. "He's too close to death. If he dies before we can read him—"

Dhumaric snorted derisively. "Get on with it, Tsingar. He'll die soon and we don't have anyone with us who can read the dead accurately."

Tsingar motioned to one of the onlookers. The man started; his eyes widened in the torchlight, then snapped over to Dhumaric.

"You," Tsingar ordered. "Get into this man's mind. Find out anything you can."

The Krotàn groaned, feebly now. He had been shot many times with arrows, one of which had lodged close to his heart. Blood ran from his mouth and nostrils into rain-darkened blond beard and mustache, and his narrow face was twisted in pain.

The man singled out to read the captive's mind edged forward. Tsingar cursed softly under his breath. He sensed this fellow was not especially talented; though he came recommended, none had ever seen him work before. But he was all they had and time was running out—the Krotàn could die in moments, taking vital information beyond their reach.

Tsingar rocked back on his heels, ignoring the rain that dripped down from the overhanging trees. Visibly ill at ease, the other warrior settled down before the arrow-shot captive. Tsingar wiped the water from his eyes and darted a glance at the kneeling warrior. *Who wouldn't be nervous with Dhumaric watching every move?*

The Krotàn screamed—a long, wild cry, it echoed for a moment in the forest's stillness. He screamed again, and again. Someone snickered in amusement. Then, with a shudder, the captive went limp, his staring eyes glazed over in death.

"Well?" asked Dhumaric, obviously bored.

No reply. Tsingar looked quickly at the man he had chosen for this task, but the warrior remained silent. Cold sweat broke out on Tsingar's hands despite the nighttime chill.

"Well?" Dhumaric asked again in an icy voice. "What did you learn, worm?"

"Dread Lord," the man whispered. "It was too late." Dhumaric tensed, coiled and ready to spring. "Too late, Dread Lord," the warrior repeated. "He was near death when I started. No one could have—"

Dhumaric stepped forward so suddenly Tsingar could not get out of the way. Knocked onto his side, he stared up at his commander, pulled his head between his shoulders, and ducked the blow that never came.

"You fool! You bungling idiot!" Dhumaric was raging now. Tsingar swallowed convulsively: Dhumaric's anger was directed elsewhere. "Do you realize what you've done?" Dhumaric's huge hand shot out, clenched: the warrior's head snapped back. "You forced his mind, didn't you?" Dhumaric yelled. "And now we're left with nothing!"

Tsingar scrambled to his feet, saw torchlight glint dully on Dhumaric's knife. Dhumaric grabbed the stunned warrior by the arm and jerked him erect. Momentary sanity came to Dhumaric's eyes as he turned around.

"Tsingar!" he snapped, gesturing with the knife at the dead Krotàn. "Get rid of that carrion. It's useless to us now." And dragging the near-unconscious warrior behind, Dhumaric stalked off.

Someone stood at Tsingar's side. He turned, and looked into Girdun's flat gaze.

"Another flawed job, Tsingar?" said Girdun, the hint of a smile on his face.

He started to reply but Girdun had already turned away, following Dhumaric. For a long moment Tsingar stood there in the rain looking after them, rage clouding his vision. Then, though he had been instructed to do the deed, he motioned one of the onlookers to drag the body off into the brush. He slowly went after Dhumaric and the other men, his eagerness for torture replaced by growing fear.

Kahsir nudged his horse into a slow canter; visibility had become far better now that the sun was rising. He, Hairon, and Vàlkir had been riding for an hour now. He glanced over his shoulder at them: they followed, shaking off the last of their sleepiness. Both had been groggy when awakened, but if they hoped to catch Lorhaiden, they would have to push beyond the pace they guessed he held.

"Lord," Vàlkir called softly. He brought his horse alongside. "How close to him do you think we are?"

Kahsir glanced at Vàlkir and shrugged. "Who knows? If the fire pit we found last night was his, we're nearly a day behind."

"It was his. I know it."

"He be crazy, Lord," Hairon said, unprompted. "Out of his mind! One man against Dhumaric? Huhn."

Kahsir laughed grimly. "All that matters to him now is his Oath. It's driving him beyond anything we can understand."

"Understand? Who wants to understand?" the stocky farmer grumbled. "Not me, that's for damn sure."

Vàlkir cleared his throat and Hairon subsided into unintelligible muttering. "He's retracing the path we took," Vàlkir observed. "He probably thinks Dhumaric will find it soon enough."

Kahsir nodded slowly, glancing at various landmarks. The logic of Lorhaiden's choice was unquestionable, but the point at which Dhumaric would turn south to pick up the refugees' trail was anyone's guess.

He glanced up at the early morning sky, then down again. *Why now, Lorhaiden, why now? How could you go off like this when I asked you to stay?* Lorhaiden's voice echoed out of the past, arguing about the importance of the Oath of the Sun's Blood. His own efforts to bring some reason into Lorhaiden's life were an apparent failure. Xeredir's voice whispered in his mind: *Keep tight rein on Lorhaiden . . . he could be one of the best commanders we have.* Kahsir winced inwardly. It was true, all too true.

"He be taking the mind-road, I bet," Hairon said from behind.

Kahsir shook his head. "Not yet. If he has, it's been for only short distances. He'll save his strength for when he feels it's needed most."

"And should we?" Vàlkir asked. "Take the mind-road, I mean."

"I suppose we could, but we need to conserve our strength, too. Besides, we don't know where he is. We could go off in one direction, and miss him with a hill between us. Worse yet, we could overshoot him entirely and land in Dhumaric's lap."

Hairon cursed softly. "Dhumaric be a dung-ball, a motherless—"

"We'll have to take the mind-road eventually," Vàlkir interrupted. "Lorhaiden's too determined. And when his Oath takes over— He probably only slept a few hours last night, if at all. Even if he wasn't traveling, he would have been too upset to sleep."

"That could help us," Kahsir said. "He might be tired enough to slow down." He frowned and looked off to the distance. *Might be.* The oath he and Lorhaiden had sworn as sword-brothers had compelled this search, yet he was tempted to let Lorhaiden go. Not only was he disobeying his father by turning back, he was going after a man equally as possessed as Dhumaric. If Lorhaiden did not bolt this time, Lords knew he would find other opportunities.

"Look, Lord!" Vàlkir pointed. A pile of horse dung lay off to one side.

Kahsir reined in, dismounted, and knelt. He picked up a stick and prodded the dung: it was not a day old. Vàlkir and Hairon rode up close behind and waited silently.

"We're getting closer," Kahsir said, glancing at them over his shoulder. He stood, dropped the stick, and reached for his reins. "Let's go."

The rain had thinned out into a fine blowing mist, only a little less uncomfortable than yesterday's downpour. One of the horse's hooves struck loudly against a rock and Xeredir started. The others must know by now how much on edge he was. Elhvàn rode at a walk alongside, equally silent and withdrawn. The other warriors followed, talking hardly at all, their hands close to their weapons.

When dawn had broken, Yalrhaci still had not returned. Xeredir had hesitated to go on, but the thought of Kahsir and Alàric in danger offered little choice: he must keep on and hope for the best.

Trusting to his scouts and old memories for guidance, he kept the mist-hidden bulk of the Golondai Mountains always to his left. When visibility permitted, he set his course by the towering height of Sijei Mountain. Where the Rodja'âno Road ran near its base, Kahsir and the refugees would have turned to the southwest.

Teeth clenched and his jaw tightly set, Xeredir tried to relax in his saddle, but found that impossible. Yalrhaci's absence weighed on his mind like a stone. Yalrhaci had made it his reckless practice to range ahead of the army by ten leagues or more—over an hour's travel through this country—returning whenever he felt it necessary to change the course of travel. Yalrhaci always laughed at Xeredir's concern, saying that any who caught him unawares would be welcome to him. His pride was justified: few could match him in the wilderness in stealth, knowledge, and cunning. But, Xeredir reflected uneasily, a man like that could run headlong into something he could not control.

"Have we seen any more markers?" asked Elhvàn, his voice loud in the silence.

Xeredir shook his head. Yalrhaci had blazed the trail, leaving signs to direct their course of march. "No," he said. "Not since the last, and that was nearly ten leagues back."

Elhvàn cursed softly. "I'm afraid something's happened to him."

"Aye."

Elhvàn fell silent again at the terse answer. Xeredir looked around, squinting through the mist, memorizing landmarks.

Dammit, Elhvàn—I'm worried, too. Yalrhaci knows this country better than any of us. If the other scouts don't get back soon, we'll have to halt.

Xeredir wiped the clinging mist from his face and looked ahead. The world was a study in grey: trees, near black, their outlines softened by the blowing mist; the land behind them, fading away into lighter shades of grey; and the sky overhead, leaden, with clouds so thick the sun could only be sensed.

And visibility poor enough that depth of vision was deceptive. An enemy attack now could spell disaster.

"Lord!" Elhvàn pointed off slightly to the right. "Here come the scouts. Maybe they've found something."

The indistinct grey forms of two horsemen grew darker and took on form as they rode closer. Xeredir's stomach tensed into a knot. There was something about the way the scouts sat their horses—

"Lord," the first said, drawing rein at Xeredir's side. His face was white and drawn in the gloomy light. One hand tightly gripped the reins; he gestured back to the way he had come with the other. "We've found Yalrhaci."

Xeredir's hands clenched. "Dead?" he asked, though he knew the answer.

"Aye, Lord." The other scout spoke, his mouth drawn into a thin line of anger. "Arrowshot. Not more than two leagues from here."

Xeredir flinched, his heart lurching. Two leagues away?

"Any sign of the enemy?"

"They camped close to where we found Yalrhaci, Lord. From the looks of it, last night."

O Lords! Xeredir turned in his saddle, looking back to the men who sat their horses behind him. "Close ranks!" he called. "Uncase your shields!" He glanced at his second in command, Sebahdyr. "Get to the rear. Make sure everyone's riding tight, with mind-shields up."

"Should we keep going, Lord?"

"Aye. Until I get a look at Yalrhaci. We're headed that direction anyway."

Sebahdyr nodded and trotted off.

"Ride," Xeredir said, and gestured to the scouts; they reined their horses around and set off at a fast trot. He followed, his mouth full of a bitter taste, and shivered, but not from the dampness. With Yalrhaci gone, he and his men would be half-blind, moving into territory they hardly knew.

A league passed, and then the second. The blowing mist thickened into a steady drizzle. Suddenly, the scouts drew rein and pointed off toward a stand of brush. Xeredir swallowed heavily, glanced around, then rode to where the scouts waited, while Sebahdyr ordered a halt at full alert.

Dead since last night, Yalrhaci's body lay tangled in the thick underbrush. Xeredir looked quickly to his right, his heart thumping loudly in his chest. A large number of men had camped nearby, and, as the scouts had said, not all that long ago. Dhumaric? Or had it been another Leishoranya company? Xeredir's flesh crawled. How close had they been to the enemy? They

might have spent the night sleeping within fifteen leagues
of the foe.

He dismounted, let the reins dangle, and stepped
closer to Yalrhaci. The guide's body was full of arrow
wounds, but his face—Xeredir shuddered briefly. That
look—that vacant, staring expression, like the man back
at the foot of Chailon Pass.

Mind-broken.

He glanced around again, fighting down a growing
sense of panic. *O Lords! If the enemy broke Yalrhaci's
mind before he died, they could have learned where we
are, how many there are of us, and where we're going.*
He hunkered down on his heels and rubbed his eyes.
*And I can't assume the refugees are still the target.
Dhumaric might be coming at me.*

He looked up: Elhvàn and Sebahdyr had dismounted
and stood a few steps away.

"Sebahdyr. Get the men in close. We're not moving
until this rain and mist lifts. The enemy could be anywhere." He turned to Elhvàn. "Tell Mataihyàr to probe
for the enemy. I want any information he can give me
of their position."

The two men nodded and walked quickly off into the
drizzle. Xeredir rubbed the bridge of his nose; a sudden feeling of loss filled his heart. Yalrhaci had been—
He frowned. *Mourn him later. Now you've got to think
fast on your feet.* He sensed the company behind him
tightening their ranks, their thoughts slipping through
their shields. Xeredir grimaced and turned away. *Lords
grant that Yalrhaci died before the enemy could get
into his mind.*

Exhausted to the point of numbness, Lorhaiden urged
his horse on though the animal was close to floundering. He looked off into the forest and licked his dry lips.
A small voice clamored for rest, but he ruthlessly silenced it. *Dhumaric! O Lords! Give me a chance at*

that motherless bastard! He blinked again. The world tilted for a moment and he nearly slid from the saddle.

Rest! that inner voice urged. *Rest now, or you'll be no good when and if you do find Dhumaric! Are you trying to kill yourself first? Idiot!*

He tried to spit off into the brush but his mouth was too dry. He reached for his water bag, unstopped it, and drank. When he lowered it, it was nearly empty. He was going to have to find a stream, some water, soon. He stopped the water bag, hung it from his saddle, and looked around. The land sloped off to his left away from the heights of the Golondai. He rode a bit aside from his path, searching for water.

He closed his eyes and drew a deep breath. He saw his father die again, his home in flames, the Leishoranya gleefully shooting down the men trapped by the burning barn. He trembled with rage, but instead of the strength the vision usually gave, he felt only a hint of energy.

I've got to rest. I've pressed myself too hard. I'll find Dhumaric yet. I can hardly miss him since he's coming this way.

His horse had slowed to an unsure walk. Lorhaiden opened his eyes and looked around. There had to be some place close by where he could rest for a few hours.

He turned his horse toward an especially dense thicket, reined in, and dismounted. His knees nearly buckled under his weight. For a moment he clung to the saddle, waiting until some strength returned to his legs, then, straightening, he led his horse into the thicket, tethered it to a small tree. His eyes went out of focus for a moment. He blinked several times, drew a deep breath, and pushed the brush back to make a place where he could lie down. He fell to his knees and eased down onto his side. Wrapping his cloak tighter, he dimly heard his horse snort quietly and shift on its feet.

Darkness washed along the edge of his vision; he surrendered and slid down the black well of sleep.

Alàric reined in his horse and turned sideways in the saddle. There, off to his left and slightly behind, brilliant in the midday sunlight, loomed the snowcapped peaks of Sijei Mountain. From here on, his course would turn more to the southwest as the Golondai Mountains gave way to the high plains. He stretched in the saddle and looked forward again down the line of refugees. *We've got hundreds of leagues left to travel before we reached the River Abhlin and cross over into Elyâsai. If we take the mind-road a few more times—*

"Alàric?"

He turned at the sound of Maiwyn's voice. She edged her horse closer.

"What's wrong?" she asked. "You've been so silent."

He sighed quietly. Sooner or later she would have to know. They had grown close enough lately that before long it would be impossible to hide anything from her.

"Your word of honor, Wynna," he said. "Nothing of this must leak out."

"Not even to Genlàvyn?" Her eyebrows rose as he shook his head. "It *must* be a secret then, if—" Her face clouded. "It's about Kahsir, isn't it? Kahsir and Lorhaiden?"

He nodded briefly. Behind, the wagons had drawn to a halt; riders let their horses graze as everyone took a welcome pause from the trek. "I suppose I should have told you sooner, but—" His voice trailed off. "We're in danger, Wynna. We're probably being trailed."

For a long moment she sat silent and stared. "Dhumaric? I thought we left him in the northlands."

"We did," Alàric said tightly. "But Dhumaric doesn't stay defeated for long. And as for Kahs . . . aye, it's as you suspected. He's gone—Vàlkir and Hairon, too. They rode out after Lorhaiden, and Lorhaiden's off to find Dhumaric."

The silence grew deeper until he could hear the sound of crickets nearby.

"Then the scouting forays," she said, "the long time spent hunting with no taking of game—"

"All a ruse. They've been gone now for two days." He drew a deep breath. "If Kahs can catch Lorhaiden, he'll bring him back. If not. . . ."

"Lorhaiden's crazy!"

"Aye. Crazy as they come sometimes. And other times, *sometimes*, he's very, very sane."

"This isn't one of them," she said thinly.

"No, it's not. When he figured out that Dhumaric was following us, he— Well, he didn't react rationally." Alàric lifted his hand, turned in the saddle, and gestured the refugees on again. He nudged his horse to a fast walk and glanced at Maiwyn riding alongside. "I'm in command, and I don't know what the Dark to do!"

"About what?"

"Anything." His jaw tightened. "I don't know where Dhumaric is, only that he's trailing us. I don't know if Kahs has found Lorhaiden yet. And," he looked directly into her eyes, silently bidding her to even greater secrecy, "when Kahs left, he told me that Father would be sending men west as reinforcements for us, in case Dhumaric attacks. I thought that was good news until earlier today. Now I'm afraid Father's leading those men himself."

Her eyes widened. "Your father? But why?"

"I don't know. Strategy, love. Something's moved him. And now, to make matters worse—" He briefly closed his eyes. "If I can sense anything at all, Father's riding into danger."

"Does Kahsir know this?"

"I don't think so, or he would have said something about it before he left. There are so many things I don't know for sure. And now I'm responsible for seeing that you and the other refugees make it to Elyâsai."

She shook her head. "Don't we have enough warriors to protect us?"

"Against Dhumaric?" He straightened in the saddle. "No. I'm afraid he's coming after us with far more than one hundred men. That's why we've taken the mind-road so often . . . to put more distance between us and him. We've got the children, the wagons, the pack horses with us, and they're all tired. We can't go faster, and if Dhumaric comes down on us, we haven't the shielding to protect us." He glanced up at the sky. "We'll be stopping soon for our midday rest. I think that would be the best time."

"For what, Alàric?"

He looked down and met her eyes. "To tell the refugees. To tell them all of it. Everything. Of the danger we're facing. To put us on alert and to increase our pace. And," he added softly, "to arm them—men, women, and all those children old enough to fight. I have a terrible feeling we'll need a hand to every weapon we carry."

CHAPTER 18

Kahsir brought his horse to a sliding stop, closed his eyes, and sought after Lorhaiden. "Vahl," he said. "I've lost him."

"He's still ahead, Lord. I can feel his presence."

"I can't, but Dhumaric's out there. *Chuht*, Vahl! We're too close to the enemy. If we're not careful, they'll find us!"

Vàlkir rode closer, Hairon following just behind. Kahsir looked at them both, at the tension and strain etched on their faces. He was equally exhausted. He closed his eyes briefly, and willed his weariness away.

"I'll lead, Lord," Vàlkir offered.

Kahsir nodded at the younger man, held his horse back as Vàlkir went ahead. He followed at a fast trot, trusting Vàlkir to know where Lorhaiden was. Behind, he heard Hairon curse softly.

A sharp sound came from his right. He whirled his horse to face it, but saw nothing. Hairon's sword rasped from its sheath. For a long moment, Kahsir sat silent, his two companions motionless at his side. Then he saw sudden movement—a big man on a dark horse, riding at a canter through the trees.

"That be him!"

Kahsir turned at Hairon's hissed words, nodded, gestured that they should go. "Vahl," he called over the sound of hooves, "see if you can stop him."

Vàlkir nodded, kicked his horse into a canter, and went off through the trees. Kahsir drew a deep breath and rode slightly off at an angle from Vàlkir's path, hoping to intercept Lorhaiden. He turned, glanced behind, saw Hairon following closely, then looked forward again. A tree limb slapped against his shoulder; Hairon cursed.

And suddenly, he came face to face with Lorhaiden, just as Vàlkir rode up behind. For a long moment he sat silent, looking at his sword-brother.

"Lorhaiden." Clipped words; precise; emotion held in control by sheer effort. "What the Dark do you think you're trying to do?"

Lorhaiden swallowed heavily. "Don't, Lord," he said, his voice trembling. "Don't try to stop me. Dhumaric's out there and I'll see that bastard spitted before—"

"You'll see nothing of the kind!" Kahsir snapped. "At least now. Tell me . . . why, in the name of all the Lords of Light, did you go off like this?"

"I . . . you'd been sent home by your father," Lorhaiden said. "He'd relieved us of any form of command. I saw this as my chance to serve my Oath—the Oath of the Sun's Blood, Lord, *not*, my sword-brother's oath. By going off on my own, by keeping you from coming after me, I was trying to save you from your father's anger." His face hardened. "And now you've ruined it, Lord. I tried to keep you out of trouble, but—"

"Turn around, Lorhaiden," Kahsir said. "As for your Oath, you've already broken your oath to me to serve it."

"I can't—"

"Dammit, Lorj! *Think* for once in your life! You don't even know how many men Dhumaric's got with him.

And he's close, damned close! Now turn around. We've got to get out of here before we're—"

An arrow thunked into a tree trunk an arm's length away. Kahsir reined his horse around, saw enemy warriors distant through the trees.

"Ride!" he shouted, his stomach knotting. "Get out of here!" He grabbed for Lorhaiden's reins.

Lorhaiden backed his horse, his hand groping for his sword. Kahsir caught hold of Lorhaiden's mind. *If you care for me*, he Sent, *follow!* Lorhaiden hesitated, indecision twisting his face. Kahsir pushed his horse alongside and snagged the reins.

"Come with me, Lorj," he grated, "or ride unconscious behind me!"

Lorhaiden jerked back on his reins, and sanity returned to his eyes. Another arrow struck a tree, as close as the first had been. Vàlkir and Hairon crashed off through the brush, through the deepening afternoon shadows. Kahsir swore softly and rode around behind Lorhaiden.

"Move, dammit!" He brought his reins down on the rump of Lorhaiden's horse, and followed his swordbrother after the others.

The trees were everywhere, thickly clogged with undergrowth, and Tsingar guided his horse as quickly as he could down the game trail. Dhumaric and the company were close now; he could hear their horses in the forest. He laughed aloud: luck was his at last.

"Master!" he called, glimpsing Dhumaric through a veil of brush. "We've got them!" He reined in his horse at Dhumaric's side. "Up ahead," he said and gestured. "Kahsir and Lorhaiden!"

Dhumaric had never looked so surprised. "What? Both?" He wet his lips, his eyes narrowing. "How far?"

"Under two leagues' ride, Dread Lord. Our scouts nearly stumbled across them."

"Did you think to send the scouts in pursuit?" Girdun asked from his place at Dhumaric's side.

Tsingar spat off to one side. "I'm not stupid, Girdun." He held Girdun's eyes, not willing to lower his own.

Dhumaric raised his hand, gesturing to the men who followed, and Tsingar looked away.

"After me! Tsingar! Lead us there!"

Tsingar bowed slightly in the saddle, turned, and kicked his horse into a fast trot back through the trees. He grinned, conscious of Girdun's eyes on his back. *Let him spoil this for me. Let him try!*

An image of the land he had crossed fixed itself firmly in Xeredir's mind. He leaned back in his saddle, closed his eyes, and thought of where he was now, of where Mataihyàr suspected Dhumaric to be. The weather had lifted; visibility was good enough now to ride forward again. Movement, the sound of horses shifting at rest, came from beside. He opened his eyes and looked at Elhvàn.

"Lord?" his shieldman asked, waiting.

"Straight ahead," he said, pointing off to the southwest. His mouth twisted into a grimace. "Dhumaric's out there. We're closer to him than I'd like to be, but I can't lose him." He glanced around, ignoring the thoughts of his men. Then something else, something familiar touched his mind—touched it and was gone. He frowned. "How far off are the scouts?"

"Not far, Lord," Elhvàn replied. "Less than a league."

"Pull them back. We're going to have to trust to our minds to probe out there. I don't want anyone caught out in front of us."

Elhvàn nodded, turned his horse, and rode off through the brush. Xeredir hitched around in his saddle, looking at the land. Behind, the forest rose in rocky hills. Off to the right lay the crest of one of those hills he had been tempted to stop at, to make camp for the evening. Well protected from behind by a cliff face, it had seemed an ideal place. He shrugged, resigned. As long as Dhumaric kept moving, he must follow.

He turned forward again. At his back was the sound of low conversation among his men, nearly as clear as their thoughts. He tightened his shields, wanting silence. Whatever had touched his mind a moment ago had set his nerves on edge. He glanced to the west, at the glare of the setting sun. The forest opened here onto several leagues of sparsely treed meadows. He would have to proceed with caution from here on out. There was too little cover for—

A hoarse, faint cry rang out over those meadows. Xeredir jerked his horse around, his heart leaping in his throat. Someone . . . no, more than one person— black dots of figures were riding in his direction. He started forward, then stopped. His men fell into defensive positions to his rear, still in forest cover.

"Who is it, Lord?"

He turned; Elhvàn was back. Xeredir looked into the sun glare and the wide grassland. "I don't know. Can you see how many?"

Elhvàn rode a few paces forward. "I'm not sure, Lord. There's more than one. I can't make out— There's—there are four, I think."

The riders drew closer now. Xeredir fidgeted in the saddle, then motioned Elhvàn to follow, and rode into the open meadows. His scouts were returning at the same moment, traveling parallel to the riders who galloped across the grasslands: the strangers must be Krotànya.

Again, something touched his mind, even more familiar this time.

"Lord," Elhvàn said. "I can just make them out—"

Xeredir cut off his shieldman with an impatient gesture. He could see them now, too. The one in the lead—the other who rode beside—the two who followed. . . .

"Kahs," he breathed. His hands began to shake on

the reins; his heart hammered in his chest. "Kahs! What in the name of all the Lords is going on?"

Kahsir clasped his father's extended arm in greeting, settled back in his saddle, and reined his horse a bit away from Xeredir's.

Xeredir's expression hovered somewhere between rage and relief. "What . . . why in the name of the Light are *you* here?"

He glanced over his shoulder to where Lorhaiden sat his horse, head bowed, next to Vàlkir and Hairon, and met his father's gaze again.

"That's something between Lorhaiden and me. I'll tell you later. Right now, we've got to get out of here. Dhumaric's following us."

His father's indrawn breath hissed in the silence. "How far away is he? And how many men does he lead?"

"About two leagues behind. I'm not sure how many."

"I've got two hundred warriors," Xeredir said, gesturing behind at the woods. His eyes narrowed. "Could you tell if Dhumaric has more?"

Kahsir swallowed heavily and nodded. "Easily twice that number."

A shadow crept over his father's face. "Damn! I thought so."

"We don't have a choice," Kahsir said. "We've got to retreat. Can we take the mind road?"

Xeredir shook his head. "Not far enough. We're too exhausted. I've only got one Mind-Born with me, and I don't think he could jump two hundred of us."

"*Chuht!* Is there any place close that's defensible?"

"Aye. A few leagues back. A hill with a cliff face behind." Xeredir turned as Elhvàn and the scouts moved their horses out of the way. "If Dhumaric's as close as you say, we're going to have to ride like the Void to reach it."

"Huhn." Kahsir gathered his strength, closing his

eyes in concentration. Then, with all the power he had left, he aimed a Sending back to the capital—to Vlàdor, to anyone who might be waiting for news from the north . . . and in that Sending, he gave his present location.

"For the Light's sake!" Xeredir bellowed. "You *fihrkken* idiot! What the Void do you think you're doing? You've doomed us with that Sending. The enemy will find us now for sure!"

Kahsir met his father's eyes and lifted his reins. "They'll find us anyway," he said, his voice cold. "Idiot that I am, I at least know when it's time to ask for help."

"Tsingar!" Dhumaric's voice cracked like a whip. "Can you tell which way they went?"

Tsingar reined in his horse, his eyes intent on the ground. The signs were there—small, insignificant, but scored into the sparse grass, they were readable by a trained eye.

"Aye, Master. Straight ahead. It looks like they met other riders here. A converging line, half a dozen more."

"Who could that be?" Dhumaric's face fell into deep concentration as he probed forward with his mind. "It's no use. You felt that Sending, didn't you?"

"Aye, Lord. But it was so brief, I couldn't swear where it came from."

Dhumaric snarled. "I can't find them, and they're too tightly shielded to Read at this distance. They could have gone off in any direction. Lead us!"

Tsingar nodded, kicked his horse savagely in the sides, and rode off across the thinly treed meadows. The company followed close behind, spreading out in search formation. The trees grew closer, then opened. His eyes never left the ground ahead. The bushes were full of broken branches, the undergrowth trampled; more than just a few men had come this way. His mouth twisted. Could he be leading them into a trap? Could the Krotànya have more men than Dhumaric?

"There's been a dozen riders here," Girdun said from behind, "more like a regiment." Dhumaric grunted in acknowledgement. Tsingar set his jaw, tightened his shields, and bit back angry words. The last thing he needed now was a fight with Girdun. Besides, Girdun had given no overt reason for such action. *Clever, clever. But one day you'll slip, Girdun, and then we'll see.*

A league passed. The land began to rise slightly under his horse's feet; the trees thickened again, then thinned out. He glanced up from the ground, his eyes straying forward. Though the land was more open, the trees still obscured the distance. The ground underfoot gave all the signs they had.

"Dread Lord!" Girdun again. "Look! That hill over there!"

Tsingar glanced up at the hillside that rose ahead, scantily covered by trees. He urged his horse to a faster pace, keeping his gaze fixed on the hill, but the trees were still in the way. He threw his weight into his off stirrup, leaned sideways for a better view.

He saw sudden if faint movement on the hillside: Krotànya! Many of them—well over the number he expected. His heart sank. What if—?

"Halt!" Dhumaric's command rang out in the forest's silence. Tsingar reined in his horse, turned, and faced his commander. "Girdun," Dhumaric said. The other, as usual, had ridden close. "It looks like they've got a good place to fight from. What do you suggest?"

Tsingar sat tense, his face expressionless, and waited.

"Let Tsingar decide," Girdun said, his voice deceptively mild. "He's ridden with you longer than I have."

Dhumaric raised an eyebrow. "Well, Tsingar? What's your advice?"

Tsingar threw a dark look in Girdun's direction. *You want to see me fail, don't you? Well, by all the Gods, I know some strategy, too.*

"Archers, Dread Lord," he said. "That cliff face behind won't let us surround them. I don't know how many men they've got, but we outnumber them. If our bowmen can keep them pinned down on that hilltop, the rest of us can assault the hill."

Dhumaric nodded slowly. Suddenly, his face changed, became more feral. "There! Did any of you—?"

"What, Master?" Tsingar asked. Girdun was silent.

"It's Xeredir," Dhumaric whispered. "Out here. Where we least expected him." A cold laugh rumbled up from Dhumaric's chest. "I couldn't have asked for anything more, except that Haskon and Alàric be with him."

"Haskon's back east, Dread Lord," Tsingar said. "Alàric's our problem. The bond of flesh—the closeness of blood. . . . He might guess what's going on here. If so, he could abandon the refugees, gather reinforcements, and—"

"Then you take care of that, Tsingar," Dhumaric murmured through a thin smile. "Alàric's got one hundred warriors with him, doesn't he?"

"Aye, Lord. If we can believe what we got from the Krotànya sentry's mind."

"Good. Send sixty men to the southwest. Alàric shouldn't be hard to find; he's likely along the roadway he's been following. And tell your men to keep their distance—I want Alàric kept busy and off our backs."

Tsingar bowed and glanced back at the hill, the nearness of battle making his heart beat quicker.

"Archers!" Dhumaric's voice was vast in the forest's stillness. "Positions! Fire at my command!"

Another shower of arrows rained down on the hilltop. Kahsir ducked behind a tree, heard shafts strike other tree trunks close by. Cries of pain and anger rose from wounded men as they fell beneath those arrows. Kahsir leaned out from behind his cover and squinted down the hillside. It was hard to see in the dusk. The enemy archers shot continuously, keeping his father's men pinned down to the hilltop.

Once more, arrows hissed past his head. Someone

grunted in pain nearby and Kahsir spun around. Teeth clenched in pain and blood dripping down his hand, Hairon pulled at an arrow in the fleshy part of his upper arm. Kahsir met the farmer's eyes. *It's his shield arm. Thank the Light for that!*

"They're coming!"

The shout rang out in the twilight. Lorhaiden murmured something, shifted his shield, and Kahsir turned back to look down the hillside. Someone touched his shoulder.

"Lord," Hairon said, his face pale in the fading light. "Help me."

Kahsir set his shield down, his sword beside it. He grasped the arrow and Hairon's arm, then glanced up at Hairon's set face.

"Now?"

"Do it," Hairon said tightly through clenched teeth.

Kahsir pushed the arrow on through the farmer's arm and Hairon gasped softly in pain. "I'll be done in a moment," Kahsir murmured. "Hang on." He broke off the arrowhead and, with a quick jerk, pulled the shaft back out of Hairon's arm.

"Get someone to bind that for you," he said. "Hurry!"

"Lord." Hairon clutched at his bloody arm and trotted off into the trees.

A clash of weapons sounded from down the hillside. Kahsir turned around and took his sword and shield from Lorhaiden. He hefted the sword a few times to loosen his shoulder muscles, met Lorhaiden's eyes, and tried to smile in encouragement.

The Leishoranya were visible now. Kahsir glanced around for his father, saw him a few paces away, then started forward, Lorhaiden moving to his left side, to the position of shieldman. An enemy warrior ran out of the dusk, but Lorhaiden was quicker: he cut the man down with casual indifference, then turned to face another. A foot slipped on rock: Kahsir whirled to his right and blocked the enemy's sword stroke. His blade met his opponent's again. He parried, feinted to his left, then struck.

The dusk deepened: soon it would be hard to tell foe from friend. Arrows fell again and Kahsir jerked his shield over his head, waiting to be hit. Nothing happened, though arrows whistled and other warriors close by cried out in the dusk. Xeredir had guessed right: the enemy must have had a large number of men if they shot at the hill now, unsure of their targets. Several Leishoranya had been struck down by their own bowmen. Again, the enemy archers fired. Kahsir cursed softly: something had to be done soon, or—

"Down!"

His father's voice rang over the hilltop. At the agreed-upon signal, Kahsir fell flat to the ground, the other Krotànya doing the same. Then Xeredir's archers fired at the enemy still standing, cutting them down where they stood.

"Attack!"

Xeredir's voice rang out again. Kahsir leapt to his feet and ran forward to engage the few Leishoranya who remained standing. Lorhaiden laughed in the gathering darkness, his sword gleaming dully as he chased down a fleeing Leishoran. Kahsir spotted his own prey, met the man's attack, and dropped him with a slashing backhand stroke.

Suddenly there was no one to fight. Kahsir blinked in the near darkness, lowered his sword, and took several long, deep breaths. He could hear nothing now from down the hillside. Dhumaric had obviously called his men back into the protection of the thicker trees below, realizing the futility of charging the hill in the dark.

Kahsir turned around, Lorhaiden once more at his side, and walked back to where Xeredir stood on the hilltop. Bodies lay everywhere. He frowned: as many dead were Krotànya as Leishoranya. If the ratio held true elsewhere, his father had lost around fifty men— men he desperately needed.

*   *   *

Arms crossed, his eyes only shadows in the firelight, Dhumaric stood looking up the hillside, the hint of a smile on his face. Tsingar estimated their losses at fifty killed in the assault—not a bad loss, for an equal number of Krotànya had fallen. He smiled: Xeredir could ill afford that number of casualties; Dhumaric still had nearly four hundred men.

Tsingar had not fought in the battle, staying behind with Dhumaric and Girdun to direct the attack. But tomorrow—perhaps tomorrow he could honor his weapons with Krotànya blood. Now, all he wanted was somewhere to stretch out and sleep. He doubted the Krotànya would attack. Xeredir was known for conservatism, and night fighting would not be to his liking.

And the block Dhumaric had ordered lowered over the hillside would prevent any of the Krotànya from taking the mind-road to safety.

"Tsingar."

He turned and hurried to Dhumaric. Girdun stood there, along with another man Tsingar thought he recognized as one of the hundred-commanders Dhumaric had left behind with the main army. Tsingar glanced at Girdun, but his fellow officer's face was a neutral blank, giving no hints of what had happened.

"Good news," Dhumaric said, gesturing to the warrior. "This man reports that soon after we started out after Kahsir, the Krotànya sent a company of three hundred infantry west. They did this under the cover of darkness, keeping each man heavily shielded. We wouldn't have noticed this company, but one of their men was careless and let his shields slip." Dhumaric's thin smile grew wider. "It was a massacre. We surprised them with one thousand men. Several Krotànya survived and we forced their minds open. It seems Xeredir didn't trust in secrecy: this company followed him as reinforcements."

Tsingar laughed, genuine mirth, not an expected response. Now Xeredir would be without men he had counted on—men who could have made it difficult for Dhumaric.

"You'll let Xeredir know about this, won't you, Master?"

"Aye."

"Tonight?"

"That wouldn't be best, Tsingar." Girdun spoke for the first time. "Why not save this news for a far more advantageous moment?"

The warrior at Dhumaric's side grinned at Girdun's words, but when Tsingar shot him a look, his face froze into immobility.

"Set up pickets," Dhumaric said, ignoring Tsingar's threatening glance. "And keep that mind-block in place. We'll attack again at dawn."

Tsingar nodded, turned, and went off to select his men. He spat into the darkness and hoped he had hit somebody, anybody. *Patience. Patience. I can't make a mistake now. That's what Girdun wants me to do.* He glanced over his shoulder and sneered, thankful for the concealing dark.

Kahsir looked up at the sky, hoping for rain. A chill wind blew down on the hilltop; the pine trees moaned and whistled before it. The clouds were thick enough to hide the sun, but they held no signs of moisture. He shook his head: a good, hard rain would not only decrease visibility for Dhumaric's archers, but dampen their bows as well.

He drew his cloak closer, felt the weariness ache deep in his bones. All morning long Dhumaric had assaulted the hill, again sending men forward under the murderous hail of arrows. *Lords! That bastard must have started out with more arrows than he thought he'd need, or he'd have run low by now.* Kahsir glanced at his father, who sat close by, wrapped in moody silence. Xeredir was as weary as everyone else, possibly more

so, but it was the loss of men that pained him, that
slumped his shoulders and bowed his head. This morning alone they had lost another twenty-five men.

Lorhaiden sat on a rock, sword unsheathed and resting point-down on the ground. Hairon crouched alongside, his wounded arm bound tightly, and Vàlkir stood
among the bowmen. Kahsir glanced back down the
hillside: the soil was too rocky to bury the dead and
bodies lay everywhere.

"Krotànya!" A voice cried out in the stillness. "Here
they come!"

Kahsir stood, threw his cloak back over his shoulders,
unsheathed his sword, and picked up his shield.
Lorhaiden already stood fully armed, the only one among
them all who seemed eager to greet this new attack.
Everyone else was exhausted from too little sleep last
night and hard fighting all morning.

Arrows coming: Kahsir raised his shield, heard a
missile thunk off it, but no one nearby was hit. Again,
arrows fell in a deadly rain. The Krotànya returned fire,
ineffectually—their targets were hidden in the thick
woods below.

The first of the Leishoranya warriors topped the hill,
followed by a rush of others. Kahsir ran forward,
Lorhaiden at his side and Hairon behind. He selected
his opponent, engaged the Leishoran in a quick burst of
sword strokes, then dropped him with a lucky blow.
More Leishoranya gained the hilltop. Fighting became
so thick Kahsir had no chance to see beyond new opponent. Blood stained his sword blade now—his hand was
spattered with it. He had been cut at least once, but
felt no pain.

More of the enemy were gaining the hilltop now.
The battle became a weary haze. Kahsir's arm moved
mechanically, his sword a simple extension of his body.
He glanced at Lorhaiden and Hairon: Lorhaiden was
laughing in joy of combat, but Hairon fought in grim

silence, his shield arm hanging useless from yesterday's arrow wound.

Suddenly, there were no more enemy warriors to face. His arm aching, Kahsir lowered his sword, his shield pulling at his other arm.

And pain burst inside his head.

Staggered by the suddenness of the inner attack, he threw the shields up around his mind.

Brikendàrya!

Kahsir gripped his sword tighter. The enemy had brought their *brikendàrya* into combat. Mind-Breakers: living symbols of what the Krotànya hated most.

"Mataihyàr!"

It was Xeredir who called for the Mind-Born's aid. Kahsir felt Mataihyàr's presence somwhere behind him and to the left. The dull pain in his head receded somewhat as the young Mind-Born threw his defensive skills into play.

Another wave of Leishoranya rushed up the hillside. Kahsir sprang forward, Lorhaiden at his side, and with his comrades met the enemy. His swordplay had degenerated into an artless barrage of hacking and slashing, but still proved effective. His swordmaster's voice echoed from out of the past:

When you're facing death, there's no time to be pretty.

Another opponent, followed by one more, then another. Kahsir's sword arm had gone numb . . . only instinct held the blade now. The entire world had narrowed to the tip of his weapon and each new enemy he faced.

And suddenly, the enemy withdrew down the hillside.

The mental pressure of the *brikendàrya* still throbbed in Kahsir's head. Panting, his legs wide-spread, he glanced around, looking for his father. Xeredir stood at the hill crest, apparently untouched. The thoughts of the warriors on the hilltop were easy to read, leaking from behind each man's shields. Death—dying—pain. Kahsir shook his head slowly. *Not now . . . not now!*

"Kahs!"

He drew a long, sobbing breath and walked to Xeredir's side, Lorhaiden and Hairon coming along behind.

"How many more dead?" asked Xeredir.

Kahsir glanced around: it was difficult to tell. The hill had been littered with bodies when the battle had begun. "Over twenty," he said.

His father cursed softly and Kahsir glanced away. The silence was broken only by the curses and moans of the wounded. His own cuts proved shallow; some had already stopped bleeding. He licked his lips, and longed for something to drink.

"Xeredir!"

The harsh cry echoed out in the quietness, coming from down the hillside. Kahsir glanced at his father. Xeredir stiffened, his face settling into hard lines.

"Xeredir!" The cry came again. It was Dhumaric's voice, Kahsir felt certain of that. He closed his eyes and, concentrating against the sustained mental attack, picked up Dhumaric's presence down at the edge of the woods.

"Sorrow for you," the voice called in badly accented Krotànji. "Three hundred your men die yesterday. No reinforcements yours! Death yours be soon!"

Reinforcements? Kahsir turned quickly to his father. *Why, by all the Lords, didn't he tell me about that?* He bit his lower lip and shook his head. Of course Xeredir would not have said anything about it: there were probably less than a handful of men who had ridden out with him who knew. The tighter held the secret, the less likely it was to be divulged by mistake.

"Do you want me to reply?" Kahsir asked, amazed at the calmness of his own voice.

Xeredir shook his head. "No. It won't do any good. He has us here. I don't see how we can escape him. Those bastards are still blocking the mind-road, even if we were rested enough to take it. They're tearing at our minds, and we've lost half our company. He still has—well, I'd guess over three hundred men."

Kahsir shifted his feet uneasily. Though what his father said was true, he still denied the possibility of their defeat. He had not Seen it in any of the futures he had glimpsed at Rodja'âno. But then he had not Seen this battle, either.

"Help me look after the wounded, Kahs," his father said. "I think we'll have a short rest from fighting now. There's no better way for Dhumaric to demoralize us than to let us brood over the fact that we're trapped here."

CHAPTER 19

Alàric rode with the wind at his back, the faint spatter of raindrops on his helm, and shivered slightly: the wind was chill, but he was warm enough. A glance around showed the refugees in a well-ordered column, by now used to the pace of travel. The thoughts of the people nearby radiated optimism. He shivered again.

"Alàric?"

Maiwyn rode at his side again. The hood of her cloak shadowed her face, but there were other shadows there.

"What's bothering you, Alàric?"

He shrugged, for the moment unable to answer. "It has to do with Kahs," he said finally, struggling to clarify his sense of foreboding. "And Father." She stayed silent, her eyes never leaving his face. "There's something wrong," he said. *Something wrong.* A quick, disjointed scatter of visual impressions darted through his mind. Fighting—a hilltop—swords spattered with blood; a cold, icy laugh from somewhere down that hillside. . . . "Dhumaric." He said the name unwillingly, not wanting to give substance to his fear. Another brief passage of visual impressions. "Aye. Dhumaric's found them."

"Lords of Light!" Maiwyn pulled her cloak closer.

"But *who* did he find? Did Kahsir catch up to Lorhaiden?"

Alàric felt about for the answer to that. "Aye. Then, somehow, they stumbled across the men Father sent after us. Father's there, too." He shook his head, trying to collect his unruly thoughts. "And Dhumaric. . . . A battle—there's a battle." He looked up from his clenched hands, felt the woodenness of his expression. "And I can't help them."

"There are other Krotànya in the north, Alàric," she said. "Perhaps—"

"No." Even as he said it, the word loomed in his mind, final, inalterable. "Not close enough." He shut his eyes, then looked around again. Suddenly, he straightened and his mouth went dry. *Lords! Could it be? Could—?* He mentally summoned Rothàr. "Wynna," he said. "Go back to the wagon. Don't argue—go! Tell Genlàvyn to spread the word that we could be in danger." He smiled to take the edge off his words, and touched her mind gently. "Hurry."

"Be careful," Maiwyn said. Ducking her head farther back in her hood, she turned and rode back to the wagons.

Rothàr cantered forward, reined in his horse, and sat waiting, his eyes shadowed in the gloom. Alàric threw up his hand, signaled a halt, and reined his horse around to face Rothàr. For a moment he was silent, looking at the refugees.

"Rothàr," he said. "Tighten the ranks. Pull in the scouts who ride on either side of us. I want all wagons to travel so they can assume defensive positions at a moment's notice."

"Trouble?" Rothàr asked, his eyes narrowing as he glanced at the land about.

"I think so." The rain had stopped, though the clouds were still dark and moisture-laden. A gust of wind whipped Alàric's cloak back from his shoulders. He grabbed at it, wrapped it closer. "And Rothàr—arm everyone who's able to fight."

It was pitch black on the hilltop, but Xeredir had given orders that no one build a fire. Now, sitting in the wind on the hill crest, he longed for something to alleviate the chill. He shook his head, rose, and walked over to his eldest son.

Kahsir sat with his back propped up against a boulder, Lorhaiden and Vàlkir sitting next to him. Hairon dozed a few paces away. Xeredir touched Kahsir's shoulder and gestured for him to follow.

Once away from the other men, he turned to face his son.

"How many men do we have left?" he asked.

It was impossible to see Kahsir's expression in the darkness. "Ninety-seven. Twenty-three of those are seriously wounded."

"Huhn." Xeredir looked off into the night. Ninety-seven, in actuality only seventy-four. *I wonder how many Kahs thinks Dhumaric still has?* He bit back the words before they tumbled out. Tomorrow—tomorrow could see the end of it all.

"That *fihrkken* bastard's got us trapped but good," Kahsir said. "I don't think many of us will ever come down off this hill."

Xeredir's chest tightened with now-familiar anger. "Thanks to you," he muttered.

"Thanks to *me?*" Kahsir's voice dropped to a hoarse whisper. "What the Void are you talking about?"

"If you hadn't sent off that message to Hvàlkir giving away our position—"

"*Chuht*, Father! Dhumaric would have found us anyway. Even if we'd had the strength to mind-road it out of there, he could have traced us . . . maybe pulled us back."

"Dammit, Kahs! We're all going to *die* here! If you hadn't disobeyed me at the very first—"

"If that's all you're going to talk about," Kahsir said, his voice very cold in the dark, "I'm going back to my friends."

Xeredir's shoulders stiffened. "I should never have come after you," he snapped. "When I did, I found you'd disobeyed me again. I ordered you home, out of the northlands. But no, you turn around and chase after that crazy shieldman of yours, right into Dhumaric's arms!"

"I'm oathed to Lorhaiden, Father. You know that. And besides, I'd renounced my command. I was subject to no one's orders . . . not even yours!"

"You stubborn, pigheaded. . . ." Xeredir felt his anger fade, drew a deep breath, and bowed his head. "I don't want to die, Kahs . . . not here . . . not this way."

The silence stretched out, grew uncomfortable.

"Neither do I."

Kahsir turned away, walked back to where Lorhaiden and the other men sat. Xeredir cursed softly, swung his arms to loosen tight shoulders, and followed.

No one looked up as he settled down beside his eldest son. Xeredir closed his eyes briefly, calmed his heart, then looked through the night at his companions.

Vàlkir stretched his legs out, dislodging noisy pebbles. "If only we could use the mind-road."

"I know," Kahsir said. "If only. But we can't, and even if we could, Dhumaric would be expecting it."

Xeredir waited for someone to say something. In the silence, he looked off into the darkness again. *Dammit! Think! You've always been good in defensive situations in the past!* A still, small voice whispered out of his heart: *But you've never been trapped like this, have you?*

"Xeredir!"

He stiffened, rose unsteadily to his feet.

"It's Dhumaric again," Kahsir said, standing also.

"Xeredir!" The cry rang out in the nighttime stillness. "Again, sorrow for you. Your son, Haskon. He—all his men—killed."

Xeredir's heart caught, skipped a beat, aching red-hot in his chest.

"That's a lie!" hissed Kahsir. "Haskon's still alive and you know it. We'd have felt his death if what Dhumaric says had happened."

"The dung-ball's trying to unnerve us!" Vàlkir growled from behind. "Don't pay attention to him, Lord."

Xeredir started to reply, but Kahsir caught at his shoulder.

"Don't. Don't say anything. Let him wonder how we took those words."

"Xeredir!" Dhumaric again. "Even sorrow more! Other son, Alàric. He, refugees, attacked, defeated. Alone, Xeredir! You stand alone!"

Xeredir bit back his curse, glanced at Kahsir's unseen face, but could detect no change in attitude. The wind swirled around the hilltop again, more chill than ever. He shuddered: there was some truth in what Dhumaric had said. Alàric *had* been in trouble—he knew that now. But how much of the rest could he believe?

"Vahl." Words caught away by the fitful wind, he turned toward Lorhaiden's brother. "Get Mataihyàr."

Vàlkir nodded and slipped off through the night. For a long while, no one moved. The wind died down, then blew again. At last, Xeredir heard the crunch of boots on rock. Vàlkir sank back into his place, and the young Mind-Born stood waiting, his white cloak a blur in the night.

"You heard what Dhumaric said, didn't you?" Xeredir asked Mataihyàr. The Mind-Born nodded. "Can you tell how much of what Dhumaric said is true?"

"I'll try, Lord. It's not going to be easy getting through the enemy block."

"At least the *brikendàrya* have given up for a while. Try, Mataihyàr . . . try."

The Mind-Born sat silent for a long moment. Xeredir

sensed Mataihyàr's mind opening and searching to the southwest. He shifted his weight impatiently, waiting for the Mind-Born to finish.

"Alàric's alive, Lord," Mataihyàr said at last, "but you already knew that. I can't tell you anything for sure, but he *was* attacked this afternoon. I don't know the outcome."

"How many did he face?" Xeredir asked. He pulled his cloak closer, chewed on his mustache, and waited.

"I wasn't able to pick that up either, Lord. But not many. Dhumaric likely sent a squadron or two south to keep Alàric occupied while he has us pinned down here. They'll probably attack him again tomorrow morning."

"Thanks, Mataihyàr. Are the wounded comfortable?"

"Fairly, Lord. It would help if we could build a fire."

"Watch over them. I'll check on them myself later."

"Aye, Lord."

Mataihyàr bowed slightly, and walked back up the hillside. Silence fell again; the Leishoranya down the hillside were quiet. Dhumaric had obviously accomplished what he wanted. Xeredir looked at the all but unseen forms of his companions. Kahsir had settled back down on his heels beside Vàlkir; Hairon muttered something in his sleep, shifted his position, but did not awaken. And Lorhaiden? Xeredir could not see him, see anyone, but Lorhaiden had not moved during the entire exchange with Dhumaric.

Xeredir sat down at Kahsir's side, drumming his fingers on one knee. He chewed on his mustache again, another nervous habit, and glanced at the sky. It was still overcast, but he could not smell rain. The trees moaned. Several men off to his right talked in low voices, their words a blur of sound obscured by the wind. He judged it nearly midnight, but felt no urge to sleep. He envied Hairon's ability to rest in the face of death on the morrow.

"Alàric's going to be all right," Kahsir said softly. "At least he and Haskon aren't here."

The gentleness in Kahsir's voice made Xeredir glance away. He shrugged, not knowing what to say. *Aye, they're not here, thank the Lords. Two of us can fight on.* He looked to the east—a futile act. Dawn was still far away.

Hidden by the darkness, Tsingar crouched behind a tree, his cloak gathered close against the chill. The camp was silent, the woods about only a little less quiet. Crickets chirped close by and an owl hooted somewhere off farther to the east.

He glanced off up the unseen hill to where the Krotànya lay. Dhumaric had tried sending a few bowmen around behind Xeredir's position, hoping they would be able to get clear shots at the Krotànya, but the grade of the ground that led to the cliff face was too steep.

Tsingar looked away from the hill. *No matter. We've trapped them at last. This time Kahsir and Lorhaiden won't escape. And we've got Xeredir, too.* He grinned. Two of Vlàdor's principal heirs faced death on the hilltop in the darkness. *What will the High-King do when he learns we've killed so many of his kin?*

The odors of what was left of this night's meal, kept warm for Dhumaric and his captains, drifted up the hillside. Dhumaric had ordered two men to keep constant watch over that pot in an effort to make sure nothing unwanted found its way into the stew.

Tsingar had not eaten since midday and, after days of nothing but dried meat and meal cakes, the smell of stew made his mouth water. His stomach growled noisily. He rose and walked farther down the wooded slope to the fire.

Girdun sat on the edge of the firelight. Tsingar glimpsed the other's flat gaze, glanced away and looked for Dhumaric, but could not find him. Girdun's presence took the edge off his hunger, but he gestured to the warrior who sat beside the kettle for a dish of stew.

He took the offered plate, turned away from the fire, and hunted for a place near enough to it to keep warm.

He sat down on the opposite side of the fire. The stew was hot: he burned his tongue on it. Then, suddenly, a shudder ran down his spine. He glanced up, but the hatred on Girdun's face vanished the moment Girdun met his eyes. *He knows!* Tsingar hid behind the comfort of his shields. *By all the Gods, he knows what I've done!* He looked away, feigning unconcern.

Dhumaric came back to the fire, stepping out of the darkness so suddenly that Tsingar jumped. Had the Krotànya believed all of what Dhumaric had said? Trying to discourage them with words had never been a sure thing.

Girdun was saying something to Dhumaric. Tsingar turned and looked at them, but could not hear what they said. Dhumaric smiled thinly. Tsingar's heart skipped a beat; he kept his face expressionless and looked away. He sampled the stew again: it had cooled enough so he could eat it. Chewing on the overcooked meat, he spat a piece of gristle off into the brush, and looked anywhere but at Girdun. Dawn was a long way off, but he longed for it, for Dhumaric's planned attack, and for the action that would follow.

Alàric drew his bowstring back, held his breath, and released the arrow. The shot was true: a Leishoran fell heavily from his horse and lay unmoving in the morning sunlight while other men of the enemy band rode by. Alàric crouched beneath one of the wagons that stood bunched together on the crest of a small hill, Maiwyn kneeling at his side. Her hand brushed his as she held out another arrow. He took it, sought her eyes, and tried to smile encouragingly.

"Down, Krotànya!"

The shout came from his left. He could not tell who had cried out, but ducked all the same. A shower of enemy arrows fell on the wagons. Behind the wagon he

knelt beneath, Genlàvyn's large white cat yowled, safe
in its cage. Another hail of arrows: some of them
had been set aflame, but the wagons' rain-soaked wooden
sides were difficult to ignite.

Late yesterday afternoon the enemy had attacked.
Before the refugees could gather their wagons into a
defensible group, they had lost over twenty men. Several women had been killed, and at last count three
children. The enemy had fallen back at dusk, camping
just out of sight down the hill. After dawn, they had
attacked again, for the most part staying well out of
arrow-shot, save for the times they shot at the wagons.
Alàric cursed, waited for another target, his arrow nocked
and bowstring pulled.

Of the sixty attacking Leishoranya, only around fifty
had survived. They had grown less bold as their numbers decreased and the refugees held fast to the protection of the wagons.

Alàric sighted on an enemy warrior riding forward,
drew aim, and fired. The Leishoran jerked back on his
horse's reins; the animal reared and took the arrow in
its chest. Alàric cursed again, angered at injuring the
animal. Maiwyn extended another arrow. He snatched
it and shot down the Leishoran who had jumped free of
his floundering horse.

He risked a sidelong glance at Maiwyn. She knelt
slightly behind him, under the wagon, protected by the
rear wheels. A smudge of dirt streaked her forehead
and her hair had come unclasped, falling about her
shoulders. She was fearless, this one, or at least held
her fear in check. Her cousin Genlàvyn yelled orders
somewhere off to his left—another woman who fought
with the ferocity of any warrior he had ever known. He
smiled at Maiwyn. She returned the smile and held out
another arrow.

The Leishoranya fought silently; his own warriors
were just as silent. Aside from the hissing and yowling
of Genlàvyn's furious cat, the screams of wounded horses

and men were the only sounds he heard. He waited patiently, saw his chance, and shot again. He was luckier this time—the Leishoran fell backward over his saddle to be immediately ridden over by members of his band who followed. Alàric frowned: this could not keep up. He had only enough archers among his men to keep the enemy from charging the wagons. He felt sure the Leishoranya knew this, yet they seemed content to stay beyond the range of Alàric's bowmen.

Alàric straightened and cursed silently. What if the enemy's objective was not to destroy the refugees? What if they had been sent south by Dhumaric merely to— *Kahs! Father!* He kept his thoughts tightly shielded. *Lords of Light! That's what Dhumaric's doing! He's keeping me from going back to help them!*

"Lord." Rothàr scrambled under the wagon. "We've got the advantage as long as we stay behind the wagons. The Leishoranya must know that. I think they'll charge us soon."

Alàric lowered his bow and nodded. "And if they break through, they can hurt us badly. We'll have to beat them to that charge. How many men do we have left who aren't wounded?"

"Fifty or so, Lord."

"Can you lead the charge, Rothàr?"

"Aye. Let me choose my men and horses, Lord. We'll ride at your signal."

Rothàr slipped away. More enemy arrows fell among the wagons. Alàric jerked back quickly, his arm thrust across Maiwyn's shoulders, pushing her out of range. He heard the scuffle of men mounting horses behind, Rothàr calling orders to them. By quick mind-touch, he commanded the other warriors to hold their fire, hoping to lure the enemy closer.

—*We're ready, Lord,* Rothàr Sent. *At your orders.*

"Now!" Alàric cried, Sending to those who could not hear his voice. He leaned around the wagon wheel, aimed, and shot at another passing Leishoran. His bowmen among the wagons fired at the same time, but not all their shots were true.

"Krotànya! *Legir! Legir!*"

Rothàr's cry rang out over the wagons, and under the cover of arrows, he led his men out toward the enemy.

"Get back, Wynna," Alàric said over his shoulder. "They'll be charging us next." He loosened both his swords in their sheaths, nocked another arrow. Genlàvyn's cat let out a wail of terror and clawed furiously at its cage. "Wynna," he said as she made no move to go. "Please. And get that cat out of here! No. Don't argue. Find Genlàvyn. You're not armed. The fighting's going to be close."

She went at last, touching his shoulder in farewell. He heard her pick up the cage, say something soothing to the panicked cat, and rush off. Readying his bow, he turned back to the battle. Rothàr's men had engaged the Leishoranya hand-to-hand now. It was hard to tell how many men Rothàr had taken, but the opposing forces appeared equal. The Leishoranya screamed now, their battle cries shrill and unnerving. One of them disengaged from the tangle of men and horses, and rode toward the wagons. Alàric held his breath, sighted, and fired. The man cried out in pain and snatched at his shoulder.

"Krotànya!"

He glanced out from under the wagon—Rothàr was in the midst of the fighting. Alàric tried to find another target, but the press of men and horses was too great. Only a few enemy shot at the wagons now; he hoped they were too busy fighting to use their bows. He still had thirty men held in reserve, but hesitated to send them into battle.

A Leishoran broke free from the fighting and galloped toward the wagons. Alàric shot at the man, missed, and ducked back behind the wagon wheel. The enemy warrior rushed at the wagon and thrust the spear he carried down under it. Alàric tossed his bow aside, grabbed at the spear, twisted and pulled. Caught off balance, the Leishoran fell from his horse. Alàric ripped out his sword, scrambled from under the wagon, and slashed the warrior in the throat with a clumsy stroke. An arrow thunked into the wooden wagonside, and he jumped back into cover.

In the next instant it was over. Alàric crawled out from under the wagon, his sword still unsheathed. There were no more enemy to fight; the few that had survived had fled the field. Alàric steadied himself on the wagonside and counted Krotànya. Rothàr was wounded— he clutched his leg with a bloodied hand—but there were at least fifteen of his men left horsed. Some of the fallen Krotànya were dead, but save those Leishoranya who had fled, few of the enemy had survived.

Alàric waited for the elation of victory, but felt nothing. Too many men had died, and somewhere to the north his father and eldest brother were facing death. Rothàr rode toward the wagons, back and shoulders stiff with pain. Knees trembling with weariness, Alàric looked up into Rothàr's face and tried to smile.

"The enemy?" he asked.

"Dead, Lord, most of them. We're giving the mercy stroke to the rest."

Alàric nodded. At last a sense of victory swept through his heart. But what of his brother, his father? He could not turn back now—he led too few men to make a tactical difference. And from what he could tell, any help he could find would arrive far too late to alter the outcome of the battle being fought to the north.

Tsingar ran up the hillside, his sword unsheathed and his shield held tightly. His comrades came behind. Even as he ran he heard their footsteps, their harsh breathing. A shower of Krotànya arrows fell from the hilltop and several men cried out in pain. Shutting the sounds of agony and dying away, Tsingar kept to his erratic path. Dhumaric's presence was overwhelming, even though he waited safely at the bottom of the hill.

Tsingar glanced sidelong: Girdun ran a few paces to his left. He looked hastily away lest Girdun notice. Another hail of Krotànya arrows—and another. Tsingar ran in an even more jagged course. *Gods! Where are they getting all those arrows? And why aren't our bowmen shooting?* Dhumaric's archers stood somewhere behind at the edge of the forest, probably acting under orders not to shoot for fear of hitting those running up the hill. Tsingar felt Girdun's gaze, ignored it, and ran on up the hillside.

The noon sun beat down on his shoulders, and Kahsir shifted from foot to foot in its heat. If only the chill wind that had blown across the hilltop last night would return. But the clouds had vanished at dawn, and the day had warmed steadily. The stench of unburied bodies was stronger and new spring flies, bloated with blood, buzzed around the corpses. Kahsir glanced up at the sky. A few distant black birds circled slowly above the hilltop. *Dammit! We're not dead yet! You'll have to wait a while for your feast!*

His father stood close by, grim-faced and pale in the sunlight. Kahsir looked back down the hill but saw nothing yet. The sound of shouting was louder as the Leishoranya ran up through the rocks and trees. Soon they would reach the fairly open stretch that led to the summit of the hill. Vàlkir and his bowmen kept a steady stream of arrows descending on the enemy. Kahsir shifted his shield closer. *Let those* fihrkken *bastards come to us. We'll kill more of them that way.* Eltàrim's face filled his mind's eye. A fierce longing for her swept through his heart, and he turned the vision away.

Lorhaiden stood silent. Hairon was at Lorhaiden's left, his stocky figure set in defiance of the coming battle. Kahsir glanced at the other men who still stood alive on the hilltop. *Our backs are to that cliff. At least we'll fall facing forward.*

Another rain of Krotànya arrows fell on the hill. Tsingar ducked behind his shield, looking for better cover. The honor of leading the attack had been his, and he had lost no time in being the first up the hillside. But what had started out as an all-out run had been halted by the Krotànya archers into a slow assault. He growled low in his throat, the killing urge narrowing his vision. The hillside was littered with bodies. Dhumaric's mind seared through his. Tsingar moved forward again, prodded invisibly from behind.

A tree grew a few paces up the hill; Tsingar darted off toward its cover. He heard arrows pass over his head, ran faster, and ducked behind the tree. Too late. A burning pain shot up his leg. He grunted in agony and glanced down: an arrow stuck out of his leg just above the knee. It had not penetrated deeply; his ring mail had turned it slightly aside.

By the Gods! He reached down to pull it out. *They're shooting our own arrows back at us!*

"Wounded already?"

Tsingar looked up. Girdun stood at his side, eyes narrowed—there was no hiding the hatred now. Girdun's hands shot out. One knocked Tsingar's sword away, the other grabbed at his neck. Tsingar struggled against Girdun's strength, saw the raised dagger, and fought the choking armhold.

"This is for Chaagut, slime-born!" Girdun grated. "You'll not find me so easy to kill!"

Girdun tightened his armhold. Tsingar gagged, struggled harder, and bit Girdun's arm. Girdun grunted in pain, lost some of his leverage. Tsingar slipped free, lunged for Girdun's ankles, and pulled him down. The arrow broke off in Tsingar's leg and he gasped in pain. He fumbled for his knife, heard arrows falling again, and scrambled on his knees back behind the tree. Girdun screeched in pain.

Tsingar turned around slowly, his leg protesting. Girdun lay contorted on the ground, an arrow through his neck and another jutting out from his chest.

For a long moment, Tsingar knelt motionless by the tree and stared, unable to believe his luck. He glanced about: no one seemed aware of what had happened. Pain clawed at his mind. He tore a long strip of cloth from his cloak and tied it tightly around the wound. Then, gathering up his shield and sword, he lurched to his feet.

Girdun was still alive, but would die within moments. His pain forgotten, Tsingar walked slowly to his side. Steadying himself, he leered down at Chaagut's cousin, spat squarely into his face, and limped off up the hill.

Kahsir took the sword stroke on his shield, stabbed out beneath the enemy's guard, and felt his blade strike flesh. The Leishoran cried out, stumbled, and Kahsir struck at him again, a clean blow this time. He backed up a few paces and nearly tripped over a body. Krotànya. He glanced up from his dead comrade, his jaw set. *Don't think of your losses! Survival—think only of surviving!*

The Leishoranya were all over the hilltop now, but Dhumaric had lost over half his men in the assault. Small comfort in that—Xeredir's men were still outnumbered beyond hope. Pushed back near where the frightened horses had been tethered, the Krotànya fought on.

Kahsir set his shield as another Leishoran ran forward, but Lorhaiden charged the man, laughing amidst the slaughter. Kahsir hastily looked for his father, caught Xeredir's eyes across the hilltop. *Lords above! He's still alive!* His heart constricted. All those angry words he had said last night . . . would he ever be able to unsay them? *Father . . . did I ever tell you how much I love you? How much I care?*

"Watch out, Lord!" Lorhaiden cried.

Kahsir turned, engaged the attacking Leishoran. He dropped his opponent with a backhand stroke, and glanced up to see Vàlkir fighting to Xeredir's right. There was no chance for the archers to shoot now: it was hand-to-hand on the hilltop.

Tahra! Her face filled his mind again. *Ah, Eltàrim! I'm sorry!*

The enemy warriors bore down on his comrades, an increasing weight of overwhelming numbers. "Damn you, you Void-spawned things of emptiness!" Kahsir bellowed. "I haven't even married her yet, and I'll see you Void-bound before you keep me from it!"

Something stirred deep in his mind—a longing to strike out mentally at the enemy, to unleash all the power that raged within. He could *see* them die—feel the power flow from deep inside his mind. He shook his head wearily. *No! Don't even think about it! Do you want to damn yourself to their darkness?*

The shrill cries of the gathering Leishoranya blocked out all thoughts of his mental powers, of Eltàrim, of his father, of Lorhaiden. He heard only the voice of death.

His sword honorably stained in Krotànya blood, his vow to his weapons maintained, Tsingar limped back down the hillside to wait for Dhumaric. The Krotànya had regrouped, their backs to the cliff face, and Tsingar wanted to be at Dhumaric's side for the final kill. His leg trembled beneath his weight. It would not fester—he had lost too much blood for that—and once the arrow had been withdrawn, it should heal cleanly.

Dhumaric came striding up the hillside with surprising quickness. Tsingar waited, leaning on his sword, favoring his wounded leg. Dhumaric's men were yelling on the hilltop as they fought; he grinned at the sound.

What happened when Dhumaric faced Xeredir, Kahsir, and Lorhaiden would be worth watching.

Dhumaric stopped, looked down at Tsingar's leg, then glanced across the hillside. "What happened to Girdun?" he asked.

Tsingar blinked. "Arrows, Dread Lord."

For a long moment Dhumaric said nothing, simply stared. Tsingar kept his shields clamped down, his eyes held level with his commander's.

"I see you were hit yourself," Dhumaric said at last, his voice expressionless. "You're a lucky man, Tsingar. Lucky, indeed."

Tsingar bowed his head, acknowledging what Dhumaric said and what remained unspoken. Dhumaric turned, gestured, and started off up the hillside.

Then suddenly, from behind: cries of startled rage, of pain. Tsingar spun around, flinching at the pain in his leg, and looked down the hill. His heart froze. Krotànya! Mounted Krotànya! Where by all the Gods . . . ? So many—there was no end to them. They rode up the hill, cutting down any of Dhumaric's men who stood in their way, their battle cries loud in the sudden silence.

Tsingar glanced back: Dhumaric's face was slack with amazement. He swallowed heavily, waited for Dhumaric to say something, to give an order, to curse, to do anything at all. But Dhumaric stood there, rooted to the hillside, his mouth working silently. Tsingar drew a deep breath, lifted his shield, and moved to stand before his master, seeing death ride up the hillside in the sunlight.

"Father!" Kahsir cried over the noise of battle. "Do you hear that?"

Xeredir turned, his helmet sitting slightly askew on his head, a thin ribbon of blood running down his cheek from his forehead.

"Listen!" Kahsir cried again. "Can't you hear it?"

The Krotànya close by paused; the enemy paused, too, hearing at last what Kahsir had heard.

"Krotànya!" The cry came from down the hillside. "*Legir! Legir!*"

"Who?" asked Lorhaiden. "Who the Dark is it?"

Kahsir laughed; a wave of hope warmed his heart. "They're ours, Lorj! My message got through! They're Krotànya, and that's all that counts!"

The enemy hesitated, bewildered by what was happening. Kahsir lifted his sword and leapt at an approaching Leishoran. "*Legir!*" he cried, cutting the enemy warrior down. "For the Light! *Legir! Legir!*"

The tide of battle was turning—confusion swept through the enemy. Kahsir caught a quick glimpse of his father, who stood, sword uplifted, yelling the same battle cry that now echoed over the hillside. He laughed, his heart soaring, and turned back to the fighting.

His leg threatening to collapse, Tsingar stumbled after Dhumaric up the hillside. The Krotànya behind drew closer now. Horsed, they had no difficulty killing any of Dhumaric's men who went afoot. Dhumaric was cursing now, his voice snarling hatred, and Tsingar kept far out of reach. Yet greater than Dhumaric's rage was his consuming urge for revenge. Tsingar knew his commander's thoughts though Dhumaric was tightly shielded: if Dhumaric was going to die, he would take Kahsir and Lorhaiden with him.

Tsingar stumbled again, cursed at his pain and disillusionment. At least he had not betrayed his weapons— they had drunk deep of Krotànya blood. When he died, he could face the Gods of Darkness with pride, knowing he had been a worthy weapon of their choosing.

He heard the sound of hooves on the rocky ground behind. Tsingar gasped for breath and kept his eyes on the hilltop, hoping he would at least make its summit. Unhurt, Dhumaric was beginning to draw away. Tsingar cursed his wounded leg again, ground his teeth in rage and pain, and limped on.

The hilltop was close now—he could see the struggle going on at its edge. The sudden arrival of reinforcements giving them new hope and strength, the Krotànya pushed Dhumaric's bewildered warriors back. Tsingar tripped again, regained his balance with difficulty. *It's not far! Only a few more—*

He sensed the sword stroke as it descended from behind, cried out briefly, and fell down into darkness beneath the thunder of galloping hooves.

"Can you see who's leading them?"

Kahsir turned to his father, shook his head, and looked back down the hillside. Rubbing his sword arm to ease the ache of cramping muscles, he glanced down: his hand came away streaked with blood. The Leishoranya were falling back now, trying to regroup farther down the hillside. Xeredir's men followed, cutting down any enemy who chose to stand and fight.

"It's Lord Devàn," Vàlkir said, certainty behind his words. He turned and met Kahsir's eyes. "Your message . . . was it your message that brought him?"

"*Someone* Heard me," Kahsir said. "Probably Tebehrren . . . or Grandfather."

Vàlkir laughed. "It doesn't make any difference! Whoever it was . . . I'll hug them when I see them!"

Kahsir glanced down the hillside, squinting in the early afternoon sunlight. The Leishoranya were all but defeated—Krotànya rode up the hill from all sides. He tried to count the newcomers but gave up: probably over five hundred horsemen faced less than two hundred of the enemy.

"Lord."

He turned. Lorhaiden stood close by, a look of eagerness on his face.

"If Dhumaric's down there, don't let anyone else

touch him." A thin, predatory smile crossed Lorhaiden's face. "He's mine! That bastard's mine!"

Kahsir nodded wearily, not having the strength to quarrel with Lorhaiden now. Even if Dhumaric had survived, it was impossible to tell if Lorhaiden would be the first to reach him. Kahsir scanned the hillside, looking for the Leishoranya commander. There—at the center of the mass of fighting men—one loomed over all the others. Dhumaric!

He heard a low sound of chilling laughter: Lorhaiden had seen Dhumaric, too. Kahsir glanced sidelong, saw the expression in Lorhaiden's eyes, and hastily looked away.

Pain. There was no end to it. He was drowning in a sea of pain. Tsingar tried to open his eyes, but one was swollen shut and he could only squint through the other. The noise of battle came from farther up the hillside. He shuddered, fought encroaching darkness, and closed his eyes to an empty dark.

The shouts and cries were more distant when Tsingar heard them again. His pain was just as fierce, perhaps worse than before. He tried to move his arms, succeeded, and touched his face. His hand came away sticky with blood. His helm was gone, but it lay within reach. His sword was there, too, along with his shield.

He struggled up to his knees, the world spinning madly for a moment. He still could not see out of one eye, and suspected it was caked with blood. He fumbled for his sword, kissed its blade before sheathing it: his hands trembled so violently that he had trouble getting the sword into its scabbard. He caught at his shield, and risked a look at the hillside.

There was no one close but the dead. Taking a deep breath, Tsingar clenched his teeth and began to crawl off down the hillside, dragging his wounded leg behind. If he could make the cover of the woods, he might be safe. He laughed, a low gurgle in his throat. *You're a lucky man, Tsingar,* Dhumaric had said. He croaked another laugh, and kept crawling.

The fighting had grown fiercer now that the Leishoranya knew themselves beaten. Xeredir looked across the field at the stubborn knots of enemy warriors: they would die, all of them, for the Leishoranya seldom retreated. He glanced over at his son and shook his head in wonder. Once again, Kahsir's luck had brought victory from defeat.

As if sensing those thoughts, Kahsir grinned and pointed. Xeredir followed the line of his son's finger and saw Lord Devàn across the mass of men fighting on horse and on foot. He lifted his sword, shouted Devàn's name, but the cavalryman could not hear.

There was quick movement to Xeredir's left. With total indifference, Lorhaiden cut down a charging Leishoran and then, not even looking at Kahsir, ran off into the fighting. *A shieldman leaving his sworn place? What the Dark does he think he's doing?* Xeredir looked for Lorhaiden's goal and saw Dhumaric.

"Let him go, Father!" Kahsir called over the noise. "Nobody can stop him now!"

Xeredir nodded. It was all too true—when Lorhaiden became possessed by his Oath, little could keep him from action. Someone cried a warning. Xeredir whirled around in time to fend off the desperate blows of an attacking enemy warrior. The Leishoran's sword grazed Xeredir's arm. Despite the pain, Xeredir kept his sword moving in automatic responses. He saw an opening, lunged, and cut down his opponent.

Kahsir had started down the hillside, Vàlkir close beside. Xeredir looked away and focused on the battle again. His shield dragged heavier and, beneath the pain, his sword arm ached all the way to his shoulder. Hairon stood at his side, shieldman now that Kahsir and Lorhaiden had gone, and Elhvàn lay wounded back at the cliff face.

Xeredir smiled grimly. *It's only a matter of time now before we slaughter them all.* Another of the enemy ran forward, and Xeredir cut up beneath the man's guard. The Leishoran cried shrilly, dropped his sword, and crumpled to the ground.

"*Legir!*" Xeredir cried, rallying those nearby. "For the Light! *Legir! Legir!*"

Dhumaric!

Raging flames! The loss of family, of friends. Screams of horses. Howls of pain and anger from the men who fell at his side.

Dhumaric!

Centuries in hopes of meeting the Leishoran face to face, of finally crossing swords with him—

Past became present again.

Lorhaiden fought his way down the hillside, dimly aware of the enemy he killed. His vision had narrowed, focused on the towering figure of the Leishoranya commander.

Dhumaric!

And Kahsir? Your sword-brother? You left him— deserted his side! What kind of shieldman are you to betray that oath?

Lorhaiden snarled at the inner voice, silencing it. His shieldman's oath? He had broken it once already, and only one Oath counted now . . . the Oath of the Sun's Blood.

"Dhumaric!" He howled the Leishoran's name, swept aside the attack of another enemy warrior. "Dhumaric! Murderer! Come face me, you dung-eating bastard!"

Suddenly, Dhumaric's eyes met his across the battlefield and, for the fraction of an instant, Lorhaiden saw his enemy afraid.

Kahsir looked around the battlefield, but the press of men and horses was thicker than ever. He found Lorhaiden at last, knew where his sword-brother was heading: Dhumaric fought a short way off across the hillside. Nothing could stop Lorhaiden now. Revenge drove him on: vengeance for his slaughtered family—his father, mother, sisters, massacred at Dhumaric's orders all those centuries ago.

Dodging an enemy's sword stroke, Kahsir cursed in exasperation. All he could do now was stay as close to Lorhaiden as possible in case something went wrong. He had no intention of interfering, but could not keep his distance. His sword arm red with blood, he hacked artlessly at his enemies. There were fewer Leishoranya standing now. He risked a quick look around the hillside: only a fraction of the enemy who had fled before Lord Devàn's arrival were still alive.

Suddenly, the battle opened and Kahsir had a clear look at Lorhaiden, who had finally fought his way to Dhumaric. Those two faced each other, circling, looking for a chance to strike. No Leishoranya stood close to help Dhumaric; he had been cut off from any support from his own men.

An enemy warrior darted out of the trees. But as Kahsir raised his shield, he felt the surge of a powerful mind nearby. Surprised, he nearly missed blocking the Leishoran's sword stroke. Vàlkir was there—Kahsir deflected another blow as Vàlkir struck out and cut the Leishoran down. Again, the strength of that mind raged on the edge of Kahsir's. He sensed enormous power, similar to that of a fully trained Mind-Born.

Lords of Light! It's Dhumaric! He's attacking Lorhaiden's mind!

Despite the mental assault, Lorhaiden held his ground. Perhaps his hatred, his rage, his unyielding thirst for revenge protected him from Dhumaric's attack.

Kahsir gestured to Vàlkir and ran off toward Lorhaiden. He waved his sword above his head, caught Lorhaiden's attention for an instant. A brief flicker of acknowledgement flashed in his sword-brother's eyes.

Lorhaiden and Dhumaric wielded their swords two-handed now. Dhumaric's shield lay broken on the ground; Lorhaiden had tossed his aside.

Kahsir stared. *Lorhaiden! You fool! You brainless fihrkken idiot! Your pride will kill you yet!*

He edged closer to Lorhaiden and Dhumaric, Vàlkir still at his side. Both men's harsh breathing, the bell-like ring of steel on steel, was easy to hear. Slowly, step by step, Lorhaiden drove Dhumaric back. Dhumaric was wounded now, though Lorhaiden appeared untouched. Suddenly, Dhumaric tripped over one of the bodies that lay on the hillside. Lorhaiden cried out in joy and leapt forward.

Kahsir heard a loud grunt of pain at his back and whirled around: Vàlkir had taken an arrow in his shoulder. Kahsir looked up and froze: a mounted enemy warrior rode down on them and drew his spear back for the fatal cast.

Kahsir jerked his shield up in time to deflect the spear cast, but the force of it nearly tore the shield from his arm. He spun around and tottered, losing his balance, and fell heavily to the ground. The Leishoran had a second spear. Spurring his horse in close, he stabbed downward. Kahsir rolled aside and the spearhead missed by a finger's breadth. A hoof struck his side—he gasped in pain, fought for breath and, lurching up to his knees, scrambled sideways to avoid a second thrust down at his back. The Leishoran jerked his horse to a stop, turned to come back again.

Lorhaiden! Kahsir Sent. *Sword-brother!*

He rolled to his left—the spear tip grazed his shoulder as he landed flat on the ground. Even through the haze of pain he could Read Lorhaiden's confusion. The world started to fade; darkness ate at the edge of his vision. *Lorj!* he Sent again.

And suddenly Lorhaiden was there. With a cry of loss, of hatred, of maddened rage, Lorhaiden ran toward the mounted warrior and leapt onto the enemy's horse. Clawing his way up behind the saddle, Lorhaiden drove his sword into the Leishoran's ribs.

Kahsir felt a hand beneath his arm: it was Vàlkir, one-handed, the arrow still protruding from his other shoulder. With Vàlkir's assistance, Kahsir struggled to his feet, and glanced behind. Dhumaric was standing now. The Leishoranya commander looked quickly around the hillside, his face white with defeat and pain. A moment of hesitation transfixed him, then he turned and ran, stumbling toward the forest's cover.

"No!" Lorhaiden cried. "By all the Lords of Light! You're mine, Dhumaric! Mine!"

"Move, Lord!"

Vàlkir grabbed Kahsir's arm and Kahsir jumped back out of the way. Howling in rage, Lorhaiden whipped the fallen enemy's horse after Dhumaric. Kahsir shuddered at the sight of Lorhaiden's face as his shieldman galloped past: this was no one he knew—this was death incarnate.

He turned around, steadied by Vàlkir, and watched the race to the forest. Face contorted in terror, Dhumaric glanced over his shoulder, saw Lorhaiden coming, and increased his speed.

"Hrudharic!" Lorhaiden's war cry, the name of his House, rang out over the hillside. Dhumaric was nearly beneath the horse's hooves now, with nowhere to go, no escape from death.

Suddenly, the Leishoranya commander disappeared, only to reappear far short of the protection of the forest. Even taking the mind-road was not going to save him. The distance between Dhumaric and his pursuer grew shorter.

"Hrudharic!" Lorhaiden cried again. He rose in the stirrups, brought his sword up two-handed, and swung the blood-darkened blade downward. "Victory!" he cried. "For the Light! *Legir!* For the Light!"

EPILOGUE

The spring wind moaned around the high walls and towers of Rodja'âno; clouds flew before it, and dappled sunlight slid in patches across the courtyard. Aeschu turned away from the window, walked slowly to the fireplace, and held her hands out to the welcome warmth.

The messenger had just left, badly wounded and in need of healing, and his report of disaster to the south still rang in Aeschu's ears. She frowned slightly, glancing sidelong at the room where her husband sat bound in his somnolent communion with the Shadow.

Dhumaric: dead; the five hundred men he had taken with him after Kahsir: slaughtered. Only a few warriors had escaped death today. And as for Kahsir, Lorhaiden, Xeredir—all the Princes of the Krotànya—once again they had pulled victory out of certain defeat.

Well, my Lord Dhumaric . . . you were not so mighty, were you? I gave you your chance, sent you the men you needed, and you repaid me with your death. Aeschu threw back her head and stared at the shadows on the high ceiling. *Have you become a God of your Clan, Dhumaric? Or are you awaiting rebirth so you can try to do it all over again . . . and this time succeed?*

373

She shivered and looked down from the ceiling, toward her husband's chambers. She would have to answer to Ssenkahdavic for Dhumaric's death, but she had played Dhumaric fair, no one could deny that. What he had asked for, she had given.

She had not sent Dhumaric to his death: he, himself, had sought it too long to be denied it.

And the men she had sent south to fill the corridor Dhumaric had forced? She foresaw a long campaign, for the Krotànya would not easily give up what was left of the Kingdom of Tumâs. And now that Xeredir and all his sons had escaped death, she faced Krotànya commanders she had grown to respect through all the centuries. No. She shook her head. It would *not* be an easy campaign.

As for her husband: Ssenkahdavic would remain quiescent perhaps as long as a year, for the taking of Rodja'âno had drawn heavily on his strength. In the meantime, she would rule in his stead, and by the Dark Gods, when Ssenkahdavic awoke, he would not find she had shirked her duties.

She moved away from the fire, strategies and plans filling her mind, the final destruction of the Krotànya more now than just a distant goal.

Kahsir, with Lorhaiden's assistance, helped Vàlkir to a tree that grew not far away on the hillside. Gently, so as not to jar the arrow in Vàlkir's shoulder, they lowered him to the ground, propping his back against the tree trunk. Lorhaiden knelt by his brother's side, all joy of victory erased from his face, his concern over Vàlkir outweighing his elation.

Favoring his bruised side and bloody shoulder, Kahsir straightened and looked over the hillside. Bodies lay everywhere, contorted in the afternoon sunlight, but the living men he saw wore smiles—even those who had been wounded in battle.

Lord Devàn's cavalry had destroyed the enemy—

between his five hundred horsemen and those few men of Xeredir's company who had survived, the enemy had not stood a chance. A few Leishoranya had escaped, mainly by taking the mind-road. Those of the enemy who had lacked the strength had run off on foot, or reclaimed their horses at the bottom of the hill.

"My Lords!"

Hairon came running down the hillside, the left side of his face covered with blood from a head wound. He crouched down beside Vàlkir, then glanced up at Lorhaiden, who had torn a strip of cloth from his cloak to bind Vàlkir's shoulder.

"Is it bad, Kahs?"

Kahsir started: he had not heard his father walk up behind him. He shook his head. "I don't think so. Vahl," he said, glancing down at his friend, "you'll be all right, won't you?"

Vàlkir's face was pale, but he managed a smile. "Hurts like the Void, but I'll be fine."

"We'll get you a healer and have that arrow taken out. Hairon, see if you can find Mataihyàr."

The farmer nodded, stood, and trotted back up the hillside. Kahsir looked back at his friend. "And, Vahl . . . for what you did. . . ."

Vàlkir grinned weakly, his hand clutching at the arrow. "It had to be Lorhaiden or me, Lord," he said. "But today, *two* of the House of Hrudharic stood at your side."

Kahsir felt a touch on his arm. He turned, saw the conflicting emotions on Xeredir's face, and followed his father a bit aside from the other men.

"I swear by all the Lords of Light," Xeredir said, once the two of them had walked a few paces away, "I don't know whether to hug you or hit you."

Kahsir lifted one eyebrow. "What have I done now?"

"It's not you, exactly . . . it's your luck—your damnable, dependable luck. If Devàn hadn't come when he did—" Xeredir shook his head and shrugged, as if leaving the subject for further discussion. "I've already Sent

news of our victory home, and I'm too damned tired to
make another Sending of any clarity. Can you contact
Alàric?"

Kahsir nodded, looking around for a place to sit, and
walked toward a large, flat boulder. He lowered himself
down on the rock, and winced in pain.

It was not over between himself and his father, not at
all: they would never see eye-to-eye on strategy. But
they had made the first healing moves, and that, at
least, counted for something.

Closing his eyes in concentration, Kahsir drew a deep
breath and sought to the southwest, along the route he
knew Alàric had taken. If his youngest brother was still
in trouble—no, he and the refugees were safe, the
enemy that had attacked them gone. At the touch of his
mind to Alàric's, Kahsir sensed an overpowering emotion of relief, and started inwardly. *He knew. He knew
of our battle, of the death we faced.*

—*We're all right, Ahri,* he Sent, layering the Sending with everything that had happened. *Keep going.
We'll be following you soon. After you and the refugees
have rested, take the mind-road. You'll be only a few
days' ride from home. And let Haskon know we're all
right. Luck to you on your way.*

Another wave of relief came from Alàric, superim-
posed over his affirmative answer. Kahsir cut off the
Sending, leaving Alàric to spread news of the victory.
Slightly weakened by the Sending, he sat motionless on
the boulder, the sunlight warming his face.

For a long moment he was content to sit there,
thinking of nothing more than his homecoming. But
much needed to be done before he left for home: the
wounded needed to be cared for, the troops Devàn had
brought north with him would have to be—

They were calling his name now, his father and the
other warriors. A few cries of victory still rang out over
the battlefield. Kahsir smiled, struggled to his feet, and
walked across the hillside to where Xeredir and Lord
Devàn stood.